THE STILLS

ALSO BY JESS MONTGOMERY

THE WIDOWS

THE HOLLOWS

JESS MONTGOMERY
THE STILLS

 MINOTAUR BOOKS NEW YORK

First published in the United States by Minotaur Books,
an imprint of St. Martin's Publishing Group

THE STILLS. Copyright © 2021 by Sharon Short. All rights reserved. Printed in the United States of America. For information, address St. Martin's Publishing Group, 120 Broadway, New York, NY 10271.

www.minotaurbooks.com

The Library of Congress Cataloging-in-Publication Data is available upon request.

ISBN 978-1-250-62340-9 (hardcover)
ISBN 978-1-250-62341-6 (ebook)

Our books may be purchased in bulk for promotional, educational, or business use. Please contact your local bookseller or the Macmillan Corporate and Premium Sales Department at 1-800-221-7945, extension 5442, or by email at MacmillanSpecialMarkets@macmillan.com.

First Edition: 2021

10 9 8 7 6 5 4 3 2 1

To the public school teachers
and librarians of my youth: thank you.
You gave me the encouragement
that made my childhood survivable,
and a foundation that now makes
living my dreams possible.

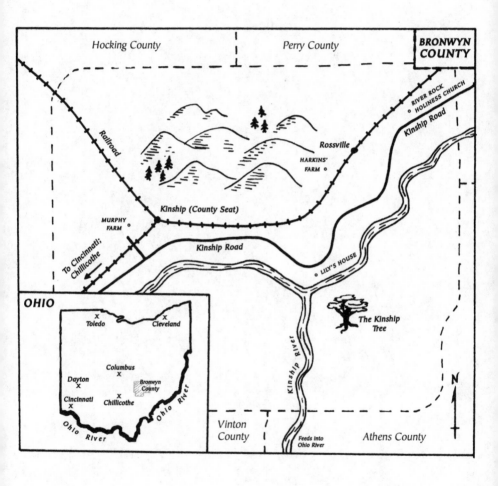

THE STILLS

PROLOGUE

Week before last, cold shooed warmth into a wish and a memory, then rattled tree limbs to leaflessness with one gnarly hand while gripping the earth with the other.

Now on this cold earth Zebediah Harkins lies belly down in the shaggy brush line by an old clearing, as if he had crawled here through the forest itself. Truth be told, this morning, as on every morning for the past two weeks, he'd turned off just a mile into the three-mile trek down Forbidden Creek Run, the dirt road between his home and the Rossville schoolhouse, then traced his way to his post along nearly hidden, almost-forgotten paths once cleared to make way for the iron-works business—itself now all but gone.

A not-yet-sticking snow teases Zebediah's face with quick melting licks. He aims his Hamilton single-shot rifle at a squirrel, over there by the old stone iron blast furnace. He'd hiked out here last Thanksgiving with his grandpa, who'd told him about working there—clear-cutting trees for burning into charcoal to be fed along with coal into the smelting fires of the furnace. All that's left now of ironworks in the Appalachian hills of Bronwyn and nearby counties are old furnaces like

1

this, still standing in uncrumbling defiance against time and vines and brush and twenty-year-old trees growing where the old ones had been, and bits of glassy slag littered in among the natural rocks and dirt, and stories like his papaw's.

Papaw had passed on this past spring, and Zebediah has learned of late the value of focusing on whatever's offered in the moment as a way to secure the future—like that unwary squirrel. Wouldn't Ruthie be right pleased if he brought the critter home for a savory stew?

But he hears his sister's weary voice, as if she's knelt beside him to whisper in his ear:

Where'd you get that, Zeb?

Where you been all day, if'n not the schoolhouse?

And he can see her take note of the dirt on his clothes, of the flashing quickness of his dropped gaze. Not for want of trying, Ruthie is the one person he can't lie to. Zebediah doesn't want her to know that he's been skipping school.

Zebediah swipes snow from his face. When he refocuses, the squirrel has skittered to just the other side of a makeshift ledge of plank on stone, on which bottles of moonshine are lined up side by side, as if the plank is a proper store shelf.

God forbid he shoots one of the bottles. Boss would have his hide.

His job is to keep watch over them and the bigger swigging jug, always set out by the time he gets here, and stowed away, he reckons, in some hidey-hole after he leaves. He doesn't know where the moonshiner's still is—probably not too far off—but that's none of his business. Boss had made sure to tell him that, along with plenty of other admonishments:

Stay quiet. Watch. Note if someone don't leave money for their bottle or swig, or overly guzzles, or pockets the coins.

He will only get a small portion—five cents for every dollar—from the coins he gathers between customers. But plenty of men are coming— he recognizes some from church, or from town—and not just 'cause it's Thanksgiving eve. In winter's bone-jarring cold, shining at small, personal stills will be hard, and with smoke rising twixt bare-limbed trees, hiding them will be harder. 'Sides, talk is that revenuers—the federal agents who work for the Bureau of Prohibition—will soon beset the land like ill-timed locusts.

And ain't it nice that the boss trusts him? Pa won't even trust him to come along hunting for wild turkey! Says he was too shaky, the last time they went out for squirrel and rabbit.

Zebediah's head throbs. As he sits up, his vision speckles, gray spots waltzing with snowflakes. His hand shakes as he reaches into his pocket, but he manages to grab the biscuit, a remnant from last night's supper and dried overnight to the toughness of hard tack. Usually, Ruthie cleans the kitchen nice and proper at night, rises early to make a good hot breakfast, and fills his dinner pail for school, but she's been so preoccupied of late.

Zebediah snaps off a bite. His mouth waters for want of the squirrel, enough to soften the biscuit.

Mayhap it's just as well if he doesn't bring home squirrel. When he complained about the sameness of Ruth's suppers last night, Pa back-handed him so hard that his vision blacked out for several moments. From the other side of this inflicted darkness, he'd heard Pa growl: *Don't go making work for your sister! She's got enough.*

By which Pa means—tending to Ma, dying.

Course Pa don't call it dying. He calls it taking a bad spell. As if Ma just has a touch of fever. But Ma knows. Ruthie knows.

Zebediah knew before even they did. There'd been that day back in early September, when the last breath of summer taunted red-tinged leaves loosening on high limbs and made the Rossville schoolhouse so suffocatingly warm that Miss Cooper, the schoolmarm, had let everyone tote their dinner pails outside when the mine's noon bell rang. Zebediah had kept right on toting over to Forbidden Creek Run. At their farmhouse, he found Ma out on the side porch, coughing so fiercely that she bent near double as she held her stomach. As she looked up at him, the glassy terror in her eyes told him something was bad wrong.

Ma took to her bed shortly after that. Ruth, who is in the eighth grade and loves school so much she has pretensions toward high school, dropped out to tend to Ma and the toddler twins, while Pa works as a laborer for Sheriff Lily Ross and others in Bronwyn County, and spent the rest of his time at the River Rock Holiness Church, praying for a miracle. Till recently. Sunday before last, he proclaimed it *good for nothin'*. At least twice since, like last night when he was backhanded, Zebediah thought he smelled liquor on Pa's breath.

Imagine Pa showing up here as a customer—a prospect both terrifying and amusing.

Both Ma and Pa expect him to just keep on going to school, even though he's the opposite of Ruthie. For him, reading is especially hard. The letters lift off the page and swim around. Why, he ought to be the one dropped out, tending to Ma, but Ruthie is older, and a girl—

A snapping sound startles Zebediah to wide-eyed alertness, in time to see that it's just a small branch, wind-flicked from a treetop to the ground near the plank.

Zebediah shifts on the hard ground, seeking a comfortable divot. The pouch of coins digs into his hip. His stomach rumbles. That hard biscuit won't stave off hunger for long.

And yet he grins, thinking about the fanciful books Ruthie covets at the Kinship General Store—most especially one that's been in the store for nearly a year, *The Blue Castle*. Soon, with his portion of these coins, Zebediah could go back, buy that book for Ruthie for Christmas—he'd memorized the cover with its goldenrod yellow binding and, on the front, the outline of a grand castle impossibly built into rocks and clouds. Maybe getting the book will remind Ruthie of who she was before Ma took sick—who she still is, deep down, below weariness and sorrow.

He'd like to earn enough to get himself something else he'd seen in town—a new Winchester repeating shotgun. Better than this kid's gun. He'd have to buy it himself—Pa won't trust him with it, after that hunting trip where he'd shook so bad.

Footsteps crunch the frozen spikes of grass on the other side of the old iron furnace.

Zebediah quickly goes back down on his belly like a sneaky snake—he grins at the notion—hidden but still able to see who approaches.

He doesn't recognize the men, and they're not the sort he expects—farmers, coal miners, hunters. One is in a fine wool coat and boots, the other in just a suit and two-toned leather lace-up dress shoes. Both wear fedora hats. Zebediah frowns. There's a speakeasy in Kinship for men like this—everyone knows that. Even the ladies and children at the church they used to attend know. The pastor, Brother Stiles, railed against it often enough.

"Here it is," the man in the coat and boots says, gesturing at the makeshift shelf.

Zebediah's frown deepens. This man's voice has the sound of the hills and the hollers, each word jangling into the next like beads on a string, but something makes him seem an outsider even more than the younger man, coatless and in fancy shoes too fragile for backwoods hiking. Are these men part of the *revenuers* people have been talking about?

The coatless younger man shivers so hard that his voice crackles as he asks, "This is it? You were supposed to lead me to Vogel's main operation!"

Vogel? Zebediah wonders who that is.

"Well, one small operation leads to the bigger ones." The older man grins as if he's clever, but he looks more like a rat baring its teeth.

Zebediah's heart pounds. Something is not right. He wants to yell at the younger man: *Run!*

The younger man says, "It had better. We're paying you enough—"

"No. The pay isn't all that I'm after. You promised—"

"You'd better not be toying with the bureau. We're deadly serious—" The younger man pulls out a revolver, but it shakes in his hand.

Damn, mister, thinks Zebediah—he's rooting for him, whether he's a revenuer or not—*stop shaking!* Maybe he can't help it, just like Zebediah can't.

The older man's expression stiffens. "Let me show you some markings on the jug that will help you believe me—a symbol that leads straight to Vogel. Put away the damn gun first."

Markings? The only marking was three *X*s, signifying that the whiskey was triple-distilled. That won't lead to whoever this Vogel is.

As the younger man puts away his gun, something blue and gold pinned to his vest flashes in the spare morning sun. He steps toward the plank.

The older man pulls out a pistol from inside his overcoat, and shoots, grazing the stone furnace. At the cracking sound, the younger fellow whirls around—and a second shot hits him in the head. Blood spurts as he goes down to his knees, dropping his weapon, grabbing at his head, knocking his fedora to the ground. But then his eyes roll back, his bloody hands drop, and he falls forward. The older man strides over, kicks the young fellow over to his back, stares down as if regarding nothing more than a fallen tree limb.

Run. The moonshiner had told Zebediah to run if there was trouble—and this is the greatest mess he's ever seen. But all he can do is stare, transfixed.

The older man's mouth curls, just the slightest self-congratulatory smile.

Startled by the odd, cold reaction, Zebediah gasps, drawing the man's glassy gaze. Zebediah holds his breath.

A chipmunk darts out from the old iron furnace, making the man jump, look away. Then he laughs, pulls a flask from his hip pocket, tries to take a swig. Frowns, irritated that it's empty. He opens the sipping jug, drinks—one gulp, two—then sloppily pours moonshine into his flask, which he caps and pockets as he walks away, whistling some merry tune, off-key and wheezy.

Tears burn Zebediah's cheeks as he waits for the man's wretched whistling to fade. Finally, the only sounds are a thin hum of breeze, birdsong, creaking bare-limbed trees.

For a long time, Zebediah lies where he is, staring at the younger man's body. What to do? Wait for someone else to come along? Run to find the moonshiner?

The man's hand twitches.

Zebediah swallows back a whimper. Surely that was just the man's body shutting down. He'd seen that with deer and pheasant out on hunts with Pa—the postdeath twitch.

But then there's a soft moan. It grows louder. Zebediah rises stiffly, as if he's aged a decade in the last minutes. His mouth is sticky, parched. He opens the sipping jug, wipes the top with his jacket sleeve. He takes three long gulps. The liquid burns as it goes down. He gasps.

The man moans again.

Zebediah moves slowly toward the man, like he's trying to run in a muddy creek bed.

The man's eyes open in a glassy-eyed stare. He does not appear to be breathing. Had Zebediah only imagined the man's moans?

The man's jacket, fallen open, reveals a pin on his vest—the flashing item from moments ago. The pin, knocked loose by the man's fall, is in the shape of a shield, with a bright royal blue background, a coin-like insignia, a *U*, an *S*, the other letters rising up, floating around, like they do in his schoolbooks. Ruthie would know right away what the letters say.

Ruthie.

Zebediah starts crying again. He wants his big sister.

Another moan. The man's eyelids flutter.

Zebediah stares at him.

"Mister?"

CHAPTER 1

※

LILY

Thursday, November 24, 1927
Thanksgiving Day
9:50 a.m.

Just a moment more.

Behind her house, Sheriff Lily Ross kneels by her garden plot. After a cold snap two weeks ago, she'd harvested the last of her sugar pumpkins and acorn squash, then hand-tilled most of the plot, turning under dried husks of tomato vines and cornstalks. Snow, sifting down into these Appalachian hills since yesterday, now shrouds the mounds of dark earth like fine white chiffon.

In one garden corner still unturned, sage yet spikes toward the cold winter sun. Lily adds another stem to her thick bouquet of the herb. Might as well harvest it all—some for Thanksgiving dressing, most to dry in bound bundles in her cellar. Lily glances up at sodden, bulky clouds, gray horns of plenty spilling an early snow. She should hurry—so much yet to do before the day's feast. . . .

Just a moment more.

This is her chance for a few minutes alone before her house fills with a houseful of family and friends—a blessing, to be sure. But it's also a blessing to have a few moments alone on a day off from her duties.

One in particular hounds her. The telegram, on her desk at her office in the new wing of the courthouse, flits across her mind: *Expect Special Agent Barnaby Sloan, Columbus office of Bureau of Prohibition, to visit Friday 25th, a.m., to review forthcoming visit by Assistant Attorney General Mabel Walker Willebrandt. She will address value of Prohibition at Kinship Opera House, Wednesday next. Requests your briefing on local situation*—Lily assumed that meant moonshining in the county's hills and hollers. She'd shaken her head in surprise and wonder at the telegram, then shrugged at the notion of a *briefing*. What could she possibly tell the highest-ranked woman in the country?

Now Lily shakes her head to clear it of work worries and plucks one fuzzy gray-green sage leaf, rubs it. *Ah.* That savory scent, a summer season's warmth infused from the earth itself.

Lily gazes across her land, past the empty clothesline strung between crosses, beyond outbuildings of barn and chicken coop and cold frame and outhouse, on down to the tree line along Coal Creek. Her twenty acres of crops—split between buckwheat and corn—are beyond view, but she imagines them now, resting under a soft thin sheet of snow, thinks back briefly to Mr. Harkins, whom she'd hired to work the fields, and who had last come three weeks ago on a Sunday just after they'd gotten home from church. Mr. Harkins had worked the fields for the previous owner, who'd told her the Harkinses were a good family. She knows them as such, from attending the Presbyterian church with them in Kinship, but they hadn't been for a few months.

Well, it's not her place to judge the Harkinses' religious practices, but still, Sunday's an odd day to be working the fields. Some would say a sure way to draw bad luck for next spring's crops. Lily isn't the superstitious type, but still she'd been startled to find the Harkins boy at the mudroom door. She almost hadn't recognized Zebediah, whom she reckons is twelve or maybe thirteen. He'd shot up since summer's end to a smidge taller than Lily's five-foot-three.

Pa's loading up the cart, Zebediah said. The boy's hands shook, imperiling a quart jar of canned apples. *For pies. Ruthie wants you to have it.*

Lily'd recollected that Ruth had come several times to help Lily in the big garden but had stopped of late. The girl was no doubt busy helping her mother with the younger children—twins, just turned two. And yet the boy looked worried as he thrust that jar of apples at her. And why was the girl proffering gifts, and not her mama?

Ruthie wants you to pray for us, Zebediah said as Lily took the jar.

Tell her thanks—though I'd pray without a gift of apples. But why—

Mr. Harkins had come around the corner, and Zebediah cast his gaze downward. Mr. Harkins said he'd be back in the spring if she'd have him, only nodding when she told him of course she would—quieter than usual. She went back in her house briefly, to get the money she'd been planning to pay him later in the week. By the time she returned, Zebediah was heading back to the mule cart.

Now Lily refocuses her thoughts on her own family. There's a fine line between trusting the instincts that serve her well as sheriff—such as how to deftly handle that upcoming visit from Willebrandt—and putting her nose in another family's business where it's not needed.

A snowflake tickles Lily's nostril, and she sneezes. Then she laughs, the snowflake spurring a childish impulse. As far as Lily can see, she's alone on her snow-gilded twenty-acre farm—the boys are frog hunting at the creek, her daughter feeding the mule and dog and cats in the barn—and so she jumps up, sticks out her tongue, and laughs again at the delightful sting of catching a few frosty flakes.

"Lily Alvena McArthur Ross!"

Lily snaps her mouth shut and sees Mama, just inside the mudroom door, arms crossed.

Usually, she'd be aggravated by Mama hollering her full name to indicate irritation. But Lily laughs again. Even as—or maybe especially as—a twenty-nine-year-old widow and mother and county sheriff, she finds something delightful in being treated as if she's a youngster, with no more concern than the consequences of lollygagging by her garden plot. Maybe for Thanksgiving Day, that can be true.

As she goes back inside, Mama lets the mudroom door slam shut hard.

Just a moment more . . . a quick walk down to the creek, to the Kinship Tree. . . .

No. She's loitered long enough while the other women toil in the kitchen.

Just outside the porch, Lily pulls the soles of her boots over the boot scraper. Warm kitchen scents lure her from the grasping cold: baking pumpkin pies spiced with fresh ground nutmeg and cinnamon, bubbling turkey broth. Lily smiles at the blend of scents mingling into the most exotic perfume. *Home.*

With now-clean boots, Lily steps inside the mudroom, briefly sets the bunch of sage on top of a stack of old newspapers and Sears, Roebuck catalogue pages for trips to the outhouse. As she hangs her coat on a hook, that jar of sweetened apples from Ruth Harkins catches her eye from a shelf filled with home-canned goods. Then she picks up the sage, holds it behind her back, quietly enters the kitchen, and whips the savory bouquet out at Mama, hollering, "Hiya!"

Mama is too caught up in a conversation with Marvena Whitcomb Sacovech to be startled by Lily's hijinks.

"You mean t'tell me this here is perfectly legal?" Marvena pokes at a brick-shaped package on the worktable.

Lily sighs and starts tearing sage leaves into a bowl of crumbled corn pone on a small table by the stove. Mama and Marvena stare at each other from either end of a longer table. Mama's dress and apron bundle her plumpness, and the softness of her round face makes the stubborn thrust of her chin endearing rather than intimidating, especially with wispy gray tendrils flying comically loose from her bun. Marvena is all wiry angles, sharp bones held taut by lean muscles hewn from years of hard farmwork and hunting and moonshining. She'd once spent time in lockup at Lily's behest for brewing corn whiskey. Still, Lily knows not to count out Mama in this standoff.

On the worktable between the two women is a paper-wrapped brick, one of two Mama had insisted on buying the month before at Douglas Grocers in Kinship. The brick is compressed dried grapes, wrapped in paper and labeled *Vino Sano Grapes.* Beneath the fancy script are detailed instructions: *Dissolve in a gallon of fresh water. Add sugar to taste. Store in jars and drink grape juice within week after mixing. Warning: storing in jug in dark cupboard will cause fermentation*

*three weeks from date of mixing. Can also add baking soda to prevent
fermentation.*

When Mama had shown her the bricks, Lily had laughed out loud,
amused by the absurd yet clever work-around of the Volstead Act, now
national law for seven years, making the manufacture, sale, and distribution of alcohol illegal. But perfectly legal dehydrated grapes with
an absurd "warning" give the company a wide-eyed legal dodge, and
"wet" consumers the exact instructions for making wine. Why, even the
most die-hard "dry" would have to admit *that* was clever. Even Mabel
Walker Willebrandt.

Yet Lily's laughter had turned bittersweet as she considered that
agents from the Bureau of Prohibition—established this past spring
by the US Department of the Treasury—were expected to enforce the
laws of the Volstead Act, so filled with loopholes that it was flimsier
than worn-out washrags. The bureau was tasked with ending criminal
syndicates besetting big cities as they bootlegged alcohol. But with just
a few thousand agents, a vast country, and seven years since Prohibition took effect for criminals to develop clever means of mostly elud-
ing capture, the Bureau of Prohibition agents—vastly outnumbered
and underpaid—may as well have been sopping up a flood with those
worn-out washrags.

Lily's laughter had drawn startled looks in the grocery. After all,
Lily is sworn to uphold the law. And she does, when she runs across
the occasional still, or a moonshiner raises too much of a ruckus, or
someone—usually a frustrated wife—complains about the speakeasy
that kept popping up in a "storage room" in the basement of the Kinship Inn. Lily has raided it twice. But in geographically large Bronwyn County, there is enough else to occupy her time and attention in
the spread-out population of mostly coal miners and farmers without
looking for trouble in the hills and hollers as well.

Now Lily regards the brick of "vino" sitting in the middle of the long
table, like an awkward centerpiece.

"Drinking alcohol is legal," Lily says. "Just not selling, buying, transporting, making..."

"So anything that makes drinking possible," Marvena says dryly.

Mama glares over the brick at Marvena. "Don't get all high-'n'-mighty with me." Mama is referring to Marvena's recent conversion to a strict Pentecostal sect, after years of being an unchurched moonshiner. "These were a pretty penny—brought in last month all the way from California. Only two per customer."

Marvena arches an eyebrow. "Convenient timing, right afore the holidays. I reckon the other brick has disappeared into a jug of water."

Lily suppresses a chuckle. The jug had been resting in the pie safe for, oh, about three weeks. And Mama had saved the baking soda for its proper use—leavening biscuits.

Mama grins mischievously and nods.

Marvena glares at Lily. "You're all right with this?"

"It's Mama's house, too. If she wants to offer perfectly legal grape juice—even if it's gone 'bad'—at Thanksgiving, that's her prerogative. Just like it's other folks' prerogative to say 'no thank you' and leave it at that."

Marvena, usually too tough to be cowed by anyone, drops her gaze. As her shoulders droop, Lily wishes she could retract her snapping tone. Marvena, who has had a hard life, too, values Lily's respect and friendship. Though sadness has always lingered behind Marvena's gaze, and worry edging on anger furrowed her brow, of late these expressions have deepened.

Lily softens her tone as she tears more sage leaves. "A grape brick's not the only frivolous item Mama picked out for Thanksgiving," Lily says. "She got soda pop for the children! Ginger ale." The store had started carrying Whistle brand.

"Well, if it's got real ginger in it, that might settle Frankie." Marvena picks up a bowl of cream and beats it. Her next words are so soft-spoken that Lily barely makes them out over the clink of the metal whisk. "She had a bit of a sour stomach this morning."

Oh no. Frankie—Marvena's daughter, same age as Lily's eight-year-old Jolene—often takes sickly turns, usually coughing fits. Lily's had to quietly tell Jolene not to play rough with her friend.

"Well, I hope she feels better," Lily says gently as she rinses her hands in the pump sink's icy cold water. She grabs a towel to dry off. "Jolene and the boys were disappointed she didn't come with you."

Marvena puts the bowl down long enough to sift in some sugar and cream of tartar—just a pinch to stabilize the whipped cream so it won't melt back down to liquid. "Her cough gets worse in the cold," Marvena says. She'd ridden part of the way from Rossville to Kinship with someone she knew, then hiked the rest of the way, all just to help with today's feast.

Marvena goes back to beating the cream, so hard now that she's going to beat it into butter, if she doesn't crack the bowl first.

"Frankie'll be along with Jurgis and the others," Marvena says, meaning her husband, Jurgis; his mother, Nana; Marvena's brother, Tom; his son, Alistair; and Hildy Cooper, the coal-mining town's schoolteacher and Tom's sweetheart—and Lily's oldest friend.

Then Marvena's eyes glint with amusement. "Well, not all the others. Your mama tells me there's one more guest coming."

Lily stops mid-dry, clutching the towel between her hands so tightly that she's in danger of rending it. "Mama—you didn't."

"I did," Mama says, a mite defensively. Then she grins. "And he said 'yes.'"

He is Benjamin Russo, an old friend from the Great War of Lily's deceased husband, Daniel. Now Benjamin works for the Bureau of Mines in the southeastern Ohio branch on safety studies in various mines in the region. Several months ago, he took a boarding room in Kinship.

"Mayhap we should drink to that," Marvena says, a wry twist to her tone.

"Are you kidding? After all"—Lily waves her hands around so hard that the towel flaps noisily—"after all that *moralizing*?"

Mama's already opened a lower cupboard, digging past jars of blueberries and pickles so fast that there's likely to be a mess on the wood floor any second now.

Marvena shrugs. "Hear tell this Benjamin—"

"Mr. Russo!" Lily snaps.

"OK—this *Mr. Russo*—is a big-city fella, from Cleveland originally."

Lily turns to Mama, though all she can see of her now is her backside sticking out of the cupboard. "You've been telling Marvena about him?"

"Figured she'd want to know about him, seeing as how she's not met him before." Mama's voice comes out muffled from inside the cabinet.

Lily and Marvena exchange a gaze acknowledging the truth—Marvena *had* met Benjamin before—once, two and a half years before, near the conclusion of the first case Lily had ever solved: the murder of her husband, Daniel. Marvena, who had been Daniel's childhood friend, had worked alongside to solve the case, while Benjamin had helped resolve a dangerously brewing conflict in the mining town of Rossville between the miners Marvena was helping organize for possible unionization and Luther Ross—the then-owner and boss of the mining company, Daniel's half brother.

Marvena clears her throat. "Seein' as how your mama is going to serve the so-called grape juice no matter what I think, we may as well make sure it's safe for your honored guest. Wouldn't want to poison the poor man, before he can even start properly courting you."

"He—he's not—" Lily stutters. Heat rises in her face. "We're not—" Well, yes, they had chatted a few times in town, at the Presbyterian church, before and after services. But he was just being polite. And beyond the fact that her work keeps her far busier outside a home than most any man would tolerate, Daniel has been gone for more than two and a half years. He will always be a part of her heart. Is that really fair to a suitor—assuming she's ever interested?

"There's a barn dance at a farm north of Rossville tomorrow night," Marvena says. "Even Jurgis has agreed to take me." Their new church frowns on worldly goings-on like dances. "And Tom and Hildy will be there. It's an easy walk from Tom's place." Marvena's eyes twinkle as she grins at Lily. "You could ask this Mr. Russo."

"I—I'm not much of a dancer—" Lily sputters.

To her relief, Mama finally emerges from the cupboard, no broken jars at her feet, holding a gallon-size canning jar filled with dark liquid. Mama's hair has now fallen completely loose from her bun and her face is red and sweat slicked, but she's grinning triumphantly.

Lily laughs, lays aside her tea towel, and gets out three jelly jar glasses.

Mama carefully pours dollops of the liquid in each glass, and each woman takes one.

"Here's to Lily being written up in *Thrilling Gumshoe!*" Marvena says.

Lily shakes her head. She'd solved a tough murder case last fall, and it had turned into a story in the popular detective magazine, in an issue that had just come out. She'd been teased and adulated far too much already over that.

"To Mr. Russo, then," Mama says.

"No!" Lily snaps.

Whoops from the yard draw the attention of all three women. Together, they stare out the kitchen window, as Jolene scoops up a snowball and lobs it across the yard so that it lands right on top of her little brother Micah's head, while Caleb Jr. laughs at Micah's shock, until Jolene nails Caleb Jr.—Mama's change-of-life baby, same age as Micah—square in the arm.

Lily grins. Her girl is showing ever as many signs of athleticism and tomboyishness as she had. Many mothers would try to tamp that down. Mama had for a while, until Daddy told her to let Lily be. She'd overheard him saying folks just have to be true to their nature, a sentiment Lily had reckoned as wise counsel. And so now Lily thinks of her own daughter, *Good for her!*

Lily lifts her glass. "How about a toast to all of our children. May they ever be joyous!"

Even as she says it, Lily's heart pangs and her grin fades. All of them—her, Mama, Marvena—have lost children. Life offers no guarantees in life, especially of perpetual joy.

But Marvena and Mama lift their glasses.

And then all three women drink the grape-juice-turned-to-wine.

Well. It has a kick—but taste-wise, Lily had guessed right. It is like gulping pure vinegar.

Lily glances at Marvena, who'd once made nearly 100-proof whiskey. Her mouth twists bitterly, upper lip almost touching her nose, as she swallows.

Lily would laugh, but Mama looks so disappointed that instead she says gently, "It's—right tasty."

Mama sighs. "Well. I don't know about that. Maybe if I add some simple sugar syrup, and a bit of blackberry juice—"

Marvena flicks an eyebrow. "Well now, Mama McArthur, you're gonna turn into a right proper moonshiner yet."

For a moment, silence hangs among the three women: sheriff, union organizer and former moonshiner, homemaker. Again, Lily wonders at Marvena's sudden good humor about alcohol. *Maybe she's backsliding.*

But then Mama and Marvena burst out laughing, and Lily joins in.

"To friends!" Marvena says.

The women gulp down the rest of their wine.

CHAPTER 2

⫸

FIONA

Thursday, November 24, 1927
Thanksgiving Day
9:50 a.m.

"Is there anything more I can do for you, ma'am?"

Fiona Weaver Vogel looks up from her third frustrating attempt to tie the floral-patterned French silk scarf into a proper bow over the low cleavage of her drop-waist dress. In Cincinnati she'd packed her most conservative clothing, and yet once she'd arrived at her aunt and uncle's farm in the southwestern corner of Bronwyn County, everything she'd brought seemed out of place. Even scandalous. Thus her effort to correct the fashion blunder with a scarf she hadn't requested Klara pack for her. And yet she had found it this morning—the first morning since arriving two days before that she'd felt up to dressing—in her trunk.

She'd felt both gratitude and irritation at Klara anticipating this need.

Now Fiona turns away from the floor mirror to note Klara hovering in the doorway of her old bedroom that is, for now at least, hers again. As usual when regarding Fiona, the older woman's eyes narrow, her lips pinch into an insincere smile. From the point of view of Klara Schneider—longtime cook and housekeeper for Fiona's husband,

George Vogel—Fiona is, as she'd overheard Klara tell another maid, a *floozy*. Someone to tolerate until, inevitably, George gets rid of Fiona.

Fiona couldn't seem to find any way to undermine Klara—not yet. The woman seemed as impervious as a cast-iron skillet. The only hint of vulnerability had come on the harrowing drive over. On a sharp turn, Klara's tote bag had fallen from her lap to the automobile floor—exposing neatly folded undergarments, a dress, a small bottle of cologne, and an old, faded photo in a glass-covered frame, of a woman, a man, and a little boy in formal dress.

Klara had snatched the photo up first. And Fiona had been too preoccupied with her own illness to ask about it—though it had struck her that the photograph must represent precious people and memories for Klara to travel with it.

Fiona has an item like that—though she hadn't brought it on this trip. A cut-glass candy dish, with a chip off one of the tendrils of the fluted edge. She knows right where it is, back at the Cincinnati mansion, tucked safely in a trunk.

Now Fiona shakes her head to clear it of thoughts of that dish, and Fiona's bow falls apart, as if the scarf sides with Klara, whose smile pinches even more tightly as she looks pointedly at Fiona's cleavage. Heat rises in Fiona's already-flushed face. Why can't she tie a simple scarf this morning? Yes, her hands shake from perpetual hunger brought on by morning sickness. This is the first morning in a week she'd been able to keep anything down—just tea and dry toast. The thought of eggs remains nauseating.

But truth be told, her nervousness comes from anticipating the conversation she's planning to finally have with her aunt Nell.

Best to stiffen her spine before facing the old, judgmental woman. Maybe practice with this one.

Fiona squares her shoulders, gives Klara a full smile as she turns her own pointed look at what Klara's holding—Fiona's chamber pot. "That's fine. Your hands are full as it is."

A comment meant to hurt. Anger flashes across Klara's face. *Careful*, Fiona admonishes herself. Though a servant, Klara is a perpetual part of her husband George Vogel's life, and though he is more than willing to dispatch her to do the most menial of tasks—like tending to his wife's personal needs—he also treats Klara with deference. As for Klara, Fiona cannot for the life of her cipher why the nearly seventy-year-old woman stays dutifully in George's employ. All she knows, vaguely, is that Klara was a distant cousin of George's mother, and the few times he'd referenced his mother, long deceased, it had been in worshipful terms.

Knowing how much Klara has George's ear and not wishing to suffer George's wrath, Fiona hastens to add, "I mean tending to everyone here." Besides Fiona and Klara, George had sent on ahead three of his men, but no additional kitchen help for Klara. Fiona says as sweetly as possible, "Please tell my aunt Nell to get on her coat and meet me by the kitchen door?"

Klara doesn't budge from the doorway. "Why?"

None of your business. Fiona looks down at her scarf, fusses with it, so Klara can't see the irritation mounting in Fiona's expression, and gives the most basic answer possible that's still true. "I want to go with her to visit my uncle's grave."

"But Mr. Vogel will be here soon, I'm sure—"

It's true; George and his two top yes-men are supposed to arrive at any moment.

In fact, they should already be here.

The image of George's shiny automobile skidding off an icy road on a treacherous hairpin turn, tumbling into a deep ravine, the occupants dying bloody and broken upon impact at the bottom, slides across Fiona's mind. Instead of despair, the notion prompts relief—though she knows that if George dies, she will only get a small stipend. The bulk of his estate will be divided between Klara and his right-hand man, Abe Miller—a fact that rankles.

She'd briefly considered, after the doctor told her she was *with child*, using her pregnancy to have George amend his will in her favor. It had been her first thought. Her next had been *no*—George would likely leave the bulk in trust to the child, and her that same small stipend.

She wants more. So much more. And she's put together a plan to get it.

"He'll expect to see you here," Klara continues.

He'll expect that I've buttered up Aunt Nell. Sending Fiona and Klara to help prepare the house for a Thanksgiving feast was a ruse; Fiona's task was much more important than that. Those hairpin turns en route had retriggered the morning sickness she thought she'd gotten past weeks before. She'd been so relieved when her and Klara's driver had finally pulled onto the gravel drive to the farm that she'd only caught a flash of Aunt Nell in the parlor, before rushing upstairs to her childhood room, eager to lie down, for her head to stop spinning.

Aunt Nell had not checked on her, not once.

"I need to talk with Aunt Nell," Fiona says firmly. "George expects that as well."

"You can talk to her here," Klara says. "Where it's warmer. Safer. George also expects that you'll be in good health. These hills are steep." Klara's tone implies that the hills are purposefully willful, just to defy her. She gives another pinch-lipped smile as she looks pointedly at Fiona's belly. "Wouldn't want you to slip or fall."

Fiona's face flares in a rush of heat, feeling exposed, as if Klara had seen her moment of envisioning George dead in a ravine. Or somehow suspects that— No, Fiona can't just talk with Aunt Nell here, in the house, full of eavesdropping ears. Between bouts of sickness, the past two days have given Fiona ample time to rethink George's plan—which Fiona had triggered with a casual suggestion in the first place. To revise it to better suit her own desires. No, she could not talk with Aunt Nell here.

"Just do as I ask!" Fiona snaps. She turns back to the mirror, tugs on one end of the scarf, tries again to make a bow.

Klara remains in the doorway, still holding the chamber pot. The expression on her face imparts that she'd love to just fling it at Fiona. Instead, she tosses this zinger: "If I may say, you're starting to remind me of Nina."

Fiona pauses, each hand clasping one end of the scarf.

"Nina Vogel. The first Mrs. Vogel."

Fiona's gut clenches. *Oh.* She'd nearly forgotten that she's George's *second* wife, the first having died just months before Fiona and George met, in the spring of 1926. Nina Vogel. What was her maiden name?

Her history? Fiona doesn't know; she'd heard only a brief explanation that she'd existed, and then only in terms of being George's wife, and that there'd been no children.

Through innuendo and gossip among the wives of George's yes-men, Fiona had learned that the first Mrs. Vogel had settled for a paltry allowance in a divorce and later died alone from a heart attack in a dingy walk-up apartment in Cincinnati.

Well, Fiona's much younger, healthier—despite morning sickness—than the first Mrs. Vogel, and has no intentions of settling for a paltry allowance, whether through divorce or widowhood.

Which leaves two options. Fall into line under George—or outwit him and take control of as much of his assets as she can.

"Too bad *she* never got pregnant," Klara says. "That might have kept her from becoming *restless* in her marriage."

Fiona swallows back a gasp. She hasn't told anyone, not even George, about her pregnancy. Only she and the Cincinnati doctor who'd confirmed the pregnancy are aware of her condition, carrying a late-in-life baby—she is, after all, thirty-seven, with a fifteen-year-old son from her first marriage. She'd explained away or hidden earlier bouts of morning sickness, planned to chalk this latest round up to the twisty-turny automobile ride. Truth be told, she's holding back the news because she wants to reveal it when it will be most useful.

Fiona says, "I've been sick because of the awful ride over—"

Klara's laugh is a short burst. "No one stays road sick for two days," Klara says. "My point is, if she hadn't gotten so *restless*," by which, Fiona thinks, the woman must mean *disobedient*, or maybe the woman had an affair, which George of course would not tolerate, no matter his own shenanigans, "or had at least had a child, then George would have not gotten rid of her."

Turning from the mirror to Klara, Fiona smiles. "Why, Klara, it sounds like you want to give me advice to keep me around!"

Klara inhales sharply, taken aback. "No, well, I—I just mean—" She stands up straighter, tilts her chin up. "It is not good to disappoint Mr. Vogel, and the worst way to disappoint him is to keep from him things that he'd want to know."

The foolish old woman means it as a warning, but Fiona takes a different understanding—Klara will pass on to George any news, information, or gossip she thinks George might find interesting or useful. Good to know.

Fiona's expression hardens, slit only by a clenched smile. "Yes. We don't want to disappoint Mr. Vogel." Her hands move so suddenly in another attempt at tying a bow that Klara jumps just a little. Fiona yanks the loops, hard. "I'd hate to tell him you didn't support me in the one task he asked of me—talking with my own aunt."

"I'm sure I can convince your aunt to take a break from cooking with me to get some fresh air," Klara says.

Fiona turns back to the mirror as Klara departs. *Well, the bow is still lopsided, but at least this knot is so tight the scarf is not at risk of coming untied.*

Moments later, Fiona walks down the hallway past the other bedrooms—there were a generous four of them, repurposed as sewing and storage rooms, except for Aunt Nell's bedroom of course, but now reverted back to their original purpose as George Vogel's people took over the farmhouse for what is supposed to be—as far as Aunt Nell knows—a Thanksgiving visit. Fiona and George will share her old room, George's top men another, Klara with one to herself, and the three men who are already here have cots in the attic.

After Fiona read of Uncle Henry's sudden death in the *Kinship Daily Courier,* which Fiona has mailed to her Cincinnati home—her only ongoing tie to her old life in Kinship—George had insisted on the holiday visit.

She's alone now. She'll want family. You're her only niece. And perhaps I can help her out . . . , he'd said. *But I need you to convince her . . .*

Fiona had been at once irritated and surprised. Irritated, because he said it as if the notion of *helping her out* was his idea, when it was she who'd broached it, months before. And surprised because at the time he'd seemed to dismiss it, and then he'd brought it up again, putting pressure on Fiona to help.

Now, as Fiona descends to the parlor, she clutches the handrail, takes each step carefully. She's wearing the most practical shoes she'd brought—T-strap, low heel—but they aren't really suitable for climbing an Appalachian hill in early winter. Oh, how much she'd forgotten about living here. How quickly it all comes rushing back.

She walks through the parlor, where three of her husband's lower-level men—they serve as drivers and bodyguards—drink whiskey, smoke cigars, and play poker. One of them gives her an appraising look.

Fiona stops cold, stares him down. "Get your feet off my aunt's table. And if you're going to smoke, do it outside!" That had been, after all, Aunt Nell's rule for Uncle Henry.

Fiona might be the second Mrs. Vogel and perhaps the first had put up with disrespectful behavior, but she won't. The man with the offending feet sits up, and all three put out their stogies.

In the kitchen, Klara scrubs her hands at the pump sink, presumably having just cleaned Fiona's chamber pot. Klara doesn't give Fiona so much as a scant glance, though she nods toward the door between the kitchen and the mudroom.

Fiona hurries out through the mudroom. Even before the door slams shut behind her, Fiona abruptly stops at a cold slap of wind, at snow prickling her cheeks and hands, and belatedly realized she hadn't grabbed her coat and hat from the rack in the parlor. Well, she's not going back to the parlor now, give George's men a reason to sneer at her, even though her arms are already cold in the thin sleeves of her dress, the silk scarf providing modesty but no warmth. But Aunt Nell is already yards ahead of Fiona, making good time in thick, practical work boots and a wool coat. Aunt Nell is already past the big barn, plunging up the hill just behind it. Soon she'll be out of sight.

Fiona plunges on, too, in the spitting snow toward the barn.

If George has his way, it will soon be emptied out. An extension will be added—more men will come to work with the ones already here—even in this cold weather, right after Thanksgiving, a tunnel dug out in the hill behind the barn, a new dirt and gravel road made to connect with the county road on the other side of the hill. One remote dirt road on the way in, ancient Osage trees on either side lacing their gnarly limbs over the road to form a natural canopy, another dirt road through buckwheat and cornfields for the way out, both entrance and egress heavily guarded. The timber and the workmen were all set to go. Once Aunt Nell signs over the property, the modifications will take a week. George, after all, employed nearly two thousand men scattered from Chicago to St. Louis to Cincinnati, and his new plans here would push his business south and east.

Fiona only knows this because George had gone over the plans in detail with her. She'd triggered the whole plan one night after dinner, lingering at the big cherry table, sipping her port, hearing George talk about his frustration over needing an additional storage and distribution location for Vogel's Tonic outside of Cincinnati, the medicinal comprising a small percentage of alcohol and mostly water with a few herbs completely legal under the Volstead Act that oversees the enforcement of Prohibition of alcoholic spirits for all but a few uses—manufacturing and medicinal, for example.

George had complained a few months ago that he couldn't seem to pinpoint a place both hidden enough and within access of decent roads for the operation.

My uncle Henry and aunt Nell's place, where I grew up . . ., Fiona had said, so softly that at first she thought George and Abe Miller—his right-hand man—hadn't heard her. Then she realized they'd forgotten her presence at the table. Easy for them to do, she'd come to realize.

But George had heard. For weeks after, he kept grilling her on her memory of the lay of her aunt and uncle's land—any stone faces, creeks, cemeteries, copses of trees to avoid? Other neighbors?

The matter dropped—until Fiona read of Uncle Henry's death in the Kinship newspaper. Upon George pressing her as to the reason for her woeful expression—*Don't I provide enough jewelry? Furs? Help so you don't have to raise a finger?*—Fiona had shared the news.

That's when George insisted they must go visit Aunt Nell, feigning concern. Of course, he wanted to check out the land. See if he could buy it cheap from a grieving widow. Fiona's letter had merely explained that she and George so wanted to visit for Thanksgiving. See how she was doing after Uncle Henry's passing.

Aunt Nell had no doubt expected just the two of them and Fiona's son, Leon, from her first marriage—not a whole entourage. At the last minute, George told her that he would not bring Leon back from boarding school for such a brief holiday. Maybe, he'd said, for Christmas.

When Fiona at last reaches the top of the hill, she enters Sandy Creek Cemetery through the wooden gate and crosses to her aunt standing next to Uncle Henry's fresh, unmarked grave. Aunt Nell stares silently across the hollow, her breath remarkably even. Fiona, panting from the effort of the climb, looks in the same direction. There, beyond the farmhouse and outbuildings, a copse of trees alongside the lane to the farmhouse. The dirt road, not far off the main road. Another hill to the west, rolling soft and low, thick with dark trees, the trees limned with snow, the limbs reaching for her. Oh, she knows this hill all too well. For on that hill, among those trees, is the cabin where she'd been born, only child of a sorrowful woman and a cruel, bitter man. Her father. Aunt Nell's brother.

Aunt Nell, too, had grown up in that cabin, when it had belonged to her parents before her brother inherited it. In this squalor and despair she and Fiona are bonded, both escaping awful beginnings: Nell not going far in physical distance yet so very far in the quiet life she'd found with Uncle Henry; Fiona at first finding respite a little farther away, in Kinship, with her first husband, kind and gentle Martin.

It strikes her, how alike Martin and Henry had been in spirit. How thoughtless she'd been to demand that Aunt Nell speak with her here, in the cemetery where Uncle Henry is buried, and from which they could both espy the location of their hurtful beginnings.

Fiona feels as if she's spinning, along with the snow, and for a moment the tree limbs across the way seem grasping, as if they might pluck her off this hill and fling her back into the horrid cabin she'd run from so long ago.

Fiona startles at a slight sound, like a wren's piping call, but no, it's a sound from deep within her, a whimper. She jumps as if slapped, although Aunt Nell's hand alights gently on her arm, blessedly warm and solacing. The old woman's hard gaze softens with concern as she gives Fiona's abdomen a knowing look. "You need to take care of yourself, so you can take care of your child."

Fiona pulls away, stares down at the hard, resolute earth, crusted with clinging snow. So much for waiting for the right time to tell George. She's fooled no one, at least not the women around her.

"Does he know?" Aunt Nell asks.

"I plan to tell him when the time is right! George will be thrilled. He'll be a good father. He's been so good to Leon. . . ."

Has he? She's told herself all along that her choice to be with George was as much for Leon as for herself. A new thought grabs her so hard it rattles her more fiercely than the wind: What would Martin think of how she'd agreed—eagerly, even—to George's suggestion that her son, Leon, should go away to a fine private boys' school in Philadelphia? The boy had sobbed at the train station the first time he left, George's man Abe Miller nearly having to strong-arm him across the platform.

Aunt Nell's eyes widen at Fiona's notable tremor, and she shrugs off her coat, shoves it at Fiona. "You have to take care of yourself," Aunt Nell says, "for the baby." Then she proffers a small smile. "Since the change, I welcome cold more often than not."

Not wishing to squander this bit of intimacy by deflecting the offer, Fiona takes the coat and drapes it over her shoulders. A scent—Aunt Nell's soap and lily of the valley, an old scent Fiona recognizes from her childhood—wafts from deep within the garment's fibers. Life with her aunt and uncle hadn't been all coldness. There had been sweet moments. . . .

"Of course Mr. Vogel wants the best for dear Leon," Aunt Nell is saying, though her patronizing tone makes it clear that she does not truly believe this. "And I know that you do, too. You always did have a soft spot." Her voice softens to show that this she does believe.

Fiona blinks hard, sniffles from the hard wind driving across her face. She knows what her aunt alludes to . . . that candy dish . . . but it's best not to think of that now. She refocuses on the matter at hand: yes, yes, she had wanted the best for Leon, opportunities to do more with his life than sweat it away on a few acres of tobacco or buckwheat or, even worse, deep in one of the coal mines, or—if he was lucky—run a small business like Martin had, a shoe repair shop. The business, being a deputy for Daniel Ross, and being her husband and Leon's father had been a big enough life for him—yet a life so small that George wouldn't even have recognized it as a dust speck floating in the corner of his eye. She had thought it, if not a big life, a comfortable one, and she'd been glad for her peaceful, cozy niche in it, until Martin died in the line of duty, working for Sheriff Lily Ross.

"Martin was a good man," she says. "But a soft man. Weak in some ways. George, though—well, you'll see when you meet him. He's strong, and, well, efficient. He knows how to get things done, and—and . . ." She stutters to a stop, unsure how to describe her husband.

At first in their courtship and marriage, she'd been happy—eager, even—to disappear in the cool grayness of his enveloping shadow. She romanticized it as a cover for a tender heart she'd surely soon be privy to. When she'd discovered him with another woman—one of the many acolytes who hover around the periphery of George's world—she quickly learned that his coolness was not an act. It emanated from a cold heart.

He'd laughed after she demanded he stop his affairs. Laughed again after she said, well then, she'd divorce him and just enjoy living on a generous alimony. Struck her. Then he'd grabbed her shoulders and said, *Never threaten me, my little spitfire.*

Though once she'd found the term complimentary, she'd come to hate it.

All it means is feisty—yet powerless.

Which is exactly what she'd been after her first husband Martin's death.

Fiona had been angered to discover that Martin had borrowed against both his shoe repair business and their house to feed a gambling habit she hadn't previously known about, engaging in poker games at the Kinship Inn's speakeasy. Fiona had gone to the speakeasy with only a vague plan for demanding to know who Martin had lost his money to. When she started asking around, though, a brute grabbed her arm so hard that she thought it would crack in his fist. Instinctive defensiveness arose quickly from a nearly forgotten past, and she'd spit in his face. He'd slapped her—and a tall, stark man in a fine suit intervened. Abe Miller, the right-hand man of the great George Vogel, acting at George's behest. Later, she'd piece together that even then George was in Kinship looking for just the right farm for his future plans.

In that moment it was her behavior—that was the first time he called her *a little spitfire*—that sparked George's interest. The realization of the power George wielded, casually yet absolutely, more than sparked Fiona's interest. Shaping herself to his desires hadn't been difficult. George had turned out to be a surprisingly thoughtful and gentle lover. Becoming his wife had brought her luxury and ease beyond her wildest dreams.

Yet, so quickly, it had also cost her her dignity. Cost her the respect of her son.

Now she has a plan to correct that. To divest herself of George but keep the luxury and ease, at least a goodly portion of it, if she can just outwit George. The first step is winning Aunt Nell over to do as George wants—but with a change that she'd thought up over the past two days.

"I think," Fiona goes on, "that you'll find George is really quite generous. He wants to offer you a good price for this farm. Didn't you and Uncle Henry used to talk about wanting to someday retire down to Florida? A cottage near the ocean?" Sentimentality crosses Aunt Nell's face. "Well, with what George is willing to offer—"

"He can't possibly know anything about farming. Why would he want to buy?" Aunt Nell crosses her arms. "And why are we talking about this here?" At last, she glances at Uncle Henry's grave, then back at Fiona, her expression conveying that such discussion here is desecration.

Fiona frowns. She hadn't expected such a strong reaction. "Well, he wants to buy it for me," Fiona says. This is what George had told her to say. "So I have a place near Kinship. . . ."

"Here? You hated it here," Aunt Nell says, flicking her gaze toward the other hill with the hateful cabin. "Only visited once or twice after marrying Martin, moving to Kinship—and then only when he made you. May he rest in peace. Martin was a good man—*not* weak. And since you left Kinship as soon as you could hitch your wagon to George, you haven't looked back."

Frustration grows in Fiona, keeping pace with the thickening snow. "George wants to buy it from you—and he will have it one way or another. For me. And . . . honestly, to convert the barn for storage and distribution of Vogel's Tonic in the area. You've had Vogel's Tonic, right?"

Aunt Nell shrugs as if to say, *Sure. Who hasn't? So what.*

"Here's the thing—if you told him you'd sell, but only to me, then I could turn it over to you at any time, later. If you didn't like Florida."

Aunt Nell lifts an eyebrow, skeptical. "Why would you do that?"

Ah, a reaction Fiona had anticipated. Aunt Nell is right to be skeptical. Fiona has no intention of ever turning it back over, but she has an answer she thinks Aunt Nell will like. "You and Uncle Henry saved my life, taking me in."

For a moment, Aunt Nell's gaze softens. Understanding passes between the two women—and then Aunt Nell gives a short, barking laugh. "Henry saved you. I didn't want to take you in. And I didn't want him to go back after you. . . . Anyway, I've already met him. Your George Vogel."

"When . . . how . . . ," Fiona gasps, sucking in cold snowy air.

"He came to visit us, just three weeks afore dear Henry passed on. Wanted to talk your uncle Henry into selling our farm to him. Told us that he knew how much having this farm, a place to stay and visit in your beloved home county, would mean to you. Course, Henry wouldn't sell. He was right polite about it. Said you could visit anytime—no need to buy the farm. And your George seemed to easily accept no for an answer." *Your George.* Fiona would laugh—George belongs to no one—but for her aunt's pitchfork gaze, prodding and stirring, seeking to unbury within Fiona some realization that Aunt Nell appears to already grasp. "Then two weeks later, Henry died. Right out in the field, running the plow for the field's final turn."

Fiona casts her gaze downward. Shadows of the bare limbs of the nearby oak weave a Spartan pattern on the dark, snow-dusted earth. Suddenly her head throbs, and her stomach pinches as if she's swallowed a handful of straight pins. "A stroke, that's what the obituary said. A stroke. I—I'm sorry we didn't get out for the funeral—"

"Look at me! Henry had a strong heart. When he didn't come back proper for supper—well, I found him fallen alongside the rig. The mule had drawn the plow back over him, gashing his head. I saw boot prints, two sets, trailing off. That's what I told Sheriff Lily Ross when she came out, but by the time she got here, too many other prints were around

Henry—neighbor men who helped me move his body. She looked sorrowful enough, but disbelieving. Like she just pitied me for doubting Dr. Goshen saying it was a stroke that felled my poor Henry."

For a moment, the women stand before Henry's fresh grave, widow and niece, connected by loss and understanding, the only thing between them the bright snow-sparkled wind.

Then these words, soft and wispy, as if the wind carries them rather than Aunt Nell's voice: "When Mr. Vogel came, he had a doctor with him—the one used to work in Kinship. Elias Ross."

Fiona swallows hard. George's newest yes-man, on his way here with George and Abe. Uncle to Daniel, Lily's deceased husband, and the sheriff before her.

"Dr. Ross kept staring at Henry, like he was sizing him up," Aunt Nell says. "I thought it strange at the time. Two weeks later . . . healthy man, a stroke? And Fiona, oh, when I found him, turned him over, well, I saw a lump on his head."

Fiona shivers, more from the image of her aunt kneeling over her uncle's wrecked body than from the snow and wind. Martin—seeing him for the first time after his passing—crosses Fiona's mind, and she blinks hard to push away the image.

"Mentioned it to the sheriff and to Dr. Goshen. He said Henry would have gotten it when he fell from the seat. Sheriff Lily said the boot prints I saw were probably from Henry doing something with the rig—or that I'd stirred in the sight of the neighbors' boot prints with his. So—what do I know, a farmwife like me?"

Fiona crosses her arms, shivers, again not so much at the cold as at the knowledge that though it's possible Uncle Henry really had died of a stroke, it's just as possible George had acted ruthlessly, like the morning after their wedding—but she pushes that memory aside.

She considers another memory—how unsurprised George had been by the news of Uncle Henry's passing. How smoothly he suggested visiting, as if for the first time. And why had he kept that visit from her?

Of course George would arrange to have her uncle removed when he would not bend to his will. It is exactly what George would do.

Just for an additional storage and distribution facility for Vogel's Tonic?

There must be more at stake than that. Something else George is hiding from her—just like his mistresses, though those have become more of an open secret.

Fiona inhales the bracing coldness. Either way, it's to her advantage to play along with her aunt's belief that George had somehow been involved in Uncle Henry's death.

Fiona looks back at her aunt. "Well then. All the more reason to make sure that this land goes to me—not to George. He will find a way to get it, one way or another. Tell him you'll sell to me, and I'll take care of . . . things . . . going forward."

Aunt Nell looks skeptical. "How?"

Fiona smiles. "I don't want to trouble you with details—"

Aunt Nell crosses her arms, pinches her lips together. Fiona knows this look all too well. Her aunt will not budge without a bit more convincing.

"Have you heard about the *US versus Sullivan* Supreme Court ruling?" Fiona asks.

Aunt Nell looks blank.

"Well, it was settled just this past spring. I read about it in the Cincinnati newspapers," Fiona says. She'd read everything then, just to keep her emotions and thoughts from racing about George's affairs. She'd started with the advice columns, which hadn't helped; moved on to serial stories, which bored her. Yet desperate to stay distracted—it still hurt her so that George had *hit* her, something Martin would never have done—she began reading crime and legal news, and found that fascinating. And much more helpful than advice columns.

"It's a case that allows prosecution of criminals for income tax evasion." Fiona can't help but let pride creep into her voice, at her own knowledge. "Even income through criminal means."

After a moment, understanding overcomes the blankness on Aunt Nell's face.

Fiona puts a hand to her abdomen. "Once George knows about his—

our—child, he will want to protect his assets for the child's future. How better than by putting assets in my name?"

She'd imagined herself asking him in a tremulous, soft voice, *But what happens, George, if somehow you are found out?* While he didn't share details of his criminal activities, he also didn't keep them well hidden from her. *And the revenuers can take all your assets? What will happen to*—and here she'd put her, no, *his* hand gently on her belly—*to our son? Your son.*

Of course, there's no way to know if she'll have a son or daughter. But she'll go with son. That would better please a man like George.

Leverage. The first time she'd thought of this new baby as just that, she'd been appalled by her own sentiment. Then she'd told herself, it could be true both that the infant would be leverage and that she'd love it just as much as Leon. *A man like George—his first child? He'll be proud. Do whatever he can to ensure its safety. Its future. This baby would be proof of his manhood—especially at age fifty-three.* Why, he'd put the interests of his own child ahead of hers, or Abe Miller's, or even his own.

Aunt Nell casts a doubtful look. "And you think you have the guts to follow through on such a plan? You never were as resolute as you liked to think—"

"I was a child!"

For a long moment, the only sound in the cemetery is the hollow wind whispering between them, as if of atrocities best left buried with the dead.

"Well, with Henry gone," Aunt Nell says, "it's true that only I can sell the farmland. And I have gotten weary of being here." She casts a spiteful look across the hollow to the hill with the cabin where she'd grown up. "I always wanted to get away from here. Early on, Henry promised we'd go far away. Put this entire region out of mind. But this farm had been in his family for generations—just like that, that patch of land and cabin was in ours. I wanted to go. He wanted to stay. And I loved him, so . . ."

So she stayed. In that trailing off is something else. A longing that never quite died to get away, far, far away, and not just because Florida is exotic and warm.

If Aunt Nell truly believes George had had Uncle Henry killed, her resolve to thwart George by not selling might be stronger than her longing to leave. Fiona resists the temptation to speak, to push Aunt Nell too hard. She lets the fragile moment play out.

Aunt Nell breaks the silence with a harsh question: "How do you know I won't just tell your George about this conversation?"

Fiona doesn't flinch as she replies, "You might. But then, I'll deny it. It won't change anything about George wanting this farm. Once he gets his mind made up that he wants something, he pursues it ruthlessly. . . ." She pauses. That had been, she thought, true of her—though she'd offered little resistance, seeing him as a quick and easy way to what she thought she wanted: riches, security. Maybe if she'd put up more resistance, he'd have at least waited longer before having affairs. "And why sell it directly to him? He'll pay the lowest he can get away with. I can beseech George to give you a much nicer price. Plus, consider your insinuations about Uncle Henry. What happens if I tell George about those?" Aunt Nell blanches, as Fiona offers up a slow, even smile. "And, come to think of it, what becomes of this land if something happens, unfortunately, to you?"

Aunt Nell inhales sharply. *That's right,* Fiona thinks. *As the only kin—I inherit anyway. So long as Aunt Nell hasn't written up a new will. And from her telling gasp, she hasn't.* "Uncle Henry would want me to do things this way. To make sure you're taken care of."

"Why do you hate me so?" Aunt Nell asks.

"Why did you hate *me*? I know I was like a daughter to Uncle Henry. I wanted to be like a daughter to you. But you would have sent me back—"

"You were nothing more than a reminder."

At that, it's Fiona turn to gasp, and cold fills her, burning as only the hardest unrelenting chill can. She stops shivering.

"It's up to you, Aunt Nell. You can have sufficient funds from this farm, in the warm land far away in Florida, knowing that you can trust me to . . . well, set things right for Uncle Henry? After all he did for both of us?"

At that, tears well in Aunt Nell's eyes. Her shoulders slump, and she looks like no more than what she is—an old, weary woman.

Fiona goes on a bit more gently. "All you have to do is agree to sell—but to me. Your only kin. No one can blame you for that. Just talk about how blood runs deep in these hills. Can you do that?"

Movement at the bottom of the hill, down on the road by the turnoff, catches the gazes of both Fiona and Aunt Nell.

Another Model T, driving slowly up the lane toward the farmhouse, a dark dot progressing under the sparkling snow.

That would be George Vogel and his two yes-men, Abe Miller and Elias Ross.

Fiona's heart quickens. She looks back at her aunt, now shivering so hard that her teeth clack together. The movement makes her seem weak, broken, but after a moment Aunt Nell manages to stutter, "I-I can do that. I promise."

Fiona takes off Aunt Nell's coat. She no longer needs it. She drapes it back around Aunt Nell, puts her arm around her, and starts to walk her back.

Aunt Nell stops, making them both stand still. She glances at the hill with the cabin, and Fiona realizes it's for one last time. Aunt Nell says as soft as the feathery snow drifting around them, "Careful, lest by hating you become what—or who—you most hate."

Are the words for herself—or for Fiona?

They walk down the hill, away from the cemetery, back to the farmhouse where George awaits.

CHAPTER 3

⇾

LILY

Thursday, November 24, 1927
1:42 p.m.

Lily gazes over her dining table laden with abundance: the wild turkey, which she and Marvena had bagged on a hunting trip just two days before, taking Jolene and the boys with them, though Mama fussed and clucked and said Jolene should stay behind with her and Frankie, then relented at Jolene's crestfallen expression. Corn-bread stuffing, aromatic with sage. Mashed potatoes in the good cut-glass bowl, gravy in the white ceramic tureen, home-canned green beans, pickled corn, even pickled eggs turned purplish red from pickled beet juice. Usually, those were saved for Easter, but Caleb Jr. had begged for them and finally Lily relented—as Mama had done with Jolene going on the hunt. Later, Lily had caught her listening with rapt attention as Jolene told her all about it.

Mama's rolls in a wicker basket, lined with washed and pressed tea towels.

Soft butter the children had made, shaking heavy cream in pint-size canning jars that afternoon—a good way to keep them out from underfoot while contributing to the lavish dinner.

And of course pies—pumpkin from the sugar pumpkins Lily'd grown, plus apple from the jar that Ruth Harkins had sent, which Lily had made at the last minute because that's Micah's favorite, and even a sorghum pie brought along by Hildy Cooper, Lily's best friend, who now teaches in Rossville, one of the coal-mining villages in the eastern part of the county.

Lily's and Hildy's eyes meet across the table, and Lily smiles at her dear friend. Nineteen twenty-six had been challenging for both of them: Lily running for reelection as sheriff of Bronwyn County while investigating the fraught case of an elderly woman's murder, Hildy insisting she must help, to the point of putting her own life in danger. Truth be told, their lifelong friendship had been strained in ways neither could have anticipated or imagined.

But 1927 has been calm thus far and there's no reason that the rest of it shouldn't be as well. Even more wonderful than the plentiful food is the abundance of people at the tables in the dining room, alight with coal-oil lamps and the candle chandelier over the dining table.

The children are gathered at the smaller kitchen worktable, covered with a pressed, embroidered tablecloth just for this occasion: Lily's daughter, Jolene, and son, Micah; Lily's little brother, Caleb Jr.; Marvena's daughter, Frankie; and her nephew, Alistair.

At the adults' table sit Marvena and her husband, coal miner and union organizer Jurgis Sacovech, and next to him his sweet mother, whom everyone calls Nana, sitting on one side of Mama. Lily smiles—within moments after "Amen" concludes their grace, Mama and Nana will be clucking away at each other, friendly old hens.

On the other side are Hildy and, next to her, her betrothed, Tom Whitcomb, Marvena's widower brother and Alistair's father. A flash of memory sends a shuddery slash up Lily's spine—two years ago, Alistair had nearly died in a coal-mining accident, but, through sheer will and the grace of God, she and Marvena had saved him. Now he's a tall, lanky thirteen-year-old, stroppy limbs keening toward adulthood, beaming with a goofy smile as he teases the others—the eight-year-old girls who snub him, and the six-year-old boys who adore him.

Then there's Benjamin Russo, between Hildy and Mama.

Lily ventures a glance at him, staring down at his plate. Lily's heart clenches. The poor man probably wishes he were back in his rented room in Kinship. Benjamin's invitation—and placement at the table—was by Mama's design. Dear Lord—please don't let Mama go on about how Lily really does have a soft feminine side. Mama will avoid the fact that Lily hunted the turkey currently on the table and chatter about the pies on the sideboard, and Lily's old county fair blue ribbons—never mind that they're gathering dust in the red bowl on the top of the pie safe, serving as a nest of sorts for her sheriff's badge.

Of course, Mama only wants what she thinks is best for Lily—but Lily still finds it amusing that Mama also thinks she's being subtle when, truth be told, she's campaigning just as hard for Lily to take an interest in Benjamin as she had for Lily to win the election last year—though Mama must know that no man would be interested in courting a woman in such an unusual job and Lily has no intentions of giving up her position, not for a man. Anyway, Benjamin's likely to only be here for a few years. People who come from elsewhere usually soon find that alongside the alluring beauty of these rough-and-tumble hills and hollers are heart- and bone-breaking challenges aplenty. They do not stay.

Lily's eyes fill rapidly as she thinks of Daniel, tears refracting candlelight into stars from nights so long ago. Lily blinks hard, clears her throat, but still her voice is scratchy and too loud as she says, "Let's say grace before dinner gets cold!"

The room silences, and all eyes, even the children's, turn to her.

She looks across the table at Mama. They'd agreed that Lily would say grace, but from the way Mama's gaze cradles her with empathy, Lily knows that Mama understands that Lily is feeling too shaky for the task.

"Well then." Mama looks at Benjamin and holds out her palm. "We hold hands when we pray in this family."

"Yes, ma'am." He takes her hand.

"Children." Mama's inferred command brings the children rushing over from their table, inserting themselves among the adults.

With the warmth of her children's hands in hers, Lily's heart loosens with gratitude. She presses her eyes closed as Mama's voice sweeps over the table, soft and sweet as a warm breeze conjured up on this cold day. And as she prays—thankfulness for the food, for the people gathered, and for the memories of loved ones—Lily thinks of those dear beloved souls no longer with them on this earth.

Her heart still yearns for Daniel, gone now just over two and a half years—both an eternity and a moment since his uncle Dr. Elias Ross came to her, with Daniel's blood blooming so broadly on his shirt that his hat, trembling in his hand, couldn't cover it, with the fateful words: *Daniel's been found.* . . . At one time, it would have been unimaginable that Uncle Elias would not grace her Thanksgiving table. Even Daniel's half brother, Luther, whom Lily had never liked, would have been welcome at her table—until Elias and Luther betrayed Daniel.

Thanksgiving. Lily considers the term, as she might an unusual flower in the woods. It's impossible to be thankful for what you have without being mindful of what you've lost.

"Amen!" Mama declares.

Lily hugs her children before sending them back to the children's table. Then she declares, her voice firm and clear, "Let's start the dishes around!"

She starts slicing off the drumsticks—already claimed by Micah and Caleb Jr.—as voices rise and overlap and weave to fill the room, and hands pass dishes and fill plates.

After everyone is sated from the meal, Lily washes up dishes in the kitchen's pump sink, while at the stove Mama tends to the turkey carcass, bringing it to a boil in the large stockpot along with carrots and celery and onions. It will take hours to render bone broth. Later, they'll make egg noodles—a simple recipe of two good-size eggs to a scant cup of flour, mixed up into a dough, rolled thin, sliced, and left out on a towel on the kitchen worktable to dry. Lily's done this alongside Mama for as long as she can recollect, and it's a cherished tradition. In a few days, once the noodles are dry, they'll make turkey noodle soup.

Now Mama admonishes, "Lily, go on and tend to our friends."

"Our friends are tending to themselves well enough." From the dining room come squeals as the children play hide-'n'-seek. All except poor Frankie—she'd had a coughing fit at the end of dinner and Marvena and Nana are upstairs in Jolene's bedroom, tending to her with tea.

Mama waves her hands at Lily. "Well then, a certain special guest."

Mama means Benjamin, of course. He'd been quiet but polite. Perhaps the raucous dinner—veering from companionable to tense and back again—was overwhelming. Lily knows nothing about Benjamin's family—if he has one. Who are his people? Is it simply too far to travel—which made sense, Cleveland being a very long day's drive even in a good Model T—or are there other reasons he shared his Thanksgiving with Lily's family and friends?

Near the end of dinner, Mama had offered to pour the perfectly legal accidentally fermented grape juice—and Hildy, Tom, Benjamin, and Lily had accepted enthusiastically, but Jurgis and Nana had gone quiet, while Marvena studiously avoided eye contact with Lily or Mama, as if the earlier moment of toasting one another were shameful. Why had Jurgis become so rigid? And why had fiercely independent Marvena fallen to his lead? A dull gray lull settled over the dinner, broken by Frankie's coughing fit. Could it have been brought on by nerves?

Now, as Lily finishes washing the gravy boat, Mama says, "Go on. See to all of our friends about that coffee."

In the dining room, Lily finds Hildy under the table with Jolene and the boys, giggling away at pretending they are living in a cabin and the white tablecloth is really heavy snow. Lily smiles at the joyous sounds.

In the parlor, though, Lily's smile fades. There, on one settee, are Tom and Benjamin, and across from them on the other are Jurgis and Alistair. Whereas Jurgis had been mainly quiet during dinner, now he is holding forth on his views on Prohibition.

"The law exists for good reason!" Jurgis proclaims. "Mining is dangerous enough, without men showing up drunk—"

"Often as not, men trying to numb the pain of their aching joints for one more day of ill-paid work—and company scrip at that!" Tom snaps. "You're focusing on the wrong problem—"

"And there's what the Good Book says against drink—"

"What, that Jesus turned water into wine? Or First Timothy: 'Drink no longer water, but use a little wine for thy stomach's sake and thine own infirmities. . . .'"

"It means to rub a little wine on your stomach, not bolt it down," Jurgis says.

"That's ridiculous!" Tom scowls, and Alistair scooches into the settee's corner, probably wishing he was with the little kids rather than insisting he was old enough to join the grown men in the parlor—though to Lily's view, neither Tom nor Jurgis was acting like a grown man.

"Not according to Brother Stiles, where we've been going these last few months—"

Benjamin clears his throat. Lily's eyes are drawn to him as he says brightly, "Look! Lily's joined us!"

Coffee. Mama had told her to ask about coffee. At least that is a noncontroversial beverage. Lily'd never seen anyone come to rough words or blows over it, at least.

Before she can ask about coffee preferences, Jurgis jumps up. "C'mon, Lily. I reckon you must have an opinion."

"In the case of Prohibition, when I have encountered violations I have done my duty, as I was elected and sworn in to do." Lily keeps her tone even and pragmatic. "It is not my job to have an opinion. It is my job to uphold the rule of law."

Lily catches herself glancing at Benjamin. His gaze glints with appreciation. Though it is for her wit and wisdom, heat creeps up her neck and face. Somehow, appreciation of her mind feels more intimate than any other kind.

Lily feels someone moving behind her—Marvena. "I've got Frankie settled for now." Marvena's voice is ragged with worry. "Nana will stay with her—" She stops, alarmed by the palpable tension in the parlor.

A hard, rapid knock at the front door makes all of them jump. Lily frowns; who would come calling on Thanksgiving Day? Another knock comes harder. Apparently, someone desperate for her help. Where the Bronwyn County Sheriff lives is not a secret.

Lily rushes past the others, opens her front door.

There, on the porch, are Dr. Goshen and Ruth Harkins. Lily almost didn't recognize the girl, her youthful face at odds with the eyes of an old woman who has experienced too many losses, borne too many burdens, and yet knows with deeply resigned certainty that a greater measure of much more of both awaits. Dr. Goshen looks more than put out to be here with her and not in his own home at Thanksgiving.

Beyond the unlikely pair on Lily's porch, snow covers the sloping yard and frosts the limbs of maples, oaks, and pines on the edge of her property along Kinship Road.

Whatever they've come for will pull her from her warm house. Her Model T, even with new tires, might get stuck, depending on where she's expected to go in the rutted dark and deep nooks of Bronwyn County. She may need to hitch Daisy to the wagon. Take along her coal-oil lanterns. Her shotgun as well as her revolver. Call in deputies.

She flicks her eyes back to her porch.

Dr. Goshen clears his throat. "Ruth Harkins showed up on my doorstep about an hour ago. Said her father didn't want to send for me—seems he doesn't think too kindly of the treatment I've been giving Mrs. Harkins—but her mother thought otherwise. Their boy Zebediah is in a bad way. Alcohol poisoning of some sort. From what she's described, I reckon he's in a coma. Ruth here walked all the way into town. Says her brother told her, before he passed out yesterday, that he'd had a drink from Marvena Whitcomb Sacovech's still. That he'd been working for her. Figured I'd find you, Sheriff Lily, to root out Mrs. Sacovech so she can tell me what went in her shine—so I can know if I can help the boy, or not. Lucky she's here."

Lily looks back at Marvena, now in the doorway from the foyer to the parlor, still as a critter, trapped between Lily and the doctor and the girl, and the men in the parlor behind her.

It can't be true—Marvena had given up moonshining the year before when she took on an official job with the United Mine Workers—but Lily's heart drops at Marvena's face, turned stiff and pallid.

CHAPTER 4

FIONA

Thursday, November 24, 1927
2:50 p.m.

The table settings are resplendent yet overbearing in Aunt Nell's modest dining room: fine linens, silver place settings, gold-trimmed china, crystal goblets. Fiona hadn't overseen packing a trunk full of their finest tableware. That must have been a task assigned to Klara.

What had George been thinking, lugging all this here for a Thanksgiving dinner? Had he really eschewed the notion of dining from Aunt Nell's ordinary tableware? Or did he honestly think that such showing off would impress Aunt Nell into selling her farm to George?

But from her end of the table, Aunt Nell's gaze flicks disdain from one piece of crystal to another. At dinner parties in the Cincinnati mansion, the mesmerizing sparkle of finery took Fiona's breath away. From pride, yes. But also from reassurance that she was sequestered, at last, from the hurt and nastiness that life heaps on those less fortunate.

Well, she'd smiled then until she'd caught George with another woman. Until he'd hit her for suggesting divorce.

And yet Fiona almost smiles now at the ironic metaphor of the gleaming plates and tumblers being, literally, empty. There is not a speck of food on the table. George sits at the head of the table where

Uncle Henry should have been, his right-hand man, Abe Miller, and Dr. Elias Ross on either side. Upon arrival, George gave her only a brusque kiss.

Now, as Klara scrambles to reheat Thanksgiving dinner, George and Abe talk quietly over business, ignoring Aunt Nell glaring from the other end of the table. Luther Ross—Elias's nephew who had rolled in from God-knows-where shortly before George—sits drinking from his ever-present flask.

Fiona can't bear to look at him. Her skin chafes as if with a rash at the feel of his gaze, crawling all over her. The first argument Fiona had with George—about a month before she caught him in bed with another woman—was over him bringing Luther and Elias into his employ. He proclaimed, *Some of your hometown boys will be joining my operation,* as if Elias, nearly seventy, and Luther, fifty, were young men. George either had forgotten—or never knew—that Luther, as the owner of Ross Mining, now bought out and run by another company, had been in charge of the Pinkerton hired guards who had fired into a crowd a few years ago, a stray bullet killing Martin. Fiona tried to tell him, but George had laughed off Fiona's protests—as if Fiona has come into his life with no past, no history, no haunting emotions.

Fiona stares at her crystal water glass, noting the coal-oil light glinting on its facets. As if resurrected by the glitter, a specific memory arises before Fiona, supplanting the farmhouse dining room—the memory that had buzzed at the back of her thoughts up at the cemetery when Aunt Nell suggested that George, with Elias's help, had caused Uncle Henry's death, that he hadn't simply died from a stroke.

George and Fiona's wedding this past summer had been at the Drake Hotel in Chicago, attended only by George's business associates, except for Fiona's son, Leon. She hadn't sent invitations to Aunt Nell and Uncle Henry, or to any of the women she'd known in Kinship.

And yet, at the reception, Fiona found herself thinking of Lily Ross, of how Lily—with her pragmatic nature and own unconventional choices—was the one person from back home who might be the least likely to judge hers. Her reverie had been interrupted by Mrs. Eugenia Chantelle, the wife of one of George's business associates, who'd stopped to congratulate her on *her surprising coup.* Fiona had stuttered some rambling reply, growing increasingly awkward as Eugenia pressed her lips together to hold back laughter, until even to Fiona's ears her accent sounded flat-footed as she drew out her vowels over much. When Fiona responded to some now-forgotten question saying she "might could" do something or another, Eugenia finally burst out laughing as she sauntered away. Later, George asked Fiona why she looked crestfallen—*Aren't you enjoying your own wedding reception?*—and Fiona confided the exchange. George smiled, told her not to worry—*I'll take care of it*—and whirled her onto the dance floor.

The next morning during breakfast in the hotel's dining room, Eugenia nervously came to their table—her husband steering her by the elbow—and told Fiona that any time she was back in Chicago she'd love to go shopping or have tea, the offer delivered with a quivering voice. A thick dusting of tinted powder barely disguised the dark bruising on her cheekbone—and Fiona realized with a shock that George must have complained to Eugenia's husband, who would have reassured George he'd get his wife to set things right.

Fiona had been horrified at what she'd triggered. Then fascinated at her ability to trigger it with just a few stray words. Then, again, horrified, this time at her own fascination with her—though she hadn't learned the term just yet—*leverage.*

Less than a year later, she'd had to heavily apply powder to her own cheekbone for daring to suggest divorce. That was when she started seeking better *leverage.* And then she'd found out she was pregnant . . .

"Fiona, are you all right?"

Fiona jumps as the question snags her back to the moment.

Elias's eyes are wide with concern, dark pools in his long face, slack and weary, mimicking the "oh" of his partially open mouth. His panting breath is audible, and though his brow is sweaty, his face is pale.

"Prob'ly just wishing George had gotten here a little earlier," Luther says, his words slipping and slurring, the alcohol on his breath hitting Fiona even from across the table. He takes another sip from his ever-present flask.

Fiona looks at George, still chattering with Abe, even as Klara sweeps in from the kitchen, finally delivering platters of food. Klara looks at him adoringly, as one might at a precious son, but George doesn't seem to notice her.

Why her devotion? Surely not because they are distant cousins. Because she's so well-appointed in his will? In any case, Klara does not look the least hurt that George ignores her.

She knows how to be—well, whatever the opposite of restless is.

Patient, perhaps.

Fiona is not patient.

She regards her husband: vulnerable flesh and bone, yes, but stolid, handsome enough even at age fifty-three, with thick black hair that would be unruly but for the pomade he always uses. George is overweight, pudgy even, but there is nothing soft or giving about him. His square jaw has a constant, uncompromising set.

Now, as Klara recedes, leaving behind dishes and platters, George abruptly looks away from Abe, turning to Fiona as if he felt her gaze brushing his cheek, like an annoying prickle of a gnat daring to glance his skin. His dark eyes meet hers and she makes herself smile, puts her hand gently on his arm, hopes her touch soothes him. He does not like being interrupted—not even by an unsolicited gaze.

"Dinner's been served," she says, willing her voice to remain steady. "I thought perhaps—a word of grace?"

George's gaze shackles her, for she dare not look away or let her smile drop. He gives a thin smile, looks across the table at Aunt Nell. "Well," he says. "Since we are mere guests, that would not be my place."

Aunt Nell gives George a cold smile. "Oh, well then. I'll be glad to offer grace—since, of course, my dear Henry isn't here to do so."

George's response is immediate, staunch: "May he rest in peace."

Fiona ventures a look at Elias, but his expression is blank, his gaze pasted to the wall.

After grace, moments pass as everyone eats. Fiona can barely swallow—the mashed potatoes are cold, the gravy scorched. The pickled red cabbage and sauerbraten George had insisted on, alongside the traditional Thanksgiving dishes, seem at odds with the bland turkey and green beans. But she'd taken several dutiful bites of the German dishes, even after the first one immediately made her stomach turn sour.

"I managed the problem you sent me ahead to take care of!" Luther blurts, his voice booming in the dining room.

The problem? George is just having the barn converted to a warehouse, a new gravel road added, for expanded distribution of Vogel's Tonic—isn't he? Increasingly, though, this explanation of George's desire for this farm seems, well, thin. And what *problem* does Luther mean? If he wasn't in Cincinnati, or here for the past few days, where has he been?

A slight frown furrows Elias's brow as he looks across at his nephew. "I don't think we want to discuss business at the table."

"Well, George and Abe were!" Luther's tone turns belligerent.

The room goes quiet as George turns his gaze to Luther, who shrinks down into his chair, pale and quiet.

"I—I believe my nephew is feeling not quite himself. He's like this when he doesn't eat for a bit—" Elias says. He pats his napkin across his sweaty, pale brow.

George turns his stabbing gaze onto Elias. "Are you saying we should not have completed our work before leaving Cincinnati?"

"No, no, of course not—" Elias starts.

George looks back at Luther. "So, you did as I requested of you?"

Luther nods.

"Exactly as I requested of you?"

He nods again, eagerly. Fiona sees, in the fear widening Luther's eyes, that he had not done exactly as ordered, that he'd modified whatever those orders were, tried to be clever.

Her stomach flips, as the thought slithers across her mind: *No one out-clevers George Vogel.*

And yet she'd just convinced her aunt to go along with her plan to attempt just that. Being in George's presence, seeing his stolid, uncompromising expression, the clench of his jaw, the way men deflect to him, inspires an overwhelming wave of second thoughts.

She could just let George convince her aunt to sell the farm directly to him. If Aunt Nell won't, will something happen to her, along the lines of Uncle Henry's suspicious stroke? Her aunt and uncle have no children, and as their own living kin Fiona would inherit this farm.

Unless Aunt Nell made up a will after Uncle Henry's passing? Fiona wonders about this, as she had earlier in the cemetery.

"Yes, yes, sir," Luther is saying. He gives a chuckle. "Gonna be some sick men in Kinship this weekend."

Elias's fork clatters to the floor. "Oh, sorry, sorry," he mumbles. He leans over to pick it up, wipes it off with his napkin.

For a moment, Elias's and Fiona's eyes meet, and she sees that his are wide with a sickening fear. Fiona stiffens. What did Luther mean by *sick men in Kinship*? What has George set in motion?

"Good," Abe says. "And the other matter we asked you to expedite?"

"Oh—oh yes," Luther says. "I had the meeting just like you said—"

"Oh, for God's sake, stop loitering in the doorway and get in here!" George hollers at a man, one of his guards, standing in the entry between the dining room and the parlor, holding a plate of food and trying to eat quietly, his forearm brushing the revolver holstered to his side with every effort to spear a bite. "I hardly think anyone is going to find me here," he adds, as if he himself had not been the one to order armed guards to precede him to the farm.

The man comes in, puts his plate at the one empty spot, hesitates.

"For God's sake, no one is sitting there. Sit!" George commands.

For a moment, the lights glinting off the crystal blur and fuse in Fiona's vision. She sees only a watery whiteness, as the legs of the chair—*that should have been Leon's seat*—rub against the thin dining room rug.

George had promised her Leon would visit for Thanksgiving—then cavalierly broken the promise. And now, sitting in what was her Uncle Henry's chair—her sweet uncle Henry, who'd saved her when she was just fourteen, whose death Aunt Nell has put at George's feet—George motions for a stooge to take what should have been Leon's chair.

Fiona blinks, and her vision is clear.

Fiona doesn't just want to survive. That's all she's done, really, all her life. Survived at the goodwill of men—Uncle Henry, Martin, now George. George's goodwill is fickle. No, she's weary of merely surviving.

She wants to be in control of her life. To thrive.

She puts her fork down, her hand across her midriff. Too soon, of course, to feel life stirring within her. She spreads her hand protectively, centers her will on the only pocket of warmth in her heart grown otherwise cold, a warmth for Leon, for this child, for their future through her.

"Well, my apologies that the turkey is a little dry this year," Aunt Nell says to the guard, then looks across at George.

"It's fine," George says gruffly. "Now, I'm sure you've been enjoying your visit with my lovely wife—your dear niece—which is exactly why I sent her ahead. I know how much she's missed being in this area, and—" George stops, freezes, at a sudden, horrific strangling sound, followed by a thready moan.

Fiona turns—as they all do—to the source: Elias, slumping in his seat.

CHAPTER 5

※

LILY

Thursday, November 24, 1927
2:50 p.m.

"Plain and simple—I wanted money to get Frankie to a treatment center for her asthma. One *he* told us about." Marvena points at Dr. Goshen. "That's why I started up a new still. For Frankie."

Marvena says her daughter's name like a sigh, the sweet, simple *Frankie* exhaling into the room, yet at the same time drawing all the air out of it. Jurgis stares at Marvena, first with disbelief, then—worse—with no surprise at all. Only disappointment.

Sorrow rushes Lily's heart. Yet she's angry, too. Not so much at the moonshining itself, but at Marvena's deceptions, her willingness to profess one belief, yet act in opposition to it.

Benjamin walks over to Lily. Sweet pinpricks run up Lily's arm as Benjamin briefly brushes against her dress sleeve, as he looks at her with a kind, reassuring gaze: *All will be well.*

He says to the group, "I'm taking a walk down to the creek." Lily understands: he is not part of this argument.

Tom looks at Alistair, says, "Come on. We're joining him."

Alistair starts to protest, but Tom shakes his head, then says to

Marvena, "Sis, you know I'd do anything for you—for my niece. All you had to do was ask—"

"For company scrip?" Marvena asks harshly. "Treatment centers don't take that."

His shoulders slump as if in defeat as he leaves the parlor with Alistair.

Lily refocuses on Dr. Goshen and Ruth Harkins, still standing in the open doorway, cold swirling into the parlor, wrapping around throats and hearts.

Ruth shivers. Lily puts a gentle hand on the girl's shoulder. "Please, come in, get warm."

Marvena clears her throat, looks at Lily. "Frankie's breathing problems just keep getting worse," Marvena says. "Nana's teas and tinctures offer ease—but they come back worse'n before." She gives a slicing look at the doctor, rubbing his hands before the fire. "We went to the doctor, here, and he done sold us asthma cigarettes, said it would ease her troubles. Now there's times she can barely breathe."

Dr. Goshen gives Marvena a hard look. "I prescribed the best—Page's Inhalers! Are you sure she's exhausting her lungs of all air before she inhales the smoke? Holding it there for several seconds?" He takes off his fine wool overcoat, so new that Lily recognizes it from the window of the men's clothing store in Kinship, and tosses it where Benjamin had been seated.

"We had her follow the directions, like you said," Marvena says. "But it did no good—"

"We were foolish to put our faith in man's medicine!" Jurgis exclaims. "We must have faith, keep prayin' for her; if you just had more faith—"

"Faith didn't work for Mama, either." Ruth's voice softly threads around the room, stitching everyone's gaze to her for a moment. "When the doctor couldn't help, we left the Presbyterian church in Kinship to go to their church." She nods toward Jurgis and Marvena. "Tried their healing ways. That didn't work, either. So we left there, too."

Oh. So that's why she hadn't seen the Harkinses at church in a while. Lily's heart cracks at Ruth's flat, resigned tone.

"Ruth's right. We've tried faith," Marvena rumbles on, steady as a train barreling down.

"But you wouldn't let Frankie—" Jurgis starts.

"If the Almighty wants to help Frankie, then he might oughta just do it—but I'm done putting my faith in him!" Tears stream down Marvena's face. "When's he ever intervened—for any of those we lost? So yes, I went back to shining, for the money to get Frankie to the treatment center *he* told us about."

Dr. Goshen shakes his head. "Don't draw me into this—"

"Faith in the *man* who sold us those worthless asthma cigarettes?" Jurgis's tone twists with disgust. "You have to have faith in *God*, Marvena, really believe—"

"I've believed! Mayhap I don't have a good enough or a deep enough heart. Mayhap I'm too evil, too dark, the things I've thought and done—"

Jurgis rushes to her then, puts his hands to his wife's face. "Don't say that, Marvena; that's not true; you're a good person . . . you just have to believe. . . ."

Marvena gently but firmly pulls his hands from her face. "No, Jurgis. I need a solution and God ain't listening, not to the likes of me. And mayhap God wants us to find our *own* answers. May be that having faith means using the wits the Good Lord gave us, best we can."

Jurgis drops his head.

Marvena looks at Lily. "You gonna take me in?"

Lily considers what she'd said earlier, about how it is not her job to have an opinion about Prohibition one way or another. It is her job to enforce the law when she knows—or has reason to suspect—it has been violated. And here Marvena has confessed.

Lily feels a tug on her sleeve. She looks at Ruth.

"My brother. All I know is he came home sick yesterday. It was late, after school woulda let out, but still some light, hanging on to the sky."

All right. So sometime between four and six in the afternoon.

"Told me he'd been mindin' her still." Ruthie nods toward Marvena. "Then he fell asleep and won't wake up. So I came today to get the doctor."

"Sadly, Mrs. Harkins has pancreatic cancer. There's nothing I"— Dr. Goshen cuts Jurgis a hard look—"nor God can do. It's just her time."

"But it's not Zeb's!" Ruth jumps up.

Lily's heart twists at the conviction of this girl. No one can know when it's their time—and maybe it is Zebediah's, young though he is.

Then, refocusing on the purpose of Ruth's desperate trek, and Dr. Goshen's visit, Lily thinks of a quote from Wayne Wheeler, an advocate from the Anti-Saloon League, headquartered just northeast of here near Columbus, Ohio's state capitol. He'd said, *The government is under no obligation to furnish the people with alcohol that is drinkable when the Constitution prohibits it. The person who drinks this industrial alcohol is a deliberate suicide. . . .*

The quote, reported far and wide and in her local newspaper just last month, had so horrified Lily that it stuck with her, word for word. It could only be deliberate if the drinker was fully informed. She finds the law requiring deadly methanol to be added to industrial alcohol to be reprehensible, no matter the twisted logic defending it. Maybe, when she meets Mabel Walker Willebrandt, she'll ask how a government that's supposed to help and educate people could do such a thing.

Now she looks at Marvena. "There have been reports in the bigger cities of people drinking industrial alcohol, or drinks made from that. But it's lethal—as of earlier this year, the law now requires methanol to be added to make industrial alcohol undrinkable. Some bootleggers have been trying to dilute or mix it to make it drinkable. I gotta ask—"

Marvena's face darkens, and her hands clench by her sides. "You think I've been using alcohol the government's tainted to kill people?"

"The doctor needs to know what you've used, maybe not knowing the industrial alcohol is lethal, maybe hoping to brew product quickly to have plenty to sell," Lily says. "Yours is not the only child whose life is at risk. I'll worry about what to do about your violation of the law later. Right now, we need to help Zebediah."

"I didn't use anything except corn. Pure spring water. Good steel kettles and pipes. Clean canning jars. My shine is pure."

Dr. Goshen sighs. "Well, something's put Zebediah into a coma—which is beyond my ability to treat." He looks at Lily. "Given how tragically the mother's case has turned, I may not be able to convince them to get to the hospital over in Chillicothe."

"I can go with you to the family, but I can't force them to send Zebediah, not by law—"

Lily stops as Ruth's hand laces into hers. "Please, Sheriff Lily. My daddy says you're good people. If he'll listen to anyone, it's you."

Lily gazes out the window at snow falling thickly now in quickening darkness. She turns to Ruth. "How slick was the road down from your place to Kinship Road?"

"The mule path was already pretty slick. From the sharpness of the wind, more sleet and snow is coming."

Lily knows neither her nor the doctor's Model T will make it all the way up to the Harkins place, not on a steep, sleet-slicked dirt path.

She looks evenly at Dr. Goshen. "You will drive up over to where Possum Creek Run branches off Kinship Road, just outside of Rossville. Leave your automobile there."

Dr. Goshen frowns, shakes his head. "I just bought the newest model. Yours, though, has the sheriff's star, so people passing by will be less likely to vandalize—"

Lily grits her teeth to hold back the hard words that fly to the forefront of her thoughts. *Dammit, what "people," on a Thanksgiving evening? Doesn't doctoring sick people matter more than his sharp new motoring machine—which, as such, would be faster and more reliable?*

There's no time to argue—or to ask Marvena the flurry of questions swirling in her mind. Between the boy's condition and the coming dark and storm, there is only time for one focus: helping the boy.

As Lily turns toward Ruth, she spots Benjamin bringing a mug of warm milk to Ruth. Oh, so he hadn't gone to the creek after all. He'd filled in Mama, no doubt, who'd warmed up the beverage. As Ruth takes the mug, gulps eagerly, Benjamin stares at Lily, eyes shining with admiration. *How much has he heard?* Lily brushes off the thought—no time for foolishness now.

Ruth licks milk from the top of her lip. Lily takes the empty mug gently from her, hands it back to Benjamin, while saying to Ruth, "Dr. Goshen will take my automobile, then. We'll follow with my mule and wagon. Then you can direct us up to your house. That way, if we get your pa to agree for Zebediah to be taken to the hospital—"

Ruth's chin tremors and Lily wishes she could scoop her up in a hug. But it wouldn't be right, not yet, for such an embrace would harken of comfort after loss, and she can't take hope away from Ruth. So instead she amends her statement. "When your pa agrees, either he or you can go with the doctor to the hospital—"

The doctor moans—this is more than he'd bargained for. Lily gives him a coal-hard look, hopes he can read her meaning: *You'll go, or I'll requisition that automobile of yours.*

Lily turns back to Ruth. "Does that plan sit well with you?"

Ruth's eyes widen, at last awash with relief and fear and hope, mingling emotions that prick tears. She dashes them away with the back of her hand and nods.

CHAPTER 6

FIONA

Thursday, November 24, 1927
4:00 p.m.

"Are you feeling better?" Fiona asks.

Elias does not react. Eyes closed, he lies so still under the chenille bedspread that for a moment Fiona thinks he's passed. But his eyelids flutter open and he gives a small nod.

"Water?" Elias's voice is a thin, crackly croak.

Fiona pours a small glass from the pitcher on the side table. She holds the glass to his lips, helps him drink.

"Luther?" Elias's eyes are wide with worry, concern for his nephew outweighing any fears he has for himself. It would be touching if Fiona didn't find Luther so grotesque, if Aunt Nell hadn't insinuated that Elias had had a hand in helping George figure out a plan to kill Uncle Henry. "Where, where is he?"

"He went with Abe to find Dr. Goshen," Fiona says. "He said he knows the heart pills you need, that Dr. Goshen should have them on hand."

She leaves off that Abe hadn't wanted Luther to go with him—couldn't Luther just tell him the type required? But as two of George's men helped Elias up the stairs, George had given a dismissive wave of his hand. *Take Luther,* he'd ordered. *Before he gives us all a coronary!* Fiona understood—Luther would fuss and dramatically holler, more so than usual. George can barely tolerate him.

And Abe, always the good foot soldier, had complied.

A few minutes after Abe and Luther had left, the two men came back downstairs, only to find George ordering Aunt Nell, *Go keep an eye on him.* Fiona quickly assessed—she didn't want Aunt Nell alone with Elias. What if she directly accused him? Blurted out the discussion they'd shared at Uncle Henry's grave?

I'll help, Fiona had said.

Klara can do that.

And give Klara a chance to grill Aunt Nell about what they'd talked about? On the other hand, leaving Aunt Nell alone meant that George might make an offer on the farmhouse and Aunt Nell—just to end the nightmare that had overtaken her house—might agree.

Going up with Aunt Nell, though, would give Klara a chance to tell George that Fiona and Aunt Nell had talked far away from the farmhouse—where Klara couldn't overhear. Of course, Fiona could talk her way around that: *Oh, George, I knew I could soften Aunt Nell up better away from the house. . . .*

Better yet, though, is to leave both Aunt Nell and Klara behind in the dining room.

Fiona smiled, imagining the awkwardness that would fall over the room. Then she gave that smile a sympathetic twist and said, *Both women have worked so hard on this meal, dear. Let them rest down here, while I tend to Elias. I'll be back in time to enjoy dessert with you.*

Now Elias sighs. "I'm an idiot, forgetting my pills in Cincinnati. But then, stress can make a person forgetful about the most ordinary things."

Fiona pulls the chair closer, leans in as if inviting confidences. "Working for my husband is stressful?" She asks this with a small smile, as if she's trying to be light, help Elias relax, rather than just slowly sliding a spade into the conversation to dig for truth—maybe something about the day he and George had visited her aunt and uncle.

Elias returns a flickering smile. "George has big plans."

Fiona nods. *Easy, easy. Don't arouse suspicion.* "Yes, he is an ambitious man. I admit, that is one reason I love George."

Elias's eyebrows lift, as if the notions of *George* and *love* in the same sentence are discordantly surprising.

Fiona clears her throat, widens her eyes. "I'm sorry, if you need to rest . . ."

"No, I think it's better if someone is with me right now. And you're a lovely distraction. Someone from Kinship, to remind me of better days."

Fiona forces her gentle smile to linger. "I also like having people around from home. It can feel so foreign, otherwise." She thinks of Leon, at the boarding school in Philadelphia, and her heart pangs. "I admit I'm curious as to why you left Kinship in the first place, and how you came to work for George?"

"We, Luther and I, left Kinship because Luther, well, he got into a bit of trouble. Over a girl that he shouldn't have been seeing."

"Oh!" Fiona widens her eyes, as if this kind of *trouble* is a new concept. "How did you find George?"

"Through my other nephew, Daniel. But we didn't stay in touch after . . . after Daniel's death. We went to Chicago, looking to establish a life there. I find that city overwhelming, but Luther loves it. Or should I say—he finds it exciting. . . ." Elias pauses, perhaps, Fiona thinks, also reconsidering the notion of *Luther* and *love* in the same sentence. "He ran through the money we'd gotten—from me selling my house, him selling the mining company—pretty fast. So he started working for a man on various . . . assignments . . . and quickly realized that the man was one of George's employees. From there . . . well, George decided we could both be useful."

"Elias, right before you had your attack, Luther was talking about men getting sick in Kinship this weekend." Elias closes his eyes, but Fiona presses on, even takes Elias's hand in hers. Let him think of her as an ally, a comforter. "It seemed to distress you so much. If you told me more about it, maybe I could do something about it. Something that might bring you ease?"

"I—I may not make it through to tomorrow and I can't have this on my conscience, too. . . ." His voice fades.

"In case . . . in case you meet our Maker?"

Elias goes stiffly still again. Has she pressed too hard after all? But then he licks his lips. He opens his eyes as she gives him another sip of water.

"If I tell you," he whispers, "will you promise to help stop it?"

"Of course."

"George isn't building a warehouse here. He's set up a plan for his own trucks of legal alcohol, for his tonic, to be hijacked, supposedly by bootleggers, but really by his own men. He'll collect the insurance, but bring the alcohol here. Reconstitute it with sugar syrup, other bootleg gin or whiskey, water, flavorings, rebottle it, and distribute it," Elias says. "More money to be made in that than in Vogel's Tonic—though he'll continue that business of course."

Fiona turns this over. It's brilliant. And she doesn't have to ask, *Why here?* It's remote. Hard to pursue. Revenuers from the Bureau of Prohibition are focused on the big cities, or the country's coasts. And here there are backwoods moonshiners and miners and farmers aplenty who wouldn't mind extra dollars, wherever they might come from.

"I see," Fiona says softly. "But . . . what does that have to do with Kinship Inn?"

Elias opens his eyes, looks at her. "Luther came early, to convince locals to help. But—he hasn't been particularly successful. I love my nephew like a son, but he tends to rub people the wrong way." Elias looks down, and again, Fiona senses he is not telling the whole truth. "It seems, well, Lily Ross and I parted with hard hearts."

Fiona startles at that revelation.

He gives a sad smile. "She found Luther's—management style—at Ross Mining too . . . harsh. Anyway, Luther has followed through on a plan of George's and Abe's I never agreed to—substituting the local brew at the speakeasy for methanol. That's why I reacted so strongly, when Luther said he'd done as asked."

Fiona stares at him.

"Methanol is wood alcohol," he explains.

She's still unsure of the import.

He sighs. "Drinking that would cause serious illness. Maybe death.

The idea is to show the people of the town and county George's power and reach. Work for him if asked—or don't, at your own peril."

Now the horror of what Elias has described strikes Fiona. Her hand goes to her mouth. She knows her husband is ruthless, but this is beyond anything she'd imagined him capable of. Who knows who could be hurt or killed? Men, or women, whom yes, Fiona had been happy to leave behind. But they were also people who had patronized her first husband's shoe repair shop, whose children had been Leon's childhood friends.

"Can you convince George to stop it?" Elias asks anxiously. "Reason with him?"

For a second, the image returns of battered Eugenia, who'd come to her breakfast table the morning after the wedding to apologize for mocking her accent, followed quickly by another flashing image, of Aunt Nell expressing her suspicion that George had conspired to have Uncle Henry killed when he wouldn't sell his land to George—a suspicion that seems all the more well-founded now that Fiona knows why George wants this particular patch of Bronwyn County under his control.

Reason with George?

If the situation weren't so dire, if it wouldn't break the trust she's building with Elias, she'd laugh.

"I will do my best . . . but first, I have to ask you something."

"Anything, my dear."

"You know something of heart trouble, of course, and I'm sorry you're having it now. Funny thing, my dear uncle Henry. He never had a bit of it. Was as hearty as could be. Now that you've confided in me, I'm sure I can confide in you and that you won't tell George that my aunt Nell says that you and George came to visit a few weeks ago. Just before Uncle Henry died. Tell me—did he look ill to you? It's just so strange to think he had a stroke."

For a long moment, Elias stares back at her. Something shifts and hardens in his eyes, though his expression stays slack, pale. Fiona swallows nervously. Maybe she's miscalculated. She'd thought of him as somewhat soft, easily manipulated by her much more savvy husband.

The flinty look in his gaze now tells her that he is capable of stone-cold action.

His voice is thin but unwavering when he finally replies. "I came with George mainly to assess the property, check the various outbuildings, see what might be suitable, or at least quick to modify, for the operation George wants to install. There are inherent dangers—fire, explosion—in the art of brewing. It is a delicate process. I know a lot about chemistry—that's why I'm useful. . . ." Elias pauses, closes his eyes again, whether from weariness or to keep her from reading his expression she isn't certain. "When George asked about your uncle and aunt's health, I did advise that they both looked fit, likely to live for many years."

Fiona freezes as cold questions run their cruel and tingly fingers over her skin.

What else had he advised George? About when and what time of day Uncle Henry would be out—by himself—plowing under the fields? Elias, who had been a gentleman farmer, would know that, whereas George, who had never farmed, would not. About the best way to have hired guns surprise and attack Uncle Henry?

Fiona takes a deep breath, forces herself to focus.

She cannot get distracted—not even by this.

Now, before anything else, she must stay the poisoning that's set up to take place at the Kinship Inn. Get word to Lily, somehow?

And then . . . after she gets George's assets in her name—for the sake of their child, of course—she can somehow get his tax records into the Bureau of Prohibition's hands. And if there's any blowback on her, she can take credit for having saved the townspeople from George's plot with tainted alcohol.

Tricky.

She will figure it out.

Somehow, later, she'll find out the truth about Uncle Henry's death—and deal with Elias if she must. For now, Elias must remain an ally.

Fiona gives Elias's pillow a gentle fluffing.

"I will," she whispers, "do as you've asked. And maybe . . . if you would like to find a way for you and Luther to get out from under working for George, I could help with that, too. . . ."

Elias does not open his eyes, but a thin smile lifts his lips.

Good. He thinks she's his ally.

Fiona rises quietly. She needs a break from him. "I'm just going to get you some broth. I'll be back in a moment."

She steps out in the hallway.

"Oh!" she cries.

For there is George, leaning against the wall just to the left of the door.

His unreadable yet sharp gaze stills her in her tracks.

CHAPTER 7

LILY

Thursday, November 24, 1927
4:00 p.m.

Daisy, Lily's mule, comes to a sudden stop at the foot of a sharp rise. As Lily'd expected, the road to Ruth's home isn't much more than a rutted dirt footpath, now covered over in a wintry mix of snow and ice. Both fall fast and slant, stinging Lily's face.

Lily gives Daisy a quick flick, enough to send them jolting up the rise after all and then come skidding into a bit of flatland. Now clear of the hovering branches in the woods, Lily notes that the sky is a sodden mass of thick gray clouds, laden barges ready to overflow with more ice and snow. Behind those clouds the sun will soon set, and there will be no moonlight to guide their return journey. Lily glances behind her, double-checks that she has a coal-oil lantern in the foot well by Dr. Goshen.

When she turns forward again, they're already upon a stone two-story farmhouse harkening back a hundred years. A porch wraps around from the front and along the east side, ending at a door into a white clapboard addition at the back of the house—a kitchen, appended probably thirty years before. Porch corners are embellished with wooden lattice curlicues, a bit of fanciness on an otherwise sternly practical house, like a dollop of just-churned butter on hard bread. Warm light flickers through both up- and downstairs windows, yet coldness seems to swirl from inside the house as much as around it outside.

Nearby, the open doors to a dull red barn reveal great stalks of tobacco hung upside down along the rafters, a disconcerting sight in this weather, at this time of year. By now, the tobacco, harvested back in August or September, is surely cured and ready for market. Such neglect is a sign of how desperate the Harkinses' situation must be.

"Go on," Lily tells Ruth. "Let your folks know we're here."

The girl scrambles down and dashes up the front porch steps.

Lily hops off and unhitches Daisy, ignoring Dr. Goshen's yelp as the wagon shifts back just a few feet. By the time she's tied Daisy to a pole in the yard and thrown a spare rough wool blanket over the beast's back, Dr. Goshen is by her side, giving her a dark look.

"You could have warned me about the wagon backsliding," he grumbles.

He'd been fairly helpful on another case a year before; Lily wonders what has turned him to precious uppityness. As with her questions for Marvena, now is not the time to worry about such.

Lily hurries up the steps, so fast she nearly trips on a cement planter at the top of the porch. The planter is filled with dead flowers, zinnias that would have been cheerily resplendent in summer. Seed pods droop, unharvested. Another sign of the grimness that awaits inside—no farmwife, especially one who has carefully taught her daughter to can apples, would let those seeds go to waste. She'd gather them, keep them in a jar in a dry cupboard, think about them in flitting moments over the long dark winter, find comfort in the anticipation of planting them in soft, yielding spring earth. Faith the seeds will last the winter; hope in the notion of yellow and red and pink summer blooms.

As Lily is about to knock on the kitchen door, it swings open to reveal Mrs. Harkins, her robe and nightgown hanging loose over her gaunt frame. Her feet are bare. Loose, greasy strings of hair hang from her bun; her skin is sallow and dry; her shoulders scoop forward. Her scent is vinegary like old sweat.

"Sheriff Lily." Her voice is a thin thread struggling to pull along each word. "Please help. Our boy—"

"Dora!" Leroy rushes to the door, gazing at his wife, not seeming to notice Lily at all. "What are you doing—you're gonna catch cold—"

"The sheriff is here. I'm hoping she and the doctor are here to take Zeb—"

"No, sweetheart, we gotta get you back in bed, keep you warm—"

Lily clears her throat. "Mr. Harkins, I can get Zebediah to the help he needs. Based on what Ruth told us, Zebediah has ingested tainted alcohol. The sooner we c-can—"

Lily stutters to a stop. Whereas at her farm Leroy often removes his hat and lowers his eyes when addressing her, now his gaze is straight and sharp as a finely honed stone arrowhead. This is his turf, his land. "You need to pull my boy in for drinking, so be it." As he starts to pull his wife from the cold door, his voice softens. "Come on, honey."

Lily's fists clench. *Damn that it's the man's legal right to run his family as he sees fit.* She relaxes her hands, tries to speak gently. "I'm not pulling him in. We just want Zebediah to be all right."

Dora jerks away from her husband, and the look on his face is as if she has shot him through the heart. "Please, Leroy! Just let the doctor in—"

"Didn't do nothing for you," Leroy mutters. "Just like that fool church didn't do nothing."

Lily's heart crackles, sorrowful for the man's loss of faith. He's already lost so much.

But not his love for his wife. As he gently turns her away from the door, Leroy says over his shoulder, "Come in then. Shut the door behind you!"

Inside the tiny kitchen, there are no scents or signs of Thanksgiving. Ruth is already busy at a small worktable, assembling bread and butter sandwiches, handing them to two toddlers, a boy and a girl. Fraternal twins.

Lily's heart flinches as Dora walks gingerly over to Ruth. She folds her arms around the girl and rests her cheek against Ruth's. Dora is past mothering, except for this: relief that her daughter is fine, wanting the boy upstairs to be fine, wanting all her young ones to be fine.

Dora says to Lily, "You'll find him in the bedroom at the top of the back staircase."

Lily rushes up, Dr. Goshen following. At the top, Lily stops, beset by the lingering smell of sick, and bleachy attempts to scour it away, and, underlying that, the scent of something herbal, vaguely mint-like. Perhaps Dora or Ruth had tried to make a healing tea for Zebediah.

The boy is curled up in the bottom of one of two bunk beds that nearly fill the room, barely space for a wardrobe to one side and a washbowl under the window.

Zebediah somehow looks both older and younger than Lily recollects. The small bed seems to be slowly swallowing him. His face is pale, waxen, his lips flecked with dried spittle.

A quilt has slid to the floor, revealing his bare feet and his pants, too short for him. The brown wool pant legs have been cut jaggedly, as if with a knife. *How odd.* Lily makes a mental note.

Dr. Goshen crosses swiftly to the boy, kneels, pulls a stethoscope from his doctor's bag, checks the boy's heart rate. Then leans forward and sniffs the thin breath rasping from the child's gaping mouth.

"His breath is too sweet," Dr. Goshen says. "Fruity. I think he has diabetes. That—combined with alcohol—could put him into diabetic ketoacidosis. The vomiting, abdominal pains, loss of consciousness, all fit."

Diabetes—she had, during the war, worked with her husband's uncle, Elias Ross, who was the town doctor then, to help patients during the flu epidemic. One had diabetes—a woman in her twenties. She couldn't keep food down and the flu seemed to affect her more rapidly, more severely, than others. She fell into a state similar to this—the shuddery breathing, the waxy appearance. And she passed away.

Lily shudders at the memory. She is also—God help her—relieved that even if the alcohol from Marvena's still hadn't helped the boy's situation, it hadn't been the culprit.

"So you'll be able to treat him, then?" Surely some fluids, or some tincture pulled out and compounded from the doctor's medicine bag, would be sufficient to bring the boy around.

But he is shaking his head. "He needs insulin, and he'll need it for the rest of his life. He's lucky—commercial insulin has been available for the past few years. He will need to go to the hospital in Chillicothe."

"I ain't taking him all the way over to Chillicothe." Leroy's voice is so low that it sounds like it's scraping the floor, as if it had dragged itself reluctantly up with him and wished it could be back downstairs, offering soothing platitudes to his wife. "He done this to hisself—he can rally out of it."

"He can't rally out of diabetes," says the doctor. "It's not something he brought on himself. He'd have likely fallen into this condition, or wasted away, even if he hadn't drunk Marvena's hooch."

Ire rises in Lily—*for God's sake, the boy is dying.* Lily swallows her rage. "I can take him over to Chillicothe. It's not that far, and he could be back in a few days, and wouldn't Dora rather see him healthy, one last time—"

Leroy's expression is overcome by a gossamer of hope but quickly resettles into even deeper hardness than before. "No. He shouldn't have done what he did."

He is, Lily realizes, putting all his pain and anger and bitterness at the dire fate that's been heaped on his beloved, at what he must surely see as the Good Lord's rejection of his prayers and acts of faith, onto his children. The only sweetness he has left is for his wife. Lily shudders. When she passes, will softness or love return to him in any measure at all to dole onto his children?

"Please."

Behind him, Dora appears, panting from the effort to climb the stairs. She already looks a specter, fading from time and place and memory.

Leroy wraps his arms around her. "You should be resting. I thought you were on the couch downstairs—I'd never have left your side."

"But soon I'm gonna have to leave yours," she says. Leroy gasps, and Lily can no longer bear to look at this couple, clinging to each other. "And I need to know you will take care of all of our children, not be too harsh when they fail or fall or get hurt."

For the next few moments the only sound in the room is Zebediah's ragged breathing.

Less than ten minutes later, the doctor and Lily have Zebediah in the back seat of her Model T. The doctor is in the back with him, settling a quilt over him, while Lily and Ruth are spreading coarse-ground corn-meal around the tires. Lily had already cranked up the automobile and the engine runs with jittery reluctance in the cold. Now the snow is settling and sticking to the road. Thank God that Ruth—smart girl—had thought to grab not just quilts for her brother, but cornmeal to give the automobile tires traction.

"Will you be all right to get Daisy and the wagon back up on your own, Ruth?" Lily doesn't like thinking of the possibility of Daisy mis-stepping in the dark and the wagon overturning, Ruth being injured or worse. "I can come up with you, hike back down—"

"Ma'am. Course I can."

Lily nods. "Just don't be afraid to give Daisy a flick, like I did. And maybe give her a lump of sugar, if she behaves on the trek."

"Yes'm," Ruth says. Then, after a moment's hesitation, she reaches in her coat pocket, holds her hand out to Lily. "Thank you for all you done—whatever happens. You didn't hafta." Lily was just doing her job. But to deny whatever Ruth is offering would be an insult. Lily holds her hand out. Something sharp presses into her palm.

She turns her hand upright, stares at the item.

"When Zeb got home, he wasn't making much sense," Ruth says. "He just said this came from a fella he found up by Mrs. Sacovech's still, that the fella was hurt. Then his speech got so slushy and jumbled, I couldn't make sense of what came next."

Lily must hurry Zebediah to the hospital, an hour away in good weather. But the item, glinting in her hand in the last of the dimming daylight, rivets her to the spot.

It is a pin in the shape of a bright blue shield, edged as well as lettered in gold:

Bureau of Prohibition Agent
US Treasury Department

CHAPTER 8

※

FIONA

Thursday, November 24, 1927
4:10 p.m.

Fiona stands as still as possible as George pulls her head back by her hair, his other hand knuckling into her lower back, pressing her body to his. She wants to avert her gaze from his hard glare, but she can't move. She wills her eyes to simply convey softness. Submissiveness. Not pleading, certainly not angry. Tipping her look toward either might trigger George to rip out her hair. Or snap her neck.

They are in her old bedroom, door slammed shut. He's never been this brutal before. Now she can't hold back tears of pain from seeping to the corners of her eyes. In the blurry periphery of her vision, she sees the angry flare of his nostrils, discerns from the slight lift of his cheeks that his lips bear a disgusted snarl. If she could see the whole of his face, from a safe distance, she has no doubt it would be like gazing upon a snare.

Then George blinks, and for a second she sees a sliver of something else. Fear. Hurt.

Hurt?

Yes. *Hurt.* George had trusted her—or at least assumed that she was glib enough not to question his actions behind his back. He must have heard something between her and Elias that set him off, but what? How long had he been standing outside the door?

Fiona forces her breath to even and slow. Forces herself to think.

The solid oak door had been shut. She and Elias had been talking at a near whisper, Elias because he was scared and in pain, Fiona because she wished to appear soothing while digging for truths she could eventually forge into a weapon to use against George.

Perhaps it is not anything he heard in particular, but simply that Elias and Fiona had been talking, and at length. George does not like anything he cannot control, and he had not been in control of the conversation. Once, at the Cincinnati mansion, she and Klara had been conferring before a dinner party when George walked into the dining room, making them both jump with his snapped question: *What are you two yammering on about?* Perplexed, she'd replied, *The number of place settings for tonight's dinner.* He'd looked relieved.

Now the scant twin slivers of hurt and fear in his eyes, just behind the cruel anger, embolden her. George Vogel is vulnerable after all. And she can use that.

"Oh, George," Fiona sighs.

He jerks her hair, but she does not yelp. Keeps her eyes soft and embracing on his.

"What were you talking about?" George asks.

"You," Fiona says as evenly as possible. Then, though doing so painfully rips several strands of hair from her scalp, she forces herself forward, just enough so her lips brush his.

George lets go of her. She staggers back. He shoves her, so that she lands on the edge of the bed. Her head and neck are throbbing and she longs to rub them. More than that, she wishes she could strike George. But she sits still, staring up at him evenly. As if they are equals.

"What?" George looks at his hands, seems surprised to see strands of her hair.

He slaps his hands together. She forces herself not to stare at her hair falling to the rug.

"Elias told me everything." Fiona waits for shock to fully cover

George's face. She savors the sense of satisfaction over spawning such a reaction, more intimate in some ways than their lovemaking. Before the sense can make her recklessly giddy, she adds in a soft voice, "About the plans for the property here. That it's not going to be a warehouse. That you're going to have your trucks of legal alcohol hijacked, collect the insurance, and then bring the alcohol here for reconstituting and reselling." She musters an admiring smile. "George, it's brilliant!"

George stares at her. "Why in the hell would he tell you that?"

"Because he thinks it's brilliant, too." So far—the truth. Or at least part of it. Now to keep her voice even for a lie. She leans forward conspiratorially. "He told me that Aunt Nell has told him that she would only ever sell this farm to me. No matter the consequences."

George plops down on the rocker. His girth sends the rocker shooting back. But it doesn't tip over. Even a wooden rocker seems to know not to make a fool of George Vogel. "Oh yeah? And when would she have told him that?"

She must answer carefully.

At last, she allows herself to look away from George, to give herself a moment to think without his gaze bearing down on her.

Her eyes trail to the armchair across from George, to a pillow in an embroidered cover. It's the first cross-stitch Fiona had ever done, a scene of a young woman walking beside a pond, in a pink dress, with a matching pink parasol, blithely unaware of the swan gazing at her from the water's edge. Fiona had so wanted that embroidery kit from the notions and fabric store in Kinship years ago, but Aunt Nell had said it was too advanced for a first-time project. Yet it had shown up weeks later under the Christmas tree, a gift from Uncle Henry.

She moves to the chair, picks up the pillow as she sits down. Now Fiona's hands shake a little as she holds the pillow in her lap. Who had been right? Both of them. She'd only finished half of the pillow, disappointed by how her lumpy stitches botched the charm of the image. Aunt Nell—never one to let anything go to waste—had finished the pillow with smooth, perfect stitches.

The pillow's half-lumpy, half-smooth scene of a genteel yet exotic place—one with parasols and swans—seemed to taunt Fiona for the rest of her time with Uncle Henry and Aunt Nell: she hadn't seen the project through, not by herself.

But this time, she was determined. She would see her plan through.

She looks up at George, replies matter-of-factly, "When you were here with him to visit Aunt Nell and Uncle Henry three weeks ago."

George stops rocking. He leans forward, elbows to knees, clasps his hands. *Steady, steady.* Fiona keeps her eyes unwaveringly on his.

"We were together the whole visit," George says.

Fiona swallows. He's not going to deny or try to explain away that they'd visited, and yet he'd told her that this was his first time on the farm.

She forces another smile, takes a risk, hedges her bet that he won't recall every detail of the visit against her observation of how much happens on any given day with George, what's more over the course of three weeks. "Were you? There was never a time that Aunt Nell and Elias walked the grounds together, while you and Uncle Henry talked business, man-to-man?"

Doubt flashes across George's face, but he says, "Well, of course there would have been—though your uncle was a tough one. Didn't want to sell, even when I told him how much it would mean to you to have this place." George gestures around the room. *Well, of course* he wouldn't have revealed his real purpose for wanting the farm. "Told him how sentimental you are." George gives a cold smile, showing only the tips of his upper teeth. *Sentimental.*

But she says softly, "That is right, darling." It takes all her resolve not to scoff. She's . . . well, she wonders—her head is pounding so hard that it's hard to think—*What is the opposite of sentimental?* There's nothing she wants to reflect back on. She only wants to look forward, to a future in which she is in control of her and her children's fates.

Not George. Or anyone else. Just her.

"Elias should have told me—not you," George says. *Ah, good.* His wrath is now turning from her to Elias. "And why would your aunt have told him?"

"Elias says she told him that she knows I always wanted to have more children."

True, but Martin had been content with one son. Said they could offer more to one child than to many.

"But she also told him that I had such trouble in my early years." Not true; she'd never had a miscarriage. Fiona looks down as if the notion of her having had relations with her first husband is shameful. Her face reddens, as if she is blushing modestly.

But the heat rises from a panicky thought: What if she's been wrong in assuming that George would be pleased with news of a child?

After all, she'd been surprised that Martin had been content with one child.

She'd been telling herself that this baby would give her leverage—but what if George feels pinned down by the news? What if, oh God, what if he insists she have it aborted?

He'd know people who could make that happen—with or without her consent.

Maybe she should hide the news. Run away. But what of Leon? How would she get to him? How would she and her children live, without George's support yet on the run from him? He'd never accept the shame of a woman abandoning him.

No, if she wants to eventually get the power to control her own life, she must trust her instinct about George's ego. Take this gamble.

Wouldn't Martin be proud?

The bitterness of the thought strikes her, makes her inhale sharply at last.

A sound, she hopes, that George might also misinterpret, perhaps as hopeful excitement.

Fiona tilts her head up just so, looks up at George through her long lashes. "But I'm not having trouble now."

Fiona holds her breath as she watches George, who has frozen and is staring at her.

Slowly, a smile tugs up George's lips. The widest smile she'd ever seen him give.

"Do you mean—are you telling me—"

Oh, thank God.

Fiona smiles, too—out of relief, but let George see it as joy. "Yes,

George, yes! We're having a baby. And that's what brought all this up with Elias, you see. While I was tending to him, he said he'd noticed that I looked paler than usual. A bit off my food at dinner. And being a doctor, he wondered, and well, I told him . . ."—Fiona pauses, thinks of her uncle Henry, of Leon away in Philadelphia, and the tears rise naturally—"well, because I have been sickly." That much is true, though of course she hasn't told Elias any such thing. "And that's why he told me about the plans, because he thought that would mean so much for us—for our child, George!"

George rushes over, pulls her from the chair—but gently—to the bed, sits down next to her, puts an arm around her.

"Oh, this is good news." He's beaming, as if just moments before he hadn't been pulling her head back so hard by her hair that she thought her neck would snap.

Fiona makes herself melt into his embrace. She looks down at the embroidered pillow, on the floor at their feet. She still hasn't figured out how to stop the planned attack of alcohol poisoning at the Kinship Inn. Maybe she could figure a way, once Abe and Luther return.

She has at least a day for that—the speakeasy won't be running tonight.

But she has only a little bit of time to tell Elias about her pregnancy, to make sure he'll back up her story.

Fiona sighs. Already, she's constructing a plan far more complex than the embroidery pattern of her youth. *This is going to be hard—*

"Oh, my little spitfire," George says, fairly cooing, apparently certain that Fiona's sigh was proffered from contentment. "Our baby!"

Or maybe it's not going to be that hard at all.

CHAPTER 9

LILY

Friday, November 25, 1927
12:32 a.m.

At last, Lily's house emerges in her headlights. She exhales—blessed relief at the sight. Since leaving Dr. Goshen off at his home in Kinship forty-five minutes before—the drive thrice longer than usual in this weather—she's had to stop and get out twice and use a spare blanket to wipe ice off her windshield. Even so, she'd soon had trouble distinguishing the edges of the road, inching along slower than if she'd been driving Daisy.

And yet also a slight sting of disappointment at the darkness of her house—no coal-oil lamps shimmering behind the panes of her parlor window. Course, it's silly to expect Mama to wait up into the wee hours—doesn't she already do enough for Lily?

Lily parks her automobile near the road, knowing it will be hard to drive up the lane from the house if it snows all night. Her fingers won't fully extend when she releases the chilly steering wheel, so hard had she gripped it on the long drive.

She treks around to the back entry—less likely to disturb Mama and the children than coming in the front door near the foot of the stairs. Despite the cold, Lily hesitates at the back porch as she had just the afternoon before, when she'd come in with sage for the turkey. Thanksgiving dinner seems more like a lifetime than just a few hours ago.

Lily alerts to a creaking sound. Her hound or the animals in the barn? But no, the animals are surely all settled for the night, and their sounds from inside the barn wouldn't carry so far. A night critter, then, movements muted by the cold and insulating snow?

The sound comes again. Steps, inside the house. Lily lets herself into the mudroom. Surely it's Mama, never having gone to sleep after all. She slips into the kitchen and sees in the entry to the dining room the shadow of a figure, rimmed by a light burning after all. Lily draws her revolver.

The figure stills, sensing movement.

"I'm sorry, I didn't mean to startle you." Benjamin, his voice tentative and somber.

Her face flames, not just for pulling her gun so quickly. His voice feels like a warm caress, reaching to her across the kitchen. Yesterday afternoon he must have parked alongside the house where she had not walked tonight, and of course she wouldn't have seen his automobile still here in the dark.

"I was in the parlor and I just heard your automobile, and you walking around the house. I thought to come back here, to start up some hot water for tea—"

"For *tea*?"

"May I light a few lamps?"

"I reckon," Lily says brusquely. Then she considers. "I never saw a light from the parlor window when I walked up to the house. What were you doing in the parlor in the dark, anyway?"

Silence for a long, drawn moment.

"Thinking," he says finally.

She swallows back the urge to ask, *About what?* She retreats to the mudroom, divests coat, boots, and hat. When she reenters the kitchen, it's now alight with several coal-oil lamps.

Lily stows her tote bag on top of the pie safe. Her fingers brush the red glass bowl, where she keeps her sheriff's badge. Earlier, she'd left in such a hurry that she'd not thought to put it on. She thinks of the other badge—the revenuer's badge, from the Bureau of Prohibition, now carefully wrapped up in a handkerchief, in her tote bag.

She turns to see Benjamin at the stove. As the kettle starts to sing, Lily realizes that the kettle has been long filled with water, her cup prepared, her return anticipated. That he has been awaiting her.

His hand shakes a little as he lifts the kettle. Had she rattled him that much with her drawn gun? As he pours into the cup, the tea identifies itself by its aroma: chamomile.

He brings the tea to the worktable—back already in the kitchen after serving as the children's table at Thanksgiving dinner; had he helped Mama return it?—and turns up the wick on the lamp, chasing darkness from the room. Exhaustion rolls over her like a boulder, and she sits down hard on a kitchen chair. She picks up the teacup, breathes in the soothing steam.

"Nana said that this is the tea you would need when you got home," Benjamin says as he sits down across from her. "Your mother agreed—though they quibbled over how much sweetening."

Despite the weariness crackling in her bones, the sorrowful turn Thanksgiving had taken, Lily smiles. She takes a sip, savors the sweet yet light tea, the warmth slipping down her throat. "Let me guess—Mama said one teaspoon honey; Nana said two."

Benjamin laughs. A dimple appears in his right cheek. The deep timbre of his laugh is surprisingly easy and soothing. "Yes. And Mrs. McArthur prevailed."

It is strange to hear her mother referred to by her formal name. And it is strange to hear his Cleveland accent—smooth as a planed plank of wood with just an occasional splintery twang now and again. She realizes how little she knows about him. She isn't even certain what, exactly, he's doing for the Bureau of Mines over in Rossville.

And she realizes that she'd like to know more, imagines for a moment simply saying: *Well, that wasn't an entirely typical workday for me. Tell me more about what you do. . . .* She'd sound ridiculous. So instead, she says of the tea, "Doesn't taste like it."

Benjamin lifts an eyebrow. "I added an extra dollop after your mother went up to put the children to bed."

Now Lily laughs. She takes another sip. As she puts the cup back down, the clink makes a tinkly echo in the kitchen. She stares at him, as if the sound asks all the obvious questions: Why is he still here? What happened after she left—between Marvena and Jurgis, and the others?

But Benjamin has his own question. "How is Zebediah?"

Her heart warms that Benjamin remembers the boy's name. "We got him to the hospital in Chillicothe, prob'ly just in time. The hospital doctor got him quickly to a room, and injected him with small doses of insulin." Lily shakes her head, recollecting how thin yet shuddery the boy's breath had sounded, like a gossamer curtain between this life and the next, stirred by deep winds. "He had not regained consciousness by the time we left. Dr. Goshen thinks it may take a day or two."

"So his condition had nothing to do with drinking Marvena's moonshine?"

"It was made worse by doing so. But in a way, it saved his life. Brought the condition forward." Lily sighs. "But that doesn't mean what she is doing is OK."

"I thought you find Prohibition foolish?"

"I do. But I still have to uphold the rule of law. My opinion can't dictate what I enforce—or don't—or who I bring in or help. And I'm not on the side of deceiving her spouse, of keeping important information hidden." She looks down at her cup. Will he read in her look that she's experienced such deception?

"Will the boy be all right after he's home?"

Lily describes the Harkins family situation.

"That poor family," Benjamin says when she finishes. Benjamin's eyes glisten in the coal-oil light, and he looks away. Lily's eyebrows lift. It is rare to see such emotion manifest in a man. Daniel was always so stoic and hard. She takes another sip of tea and considers. Her face reflames at the realization: this softer approach intrigues her.

Then she admonishes herself. She must be really weary to let her mind wander so. She has enough to deal with: not least interrogating Marvena. And most alarming, trying to find out the truth about what Ruth had told her as she gave her the revenuer's badge: *When Zeb got home, he wasn't making much sense . . . said this came from a fella he found up by Mrs. Sacovech's still . . . the fella was hurt.* Plus, she has the meeting in the morning with Special Agent Barnaby Sloan, from the Columbus field office of the Bureau of Prohibition. She'll have to tell him about the badge. She hopes he'll just say, *Oh, we've had an agent or two come down this way the past few months. Must have fallen off a lapel.*

But she knows better than to think it will be that simple.

She should get to bed, sleep a few hours before pursuing these tasks. But there's one question that's going to keep her awake if she doesn't ask it. She drinks the last of her tea and then says, "Thank you. But why are you still here, Mr. Russo?"

Benjamin's eyes glint with a spark of hurt at the formal use of his name. He clears his throat, says, "After you left, everyone else did, too, abruptly. It was probably just as well—though Jolene and Frankie were particularly upset at parting sooner than they expected." He smiles, shakes his head. "I grew up with three older brothers, no sisters, so I didn't know girls could wail so loudly, as if life was ending."

Lily smiles, both at his good humor and at his tiny divulgence of personal detail.

"I lingered to help your mama and Jolene with the cleaning up," he says. "They didn't seem to mind the help."

Lily glances around. Indeed, everything is in order. She's relieved at the notion of no household chores awaiting her. But it is unusual that a man would volunteer for such work. Her eyebrows rise, questioning such beneficence.

Benjamin grins. "I have to clean up after myself all the time. I rent a bedroom from Mrs. Lumpkin, but it's up to me to do my own cooking, and she doesn't tolerate a mess. Plus, my own mama didn't stand for boys not doing household chores."

"Good for her."

"And I'm always happy to help your mama," Benjamin says, the corners of his eyes crinkling as he smiles.

Ah. Of course. Occasionally, Mama and Lily run into Benjamin in Kinship and she watches the two strike up a conversation. They've become friends, of sorts. They have, after all, Lily's brother Roger in common. Every now and again, Lily used to catch Mama asking Daniel about Roger and how he had fared in the army—up to that last terrible second. Daniel was always soothing: *Roger had friends. Everyone liked him. He died quickly, no pain.*

Benjamin's expression retreats into seriousness. "I was going to leave hours ago, but as we were finishing up, a knock came at the door. . . ." He hesitates in a way that only portends bad news. Lily braces herself.

"It was a man who introduced himself as Abe Miller. There was another man with him—though it was clear Miller didn't want him at the door, told him he was supposed to have waited in the automobile. Lily, the other man was Luther Ross."

For a long moment, Lily stares at Benjamin. Surely she's not heard properly.

Luther Ross—her deceased husband Daniel's half brother—would not dare come to her county, what's more to her house, would he? Luther and Elias Ross—Luther and Daniel's uncle—had each played a role in events that led to Daniel's death. She could have tried to bring them to justice through the law two years before, but doing so would have upended the community in hateful ways, the thought of which still makes her shudder. And so, after reluctantly accepting George Vogel's help to enforce their demand, she and Marvena had made them agree to leave, never come back.

But now . . . Luther Ross was back in Bronwyn County.

Coming to her door late on a snowy Thanksgiving night.

And if Luther Ross is with Abe Miller—George's top man, his right hand—then George has for some reason gone back on his promise to keep them away from here.

How wrong she's been to think she could banish them forever. Their faces—George, Luther, Elias—emerge from the recesses of memory. Specters that will always glimmer just outside of her mind's eye, haunting her, for as long as they live. Maybe even after that.

"What—what did they want?" Lily jumps up, as if to shake off the great pressure resting on her chest. She can barely breathe.

"Lily—my God—you've gone so pale. Here—let me help you to the settee—" Benjamin reaches for her, touches her arm.

Lily jerks away—both shocked by the touch and how it ricochets through her and impatient at being patronized. "No! I don't need to sit down! What did they want?"

"Abe Miller said they were looking for Dr. Goshen. They'd gone to the doctor's house and his wife told them he had come here with Ruth Harkins."

"Why did they need the doctor?" Lily snaps.

Benjamin's face shutters at Lily's biting tone. "For Luther's uncle, Elias. Luther seemed to believe Elias had a stroke or mild heart attack, but didn't have his heart pills with him. He was desperate for any help he could find."

Lily sits back down, presses her eyes shut. She hears Benjamin rise, walk away, no doubt weary of the drama surrounding Lily and at last eager to get back to his boarding room. She can't blame him.

She forces herself to breathe, to focus on this news. How worried should she be about the sanctity of her home? Why is George Vogel in this area—and on Thanksgiving? As far as she knows, the only connection George now has to the area is his wife, Fiona, who grew up here. Fiona had been more acquaintance than friend with Lily, even when they both lived in Kinship proper.

Something glints in her mind's eye.

The Prohibition agent's shield.

Which Zebediah Harkins had claimed to find near Marvena's still.

Surely this couldn't be connected. Yet with Vogel in the area, surely it must be.

Hot tears run up behind Lily's eyelids, at the overwhelmingness of this situation.

And a tiny voice teases her, with sorrowfulness at Benjamin's departure.

But then she hears his steps returning. She opens her eyes, gazes up at him holding a glass of water out to her. She takes it in both hands, as a child would—embarrassing, but she is shaking so that she can't help it. She takes a long sip.

Benjamin waits, says nothing. His presence is calm, relaxed. He's not going to go anywhere, she realizes, but neither is he going to do anything other than wait for her to tell him what she needs.

Lily takes another sip. Her shakiness settles. "Did either say why they are in Bronwyn County? Where they are staying?"

"No."

"What time did they arrive?"

"Just after three thirty p.m." Benjamin nods toward the grandfather clock. "The half hour had just chimed."

So shortly after she and Doc Goshen and Ruth had left.

"Did anyone tell them where we went?"

Benjamin shakes his head. "I was about to—I was the one who answered the door. But by then Mrs. McArthur had come to the door, and she looked so spooked by the sight of the men."

Oh, poor Mama. Even Mama, whose instinct is to give everyone the benefit of the doubt, doesn't like or trust Luther—he had, after all, made decisions when he ran the mining company in Rossville that led to a tragic cave-in, and both Lily's father and Marvena's then-husband had died while working on rescue efforts. Mama only knows of Abe Miller as a shadowy sight who has from time to time appeared in Kinship—and once, over a year ago, Miller had aided Lily only at George Vogel's behest, because Lily had desperately turned to him.

And George hadn't said it then, but Lily knew that eventually he'd expect a favor of her in return. George never does anything without expectation of eventual recompense. Maybe he has some reason to bring Luther and Elias into his fold—and all he will expect of her is to accept their presence back in Bronwyn County.

Lily's stomach turns.

She can't do that.

"So neither of you mentioned the Harkinses?"

"No, Lily. They just turned around and left."

"Did you happen to see which way they went?"

Benjamin shakes his head. "No, I'm sorry."

Lily clears her throat. "Did—did the children see them? Or hear them?"

"I don't think so. Jolene was back in the kitchen, and the boys were outside, settling the hens for the evening. I'm sorry for this bad news. I hope your uncle is all right. Daniel didn't talk much about his brother—

and just that brief encounter makes me see why—but he talked often about how kind and supportive his uncle Elias was. Like a father to him."

Lily's heart squeezes at this revelation. Tears run up into her eyes. *Oh God.*

"I wish I could tell you more," Benjamin says. "I promised Mrs. McArthur I'd stay until you got back. She seemed so rattled. . . ." He pauses, adds more softly, "But I can still stay. Do you need me to?"

Benjamin's dark eyes gather her to him. Something flutters beneath her ribs, the twin wings of hope and nervousness. But Lily shakes her head—wrong feelings, wrong time.

Disappointment crosses Benjamin's face. But she doesn't stop him as he walks to the mudroom. A gust of wind blows in as he hesitates after opening the door. "Let me know if you need anything!" he calls softly. Then the door clicks to.

As Lily climbs the stairs up to her cold bedroom, questions shout for her attention. She shakes her head at herself; the loudest is the one she's likely to never get to ask, one for Benjamin: *What were you thinking about, sitting in my parlor in the dark, awaiting my return?*

CHAPTER 10

FIONA

Friday, November 25, 1927
1:00 a.m.

In the dismal dark, Fiona lies wide awake. Next to her, George sleeps deeply but not peacefully. He moans and occasionally cries out—"Oh! Oh!"—lost in some nightmare.

Though it's not unusual, Fiona has never brought this up to him or asked him about it. She's speculated, of course: *Something from child-hood, from immigrating?* She only has a sketch of George's life from before he became George Vogel, the feared bootlegging kingpin, and what she knows is this: He grew up in Germany, immigrated to the United States with just his mother and distant cousin Klara, grew up in poverty in Chicago, somehow made it through law school, spent a few years in traditional practice, and then began finding ways to make legal loopholes work to his benefit. One previous, childless marriage ended in divorce.

Klara could fill in many details. But she and Klara are not allies.

Abe, too, could offer up details, if he trusted Fiona. But he does not.

On the other hand, Klara and Abe are not allies, either. Maybe she could play them off each other, find a way to turn George's trust toward her, and only her.

Whatever torments some tender, deep part of George Vogel is not what keeps Fiona awake.

Ice taps the windowpanes, as if the hand of the past is relentlessly knocking, asking her to let it in. And oh, how she resists, as if she can will away both weather and memories of her earlier life in Bronwyn County, memories that have, since entering the whirlwind of life with George, become so flat and distant, no more than flowers long ago plucked and pressed in between the pages of a book, near to crumbling into dust.

Another moan from George, as his body jerks and twitches.

Though she can barely make out his shape in the dark, Fiona looks over at him.

Did you conspire to kill my dear uncle?

She wants to know, and yet she realizes the answer doesn't matter. Even if Aunt Nell is simply being paranoid, her belief makes her willing to help Fiona take control of George's assets. That's what matters. It's the first step in getting George put away—for good. Even if he hadn't been behind Uncle Henry's death, Fiona is sure George has committed plenty of sins to justify miserable punishment and the loss of all he holds dear.

Meaning money and power. Oh sure, he would say their child, but after the first flush of excitement wears off he will revert, quickly, to focusing only on money and power.

But she has a little time, while he's still caught up in that first flush. It gives her, as she'd thought yesterday, *leverage.*

First, though, to shake his confidence. Stir doubts within him. Fiona gives his shoulder a little shake and, when that does not break his deep sleep, a harder one.

"Wha—what?" George bolts up, fists flailing. Fiona barely jumps out of the way before his hand lands on her pillow near to her head.

"Oh, oh, George!" she cries. "You were having a nightmare!"

"I—I was?" His voice is thick, confused.

Fiona sits up, lights the bedside lamp, turns the wick so just a dollop of light thins the darkness. Then she lies back down beside him, strokes his head. "You were . . . ," she says. She hesitates, hoping that she's guessed correctly, that in his adult life other women have refrained from telling him about his troubled sleep patterns. "I—I'm sorry to wake you, but I've never heard you have a nightmare like this. I was sound asleep myself and your cries awakened me."

George sits up, fumbles for his glasses on the night table, puts them on at an askew angle. He stares forward, perplexed, as if clarity might stumble forth from the shadowed corners of the bedroom. "Have I, have I done this before?"

Fiona exhales, relieved. He doesn't remember having nightmares. Fiona leans into him so that her breasts press into his shoulder. "Not like this. This one seemed really bad." She strokes his hair. "Do you—do you remember anything of it?"

George frowns. "Something about running. A ball in the street. I—I think it was a nightmare I had when I was a boy. My mother would wake me occasionally—"

A rapping on the bedroom door makes them both jolt.

George swats her hand away, throws back the quilt, gets out of bed.

"I'm sorry, I heard voices, saw the light under the door—" It's Abe Miller. Fiona sighs, sits up in bed, pulls the quilt up to her chin.

George steps back, impatiently shoos him inside. Abe keeps his eyes averted from Fiona as George shuts the door.

"Turn the light up, Fiona!" George snaps, as if she is foolish for not anticipating that she should do so.

She turns up the wick.

"What time is it?" George plucks his watch off the nightstand. "Good God, one in the morning. How long have you been standing outside the door?"

"I got back shortly after midnight," Abe says softly. "I—I wanted to tell you, as soon as you awoke—" Abe rambles to a stop, already second-guessing his intrusion into George and Fiona's privacy.

"What?" George snaps the word like a whip.

"It's—Luther. He's—disappeared. He was with me—but then we ran into trouble—"

Silence thickens in the chilly room. Suddenly George backhands Abe.

Blood oozes from Abe's nose, but he doesn't react, doesn't cry out or step back after the first blow lands, doesn't make a move in response.

George grabs a handkerchief from the nightstand, wipes Abe's blood from his hand, but doesn't offer the handkerchief to Abe, who stands stock-still, awaiting his boss's next command—or another blow.

"Stop stuttering around like a fool. What happened?"

"We went to find Dr. Goshen for Elias. He was not at his home. His wife said some young girl had showed up—something about trouble with her brother—and they'd gone to find Sheriff Lily Ross."

At this, it's George who goes still.

Fiona turns this over. This is twice in less than twenty-four hours she's been reminded of Lily—first her aunt, saying she'd come out here after Uncle Henry died, and now Abe.

"Mrs. Goshen didn't know the name of the girl or the family, just that her husband had left with her. So we went to Lily Ross's farmhouse. I know where it is from last year—"

"I don't want details I don't care about." George tosses the handkerchief at him after all. "Clean yourself up! We don't want you bleeding on the lovely rug and furniture here," he says with a nasty sneer.

Fiona keeps her expression placid, but the comment—of all things, in the midst of everything else that's happening—stings. Aunt Nell had taken great pride in her home, keeping it neat and tidy all these years.

As Abe dabs his nose, he says, "We went to Lily Ross's house, hoping to find the doctor or someone there who could tell us where they went—"

"You went to Lily's house *with Luther*?" George says, putting emphasis on the last two words.

"I told Luther to stay in the automobile. But he got out and came up to the door, too. Sheriff Ross wasn't home—but I spoke with her mother and a man who was there. Unfortunately—Luther spilled the news about Elias's condition."

"So now she knows we're all here. Do you realize how stupid that is?" George clicks his teeth. His voice is cold, hard.

Fiona has pieced together that George had been involved in the life of Daniel Ross, both when he was a boxer for George before Daniel met Lily and later, when Daniel became sheriff shortly after he and Lily married—but she doesn't know the details of Daniel and George's connection. And she understands that Lily and Daniel's uncle Elias, once close, are now estranged—but she doesn't know why.

In a way, George and Lily are alike in that they are both impossible to cipher, only giving hints about who they are in the most stressful of moments. A little over a year ago, Lily had come, once, to the Cincinnati mansion to ask George for help in tracking down a person connected to a murder investigation—something about an elderly woman, killed along the train tracks in a remote part of Bronwyn County. Fiona had regarded Lily from across the expanse of the mansion's well-appointed parlor— and found her expression closed, tight as a box nailed shut. Later, when Lily and the case were written up in *Thrilling Gumshoe*, Fiona read the article—and though she found the case itself fascinating, at the end she knew no more than she had at the beginning about what motivates Lily. Is she, too, after control? Power? Or something else altogether?

"Yes," Abe says, weariness fraying his tone. "Luther wanted to hunt down the doctor for Elias, but I drove us back to the Goshens'. We waited at his house—"

Fiona can just imagine how anxious Mrs. Goshen must have been with Luther and Abe waiting in her parlor on Thanksgiving night.

"—and he got back around eleven p.m. He dispensed the medicine Elias needs, gave the bottle to me—and I've given that to Elias, by the way."

George lifts an eyebrow. "You gave the medicine to Elias?" He smirks. "Let me guess—Luther was passed out by the time you got back here."

Abe looks down. "No. Luther ran out as soon as he saw I had Elias's medicine. I gave chase, but I couldn't find him. I came back here, and—"

George grabs Abe by the jacket. Though Abe looms over George by almost a foot, his usually placid expression crinkles with fear. Through gritted teeth, George says, "So you're telling me that Lily knows Elias and Luther are back here? Isn't that going to make it harder when they disappear? What if she gets curious about their presence, starts asking around, comes here?"

A chill runs over Fiona, sharper than the coldness of the room, like a knife's edge scraping along her skin. *Disappear.* George and Abe mean to use Elias and Luther for their knowledge and connections to set up the operation here on the farm and then kill them.

"What made him run off? Did Dr. Goshen or his wife say something to set him off?"

It had to be something incredibly important, for Luther to trust Abe with Elias's medicine.

Abe shakes his head. "He's a wild card. Always has been. Too hot-headed for our operation. I'll find him—and deal with it."

"Find him—but don't deal with him until we have all we need from Elias," George says. "We'll have to come up with something to explain Luther's absence, and now we've got the problem of Lily knowing. She'll want to snoop around, so now she's a problem to deal with, too." George grins. "I kind of like her, even better than Daniel in some ways. She's a scrappy fighter. But she won't be easily bought. Maybe it's time for a new sheriff."

Abe nods eagerly, relieved that George is giving him a new task to focus on. "I can work on that."

Oh God. They don't mean . . . Fiona's heart sinks. *Yes, yes, they do.*

"Maybe Lily knowing about Luther and Elias can be used for good," Fiona says.

Both men pause, turn, look at her. As if they'd forgotten she was in the bedroom.

Fiona forces herself to smile softly. "What I mean is, I could go to Lily. Just *tell* her Luther is missing. I *know* Lily. Always one for precise rules and regulations. Filling out the proper forms. Back when she was jail matron. Irritated Martin to no end." She checks George's expression to see if he's upset that she's referenced her previous husband, but he's still staring at her as if she'd just popped out of the wall. It wasn't true in any case—Martin admired Lily's penchant for precision as much as he did Daniel's bravery. In a mocking tone, as if speaking as Lily, Fiona says, "'The rules apply to everyone,'" giving her head a little shake as if to say, *Silly Lily.*

The rules really don't apply to everyone, Fiona thinks. Prohibition had confirmed that to her. As had living with George.

"So Lily will of course look for Luther. And she'll find him for you," Fiona says.

Then she stops, waits for the inevitable question.

George glares at her, irritated by her interruption. "How in the hell does that help us?"

Ah, there it is.

"Because why would I go to her if there's anything to hide?" Fiona smiles, demurely. "It will be easy to explain, woman-to-woman. Yes, yes, you hired Luther to work in your business—Vogel's Tonics. He approached you. He has management skills, after all. And I can explain that I really wanted Elias around as doctor since I trusted him with the birth of Leon. . . ." Fiona pauses, just a hair of a second to see if George reacts to her son's name. But no. George's expression remains skeptical about where she's going with this plan. "And so of course I'd want Elias as doctor again now, since I'm, well, in the family way. . . ."

She pauses longer this time, to take in Abe's expression—a slight lift of the eyebrows the only change, but enough to tell her that he is turning this over in his mind: *How will this change things, George becoming a father?*

Indeed, George's expression softens, just at that phrase—*the family way*—the curl to the ends of his smile becoming if not loving, at least less cruel. *First flush of excitement,* Fiona thinks. And: *Leverage.* "Go on," he says, intrigued.

Fiona's hands tremor. She clasps them to hold them still. She hopes she's not giving away too much by showing that she's willing to use her pregnancy to manipulate others.

"And I can tell her that Elias is better, but upset that Luther is missing, and that's why I want Luther found—so Elias can settle down, and take care of me. . . ." Fiona hesitates. Is what comes to mind next a step too far, a betrayal of Lily? But she plunges ahead. "Lily has lost babies. Just after Daniel died. She will understand."

There, a flicker of surprise—and a little fear—in George's eyes. He did not know this about Lily, then. And the notion, of a woman losing a baby, scares him—now that Fiona is bearing his.

Fiona adds that to her mental list of George's vulnerabilities: His nightmares—his reference to his mother—prove he's haunted by something. His dislike of being questioned. His disdain for any incompetence—the way he'd treated Abe just moments ago! And where did Abe's complete loyalty come from? Maybe finding out the root of that would be useful, too.

But in the next moment George is again sneeringly doubtful. "And if Lily finds Luther, what if he tells her about our operation here—just like Elias told you?"

At that, Abe gasps, a sound that brings Fiona a small bit of satisfaction. Abe always ignores her, as if she doesn't matter, as if she's just another of George's conquests.

Still, she must be careful. If Abe sees her as a threat, he could undermine George's trust in her. She doesn't want to turn Abe into an enemy. She just wants him to see her as someone he must also fear and respect.

"Luther hates Lily. He won't tell her anything."

And, Fiona thinks, in getting George's permission to go to Lily she'll have a chance to forewarn Lily about the tainted alcohol.

Finally, George says, "Very well. Go see your Lily tomorrow."

Fiona nods. "I'll need one of the drivers." Martin had never taught her to drive, as Daniel had taught Lily.

But George shakes his head. "Abe will take you."

Dammit.

Abe gives Fiona just the slightest smile, as if to say, *See. He doesn't completely trust you.*

Then George looks at Abe. "I'm going to trust that you won't foul this up."

That's enough for Abe's smile to disappear. "Of course not," he says.

George sighs. "Maybe we'll get lucky and Luther will stumble back somehow, sometime tonight on his own. Or freeze to death between here and Kinship, trying to get back to his precious uncle." George gives a hard laugh. "If not—we'll try Fiona's plan with Lily. Simpler, after all, if fewer heads have to roll to make this work out. Right, Abe?"

Abe nods.

George moves over to Fiona, strokes her hair, and Fiona's scalp throbs, a visceral reminder of how earlier he'd grabbed her hair as if he wanted to snap her neck. "Big day tomorrow, my little spitfire."

"Oh, convincing Lily to think nothing of our presence here will be simple; after all, she's so—" Fiona stops short of saying *gullible,* as George's brow descends toward a glower. *Careful,* Fiona thinks. George may see Lily as an enemy—but he respects her. And, truth be told, Lily may have once been gullible, but that has not been true for a long time. "—so sentimental about her friends," Fiona finishes. Well, Lily is a bit sentimental. Though she would not count Fiona among her friends.

George laughs. "That's sweet. No, I mean tomorrow you need to convince your aunt Nell to sell this property to me—before Kinship Trust Savings and Loan closes at the end of the day." He looks at Abe. "I'm assuming the paperwork is in order?"

Abe nods. "Yes, sir."

"Oh, well, of course you thought of everything, dear," Fiona said. "Except, well, it will take Aunt Nell some time to pack, and I'm guessing it will be heartbreaking for her to observe your, ah, renovations on her old home. But I'll help Aunt Nell gather up tomorrow morning's eggs. Tell her you are prepared to make her a most generous offer, and sweeten it by another ten thousand—if she'll leave tomorrow."

George looks shocked, perhaps by the amount Fiona had stated or by the audacity of Fiona's plan. But she hurries on. "She just needs to pack a few things. The one o'clock train goes to Cincinnati. Believe me, after years of living in Kinship, before finding you . . ."—here, Fiona pauses to put one hand on George's arm—"I know the train schedule. We can ship furniture, anything she wants from the house, down to wherever she settles in Florida. I know she already has a location, a great spot for fishing—"

"Your aunt loves fishing?" Abe starts to laugh, but George scowls at him.

Fiona squeezes George's arm lightly, drawing his attention back to her. "Yes, she loves fishing. I think she'll be willing to go quickly—if you'll let me talk with her. Then you have no delays, no risks from her remaining on."

George says thoughtfully, "It's an interesting plan."

Fiona pulls his hand to her belly. "Mothers are used to cleaning up messes." She nearly smiles at her own genius: a pointed jab at Abe, for making a mess, and a reminder of George's child. "And once I tell her that, well, I want to raise our son at least part of the time here, she'll agree. She never had children of her own, you know. Then after that, I'll go visit Lily."

Again, from the corner of her eye, Fiona observes Abe's reaction. This time, he's gone utterly pale. He knows that nothing will give Fiona more leverage than her being with child.

Indeed, George cups Fiona's face gently. "Ah—beautiful and brilliant." Then his voice hardens a little. "If I didn't know better, I'd be a little worried by you."

Fiona smiles, widens her eyes. "Oh, George."

"Very well," he says. "Better get some good sleep if you're getting up early to gather eggs—just you and your aunt Nell."

Abe casts his gaze downward, dabs at his nose. He's been thwarted—for now.

"But no more nightmares, all right?" George says with a little laugh.

All right then. George wishes to pass off his nightmare moans as if they had been hers—though both she and Abe know better.

But they will all pretend otherwise—for George's sake.

And for their own.

So Fiona smiles again. "Of course, darling."

CHAPTER 11

LILY

Friday, November 25, 1927
7:42 a.m.

After parking her automobile on a side street, Lily had meant to hurry to the courthouse but found herself pausing by the house that had been the sheriff's house—her and Daniel's house for all of their marriage and up until last year. She'd had their children there. Now the house is empty, as the county commissioners debate renovating it into either county government offices or space for a small police department for the town.

For a moment, she stares at the house from across the street, watching the snow sift down around the trim two-story, its neat porch. So many precious memories—already, they seem to occupy a place that can only be conjured, but not revisited. The structure that had once been her home is now a building destined to be repurposed. She's been stopping to stare at it less and less lately, and someday soon she'll hurry past without giving it a second look.

Once in her new office, though, as has become her habit, Lily pauses after neatly hanging up her coat and hat on the rack by the door—just long enough to appreciate the satisfying tidiness of her cozy though sparse office: polished wood floor, sturdy wood desk and swivel chair, clean white plaster walls, filing cabinet.

In particular, her gaze lingers on her one personal touch: a war bond poster that Mama had found in packing up her house, of the Statue of Liberty in front of a sunset rendered to look like the American flag, the admonition imprinted over the sparkling water at her feet: *Before Sunset Buy a U.S. Government Bond of the 2nd Liberty Loan of 1917.* Once, it had hung in the grocery store when Papa had owned it.

It's so ratty, Lily! Mama had fussed. *Shouldn't you have a photo of your children?*

Lily had bitten back the first retort that came to mind: *I'm not likely to forget—and I don't need to remind some folks that they think I should be at home.*

Instead, she'd just smiled at Mama, who, after all, had not thrown away the poster all those years ago and who now does so much to take care of all of them. And then Lily had it framed and hung it in her office anyway.

She is not, after all, completely without sentiment.

Now Lily tucks her tote bag under her desk and settles into her chair as Lady Liberty peers over her shoulder at the telegram confirming a visit this morning from Special Agent Barnaby Sloan, from the Columbus field office of the Bureau of Prohibition, to discuss plans for the big visit from US Assistant Attorney General Mabel Walker Willebrandt at the middle of next week.

Lily picks up her notebook to the right of the stack and opens to the notes she'd made from articles she'd been reading about Willebrandt. It's striking how much Willebrandt has achieved at only thirty-eight. She'd grown up in Kansas, gone to college in Arizona, law school at the University of Southern California, divorced, become Los Angeles's first female public defender, and—Lily liked this in particular—led courts to allow women, as well as men, to testify in cases. She wasn't the first woman to be appointed assistant attorney general—that designation belonged to Annette Adams, who'd held the post briefly in 1920–1921—but Willebrandt had held the office since 1921 and was nicknamed the First Lady of Law. The moniker was not always applied with favor. It could also be a snide reference to her status as a divorced woman. A woman without a man.

Though rumored to be personally against Prohibition, Willebrandt was for the rule of law and tirelessly fought to enforce the Volstead Act, earning her even more nicknames: Prohibition Portia, Deborah of the Drys, Mrs. Firebrand.

Perhaps Willebrandt was only drawn here because Ohio had been a central battleground for Prohibition for more than fifty years. Why, the Anti-Saloon League, which had long been a leader in favor of Prohibition, is headquartered up in Westerville, near Columbus—and it still publishes many a tract about the ills of alcohol.

Maybe Willebrandt is stopping there and then coming here to make a grandstanding speech right in the midst of moonshining territory. She'd get as many "boos" as "yays." Well, Lily'd have to round up some extra deputies for protection.

But she pauses after jotting a few names for a list of deputies, as her nerves jangle at the notion of meeting someone so intimidatingly famous. Lily puts her hand to her tightly pinned-up hair. What would the woman make of her?

Lily shakes her head at herself. *Foolish.* All Lily will be able to offer the assistant attorney general is the insight that some form of brewing has been going on in these Appalachian hills for many years— never mind that the county went dry a full decade before the US Constitution's Eighteenth Amendment officially turned the whole country arid.

And that she, like Willebrandt, believes in the rule of law, personal feelings aside.

Yet her stomach flips again, this time in anticipation of tracking down her friend Marvena and likely having to bring her in on moonshining charges.

Lily sighs. She'd like to tell Willebrandt that though she, too, believes in the rule of law, she'd rather have laws with no—or at least fewer— loopholes for the rich and powerful to get around the law, while punishing everyday people like Marvena. Maybe even laws that work with human nature instead of continually fighting against it.

Lily glances at her watch. If the bureau agent doesn't arrive in another fifteen minutes, she'll head out to Marvena's and the Harkinses'— she needs to fill them in on Zebediah.

But just as she finishes her notes, a knock comes at her office door.

Lily looks up at a middle-aged man on the stocky side with graying temples and a ruddy face. He wears a thin coat with fraying lapels, elbow patches barely covering worn, shiny material. A man who she'd normally assess as down on his luck, but as if to show he's found a new lease on life, he not so subtly pulls back his thin coat to reveal his blue-and-gold Bureau of Prohibition shield, proudly pinned to his jacket lapel.

"Special Agent Barnaby Sloan," he says, pride adding zest to his voice. He steps into Lily's office, and she gasps.

Not at Agent Sloan. At the man coming in just behind him.

Luther Ross.

Her stomach turns at the sight of him. At the smell of him, body odor and stale alcohol. He looks disheveled and rumpled, like he's been out all night.

"Sheriff Ross?" The agent looks perplexed by Lily's shock.

"Please, come in," Lily says flatly.

Barnaby takes off his worn coat and puts it up on a hook. He takes Luther's coat and hangs it for him.

Lily's office has just one guest chair. She watches as Barnaby gestures for Luther to take the seat, but Luther leans against the wall, grins down at Lily. *Thought you'd get rid of me? Gotcha, Lily!*

Barnaby shuts the door. Lily's office, cozy just moments ago, now feels suffocating. She forces herself to breathe in and out slowly, evenly, as Barnaby sits in her guest chair after all.

"And of course you know Luther. He's told us he's your husband's brother."

Us. That sounds ominous. "Half brother," Lily says. "And my husband's dead."

"Now, Lily," Luther says. "Relation don't end with death."

She looks at him. Lets her gaze convey: *No, but it ends with betrayal.*

Luther stops grinning. He looks down at his shoes. Lily snaps her attention back to Barnaby. "I thought your agency was sending someone in advance of the assistant attorney general's visit. To provide a specific date and time, requirements for her security—"

"Yes, that's one reason we're here," Barnaby says. Lily's heart thuds at the *we're*. "But we're also working with Luther, as an inside man, to finally break George Vogel. Luther, here, thinks George might be planning to make a move in this area again. Not the, ah, purchase of moonshine that Luther says Vogel sometimes got away with under your husband's watch. Something bigger."

Lily looks back at Luther. "What does Elias think of this?"

"He doesn't know," Luther says. But he picks at his fingernails—his tell that he's lying. He flicks the dirt to Lily's floor. She'll have to thoroughly clean her office to rid it of the stink and filth of him.

"So he's working with George, something to do with his tonic?"

Luther looks up, alarmed. "No, no, as I told Agent Sloan, Elias is simply George's personal physician. I mean, he knows of George's reputation, but he has nothing to do with his operation—or with my connection with the bureau. If he did, well, he'd have us just walk away."

She gives him a cold smile. "How is Elias?"

Luther stiffens. "Fine."

She looks back at Barnaby. "It seems Luther and one of George's men, Abe Miller, came by my house last night, looking for the town doctor, whose wife had told them the doc had come out to my farm," Lily says.

Barnaby turns to Luther, concern and doubt finally showing in his expression. "What? You were supposed to stay put on the farm, until I drove down this morning." He looks back at Lily. "Our plan was that Luther would make up some excuse to come to town this morning, but instead meet up with me behind the Kinship Inn, then come here. It was never meant for him to disturb you at home—"

"Elias wasn't well!" The words tear out of Luther, a ragged cry.

Lily gives him a flat look. He recoils at what it conveys: she doesn't care.

"He—he's better now," Luther says defiantly, picking at his nails. Still lying. "Just a bit of indigestion, too much dinner. I worried it was a heart attack. And . . . and we returned right away to the farmhouse."

Barnaby already looks eager, again. "He means the farmhouse that belongs to the aunt of George Vogel's second wife—Fiona. Luther tells us you know where it is, that you were out there, after Fiona's uncle passed away."

Oh, he had told them this, had he? She counts back—that had been about six weeks ago. So to know that, he has to have been in George's employ at least that long. And so has Elias. George is cruel and ruthless, but he's not stupid. He'd hire Elias, but never just Luther, who would only be accepted if Elias insisted.

Was serving as a mole for the bureau Luther's way of extricating both Elias and himself from Vogel? As well as a way to prove his cleverness to Elias? No. Luther was the sort whose ego would be stroked by thinking himself a big man in an organization like Vogel's. Lily stifles a groan. *Oh God.* Either Luther is actually a mole for Vogel—or he's trying to play both sides.

"I called on Mrs. Murphy after her husband passed away," Lily says.

"So you're familiar with the farm? The layout?" Barnaby asks.

"It's a standard farm. Nothing special." Or was there? She thinks back—*Isn't the farm situated between a road just off the main route and a rural road known just to locals?*

"Well, here's the thing," Barnaby says. "We need for you to raid the farm. Preferably before Mrs. Willebrandt's visit next Wednesday, when she plans to give a speech at the opera house. Arrangements have already been made, and an announcement will come out in the newspapers on Thursday. Word's come down that she thinks it would really establish the bureau if we could catch a big operator like George Vogel, especially in a place like this."

"You mean—in Appalachia? The backwoods? The heartland?"

"It's one thing to catch bootleggers in the cities, folks expect that, but if we show big-city crime is coming even to small towns and counties, well then . . ." Barnaby trails off as if the conclusion is obvious.

"I don't see why the bureau needs my help, if you have Luther here, working with you," Lily says. "You can get a warrant more easily than I can."

"Several reasons. One is that, well, too many sheriffs don't want to work with the bureau. Just as likely to warn the locals. But Mrs. Willebrandt read last month's *Thrilling Gumshoe*, you see, about how you solved a really tricky case last year."

Lily bites back a sigh. It had been fun—for about a day—to see the issue on display at the general store, and then it got embarrassing to be both complimented about the press and teased about being referred to as a "female novelty."

"She was impressed," Barnaby is saying. "And since you—you're—" He stops, turns red.

"A female novelty?"

"Since you're a woman, if you work with us to bring in a big operator like Vogel, it'll make for good press—"

"Agent, I can't arrest Mr. Vogel without cause. Or raid a private citizen's property without a warrant. Mr. Vogel is free to accompany his wife to visit her bereaved aunt over a family holiday."

Even as she says it, it feels off. George Vogel is always self-serving. So the chances he's spending his Thanksgiving at his wife's aunt's farm just to be kind are low. But that opinion is not enough for a warrant or a raid.

"The Eighteenth Amendment to the Constitution has banned the sale, prohibition, and transport of alcohol, except under very specific circumstances, since 1919," Barnaby says. His tone and smile are proud, as if he is a schoolboy who's properly memorized his lesson. "If we have cause to think Mr. Vogel is in violation—"

"Do you?" Lily snaps. "Have cause?"

"Well, that's why Mr. Ross here is working with us—"

"How long?" Lily looks at Luther. "How long have you been working for the bureau?"

"Let's see now—oh, about two months."

"And you haven't found cause yet?"

"I think you know, Lily, that Mr. Vogel is a clever man. Complex."

"True." *And yet,* Lily thinks, *he's trusting you.* Or pretending to. No one should trust Luther, ever. The image of the badge in her tote bag flashes before her. "Do you know when he arrived at the Murphy farm?"

"Sure. Thursday afternoon."

"And Fiona?"

"A few days earlier, I guess. For cooking and such. I don't keep track of women's doings."

Lily doubts Fiona's doing much cooking these days. "When did you arrive?"

"Thursday."

"With George Vogel?"

"Yes, yes. And Elias and Abe Miller."

"Anyone else?"

"Housekeeper. Guards."

"That's quite an entourage, for a Thanksgiving visit to a grieving relative of Fiona's."

"That's how George travels," Luther says.

Lily turns her gaze back to Barnaby, who looks a bit bewildered by Lily and Luther's exchange. "I'm assuming you're paying him." She jerks a thumb in Luther's direction.

Barnaby frowns as he gives Luther a doubtful look. "Well, yes."

On the bureau's payroll. Probably on George Vogel's as well.

"I'm close." Luther's tone turns defensive. "Soon, I'll have the proof the bureau needs—"

"In the meantime," Lily says, "I think Assistant Attorney General Willebrandt would agree with me that we can only proceed within the rule of law. After all, the Fourth Amendment has banned unjust search and seizure, without cause or warrant, since 1791." Lily leans back, steeples her fingertips together. "I read the entire Constitution, you see, before swearing to uphold it."

"But the new search and seizure laws say we can raid any establishment, without warrant, if only on suspicion of violation of Prohibition," Barnaby says.

"What legitimate suspicion do we have? We only know Fiona Vogel is visiting her bereaved aunt over Thanksgiving—with her husband and a few of his employees in tow. That's not illegal. Luther hasn't given you anything that would hold up in a court—"

"Maybe you don't want to help *us*?" Luther interjects. "Maybe you're working with Mr. Vogel, just like Daniel once did? And you and Fiona were once close friends—"

Lily turns her hard gaze on Luther, and he stutters to a stop.

Oh, doesn't he think he's clever! Not only living on George's largesse while drawing pay from the bureau—and probably a promise of immunity later—but also attempting to goad Lily into proving her honesty by rushing onto the farm, drawing George's attention and ire. Luther blames her, after all, for manipulating him into leaving the area after selling his family's coal-mining company to a bigger operation. More than that, he hates her for it. In his awful grin, she sees that he'd love to see her hurt—or worse—as vengeance for that. Is he trying to get her killed? She wouldn't put it past him. And she won't fall for it.

But what if Vogel really is planning something big at the Murphy farm? It's just not like him to want to spend a long weekend at such a rural location to be with his new wife while she comforts her grieving aunt.

Lily nearly tells Barnaby to send Luther out of the room, so she can fill him in on Luther's background, his deviousness, his foolishness. To tell Barnaby his plan to outwit George will backfire unless they have hard evidence and sufficient backup. Luther is a fool. He's going to get himself—or, worse yet, others—killed. Lily's had enough experience with George to know that no one walks away from him unscathed.

The image of the bureau shield that Ruth had given her again crosses her mind. She should get the shield out of her tote bag, show it to Barnaby, tell him how she got it and where it came from . . . except Luther is here.

And so she doesn't trust Barnaby.

What's more, now Barnaby's gaze has turned skeptical—thanks to Luther. "I know your husband and Mr. Vogel were friends, even after Mr. Ross stopped boxing for him. The bureau is aware of this, and would see your cooperation as a way to, ah, keep all of this out of the background of any pieces that might run in the newspapers, after we finally snare Vogel. I'm sure you'd like that for your children's sake. . . ."

His voice trails off as Lily's eyes harden, stone cold. He clears his throat, looks down as he goes on. "Here's the thing. Luther came to us a few months ago, told us that Mr. Vogel has big plans for the area."

"Which are?"

"I'm not sure yet," Luther says. "I'm still working on sussing that out."

"We wanted him to come along for this visit today because we assumed you'd be eager to cooperate—not just with the agency, for the reasons I've given, but also with your former brother-in-law," Barnaby says. "We want you to work with him to find a way to visit the farm, find evidence to support a raid. Then we can provide backup."

She wishes she could demand Luther to leave, show Barnaby the badge. Ask directly if they should be concerned about a possible missing agent. But it's clear that Barnaby trusts Luther, which means—especially with the doubt Luther's put in the agent's mind about her—that she can't trust Barnaby not to tell Luther about the badge.

Plus, that solicitousness at the beginning, with Barnaby hanging Luther's coat for him, offering him the chair. It could be just that Barnaby is showing deference to an elder man. Or—she eyes again the thin, fraying spots of Barnaby's clothes—he could be taking bribes from Luther.

Then why bother coming here, to see her? Lily sighs. Until she's sure what that badge portends, she doesn't want to put another agent's life at risk. Luther's very presence shakes her faith in Barnaby—and in her own judgment.

Lily forces her voice to remain steady, cool, as she says to Barnaby, "You keep saying *we*. Do you mean the agency? Or do you have other agents already here?"

"Agents?" Barnaby chuckles. "We're spread thin, Sheriff Ross, which is another reason we need your help."

"So it's just gonna be you, and a few of my deputies, on this theoretical raid, if"—Lily hesitates, her gorge rising again at the very thought of the phrase she's about to use—"if Luther and I find sufficient evidence? No one else here, no one else coming?"

Barnaby frowns. "Well, there is a young fella—cock-of-the-walk attitude, if you don't mind me saying, ma'am—who has been with the bureau a bit longer than me. He's a *senior* special agent, Colter DeHaven"—Barnaby snorts at the designation—"from the Chicago office, and is working with our field office on the case. He is supposed to come in next Monday."

Was it possible Agent DeHaven had come early, for some reason that Barnaby doesn't know? Maybe he, too, isn't sure if to trust Barnaby? Does the badge Ruth gave her belong to this DeHaven? Lily considers that badge, same as the one Barnaby had flashed at her—no rank, no name, no number, just a designation of authority that's as likely to get a revenuer shot as not.

"I'll be at the Columbus office, of course," Barnaby goes on. "You can call—"

"I can telegraph from here," Lily says. "Or call from Chillicothe. Might as well, in that case, drive up to your office."

Barnaby frowns. "I see."

Lily smiles. "Part of the downside, I reckon, of building a case in a place like this."

As Barnaby flushes, Lily regrets teasing him. "Special Agent, thank you for filling me in. I'll be sure that we have deputies to keep an eye on Mrs. Willebrandt, and I'll of course look forward to meeting her Wednesday next. Meanwhile, I'll keep my ear to the ground and contact you if I have any reason to regarding Mr. Vogel."

For a moment, the silence in the room leavens, as Lily and Barnaby regard each other awkwardly. Then Barnaby clears his throat, says, "I'm sure Luther will soon be able to provide more specifics to aid in getting your search warrant." Lily resists giving a derisive snort. Doesn't Barnaby suspect at all that Luther is playing both sides?

But Luther just stares into the middle distance, seemingly no longer interested in either the conversation or in taunting Lily. *Worrying about Elias?* Lily wonders.

"Right, Luther?" Barnaby pointedly asks.

Luther jumps. "What? Oh yes."

"Well. I guess that concludes our business, then," Barnaby says.

Lily looks at Luther. "Tell Elias I hope he feels better soon. From his indigestion, that is."

Luther shoots her a hate-filled look. He turns and leaves. Barnaby follows.

Lily waits a few minutes and then goes down the hall to the custodial closet. She retrieves a broom and dustpan and, back in her office, cleans up her floor. That task finished, she dons her coat, scarf, and hat and grabs her tote bag and notebook.

Out on the steps of the courthouse, Lily stills for a second, a cold gust snatching her breath away. She takes in the town, quiet this morning. Snow falls gently from a leaden sky. She looks east, where the sky is lighter. Maybe she'll be lucky in her trip to see Marvena.

When she looks back, she sees that two Model Ts have pulled up in front of the Kinship Trust Savings & Loan. A woman in a fur coat and hat stands on the sidewalk, between the automobile and the bank. A man holds the door open for her, but the woman stares up at Lily. Even at this distance, there's an intensity to the gaze.

Lily does not recognize the man. But there's something familiar about the woman, who leans forward, and for a second Lily thinks she is going to run up the courthouse steps to her.

The woman takes off the hat, and then Lily realizes who she is.

Fiona Weaver Vogel.

But Fiona swivels back toward the door. A moment later, Lily steps down, overcome with an impulse to rush to Fiona, to ask her if she is all right, to see what she might learn, woman-to-woman.

By then, Fiona has disappeared into the savings and loan.

CHAPTER 12

FIONA

Friday, November 25, 1927
9:12 a.m.

Maybe she shouldn't have taken that moment, when she'd spotted Lily Ross at the top of the courthouse steps, to stare up at her. But there'd been something powerful in Lily's figure, stark and still against the white of the stone courthouse, snow drifting around her.

So powerful that it inspired an impulse to run up those steps to Lily, tell her right away of the danger of George's tainted liquor being served tonight at the speakeasy. She could tell Lily, be the hero for sharing this information, turn over what she knows of George's plans, power and control and money be damned, seek sanctuary.

But doubt arose to deride her with questions: *What proof do you have? Even if you did, do you really think Sheriff Lily, in this remote place, could protect you from George's reach?*

But then Fiona realized that Lily didn't recognize her, not at first.

And maybe she shouldn't be surprised. After all, Fiona has changed so much, and the last time Fiona had seen her was last fall, when Lily came to their Cincinnati house on that *Thrilling Gumshoe* case. Then, Fiona was still naively basking in the attention, the protection, the generosity of her lover but not yet husband. Lily hadn't even recognized her at first, and when she did her expression shifted to what Fiona took to be small-town judgment.

Now Fiona realizes it was pity.

She'd seen that reaction again, even at a distance, after taking off her hat. As their gazes connected and Lily finally recognized her.

Yes, of course Lily would act on her tip.

Would probably try her best to help Fiona.

But how much could Lily do for her, really? And what would become of her—of Leon—once George wondered why Fiona hadn't come inside, saw Fiona on the steps pleading for Lily's help? She'd still be entangled with George. Married to him. Bound to his will.

The leverage she has by carrying his child would be cast aside.

Her whole life has been at the mercy of men. She is on the edge—she can feel it—of finally having power over her own life. And so she turned away from Lily, let the heat from inside the savings and loan draw her in.

She will not ask Lily to rescue her. Fiona is done with being rescued.

Now Fiona composes a lingering smile as she, Aunt Nell, and Abe wait in the meeting room. Abe looks annoyed—stuck with the women. George apparently doesn't trust Fiona and her aunt to be alone together, even though the conversation over breakfast had gone well.

Mr. Vogel, my niece tells me you'd still like to buy this farm for her, Aunt Nell had said.

George had smiled. *That's right. The paperwork will take a while—technicalities—but I can give you a portion of the sum today. We'd just have to go into Kinship, to the savings and loan.*

Well, I'm willing—but only if you also provide enough funds to cover a train ticket for me to leave right quick, Aunt Nell had said. *I—I just think it would be easier if I didn't linger. I can quickly pack a small bag.*

The tremble in her chin had been genuine, and for just a moment Fiona had felt sorry for her aunt—but more than that, relieved that she'd followed the instructions Fiona had given her when they were out gathering eggs.

If she can follow Fiona's coaching in the next few minutes, then everything will work out. Aunt Nell will get away and get to live out her days in Florida.

Fiona will have the farm in her name—the first step to getting George to trust her, so that soon she can get him to sign over other assets to her, to protect them from being seized if he's ever caught in the Bureau of Prohibition's snare. Which she'll make sure he will be.

For now, Fiona can't bring herself to look at her aunt. That conversation from when they gathered eggs is still too fresh.

Listen—we don't have much time. George is willing to make you an offer. . . .

And then she'd laid out the terms for her aunt Nell, as George had instructed her to.

Gave her aunt a moment to stare in shock.

Told her the counteroffer to make—both financial and otherwise.

But he won't pay that—

Yes he will. Just tell him you will take no less, for the trouble of leaving today, and it must be in my name. He has to believe it is your idea.

And if he won't accept my demand? Aunt Nell had added.

You've dealt with worse men than George. You can do this.

They both knew who—and what—she'd meant. Aunt Nell's expression had turned hard, cold, and Fiona knew that, yes, her aunt could handle George, at least for the time it would take at the bank. But then the specter of the cabin on the hill across from the farm arose between them, and they looked away from each other.

Their eyes had not met at breakfast. Nor as they'd ridden together in the second automobile, one of George's men driving them, while George and Abe went together in the first automobile. They hadn't spoken, either—of course, because of the driver. But also because of the magnitude of what was to come. At the bank, Aunt Nell had rushed out of the automobile, hurrying after George and Abe.

Fiona, though, had lingered, wanting a moment to just herself, to breathe in the cold air, to clear her head. And then she and Lily spotted each other.

Had the driver noticed them exchanging a look? Would he mention it to George or Abe?

Well, the driver—a newly hired man from Cincinnati—would have to know that the woman at the top of the courthouse steps was actually the county sheriff. And he wouldn't know that. And if somehow he did and troubled George, Fiona could easily explain away the silent exchange: *She noticed me and smiled, George. What would you have me do?*

Such small lies have become so easy, in dealing with George. Habit, almost.

As Fiona looks around the bank's meeting room, she recollects the awful, suffocating moment a few months after Martin's death when Mr. Chandler had smugly informed Fiona that the shoe repair business Martin had left to her was barely afloat, the payments on their tidy house in Kinship behind, and Martin had lost most of their money in illicit gambling in the basement speakeasy at the Kinship Inn.

Then she'd felt intimidated not just by Mr. Chandler, but by the room itself—its polished woodwork, the ornately patterned wallpaper, the Queen Anne–style upholstered chairs, the grandfather clock dominating one end of the room, formidable in its insistence on metering out the passage of time in even ticks.

Now she notes scratches on the table, spots where the wallpaper has lifted and started to peel, the lumpiness of the chairs, the tick of the clock as annoying as evenly spaced hiccups.

As Mr. Chandler and George walk in with a sheath of papers, Fiona's lips curl in satisfaction at Mr. Chandler's palpable nervousness, evident in his deferential manner with George—and how the banker can't meet her eyes. So different from before, when he'd looked at her as a pitiable widow.

George sits at the head of the table—even in the bank, he is in charge—while Mr. Chandler sits across from Fiona and tap-tap-taps his stack of papers to make them perfectly even before laying them down. "Everything is in order, so this should take only a few minutes."

"I've been thinking," Aunt Nell says, so softly that her words are a hiss requiring everyone to lean toward her to hear, "about the sale of *my* property."

The slight emphasis on *my* inflates the room's tension. All eyes turn to Aunt Nell, who smiles innocently, her cheeks rising into soft pink puffs, as if she'd simply asked if someone could pass the sweet pickles.

What is Aunt Nell playing at? Fiona clears her throat. "Now, Aunt Nell, remember we all talked this morning at breakfast. My generous husband is willing to pay thirty thousand dollars for the farm, once all the paperwork is sorted out, and will give you an advance on that now so you can be on your way to Florida."

Fiona gives her aunt a hard look. *All you have to say is, "I need that to be thirty-five thousand dollars and for the farm to go into my dear niece's name. . . ."*

Then Fiona can look shocked and say the part she's prepared on her own.

George's smile tightens as he says, "And if you're concerned about when you'll get the full amount, my understanding is that the paperwork was put in place a few weeks ago. For whenever you're ready." His gaze clicks over to Abe.

"It was." Abe sounds insulted at the notion of anyone—even George—questioning his crisp efficiency. "We have an account already set up here, so we can transfer funds to your account here—or wire funds to a bank of your choosing. This will enable you to immediately pay the back taxes we discovered on your property, before our, ah, earlier visit."

"Since your husband died intestate, we will need some time to expedite the property going through probate, but I'm an attorney with, ah, certain connections, so I will be able to move quickly," George says. "We just need you to sign paperwork agreeing that I will represent you in this matter. In the meantime, we are prepared to pay you fifty percent of the amount offered, immediately transferred from our account here, to yours, in good faith that there will be no issues, along with a waiver that we can begin modifications to the property—my wife has privately expressed that she would, for example, like to modernize the kitchen—as much as possible, of course, given the property's, shall we say, remote location."

Intestate. How would George have known that? A chill runs through

Fiona at how widely and deeply George's connections must run—even here, in Kinship.

Aunt Nell looks at Mr. Chandler. "Do you wish to tell them, or shall I?"

Fiona's heart does a double beat. *Oh God. What is Aunt Nell up to?* All she has to do is say she'll sell—but only to Fiona.

"I guess I will." Aunt Nell sighs, as if disappointed in the banker, but the curl to her lips tells Fiona that her aunt is relishing this moment. "The property is already in my name." Aunt Nell clasps her hands as if in gentle prayer. "It seems Henry got to thinking after you visited last." In the strained room, Aunt Nell's thin voice seems almost bellicose. "My husband knew how men can sometimes take advantage of women, especially bereft widows, and, since he was nearly ten years older than me, thought to put all the property in my name just shortly after your visit. So as it happens, it is up to me to do as I wish with *my* farm. Of course, as you know, farming it alone could well be the death of me." She gives a little laugh. "In which case, my will—just like Henry's was at the end—is airtight and up-to-date."

She looks at Fiona, gives a stiff smile.

What the hell is she playing at? Fiona had already, back at the cemetery yesterday, pointed out that once Aunt Nell dies, the farm goes to Fiona anyway. What does it matter if it's by law or through a will?

Aunt Nell's smile curls wider. "It all goes to the Kinship Presbyterian Church. I'm sure you understand why I set it up that way, dear. You've done so well, marrying your dear George."

Fiona's shock is unfeigned.

Aunt Nell had not given any hint of this yesterday—had she? Fiona desperately thinks back. Nearly moans as she recollects—no. Aunt Nell hadn't given any affirmation when she'd pointed out she'd inherit the farm. Just let Fiona's comments slide by, up on that cold cemetery-topped hill.

What now? Tears spring to Fiona's eyes as she senses her plan unraveling.

"Well, I know how much the church means to you." Fiona hates how shaky her voice is. "But why waste our time today if you don't wish to sell?" Genuine ire rises, filling her throat. "Such a remote, hidden location. Are you really saying you do not wish to sell, that you wish to live out there? What if something happens to you? It could be days before someone finds you. At least you were there when Uncle Henry passed on. To find him."

Aunt Nell blanches at this.

"And wills can be contested—"

At this, George grabs Fiona's wrist, squeezes it so hard that she cringes. She ventures a quick glance at him, nearly winces at the stone-cold stillness of his expression. She had failed him. George did not like failure.

Her aunt says, "Oh, I did agree to come here to sell. But not to you, Mr. Vogel. To Fiona. She told me yesterday about your baby, not long before you arrived. Congratulations."

George's grasp tightens so much she is sure he must feel her speeding pulse. "You told your aunt? Before me?"

"I—I—had some morning sickness. I needed her help—" Fiona stumbles to a stop. *Oh God, what is Aunt Nell playing at?*

"Klara could have helped you," George says. "I've told you, you can trust her—"

Aunt Nell interrupts. "Anyway, I got to thinking about how you're in such a, well, complicated business, Mr. Vogel. *Competitive.* What would happen to my niece if something happened to you? To her children? Your child?"

"That would sound like a threat," George says, "coming from anyone else."

Aunt Nell shakes her head. "Oh, not at all. I just mean—if property taxes on a farm are complex, what of your taxes, for income from your businesses? Other property? What happens to those assets if some paperwork goes, well, awry? After all, your man here"—Aunt Nell nods at Abe—"wasn't able to suss out that the situation changed since your visit with me."

At last, George drops Fiona's wrist, turns his wrathful glare onto Abe. To keep from sighing with relief at being at least temporarily released, Fiona clasps her hands together so hard that the edge of her wedding ring nearly cuts into her finger.

Abe protests, "This is ridiculous! Why would I think to ask about this old woman's property taxes—or will?" He glares at the banker. "Why didn't you tell me?"

Mr. Chandler looks terrified. "You told me you needed to set up an account for Mr. Vogel's wife's aunt. I assumed he was just setting up a gift to help her out."

Fiona composes yet another smile, puts a hand on George's arm. Her heart pounds as George turns his gaze to her. She forces her eyes to widen. Her voice to be soft. "Darling, I think what Aunt Nell is saying is that she knows I want to protect my children." George's gaze is hard, unmoved. Fiona forces herself to say, "Especially *our* child." *Forgive me, Leon.* But George's expression is already yielding. "And, darling, well, you *are* in a dangerous business."

"I make sure he's well protect—" Abe starts, outrage in his voice.

But Aunt Nell interrupts. "You know, word of *US versus Sullivan* has reached even our little burg."

What is Aunt Nell thinking? Trying to force George's hand—

"Oh, has it?" George says.

Mr. Chandler says timidly, "There was a piece in the *Kinship Daily Courier.*"

Fiona clears her throat, trying to look a little bewildered. "Well, we can worry about . . . whatever that is . . . later, I guess. Maybe we should just—"

Abe glares at Fiona. "If such news made the paper here, surely it's in the Cincinnati papers, too. Which I've noticed you reading quite a lot."

Fiona's gaze turns to Aunt Nell, a desperate plea for her to retract, somehow, what she's just let slip. But Aunt Nell gives her another encouraging look. *C'mon, girl. Run with it. You know how to run, don't you? To protect yourself?*

And so Fiona looks back at George. "You know I just like to read the advice columns and serial stories, dear." She slides a quick, damning look at Abe. "I think, maybe Aunt Nell is worried about what happens to your assets if there's a, well, error in paperwork? But if it is all in order—this was just supposed to take a few minutes, after all—and if it would help my aunt feel better, and ease the sale, I'd be willing to sign the paperwork."

And then she gives him her most coquettish smile. *And then turn the property over to you, my darling.*

A move she has no intention of making.

"It would make me feel better," Aunt Nell says. "Though if something happens to you, George, to your property, under the *Sullivan* decision, well, would you really want her—and your son—to have to live out here? Especially in a few years when he's in school?"

Aunt Nell is pushing too hard, too soon, for too much. *Why is she doing this?* Fiona forces herself to keep breathing evenly, to stare deeply, innocently, into George's eyes.

For a long moment, no one speaks.

Just breathe in, out, in, out, slowly. As if she's calm. As if she doesn't feel as though George's gaze is a lariat, looping around her neck.

"George, I don't think this is a good idea . . . ," Abe starts.

"It's a brilliant idea," George says. "If my property is in her name, the damned feds can't touch it."

George turns to the banker. "We will do as Mrs. Murphy wishes. Open an account in my wife's name immediately, and transfer in funds from my account here. Set up the sale of the farm. And while we're at it—" He looks back at Fiona. "But do you have the energy to wait here, while I set up similar paperwork for the Cincinnati properties? House, factory, warehouse?"

"Oh my God, George, you can't be serious!" Abe exclaims.

This is better than Fiona could have even hoped for. She turns to Abe, glaring. "You are questioning my husband's judgment? After demonstrating you can't be trusted with a simple errand?"

It's cruel, this lashing reminder of the previous night's events—Abe returning without Luther, the odious man turned to the four winds, likely to show up God-knows-where to stir up trouble, reveal George's vulnerabilities. Shame dampens Abe's eyes, bows his shoulders.

He's been a loyal soldier to George for years, never making a mistake. But somehow, chaotic Luther had managed to cause even Abe to err.

Fiona presses her advantage. "What if"—what to call Luther?— "what if your *charge* is, at this moment, running his big mouth to the wrong people?" She reflects back on the awful Thanksgiving dinner from yesterday. "He said at dinner last night that he took care of what he was supposed to—whatever that was—but what if he didn't?"

George lifts his hand, and for a sickening moment Fiona thinks he means to strike Abe as he had the night before—or maybe her. Maybe she's pressed too hard, too far. But George brings his hand down hard on the table, making the paperwork jump.

For a moment, George's and Abe's gazes are locked. An understanding passes between them. What that means specifically, she can't possibly know, but Fiona's startled to recognize something she thought she'd never see in either man's expression: fear.

Good Lord. Why had they trusted Luther with a task so important that if he failed they'd both be imperiled?

But it must have been important enough for Fiona's question to strike at George's confidence. For George says quietly, "I am serious. Property and other assets being in my name alone makes me too vulnerable."

He looks back at Fiona. She blinks a few times, as if trying to understand, and then says, "I can wait however long you wish, darling, to sign paperwork. Though—perhaps—while you and Mr. Chandler get it in order, Abe should take me to take care of the, well, the other errand?"

She keeps her expression open, eager. She means the visit she's to make to Lily—and hopefully pass on information about the tainted alcohol. Later—but only after she is sure George's assets are securely hers—she can get word to the Prohibition agency, perhaps through Lily, about the farm being converted for bootlegging, and claim she had no idea that that had been the plan all along. Won't getting word to the county sheriff about the tainted alcohol help prove her innocence?

She'd rather George never know she'd told Lily about the tainted alcohol—assuming she gets the chance—but if, God forbid, George somehow finds out *before* she's able to betray him to the revenuers, well, she'll just say that she learned about the tainted alcohol from Elias, say he'd implied that Abe and Luther set up the plan against George's will, so Fiona thought she was protecting George by telling Lily. . . .

There are all kinds of ways to weave a few small lies in with the truth to make a shawl she can wrap herself in to appear innocent, beguiling, devoted to George—which is what he wants to believe about her, especially now that she's the mother of his child—and innocent, guileless to the law and society, which is what they want to believe about women.

Why hadn't she seen earlier in life how easy it is to use those expectations to turn the game in her favor, rather than trying to live by them?

Even her aunt—whom she'd always seen as a simple farmwife—had just used similar expectations to her advantage.

Aunt Nell's plan—to get as much of George's assets into Fiona's name as possible in this meeting—wouldn't have worked if Fiona had known. For one thing, Fiona would never have gone along with it—her plan had been to slowly, steadily get George to turn over those assets.

But then, Fiona now sees that that approach would have given George too much time to have second thoughts, and Abe too many chances to talk him out of it. Aunt Nell had been clever—as well as wise in knowing Fiona would need to be genuinely shocked at the idea, so George would not suspect the idea had been Fiona's.

Fiona ventures a glance at her aunt, longing to ask why. Why had she pushed so hard, nearly ruined everything? But of course she knows: her aunt didn't trust her to be strong willed enough to follow through on her plans.

Aunt Nell had said as much, up at the cemetery, though God only knows it's unfair. Fiona had been a *child.* And yet she also sees sorrow on her aunt's face, and a flash of something else: *I'm sorry.*

Fiona wishes she could nod, acknowledge that she understands the apology isn't for taking over, speeding up the plan she'd shared the day before.

It's for the past.

That silly needlepoint pillow—the lumpy half she'd stitched, the smooth half Aunt Nell had finished—comes to mind. They'd finished the project, in their own awkward way, together.

Tears spring to Fiona's eyes. She blinks hard. In the moment it takes for her vision to clear, Aunt Nell is already looking back at George. "Can we get on with the paperwork? I want to catch the next train out."

CHAPTER 13

LILY

Here on Devil's Backbone, farther southeast but higher up than in Lily's spot in Bronwyn County, the snow falls heavier yet more languidly, as if a heavenly pillow has just given itself a little shake and loosed a few feathers.

After she'd left the courthouse, Lily had first stopped at the Kinship Inn.

No, the hotel clerk had assured her, *Luther Ross did not check in earlier this week. We'd know Luther Ross if we saw him.*

So maybe he had come on Thursday, as he'd said, with George and Elias and Abe.

Then Lily had headed to Marvena's. With the thickening snow, she'd felt nervous that her Model T would get stuck, so when she'd stopped at home to get her bloodhound Sadie, she'd also left her automobile with Mama and hitched up Daisy.

Her instincts had been correct. Now Daisy clomps over snow-shrouded ruts and rocks that would have caught the tires of Lily's Model T and then slickly held them spinning.

At last, they come to the clearing where abides Marvena's log-and-mortar cabin. From the chimney, smoky tendrils rise, their caresses barely visible against the gray sky.

Lily stops near the towering woodpile. The squeak of her wagon wheel would have alerted Marvena to someone's arrival. Sure enough, after a moment, the cabin's front door opens and Marvena steps out, forgoing her customary wave. Her shoulders slump, as if from a deep sigh of foreboding, as if knowing that of course Lily'd be coming.

As Lily spreads a blanket for warmth over Daisy's back, Sadie jumps down and runs up to the cabin to joyously greet Shep, Marvena's old coonhound, as he emerges from under the porch.

Inside the cabin, the greeting between Lily and Marvena had not been so jovial.

Now Lily sips her cup of boiled coffee, offered up by Nana, who stands watch at the stove over a pot simmering with herbs and onions. Ordinarily Lily would tease Nana about her concoctions and Marvena for letting her mother-in-law take over her kitchen. But on this morning of stilted cordiality, Lily notes the redness of Marvena's eyes. She had been crying—rare for Marvena, but Lily can imagine that Marvena and Jurgis would have fought after last evening's revelations about Marvena's moonshining.

This morning, Jurgis would be back at work in the coal mines and Frankie should be back in school, but Marvena had explained that Frankie was still asleep on her cot in the new sleeping room addition Jurgis had built off the back last summer, with a thick curtain dividing the room in half for privacy for Nana and Frankie.

"How is Zebediah?" Marvena asks quietly.

"Recovering at the Chillicothe hospital," Lily says. "He has the sugar."

Both Marvena and Nana look worried. All know that sugar diabetes is serious, especially in one so young.

"So, he wouldn't have had to drink much alcohol to trigger his state." Lily takes another sip of the good, strong coffee. "He would likely have ended up in a coma sooner rather than later, they say, and it may be a blessing the alcohol triggered evidence of the sugar now—well, at least since he was lucky enough for it to come on at home 'stead of when he was out alone."

"Zebediah's mama—Dora—how's she doing?" Marvena asks. "We ain't seen her at church in a month of Sundays, seems like."

"She might have days left."

"I'm right sorry to hear that." Marvena tries an offhand smile, but it's wobbly, like her next statement. "In light of that, I've got no right to complain that you've come to take me in."

Nana, who has turned back to the bubbling pot, stiffens.

"Thought to," Lily says. "But a possibly more pressing case has arisen, and I could use your help. You cooperate with me, and I'm pretty sure the judge can be convinced to let you off with a fine—so long as you bust up your still and foreswear future moonshining."

"I'm listening."

"You said you went back to it just for Frankie," Lily says.

"Yes." Marvena leans her forehead against her fists.

"Could you tell me more about Frankie's situation? That might help me convince the judge to ease up on you."

"The asthma cigarettes Doc Goshen lauded don't do much good, so Jurgis is ready to write off all doctors as quacks, and for all I know, he may be right." Marvena's voice goes so downy soft that Lily must lean across the table to hear the rest. "Breathing steam from Nana's teas soothed Frankie through the fall, but now even that doesn't last long. Doc says there's a new place in Cincinnati, a children's hospital that helps children like Frankie. But just getting her there, what's more, finding money for treatments—" Marvena's explanation staggers to a stop.

Lily understands. Marvena doesn't need to explain that though Wessex Corporation—owner of the mines formerly known as Ross Mining—offers better safety practices such as not using young boys to set dynamite lines—as Marvena's nephew, Alistair, had once been forced to do when the mine had been under the control of Luther Ross—and pays better, it's still in scrip. And Marvena's pay, from working for the United Mine Workers to help miners throughout the region campaign for the right to vote on unionization in their companies, is welcome but surely not sufficient for the cost of getting Frankie to Cincinnati for such advanced care.

Yet Lily is still angry at her friend—but not really for breaking the law. Why hadn't Marvena trusted her? Had enough faith in their friendship to fill her in before now, ask for help? Now—in front of Nana and with Frankie in the back room—is not the time to ask.

Lily picks up her tote bag, pulls out the revenuer's badge.

In the coal-oil lamplight haloing the table's center, the badge shines brightly. Marvena stares at it, brow furrowed. Lily waits, knowing Marvena, who has just learned to read over the past year and is making slow but steady progress, is sounding out the gold words on the cobalt blue shield-shaped badge:

Bureau of Prohibition Agent
US Treasury Department

hough a slow reader, Marvena is a sharp woman, and after she sounds out the words, the meaning and implication quickly dawn, and alarm tightens her face.

"Has a revenuer been around your place?"

Marvena shakes her head.

"Heard of any poking around these parts?"

"Nope." Marvena looks up at Lily. "Where'd you get this?"

"From Ruth. She slipped it to me last night, just before the doc and I left with Zebediah. Said her brother had given it to her, just before going under. She gave it to me in such a way that it's clear she didn't want her folks to know about it."

"So you're saying Zebediah got it at my place—when he was watching my stock."

"Looks like."

"I never saw any revenuer at my place."

"But somehow a revenuer found it. Someone sell you out?"

"Can't see why. Everyone keeps to their turf."

"But you've started up again after more than a year being out of the business. Wouldn't that make some folks mad?"

Marvena gives a wry grin. "You know, Jurgis split most of the wood out there last night and this morning. So I reckon so." Her smile drops, and her eyes glisten. "United Mine Workers gets wind of this, I'll lose my job!"

Lily forces her spine to stiffen, her voice to sternness. "I gotta do my job, too. One way or another, I have to let the bureau know about this badge showing up in my neck of the woods." She thinks of Agent Barnaby Sloan—and Luther Ross—in her office earlier. Should she have shown this to Sloan? Not in front of Luther. Should she tell Marvena about Luther's presence in the county—that he's supposedly working with the agency as a mole in Vogel's operation? Yes. But she can't tell her. Not until she knows for certain that Marvena didn't know about the missing revenuer. Agent DeHaven.

"So I need to go check out the area," Lily continues. "Need you to take me there. We can do it quietly, with you cooperating, and I'm thinking the judge will go as light as possible on you. You'll lose your still, pay a fine, maybe, yes, lose your job, but you'll still be here. With Frankie." Lily nods toward Nana, now turned to stare at them, wide-eyed. "With your family. Or I can get a warrant, bring deputies, come back, force the situation."

"Mama?" Frankie appears in the entry from the new back room. Her word comes out a strangulated plea as she gasps for air, as if she is not standing in a cabin but underwater.

In a flash, Marvena is up.

"The water's not steaming yet!" Nana cries.

Marvena grabs a bowl from a shelf, gets out a pack of cigarettes. Quickly, she flicks a lighter, lights the end of the cigarette, kneels next to Frankie.

The child's gasps have intensified into desperate barking wheezes.

Helplessness washes over Lily, just observing this. Marvena rubs Frankie's back with one hand and with the other holds the asthma cigarette to Frankie's mouth. The cigarette quivers between Marvena's thumb and forefinger, but Marvena's voice is cool, steady.

"Just close your lips over it. That's right. Now inhale. C'mon, child, inhale!"

Frankie does so, as tears stream down her face.

"Hold in that smoke," Marvena demands. She counts to five. "Now let it out, slowly."

They repeat the process twice more. Finally, Frankie's breathing evens out.

Marvena stubs out the cigarette, checks its tip. "There's menthol in the tobacco, and other medicines. Stills these little hairs—cilia, doc calls them—in the lungs." She shakes her head as she puts the cigarette in the pack, the pack in the bowl, the bowl on the shelf. "Ain't that something? Hair in the lungs! Well, it stops the attacks—but it ain't a cure. And each attack seems worse than the one before."

Marvena scoops up Frankie, who lowers her head to her mama's shoulder.

Tears stream down Nana's weary face. "I'm sorry I didn't have the herbs steaming—"

"It's all right, Nana. Just give her the treatments every few hours." Marvena peers up at Lily. "Nana's treatments help, in between the cigarettes."

But neither, Lily reads in both her friends' faces, is sufficient, not in the long run.

Marvena says to Frankie, "I gotta go help Sheriff Lily." She grabs her coat from a peg by the door, and wraps her head and neck in a red hand-knit scarf—no doubt one of Nana's creations. Then she turns to Lily. "Ain't far. We can walk."

The cold snatches Lily's breath, thins it into a sip of air. *Is this a taste of how Frankie feels when she's having an asthma attack? Poor child.*

Lily trudges on, pushing herself to keep up with Marvena's hardier pace. Snow restlessly tosses about on a swirling breeze. Sadie, Lily's tracking hound, trots alongside, leaping from time to time at a random snowflake—a welcome sight of innocent glee on this somber trek.

"I get the feeling there's something you're a-holding back," Marvena says. "You've been right touchy all morning. I mean, aside from being put out with me."

Luther Ross.

God help them all. Lily's thoughts on the trek had wavered, pro and con, about telling Marvena about Luther and Abe's visit last night to her house and about her encounter with Luther and Agent Sloan.

If Marvena finds out Luther's back in the area—and working with an agent—she's likely to set out with a shotgun to shoot him dead. Not that Lily blames her. In addition to his and Elias's contributions to Daniel's demise, Luther had also played a role in the final days of Eula—Marvena's older daughter.

When she does tell her, Marvena will be furious about her not sharing this information right away. Lily hoped she'd come to understand. For now, the focus must remain on finding out if this revenuer's badge means anything—or not. Then Lily can face her friend.

Marvena comes to such an abrupt stop that Lily nearly stumbles into her. Marvena shoots an amused look her way, then points. Lily spots, then, the rocky overcrop, dark stained with ancient drippings of rain runoff, earth draped with tangled vines turned sere and brown by winter. In summer, with such growth thick and green and ropey, and rocks coated with moss, the rock ledge and the shelter it created below would be nearly impossible to find.

Lily follows Marvena. The natural shelter gives just enough space for Marvena's still. A smaller operation than the one Lily busted up nearly two years ago, shortly after meeting Marvena. But better hidden. She'd never have found it on her own.

Lily surveys the copper kettles, the tubes, the canning jars just like the ones both women use to put up fruits and vegetables for the winter. An axe is buried deep in a piece of wood on top of a woodpile, protecting the blade against dampness and eventual rust.

Marvena gives a tenuous smile. "Haven't brewed in a while, given the weather. Sold off most of my stock earlier this fall, and was reckoning to get rid of the rest right afore Thanksgiving. Got enough to at least get us one-way to that children's hospital in Cincinnati. Mayhap talk to someone. But not enough for what I reckon treatments would cost."

"You know what I gotta do, Marvena."

"Then do it!"

I'm sorry rises in Lily's gorge. But she swallows the words back. She cannot—will not—apologize for adhering to the rule of law. Not even to a friend in dire, understandable need.

Lily steps forward, yanks the axe from the wood. There's no point in trying to bust up the kettles. She'll have to come back later with some deputies and pull these out. She focuses on the carefully rigged tubing, then on the remaining jars. Each crashing strike of the axe echoes into the hollow of the ledge, reverberates up her arms.

When she finishes, sweating even in this cold, she finally looks for Marvena.

She stands with her back to Lily, staring into the snowy woods. A soft tendril of smoke rises over Marvena's head, like a wisp of gray hair. The only spot of bright color in the gray day is Marvena's red scarf.

Marvena pulls a small pestle from her pocket, carefully grinds out the remaining tobacco in her pipe. Then she wraps both in a handkerchief and tucks the items in her tote bag.

Lily turns, lifts the axe once more, to bring it thuddingly down into its resting spot on top of the woodpile.

When she looks back around, her friend is gone from sight, and she must hurry to catch up with her in the thick woods.

Fifteen or so minutes later, they come to a small clearing, at the back of which is an ironworks furnace, in the shape of a ziggurat, built into a hill. Dotting these hills are several such furnaces, leftovers from the era of small operations employing a hundred or so men to dig out ore and put it through fire hot enough to burn out the sulfur and reduce the ore to iron. A laborious process, followed by the just-as-difficult effort to haul the iron out of the hills and ship it back east. By the early 1900s, the ironworks era was mainly over, replaced by coal as king.

Marvena points to a split log, either end on rocks—a makeshift shelf. A brown jug sits on the ground in front of the shelf. The tableau of shelf and jug blends into the muted earthy background. On the other hand, the ironworks is a handy place marker, easy enough to find for anyone knowing the rough coordinates.

Marvena goes over by the log, picks up the jug, gives it a shake. A bit of shine sloshes around. "Zebediah told Ruth a man was hurt?" Marvena asks.

Lily nods.

"Well, if'n I was out here, and I needed to crawl for shelter, I know where I'd go." She flicks a glance to the furnace.

Lily walks over to the furnace, opens her tote bag, pulls out her flashlight. She kneels to put the tote bag by the base of the tree closest to the ironworks. As she stands back up, she notes an unnatural splintering in the tree trunk, about the height of a small man's head, a few inches taller than her. She looks more closely. It's a bullet, lodged in the tree.

Lily kneels again, retrieving her pocketknife out of her knapsack, digs at the bullet, which hasn't gone far into the trunk. The cartridge she digs out is too small to be for hunting. It's from a pistol or revolver.

Maybe the bullet and the revenuer's shield badge have nothing to do with each other. But maybe they do. Lily wraps the bullet in a handkerchief, tucks it in her tote. She retrieves her flashlight, turns it on, drops to her knees in the snow in front of the opening to the ironworks. She crawls in.

The base of the old furnace is huge, certainly big enough for her to stand up. A bit of snow has drifted in, but not much. Lily slowly guides her light around—nothing but dirt and crunchy leaves. A rustling. She focuses her light up, spots brown bats sleeping in a row. She trains her flashlight toward the ground. Could be a chipmunk. Could be a snake—a harmless one. Or it could be a timber rattlesnake, the more common of the three poisonous varieties in the area. She's only spotted a few rattlers in all her forays into the hills, and though she knows logically they're as afraid of her as she is of them, just the thought of them churns revulsion.

The rustling stops. Lily's flashlight picks up a still brown shape, about the size of a hefty squirrel. Lily walks over—a fedora. She squats by it.

There's a tear, just above the brim, at the bottom of the hatband. Lily moves her flashlight closer to the spot. There, in the felt, is a dark stain, something thick and dried, with a few short black fibers. Blood and hair.

Lily picks up the hat, exits, and holds the fedora out for Marvena to study. After a moment, Marvena looks back up at Lily.

Lily sees that she's calculated as she has: A fedora is for fine in-town churches, or weddings, or funerals. For businessmen. Or for revenuers. Not so usual among the miners or farmers or hunters dwelling in these mountains. And the tear with the blood—hard to say for sure, but when combined with that stray bullet in the tree by the ironworks, it wouldn't be surprising if another bullet had hit—or grazed, anyhow—its mark. But where's the man to whom the hat belongs?

Lily looks around, spots her bloodhound, nose snuffling eagerly along the ground by the makeshift bench, the scent of some squirrel or chipmunk likely stirring hunger.

"Sadie!" Lily calls. The hound obediently trots over. "Good girl," Lily says, scratching between her ears. Then she holds the hat out to Sadie.

At first, Sadie gives a reluctant sniff. Next a more eager one, and finally her nose begins twitching rapidly. She takes off, through the woods, and Lily and Marvena run as fast as they can after her, hoisting their skirts to avoid being snagged back by brush and limbs.

Soon the hound is out of sight. But they hear her, howling in the distance. Breathless, they finally catch up to her.

There, from a snow-caked limb, dangles a strip of wool cloth. Brown, jaggedly cut on one edge, and neatly hemmed on the other. And there, a stain darkening the strip. Blood.

Sadie had just connected the hat to this strip of cloth.

Lily considers: Plenty of boys wore pants made from dull, practical, and rough cloth like this. But the likelihood of that same cloth here, so close to where Zebediah had been hiding out to keep an eye on Marvena's stock, in the same proximity as the bullet, that can't be coincidence.

Lily looks over her shoulder at Marvena.

"Zebediah didn't carry a gun, did he?"

"Could have come out with a hunting rifle, though I sure didn't advise such. Told him if any funny business started up, he was to take cover till it was over or to run—whichever was more likely to save his hide." Marvena sighs. "Poor kid."

"Lucky kid," Lily says. "Having a sister willing to defy his parents, trek to the doctor."

Lily stares up through the tree branches, so tall it is easy to fancy they tickled the underbellies of the gray clouds to set loose new snow. By the time she gathers men, explains the situation, it will be after noontime, and a search could take hours.

The wind stirs the trees, but softly now. The snow has lessened since last night. They have a better chance of getting to Chillicothe and back before nightfall.

She looks back at Marvena, says casually, "Well now, I reckon you won't mind going with me to call on Zebediah Harkins in the hospital."

Marvena looks taken aback. "What? Now? Why'n the world—"

Lily chuckles, which swirls more confusion in Marvena's expression. "I reckon the boy's a bit afraid of you."

Marvena shrugs. "Sure. I guess."

"Well, he should have come around by now," Lily says. "Boy'll be wishing to see his mama, or sister, or even his pa. But between seeing me and you, he'll tell us what he might have seen. What the badge, the blood, and the hat might add up to."

Marvena's eyes narrow, harden. "Lily Ross, you can have a right cold heart."

Lily plucks the bloody brown strip of pant cloth from the bush, folds it carefully, and tucks it in her tote bag.

Zebediah takes a sip of water from the cup Lily holds to his lips. A moment later, a retching spasm makes him shudder. Lily withdraws the cup. *Poor kid.* His stomach is so empty, it will take time before he can hold light liquids, what's more solid food.

Lily looks away, giving the boy a moment to regain his composure, and chances a glance at the starched, crisp nurse standing by another child's bed, side-eyeing both Lily and Marvena. The nurse had tried to turn the pair away. Even Lily pointedly telling her she was at the Chillicothe hospital on official business had only gained a sharply dismissive glance at her badge. To Lily's relief, the doctor who had been on duty when Lily and Dr. Goshen first brought Zebediah in happened by.

Still, Lily can't blame the tense nurse, tending to the children by herself, in the large room of ten beds on each side, only curtains for privacy between each bed. The younger woman reminds Lily a bit of herself in her nursing days, alongside Elias during the 1918 influenza outbreak while her husband was away at war. Once, she'd taken pride in the memory of those days. Now the recollection brings more sorrow than satisfaction. Lily shifts uncomfortably in her chair, as if she can scoot away from her swirling thoughts.

A modern ceiling gaslight creates a halo in the middle of the room, but the light barely reaches Zebediah's bed. A window at the far end allows a thin smear of opaque light to cover the room. Lily calculates: it's just past 1:30 p.m. now. It had taken them more than two hours to get back to Lily's house on Daisy, retrieve the automobile with no explanation for bewildered Mama—who'd insisted on packing up turkey and biscuit and apple jelly sandwiches, which they'd not yet eaten—and then make it here, Lily speeding as fast as she dared, Marvena yelping at every bump and swerve.

Maybe they should have formed a search team after all, looked for a possibly shot and missing revenuer. Ever since Ruth had shown up on her doorstep on Thanksgiving, it seemed that Lily had been faced with paths that only led to junctures with more paths, and no clear sign as to which to take, each looking as dismally thorny as the others.

"It's all right, child." Marvena's surprisingly soothing voice, concern blunting the usually coarse edge, calls Lily back to the moment. "You don't have to drink more'n you want."

Marvena dabs the boy's chin with a handkerchief. She's had practice soothing Frankie, and indeed the boy gazes up at Marvena, fearless, trusting. But when his eyes shift to Lily, they widen with fear after all. "I'm in trouble, ain't I."

Lily shakes her head. "No, no. But—"

He struggles to sit up. "Oh! Mama, is she—"

"She's still with us," Lily says quickly. Well, at least she was as of the night before. "And she wanted you to come here. Ruth was right to come get Dr. Goshen. Later, she was also right to pass this on to me." Lily pulls out the revenuer's badge and shows it to Zebediah.

As pallid as he is, his face blanches even more.

Marvena puts her hand carefully but firmly on his arm. "Zebediah, you gotta tell Sheriff Lily the truth of whatever you seen out there." She takes a deep breath. "I was wrong to hire you. I put you in danger, and I'm sorry. But you're not in trouble, no matter what you saw. We also found something else—a fancy men's hat. Looks like whoever was wearing it was shot, grazed at least. And Sheriff Lily's tracking hound traced the hat to a strip of cloth nearby."

"The cloth looks like it could have been cut from your pant legs, Zebediah," Lily says. Though he's now in hospital pajamas and covered up by a blanket, she gives his lower legs a pointed look, as if he's still wearing those brown pants.

Zebediah leans back into his pillow. "I saw two men I didn't know, talking and coming up the rise. Something didn't seem right." He looks searchingly at Marvena. "The older man said something about another man—a name with a *v* in it, I think. And he shot the younger man. Left him for dead. I thought he was, too."

"That is a serious charge," Lily says.

"I swear it! But I did what Mrs. Sacovech told me to do if there was ever any trouble—I stayed hid. And then when the older man left, I heard a moan. I went to the younger man, and saw he was hurt, bad, but not dead yet. I bound up his wound—it was bleeding awful fierce—using the pieces from my pant leg. I wanted to get him to town, to a doctor, or"—he looks at Lily—"to you, but he said no. He needed to lay low for a few days, sort out what to do next. So I took him to the church." He looks back at Marvena.

"Sanctuary." Marvena sighs the word. "Who took him in?"

"I don't know. Honest to God, I know I meant to get him there, but I don't rightly remember if'n I did! I started feeling funny, light-headed, by the time we even got to the bottom of the hill," he says. "And next I knew, I was comin' around here."

"Did you at least get the man's name?" The boy's eyes flash hurt. But Lily keeps her gaze hard on him, even as she feels Marvena's drilling into her.

The nurse comes over. "I think it's time for you to go. . . ." She trails off as Lily puts up her hand: *Stop!*

Zebediah studies her, considering. It's not, Lily realizes, that he doesn't know the name. He just feels protective of the man. Uncertain where to put his faith, who to trust.

Well, that she can sure empathize with, especially with Luther and Elias back in the area, reminding her of how her world and her certain trust in what she knew and the people around her had been upended two years before.

Lily puts her hand gently on the boy's. "You did the right thing, helping him. And giving the badge to Ruth. Did you read it?"

Zebediah shrinks back into the thin pillow as far as he can, gives his head a little shake.

"Well, it's from the Bureau of Prohibition. The man that you saw shot is a federal agent. A revenuer. Sooner or later, the bureau is going to notice one of their own missing, come looking around." She'll have to notify Barnaby Sloan—and she doesn't like the idea because of how enthralled he seems to be with Luther Ross. Is it possible Luther is the older man Zebediah had seen? She's not sure that makes sense—unless Colter DeHaven had come early for some reason. And Luther wanted a dead Prohibition agent found near Marvena's still.

Revenge on Marvena, who'd helped her root Luther and Elias out of Bronwyn County the first time. Revenge on Lily, if he could get her to rush into coming after Vogel.

Lily goes on. "If the older man who did the shooting gets wind that the man he thought he killed is alive—and was helped by you—then . . ." Lily lets her voice trail off, shakes her head. Even as her gut flips at the kid's terrified expression, Lily sharpens her gaze. "If you give me the man's name, I can make sure your family is protected."

Zebediah says the name, soft but distinct. "Colter DeHaven."

"Dammit, Lily, slow down!" Marvena yelps.

Lily scowls. It's early afternoon, but there's more to do than there is daylight left. They're close to Kinship—just a few more turns and the church spires and county courthouse dome of Bronwyn County will be in sight. Since leaving Chillicothe, Lily's turned her options over and over: First, go to the church and see if Zebediah had made it there with Colter? Maybe, if she's lucky, find Colter still alive, on the mend.

But she also needs to call on the Harkinses. Tell them their boy has regained consciousness. She hopes Mrs. Harkins is still alive to receive at least this good news.

"Lily!" Marvena snaps as the automobile jolts into and out of a crack in the road. "Dammit, I mayn't know how to drive, but I know it's not good to blow a tire!"

"Have one of Mama's sandwiches, if you're feeling puny!" Lily snaps.

"Lily, I know you're angry at me for shining, but—"

"That's not the issue, not really."

"What then?" Marvena rustles in her tote for the sandwiches Mama had packed.

How to tell her about Luther and Abe's visit to her house last night? Luther and Agent Sloan's visit to her office this morning? She'd started several times to fill her friend in on the drive over to the hospital this morning but couldn't find the courage. Now, with Zebediah's news about Agent Colter DeHaven—and Lily's suspicion that the older man whom Zebediah had seen shoot the agent was actually Luther and that he'd hoped to set up Marvena—she can't put off telling her any longer.

Marvena holds one of Mama's sandwiches over to Lily, who starts to decline it. But that apple jelly and turkey smell good, and her mouth waters. She slows enough that she can control her automobile with one hand on the steering wheel, takes the sandwich, bites into it. As she eats, she focuses on the snowy ribbon of road before her, the sweep of the struggling windshield wipers. But Lily can't sweep away her troubles—or the need to tell her friend the truth.

"Marvena, I have to fill you in on some hard news—" Lily starts, at the same time that Marvena says, "Lily, you oughta know—"

Words are snatched from both of them as the automobile skids on a patch of ice, careens off the side of the road, and plunges into a deep ravine.

CHAPTER 14

FIONA

Friday, November 25, 1927
Noon

Fiona sits quietly while Dr. Goshen presses a stethoscope against her back.

"Just breathe normally, Mrs. Vogel," he says. "I know my stethoscope is cold—but then your latest fashions don't provide modest coverage. Relax."

Fiona forces her breath to ease, even as her hands and jaw clench. If only her problems were as simple as the fashionably low cut of the back of her modern dress revealing skin against which the doctor is pressing his cold stethoscope.

Normal? Nothing is *normal* right now.

Even getting herself here had required more than simply walking over to the doctor's office after the train bearing Aunt Nell pulled out of the Kinship station. Such a direct act would have raised questions, even suspicions.

"I'm going to shine this light in your eyes," Dr. Goshen says. "Try not to blink."

So Fiona had faked becoming faint, falling back into Abe, who'd been sent with Fiona to drive her and Aunt Nell to the station, while

George remained at the savings and loan and worked on putting his real estate holdings in her name.

"Open your mouth. I'm going to check your tonsils."

Fiona is still astounded that George had gone that far. If she hadn't been able to cast doubt on Abe and his dunderheaded loss of Luther, she's certain she would not have been able to manipulate him to do so.

"All right, I'm going to press your abdomen," Dr. Goshen says. "Let me know if you have any tenderness."

Still, the realization that in a few days all that property would legally be in her name had sent her head spinning and her stomach churning as the train pulled away, and so it had not been hard for her to do a decent job of playacting her sickness.

Abe had seemed reluctant, but Fiona knew he wouldn't want her to tell George he'd refused to escort her to the doctor when she'd asked. Abe is sitting out in the waiting area.

"You are perfectly healthy, Mrs. Vogel," Dr. Goshen says now. "I see no reason for concern about your dizzy spell. I'm sure it's due to the stress of saying good-bye to your aunt—and of being pregnant."

"I wasn't dizzy when I was pregnant with my first child," Fiona says. This much is true.

"Well, how old are you?"

"Thirty-seven."

"Oh my, yes, yes," Dr. Goshen says—as if she's the biblical Sarah becoming with child when *already stricken with old age.* Dr. Goshen makes a note. "And when you had your first child, you were—"

"Twenty-two."

"Well, quite a difference in age right there, yes?" He gives her a patronizing pat on the arm and makes another note.

"The morning sickness is extreme, though. Is there anything you can give me?"

"I can mix a mild tincture of bicarbonate of soda and aspirin. That should help."

Fiona studies him as he opens cupboards, gathers bottles, mortar, pestle. She notes the drooping dark bags beneath his eyes, the weary slope to his shoulders.

As he methodically crushes and measures and mixes his ingredients, Fiona considers the question: Why would Luther—whose top priority is always Elias—have run off last night? What if Abe had been lying about that and something else had happened to Luther?

If that was the case, then Fiona could report that back to George later. Abe is already in dangerous territory with George, as had been painfully clear in the meeting at the bank. Proof of Abe lying about Luther might be just enough to finally undermine Abe in George's mind so that she could be rid of Abe once and for all.

Then there is the matter of Uncle Henry. Elias had said that it was Dr. Goshen, after all, who'd claimed Uncle Henry had a stroke. If she can get Dr. Goshen to talk, just a little, about Uncle Henry, perhaps she'll have a better idea of how much—if at all—to trust Elias.

"I think," Fiona says softly, "that Uncle Henry's death might have affected me more than I realized."

Dr. Goshen stiffens, stops grinding down the tablets. A dull silence follows. Fiona lets it leaven for a few moments and then punctures it with a tittering laugh. "Isn't it odd? Uncle Henry, healthy as can be, no issues, and then he just keels over one day—"

"He had stomach issues," Dr. Goshen says. He goes back to pummeling the tablets. "I was treating him for ulcers."

Aunt Nell hadn't mentioned that. "Ulcers . . . did that contribute to his death?"

"He had a stroke. He was worried about—farm concerns. Stress led to his stomach problems. And, I'm guessing, may have contributed to his stroke. So his tendency to worry didn't help either issue, but an ulcer wouldn't directly trigger his stroke."

Fiona considers. Uncle Henry *was* a worrier. But what *farm concerns* would he have had—until George and Elias showed up? "Aunt Nell never said anything about this."

"She didn't know." Dr. Goshen squashes each word of his reply, like it's a troublesome bug. "Your uncle Henry didn't want her to worry, too, and I respected that. I compounded my version of milk of magnesia for him every month or so—less magnesium hydroxide than the over-the-counter product, plus an analgesic. He'd find a reason to come into town, or I'd come by the farm on some excuse."

"So . . . other than the stomach ulcer, he seemed fine, the last time you saw him, a month or so before he—"

"A few days before he passed, I came by with a new bottle of the medicine for him." Dr. Goshen's small smile manages to be both amused and sad. "I'd come by with the excuse that he was teaching me a few woodworking tricks. We were in the men's group together at church, so your aunt didn't question it."

Someone knocks at the door. "Yes?" Dr. Goshen says.

"It's me." Mrs. Goshen's voice filters through the door.

"Come in." He looks at Fiona. "My wife is better at packaging my tinctures anyway—less spillage."

The door opens long enough for Fiona to note Abe sitting in a chair directly across from the door. He gives her a little smile, a sharp look.

Mrs. Goshen walks in, an ample woman as round as a turnip, swathed in a too-large modest brown cotton dress on which a pattern of blue flowers somehow makes the cloth even duller. She gives Fiona a stern look, then gazes back at her husband. "The other patients are getting restless. They've been waiting awhile." The door clicks to.

"I see," Fiona says. "Well, we are certainly grateful for your kind concern today—taking me in ahead of your other patients. Goodness! I'll be sure to tell my husband of your kindness. Oh—and we thank you for sending along the heart pills Abe and Luther requested for Elias. So, well, so kind of you to do so, without insisting on checking on Elias yourself."

Dr. Goshen looks stricken. "Well, he—he's a doctor himself, of course. And—I've met him. Just a few times."

"Yes, of course. He's doing much better now, with his heart pills."

"Oh, good, good," Dr. Goshen says hastily. "I was going to ask."

No, you weren't. "Thank you," Fiona says, "but I'm not sure they'll do much good if Luther doesn't return soon. Elias worries so, about his nephew."

Dr. Goshen frowns. "Luther didn't return?"

"Odd, given how he's always so concerned about his uncle," Fiona says.

Mrs. Goshen puts a lid on the bottle, brings it to Fiona. There's a label affixed, with carefully handwritten instructions about how to take the medicine.

"Did Luther say anything about wanting to go elsewhere, while he and Mr. Miller awaited your husband's return? Somewhere he and Mr. Miller might have gone after they left here?" Fiona asks as she takes the bottle.

"No," Mrs. Goshen says. "They were quiet—for the most part—waiting in the parlor. My husband came home, saw they were here. Explained that he'd been summoned by a farm girl who said that her brother had been watching over some hill woman's still, and taken ill, apparently drinking tainted alcohol. Mr. Ross became agitated, demanded to know who."

"And did you tell him?" Fiona asks. Abe had said they did not mention specifics the night before. Why would Abe—ever loyal to her husband—withhold such information? "You can trust me," Fiona adds, smiling as beguilingly as she can manage. "When I tell my husband that I asked after Luther, he will appreciate knowing that you trusted me with the information."

Dr. Goshen looks stricken by her implication she'll report everything to her husband. Even here, George Vogel's reputation is formidable—and frightening.

"I said I'd gone with Lily Ross to the Harkins family farm. That the girl, Ruth, accused a woman named Marvena Whitcomb Sacovech of letting her brother work for her keeping watch at her stand where customers could pick up their shine, and sadly, the boy—who has diabetes—had fallen into a coma. Luther wanted to know if the boy would come around. He seemed quite agitated. As soon as I finished the medicine, Luther looked at Abe and told him to get it to Elias—or he'd live to regret it. Then Luther took off running, and Abe followed."

A silence ensnares the room, as Fiona considers what she's learned and as the doctor and his wife look at each other worriedly. Had they said too much?

Mrs. Goshen's hand—she's been holding out Fiona's bottle of medicine this whole time—starts to quiver. A light flashes off her hand. Fiona notices a ring, beset with a gorgeously cut sapphire. So sophisticated, for a simple country doctor's wife. So at odds with the dull blue field of flowers on her worn brown dress.

But then—hadn't Fiona hinted, not so subtly, for Martin to buy her fancy things? Things a simple country shoe shop owner couldn't afford? Had that been why he'd gambled, to give her the necklace, the cupboard, the fancy blue vase—all of which she'd later sell for pennies on the dollar?

The only treasure she'd held on to was the candy dish from her youth—besides, with the chip in its side, it would not sell anyway.

Fiona shakes her head to clear it as she takes the bottle. She turns a thin smile on the doctor. "Thank you. I will have my husband send payment if you'll just tell me how much—"

"Oh, no need." Dr. Goshen waves his hands. "Consider it a . . . a . . . congratulatory gift."

Fiona tucks the bottle into her handbag. She does not wait for either Dr. or Mrs. Goshen to open the door for her. She readies her thin smile and direct gaze for Abe and opens it herself.

CHAPTER 15

LILY

Branches fly into the windshield of Lily's automobile. She clutches the steering wheel with her left hand, bracing herself, and throws her right arm across Marvena's chest to hold her back.

Lily hears a sickening pop as her automobile jolts to a stop. For a moment, in the thudding stillness, Lily stares at the branches covering her cracked windshield. Then looks over at Marvena, eyes wide with shock but all in one piece. Darts her gaze back to the windshield. Thank God no branches had broken through, stabbed them. Assesses the view as best she can through branches and windshield cracks. They're at the bottom of the ravine. Better than her automobile being caught temporarily in thick branches, only to plunge farther.

Pain shoots through Lily's left shoulder, so swift and intense that she's nearly overcome by nausea. Oh—the sickening pop was dislocation. She moans.

"C'mon, Lily." Marvena's voice, like her tug on Lily's coat sleeve, is gentle, coaxing.

Lily's door is stuck, so she slides out after Marvena. Lily notes the crumpled front end. She's not going to be able to drive her automobile for a while. "You all right?"

Marvena nods. "Might have a few bruises later from you holding me back so tight—hey!" She catches Lily as she starts to slide to her knees, and Lily yelps.

"Dislocated my shoulder," Lily says. She grits her teeth, tries to roll her shoulder back in place. Gasps, as the pain worsens. "Need you to get my shotgun out, unload it."

Marvena complies as Lily eases out of her overcoat, lets it fall to the ground. When Marvena turns back around with the unloaded shotgun, she gasps at the sight of Lily's skewed shoulder.

Lily sinks to her knees on top of her coat. "Use the butt end."

"Lily—"

"Make it fast. And don't go all gentle on me."

Lily stiffens her left arm, grasps her wrist tight with her right hand. Grits her teeth.

For a moment, Marvena is so still that Lily fears her friend has frozen in shock at the situation. But then she swiftly hits Lily's shoulder. Lily yelps in blinding pain, but as her vision returns she feels her shoulder back in place. Throbbing, painful, but such a relief.

Marvena helps her up, gets her into her overcoat, gathers tote bags and weaponry. Then both women stare up the steep bank. Marvena takes Lily's right elbow, and Lily starts to shake away—*I can do this myself*—but then she lets Marvena help her.

At the top of the rise, they stare back. The automobile is barely visible, and soon, with the falling snow, the gap created in the brush by their accident will be hard to spot. Marvena pulls the red knit scarf from her neck, ties it around a nearby branch.

She grins at Lily. "Don't need the tow truck sliding around later, looking for your T. Now, how far out of town you reckon we are?"

"R-r-reckon f-f-four miles," Lily manages. Her teeth are chattering hard—not so much from the cold wind as from shock of their situation just now hitting her.

Marvena hooks her arm through Lily's uninjured arm, starts them in the direction of Kinship. "You were 'bout to tell me something, afore that patch of ice rudely interrupted."

Lily's mind is blank, and then it comes back to her. She bites back a groan. Now, of all times, to tell Marvena about Luther's presence— his visit to her house last night with Abe, his visit with a bureau agent to her office, her suspicions that Luther is trying to not only outwit George but set up both Lily and Marvena.

"Or I reckon I could sing a hymn to pass the time," Marvena says, the offer a jovial threat. Her sweet daughter, Frankie, had inherited her lovely voice from her father, Marvena's first husband, a coal miner who'd died alongside Lily's father a little over three years before, trying to save other coal miners in a cave-in caused by poor decisions Luther had made.

Tears, not just from the brisk wind, sting Lily's eyes.

There's not going to be an easy or right time to fill Marvena in— other than immediately, and that chance is past. And Lily's already for-given Marvena for moonshining again, especially knowing her reason.

Maybe Marvena will forgive her for not filling her in immediately.

Lily stares at the toes of her boots, crunching on the icy road. She swallows back another wave of pain-induced nausea and says as care-fully as she walks, "Well, what I gotta tell you isn't gonna be easy to hear."

The white clapboard church is barely more distinctive than a ghost perched in the cleared dale below, surrounded by bare trees with limbs stretching up to the gray, snow-swirled sky like arms raised in prayer. Though impatiently waiting for the plain wooden door to open, for Marvena to appear and wave her on down, Lily is grateful for this mo-ment to be silent. Still.

When Benjamin comes up alongside her, Lily stiffens, not ready for the moment to be shattered by conversation.

But he is silent, other than panting from his trek. From his slight smile, she gathers that he isn't silent only to catch his breath. He, too, knows how, and when, to be still.

It is not uncomfortable, this being silent and still in each other's presence.

Better than the last silent half mile of Lily and Marvena's walk into Kinship, after Lily finished explaining about Luther.

Once at the town's edge, Lily'd sent Marvena to ask one of her deputies to loan Lily his automobile—after all, she still needed Marvena to guide her to the church. Expressionless, Marvena nodded and walked off. Lily then went to Kinship's only mechanic's garage to arrange for her automobile to be towed back. Then she'd gone to the courthouse, left a message with the commissioners' office that she'd wrecked her own automobile and would need a loaner until hers was fixed and would like official permission to request a loaner from the one automobile dealer in town. In her office, she'd allowed herself the luxury of dry-swallowing two aspirin and, quickly but shakily, made notes about what had transpired, what they'd learned from Zebediah.

When she emerged onto the courthouse steps, Marvena was waiting for her, but not with the deputy Lily'd requested—with Benjamin Russo.

I reckon you're not just going to loan me your automobile, Lily'd said to Benjamin at the bottom of the steps.

Benjamin had shook his head. *No, ma'am. Marvena told me about the wreck—*

Doesn't mean I can't drive—

Didn't mean to imply such. But your shoulder could use a rest.

Well, clever. Marvena knew Lily'd not goad her to talk in front of Benjamin.

But Lily'd accepted riding in the back seat, while Marvena sat up front with Benjamin to give directions. Truth be told, sitting back there and closing her eyes for the ride had done her good. But when they got to Rossville and needed to start walking, Benjamin parked his automobile and got out with them. Lily had said, *Thanks for the ride, but we don't need your help.* He'd just grinned: *Need to stretch my legs.*

Now Benjamin breaks the silence, quietly asking, "What are we waiting for?"

"Marvena didn't expect people besides the pastor and his wife to be here and she wants to ease the way," Lily says. Since tersely claiming she'd run into Benjamin on the way to the deputy, all she'd said to Lily was, *Wait here*, when they got to the top of this hill. "Or so I'm guessing. She wants me to get the information I came for, without scaring anyone."

Lily hopes Marvena can find someone at the church to confirm what Zebediah had told them, that he'd brought the revenuer here. Could she have some luck, discover the revenuer is here?

She shifts her stance, then winces. Climbing the hill with one decent arm was simple, but going down to the church in the clearing, she'd need balance. Tricky, with her left shoulder still throbbing. As she looks around for a branch that might be suitable as a walking stick, she notes Benjamin pulling out a cigarette and a silver Zippo lighter.

He looks from the cigarette to her. "You mind?"

She shakes her head.

"Some ladies don't like the sight or smell of cigarettes."

Lily sighs—there it is. Assumptions about what she does, or doesn't, like, simply based on her being "the fairer sex." Of course she'd dealt with that with Daniel in myriad small ways—he would have been shocked at her and Marvena hunting the Thanksgiving turkey, even though he knew her daddy had taught her to hunt, and that she liked hunting.

But now, nearly three years since his death, and almost as long as sheriff, Lily has no patience for pretending she's anything other than what she is. She'll have no patience with such with Benjamin. . . .

She dismisses the thought with a reflexive shrug, and winces from a jolt of pain.

"I had a buddy dislocate his shoulder like that. In the war. Fell to the ground at a funny angle. Howled like he'd been shot. Medic got it back in place, told him to rest up—"

"I don't have time for a sinking spell while someone fetches my smelling salts."

Benjamin looks annoyed. *Good.* She is starting to think he would accept any snotty thing she said, and while she didn't want to be courted by a man who made assumptions about what a woman might or might not want, she also didn't want to be courted by a man who could be pushed around—

Lily catches herself. What is she thinking? He is not courting her. She does not want to be courted.

Benjamin gently touches her arm. "In all seriousness, do you need to sit down? An injury like that, doesn't that hurt like h—"

He stops short, turns red, and Lily catches herself about to roll her eyes.

"Hurt like hell?" Lily says. Benjamin looks shocked, but then grins. She can't help but smile—pleased that he at least doesn't care if she curses now and again. "Yes, it does." The aspirin had barely touched the pain. She looks around again, then spots a branch, about the right thickness and length for a walking stick.

Lily steps over to it, picks it up, pokes it a few times in the snow. Yes, this will do.

She glances at Benjamin studying her, but not in a pitying way. He's not insisting on playing savior to her or on casting her as a damsel in distress.

For that, she lets her heart relent a little. "You handle the woods better than I reckoned you would."

"Learned from Daniel. Funny—these woods look so much like the woods in France," Benjamin says. His gaze is distant as he stares down at the simple church in the snowy clearing. Is he seeing his fallen mates in the Meuse–Argonne offensive—her brother, others—twisted and bloody and lifeless, on and around the rocks and brush of the forest? It's odd to think—a forest a half a world away, but looking like this one in remote Appalachia—and memories a decade old, but as if in this moment.

"I guess they would. Daniel didn't talk much about the war." Sometimes, though, he'd cry out in his sleep and she'd carefully wake him up, try to comfort him. But he never shared details of the war. None of the men who survived to return home to Bronwyn County did. She reckoned that was true of soldiers no matter where *home* was.

Benjamin's gaze retreats from the past, and he focuses on her. "Daniel didn't talk much, at all, was my experience. Except, sometimes, about you. Less often, about boxing." Lily's heart pangs, thinking of Daniel. "Though he said I talked too much." Benjamin lifts an eyebrow. "And could be too pushy."

Her husband and this man had spent only a few months together as soldiers, and yet they'd found a lifetime friendship. Perhaps horrors do that—bind people. That had been the case for her and Marvena. They'd get past their current tiff.

Lily clears her throat, changes the subject. "Why'd you follow us up here?"

"Daniel and Roger and other guys from the country gave me plenty of teasing about being from a city. Guess I'm still a little sore." A smile tweaks the corners of his mouth.

"Do you ever miss the city?"

"Sometimes," Benjamin says. "My brothers are all still in Cleveland."

"But you didn't go home for Thanksgiving."

"I got a better offer," he says.

"Mama can be awfully persuasive."

"Sure—but it wasn't just the prospect of your mama's cooking that brought me to your Thanksgiving table," Benjamin says. "And I followed you today because I figured the sheriff might need me to drive more than just today, at least until her automobile is repaired. So I thought I should prove my mettle."

"You aiming to be deputized? There's little pay in it."

"I'm a civic-minded fellow. And, well, I like the notion of following you around."

Lily feels heat rise in her cheeks. What can she say to this? That, yes, she feels a pull toward him, too, but she's not ready? Certainly not while in the thick of searching for a missing revenuer, dealing with the re-emergence of Luther and Elias, with sussing out George Vogel's alleged plans, with the impending visit from Mabel Walker Willebrandt.

"Yoo-hoo!" Marvena calls up the hill from the church door.

Though she'd just been waiting impatiently for Marvena, Lily's heart falls. She glances back at Benjamin, sees he's not going to follow, after all, unless she shows him it's fine. *Well.* There's no need for him to wait out in the cold. At least there will be some warmth in the church. She gives a quick jut of her chin: *C'mon, then.*

CHAPTER 16

FIONA

Friday, November 25, 1927
2:00 p.m.

Fiona had meant to ride in silence alongside Abe all the way out to Lily's.

But the silence has become suffocating.

"How's your stomach?" Fiona asks.

Somehow, what she'd meant as an amiable inquiry—a follow-up to his claim back at Dr. Goshen's office just as she exited the examination room—comes out as sarcasm.

Abe cuts a hateful look toward her just as they come upon a hairpin curve. The automobile sways, nearly careening into a ditch. Abe straightens the wheel just in time but then pushes the Model T to go faster, so fast that at the top of the next rise it feels as though the vehicle is airborne. She grabs for the dashboard to brace herself.

Fiona starts to cry out, but as the automobile lands with a thud on the other side of the rise, she catches her tongue between her teeth. Wetness and the taste of iron fill the front of her mouth. Blood.

The bag of candies she'd been holding flies to the floor, and the peppermints and taffies tumble out.

Abe slams on the brakes, and the Model T skids again, stopping perpendicular to a sharp drop-off. Another few feet of skidding and they'd have plunged into brush and tree and vine.

For a long moment, Fiona stares into the snowy woods, a tangle of frosted limbs, dark and white lace that follows no pattern.

Fiona swallows blood and spit. Presses her tongue to the tender spot on her lip. Turns toward Abe, expecting to catch him grinning at her distress, but he's glaring at the scattered candies, as if affronted—his perpetual expression, it seems. That's how he looked at her when she'd come out of the examination room, and then at the older woman—Mrs. Cooper, Hildy's mother—who sighed as he jumped up and growled that he had to see the doctor next due to a sudden stomachache. But Mrs. Cooper hadn't dared protest—nor had Dr. and Mrs. Goshen—as Abe rushed into the room.

As soon as the examination room's door shut, though, Mrs. Cooper had given Fiona a frosty look and sighed anew. Well, damned if she was going to wait under the judgmental glare of Hildy's mother. Besides, this was a chance to act on the plan that had been brewing at the back of Fiona's mind.

And so Fiona had given Mrs. Cooper a curt nod and hurried on to Douglas Grocers, smiled at her plan as she crossed the street. Oh sure, she cares about saving people in her old hometown—even if it's inhabited by busybodies like Mrs. Cooper. But she can't help but feel glee that forewarning Lily about the tainted alcohol will make her look good later.

By the time she reached the grocery and the bell tinkled over the door as she opened it, she nearly ran into a housewife exiting the store, so wrapped up she'd become in imagining herself at some later date, teary and wide-eyed, testifying at George's trial, *Oh, I just couldn't let people I'd known my whole life be hurt by my husband's plans. . . .*

At the store she'd purchased the candies—a gift for Lily's children. Abe was waiting for her when she came back out, standing by the automobile parked right in front of the store, his arms crossed. Still glaring from under the brim of his fedora.

Now she takes in his disappointed assessment of the candies. Had he suspected she'd be so foolish as to write a note to Lily while in the grocery and tuck it in the bag? Of course she wouldn't.

Abe grabs the empty bag from her lap, stares inside. No, she hadn't somehow written a note inside the bag, either.

She'd assumed he'd be with her at the store, for one thing, and had only hoped to get an extra candy bag to write on later. But without Abe there, it was easy to chat amiably with Mr. Merle Douglas, the grocery owner, while he scooped the pieces she'd selected into one of the bags. While he looked down, she snagged an extra bag from the counter.

Merle had looked up almost in time to catch her doing so—almost, but not quite. Then he'd said the oddest thing: *Do you ever see Hildy Cooper?*

Not of late.

Well, if you do, could you tell her I didn't get rid of the penny candy?

Fiona of yore would have been fascinated by that question, would have dug around for possible gossip. She vaguely recollected hearing, on her last visit to town with George more than a year ago, that Mr. Douglas had been courting Hildy. But the Fiona of now pushed aside the distraction.

Still, she took advantage of the moment. *Sure,* she'd said. Then smiled. *If you don't mind checking for me for aspirin? I couldn't find it earlier!*

She'd walked right past it and didn't need more, but her promise to pass along a silly message was enough to send him scurrying off. He was gone long enough for her to grab the pencil he'd been using to tabulate the candy, write her note on the extra bag, return the pencil, and fold the note and tuck it in the front of her dress.

As with George trusting her and her aunt at the bank, writing a note to Lily worked out more easily than she hoped. Still, once at Lily's farmhouse, Fiona was certain Abe would not let her out of his sight to talk privately with the sheriff. Somehow, she'd have to find a quick and clever way to pass on the note.

Now Abe tosses the bag back into her lap, then grabs Fiona's arm so tightly that even through her coat sleeve it feels like the sudden bite of a clamp. "Why do you want to see her?"

Fiona forces her breath to remain steady. "I've told you."

"If you think you'll be able to tell her about our plans for the farm . . . betray George . . ."

"Why would I do that?" Such a good actress she's become.

"Now that he has turned over his property to your name? You think I don't see the hurt and anger on your face when he comes back with some other woman's perfume on his clothing? And it will only get worse when you're distracted with mothering—you must know that."

He laughs as he stares at her. *Oh, of course.* He expects her to well up, maybe start crying. At least look hurt.

She doesn't look away as confusion fogs Abe's expression at her indifference. She takes a moment to study him, the angles of his bony forehead, sharply turned nose—broken and reset from various altercations—hollowed cheeks, thin lips, jutting chin. Yet somehow, even with all the arrowed lines of his face cruelly gouging one another, there is more softness in his features than in the corpulent, fleshy face of her husband.

She focuses on his deep-set, weary eyes. Usually, she thinks of them as empty, reflecting only whatever George wants to see in them. Abe—George's perfect made man. Abe—George's loyal enforcer.

Now she sees something else—fear. Not of George.

Of her.

Because she's managed to shake George's faith in him?

Or because she is not backing down, not trembling before him as everyone—except George, of course—always does?

This prospect—that she could frighten Abe Miller—first thrills her.

Then it triggers an impulsive plan, as she considers how fear clouds judgment, as does weariness, and Abe is suffering from both— otherwise, he'd know that as hard as he's pinching her upper arm, she'll have a bruise by this afternoon. And he'd know that George would not like him hurting his wife—not without it being an order, not when she's pregnant.

Fiona twists her arm, which of course makes Abe grasp harder.

She snaps, "Let go of me now!"

Abe tightens his grip. Yes, the bruise will be ugly and mottled by suppertime. So be it; she'll recover. And so Fiona gives him a pinch-lipped sneer.

Abe jerks her toward him, so close that she smells his sour breath, his cologne meant to mask body odor. No running water at the farm-house, and when would he have had time to bathe anyway? But Abe's slipping fastidiousness speaks to his distress.

"You're lying. And you're lying about why you want to see Lily. I'm taking you back—"

She grins wildly, so he can see the blood coating the inside of her lower lip—such a shocking, grotesque grin that it's Abe's turn to gasp.

Fiona chuckles, the sound throaty, like she's gargling her own blood. "If you do, I'll tell George that my mouth got hurt because you hit me."

Abe's free hand arcs over her, the trajectory of a hard slap.

"Go ahead. The welt on my face will just prove your abuse. George is already angry enough with you—losing track of Luther. Not knowing why he ran off. How do you suppose he'll react if he knows you hit his pregnant wife?"

After a long moment, Abe's hand floats slowly back down. He re-leases his grip of her arm. "Whatever game you're playing, George will see through you sooner or later, and then he'll—" He stops abruptly, grips the steering wheel so hard that his knuckles whiten as he stares out at the falling snow.

"What? Have you take care of me, like you did the first Mrs. Vogel—no alimony payments that way!" The rash words shock Fiona even as she says them.

Her heart races as he turns to look at her. She swallows hard, the iron taste of her own blood sickening. Has she gone too far? But she adds, "That's what Klara told me yesterday morning. Hinted, anyway."

Well, no. But Fiona has no doubt, as Abe's eyes narrow, that there might be some bit of truth in her wild conjecture. Or at least truth that Abe would be willing to go this far for George.

Abe lets go of the steering wheel, reaches inside his jacket, tosses her a handkerchief. "Clean yourself up," he says.

Fiona notes that it's one of Abe's monogrammed handkerchiefs. She dabs blood from inside her lip, then bends down, slowly picks up the wrapped candies, one piece at a time.

He grunts impatiently and backs up slowly, carefully onto the road, and by the time she's sitting up he's heading again toward Lily's house.

And the reassembled bag of candy is in her lap, the bloodied handkerchief folded and tucked in her pocket.

"Why do you suppose Klara would say such a thing?" Fiona presses. Abe remains silent.

"Do you suppose she was trying to make you look bad to me?"

She side-eyes Abe, notes his forced concentration on the road. "Foolish, really. You've known George the longest." She points this out to warm Abe to her, at least a tiny bit. Enough to see if, while he's tired and disheartened about George's flagging trust, he'll share anything about Klara that she might be able to use later.

"Maybe that makes her jealous of you."

Still no reaction.

"Or maybe she's jealous of me? I've seen the way she looks at George—all caring—"

Abe's laugh is so harsh that for just a moment Fiona pities Klara. "She's old enough to be his mother," Abe says. "And besides being distant cousins, Klara and his mother were good friends since childhood."

"George told me that he and his mother came here from Germany when he was a boy." All that Fiona has been able to pry out of George is that he was seven when he arrived in America with his mother—he only referred to her, had never referenced his father or Klara's family—and that they'd settled first in Chicago. That would have been in 1881. "Did Klara come with them?"

"Yes. Along with George's father, and Klara and her husband and son."

"But then—" Abe stops, his teeth clenching, as if he's said too much, though he's barely said anything at all. "What happened to George's father, and Klara's husband and son? George, well, he doesn't talk much about his past—"

"Ah, but you'll have a long, long lifetime to get him to," Abe says wryly. He ventures a glance at her abdomen. "As the mother of the son he's always wanted."

Fiona stares out the window at the thickening snow, not in the least reassured by Abe's comment. Once this child is born and is found to be healthy and strong, being the mother won't safeguard her if she doesn't meekly comply with George's wishes.

"So you came into George's life well after Klara," she says softly.

"What?"

"I'm just saying—Klara's been in his life the longest. Has a connection to his mother. And I know that George reveres his mother."

"Uh-huh."

"So you've always been second fiddle to Klara."

Abe grunts, pulls out a cigarette and lighter. The automobile weaves as he lets go of the steering wheel long enough to light his cigarette. Fiona forces herself not to grab the dashboard. *Mustn't show fear.* She nearly yelps, though, as the Model T again slides on an icy patch, but Abe rights it just at the edge of a ravine. She glances at him. Somehow, he'd managed to tuck his lighter away, and is now smoking as calmly as if he'd lit his cigarette in a parlor.

"Doesn't work like that. Klara runs the household. I run the parts of George's business he tells me to."

"Oh, I see. You're both just hired help, then."

"No! I'm a trusted advisor."

Merely an enforcer. A goon, Fiona thinks. But she says, "That's true. I've heard Klara give George advice, too, though."

"About what? She's nothing more than a maid—and only that out of pity."

Interesting. Fiona's never noticed George feeling pity for anyone. "Why would he feel sorry for her? Just because she was friends with his mother—"

"She lost her husband on the boat over, and after they were in Chicago for a few years, her son—" Abe turns red.

Now that's really interesting. The notion of Abe turning red—from shame or even anger—is even more unlikely than George showing pity.

And Klara with a husband and son . . . just as Fiona had moments ago dropped the candy on the floor, Klara had spilled her bag on the ride over from Cincinnati. That old-time photo that had fallen out . . . could it have been of Klara in years past, with them?

"Well, it doesn't matter!" Abe snaps.

"It must to George," Fiona says softly. "After all, you've known him for years, but Klara goes back all the way to George's childhood, for as long as he can remember—"

"We grew up together!" Abe snaps. "In Chicago. In the neighborhood. In school. Long enough."

"So George has known you nearly as long as Klara's son, and George is loyal to her—so why isn't Klara's son working with you? Or taking care of her?"

"There was an accident, it wasn't really anyone's fault, if Klara had been paying attention—"

Abe lifts his right hand, claps it over Fiona's neck, pressing her back so tightly against the seat that she can't move her head. His words snarl around the cigarette still pinched between his lips. "How do you do that? Get people so twisted up they say things they shouldn't. . . ." He pauses, then mutters, "Might be useful, someone like you, in the organization. If you weren't a woman. And George's wife."

She twists. Let there be bruises on her neck, too, then, or red marks at least.

Abe pulls his hand away, as quickly as if he'd just been struck by a snake.

Abe speaks softly: "Don't try and turn Klara into a foe. And George never questioned my loyalty or competence until you came along, Fiona."

The rest of the trip is made in silence as gray and suffocating as the laden sky. It's only when they reach the turn off Kinship Road, where at the bottom of a scant hollow sits Lily Ross's farmhouse, snug under a soft mantle of snow, gray tendrils of smoke rising from the chimney, that Fiona fully exhales and realizes she's been holding back her breath.

CHAPTER 17

LILY

Friday, November 25, 1927
4:00 p.m.

Lily sits in the back pew of the simple church. She wipes her hand-kerchief across her sweaty brow. She's kept on her coat, because of the scarf sling holding her throbbing shoulder still. The sanctuary is overly warm from a coal stove burning in the corner behind her.

The heat, and the scene unfolding in front of the altar, make her light-headed, as does fighting the impulse to rush forth, to put a stop to what she is witnessing, to cry out against its madness, its danger.

But such action is not her place. All she can do is force herself to sit still.

There on the simple platform, beneath a cross twined together from two branches as rough and unhewn as Lily's impromptu walking stick from minutes ago, stands the preacher—Brother Stiles—speaking so fast, so thickly, that Lily must guess at the words he is saying. A few other people stand in front of the simple bench pews, hands aloft, eyes heavenward, swaying back and forth, some mumbling, some crying out, "Yes, Jesus. Praise Jesus!" Others sing, old hymns that seem as an-cient as the earth, the sounds emitting from some place deep within the singers' souls. A few dance—though they'd not call it that—stomping, jumping, or whirling in circles. One or two are stock-still, as if struck by the hand of God.

A few speak in words that sound like language but not English or the languages sometimes heard from immigrants in towns like Rossville: Lithuanian, Italian, German. "Speaking in tongues." It's a phrase Lily knows, referenced by her Presbyterian church's pastor in a sermon condemning the practice. He'd cited Paul's teachings in 1 Corinthians 14, exhorting believers in the value of preaching plainly: *If therefore the whole church be come together into one place, and all speak with tongues, and there come in those that are unlearned or unbelievers, will they not say that ye are mad?*

And, indeed, this looks like madness.

The greatest madness, though, is Dora Harkins lying on a homemade stretcher at the front of the altar. Over her stands Leroy.

Tears stream down his face.

Standing several feet away is Ruth. She has her arms wrapped around her siblings, the twins, holding their faces against her skirt, as if she does not want them to see, even as she looks on, transfixed, at her father.

In both hands, outstretched as far from his body as he can, Leroy holds a snake.

A timber rattlesnake.

"Blessed be this man, asking for forgiveness! He has confessed his sins and prays God shows mercy for his faith, prays that God will release his Holy Retributions, which he has smote upon Leroy's wife, will see this act of belief and faith and respond in kind! Remove this cancer from her, O heavenly Father, that this sinless woman might live, and in living might show the heathens your mighty power!"

The snake's head and upper third of its body, from Leroy's hand forward, is still as a stick. The rest of the snake's body droops, undulating.

Lily is as rigidly still as the snake's upper body and—for now—its rattle.

But her mind is aswirl.

Is the snake terrified? Or perhaps mesmerized by the activities of the people before it, unsure how or where to strike?

If it does come back to itself, Leroy has easily allowed enough of its body length to bend back so it can strike the underside of his wrist, his forearm, or inside of his elbow.

It is possible to survive a rattlesnake bite. Death is not certain.

Snake handling—or *serpent* handling, to signify that the snakes used for the rite are poisonous—began to be taken up in parts of Appalachia just seventeen years ago, in a Holiness gospel church, based on one Bible verse from the book of Mark. Lily's pastor had warned against this new movement, based on a verse taken out of context.

Forcing the will or word of God through signs, he'd said, is its own blasphemy.

Lily agrees.

And yet.

She also understands what drives Leroy, what drives these people.

From the fraught look on Leroy's face, he wants only to conjure a miracle to save his wife's life.

Perhaps this is why the others are here, too. In solidarity with Leroy's deep, desperate need. Perhaps they'd been drawn to this church for similar reasons. Or their own deep unease with their wrongdoing. Or the fear of death. Or from other fears and questions that plague every human in an always uncertain world, yet always feel so private, so individual.

She, too, had lain in the stolid darkness of the night, yearning for that still small voice to speak and give her hope, comfort, direction.

And heard nothing.

Such silence could drive one to extremes.

So all she can do is sit in silence, in stillness, considering: power, money, drink, rationalizations, even rites of belief—masks to hide from facing the darkest of all truths: No one can control much of what happens to them or their loved ones. Death and illness, pain and sorrow, will come.

But without those masks, what is there to make that darkness tolerable?

She ventures a glance at Benjamin, sitting next to her. He looks completely shocked at what is unfolding.

Then she looks at Marvena, a few rows up. She, too, is swaying, arms heavenward. Lily cannot tell if she is adding to the cacophony of voices. But she notes the tightness in her friend's shoulders, the rigidity in her back, as if she is forcing herself to participate, as if she can will herself toward belief.

And then it hits Lily—this is what Jurgis meant when he'd snapped at Marvena, *You haven't given our way a try!*

Marvena had not taken up a snake. Or allowed Frankie to do so. As Marvena had said at the still, she believes snakes to be creatures best left to their own devices.

And Lily cannot blame her.

But though Lily is angry at Jurgis for trying to push the choice, neither can she blame him for the desperation that's driving him.

The preacher swiftly moves a stick, with a thin wire loop on the end. He swoops the loop over the snake's head, harnessing the creature, which begins to thrash, but the preacher pulls on the end of the wire, tightening the loop around the snake.

Lily gasps, worried on behalf of the snake. *Surely he's not going to decapitate the creature?* But then another man steps forward with a box, sliding back a lid that must fit in carved grooves at the top, and the preacher lowers the snake in the box. The man—a deacon, Lily supposes—slides the lid closed over the snake.

Wait—Lily recognizes the man. Arlie Whitcomb, a distant cousin of Marvena's. He'd worked for Marvena near on three years ago at her still. And he'd betrayed her, forcing Lily's hand to bust up Marvena's operation and haul Marvena into jail. And now they're both worshiping here? Have they put aside their differences—or has Arlie gone back to working for Marvena's new operation?

But such concerns quickly slip aside as Leroy drops to his knees beside his wife, whether in relief or supplication to her or to God it is impossible to say. Sobs wrack his body as he lowers his head to her chest.

At this, Lily must look away, though the congregants continue as before.

Benjamin catches her eyes. She'd expected to see disgust or revulsion for what was happening before them, and indeed he might feel those things later. But in this moment, his eyes glisten with sorrow, and she knows it is for Leroy and Dora.

Instinctively, Lily reaches to put a comforting hand on his arm, but Benjamin catches her hand mid-reach.

Ah, there it is. The answer to her earlier question: *But without those masks, what is there to make that darkness tolerable?*

There is connection. Community. Sometimes, love.

She does not pull away.

After some time, the service ends.

Then Leroy and Arlie come back up the aisle, carrying Dora on her stretcher. As she passes, people cry out with shouts of praise and thankfulness, as if Dora has already cast aside illness and miraculously risen to walk healthy and whole. As they approach the back of the church, Leroy ignores Lily completely, his face turned so she can't catch his eye. Ruth and the young twins are still at the front of the sanctuary, taken over by several of the churchwomen, fussing and clucking over them.

Dora calls out, "Sheriff Lily!" Her voice is thin, watery. If she'd uttered a word during the earlier events, Lily had not been able to hear it.

Lily moves toward the end of the aisle, but Leroy and Arlie keep walking.

"Please, please, stop!" Dora cries.

Leroy takes mercy on his wife. They lower Dora to the floor at the end of Lily's aisle.

Lily rushes over, drops to her knees quickly. She'd nearly forgotten about her shoulder with all that has transpired, but the jolt to the floor ricochets up her body and into her shoulder, and she almost winces. She gulps a cry of pain back just in time as Dora reaches her hand out from under her blanket.

She grasps Lily's good arm, her hand surprisingly strong but oh so cold. The coldness of granite. Lily meets Dora's seeking gaze, the woman's watery blue eyes nearly twitching with a need to know.

"My boy . . . my boy . . ."

Lily hesitates just a moment. Zebediah had led a revenuer here—or tried to. But Marvena was a moonshiner as well as a worshiper here, and hadn't Marvena snapped just yesterday that some of her best customers were also worshipers here? She does not yet know if the revenuer is here—if he'd found sanctuary. Or if she would need to come back with more bloodhounds and men and search for him.

Lily leans forward, whispers gently, "He has come around. He will live. He will be fine."

Lily sits back up. Now Dora's eyes overflow, but there is a spark of joy in them. And something else—a release. Knowing her boy will be fine is all she needs to finally let go.

Lily blinks hard but does not pull her gaze from Dora.

"You the praying kind, Sheriff?"

Lily nods. She is. Intermittently. Often in anger, asking *why* or *why not*. Not often enough with *thank you,* as at dinner yesterday.

"Pray for me, then?" Dora asks.

She does not mean pray for her to be saved from cancer, Lily realizes. She means for her journey from this life to whatever awaits on the other shore to be swift and merciful.

And so Lily nods. "I will."

Lily stands, watches the men bear Dora out, hears the shouts of praise and thanks rise again. But to Lily, Leroy and Arlie look like pallbearers.

Marvena comes up alongside her. By the sorrowful look in her eyes, Lily knows her friend is thinking the same.

"Come," Marvena says.

There is a small private room, built off the west side of the church, the only other room besides the sanctuary.

Lily notes that storage shelves fill one wall of the windowless room: the bottom ones holding several boxes like the one she'd seen the rattlesnake returned to, the other shelves fitted with wood and wire cages.

Arlie opens an unoccupied cage. A rattle shivers from another cage through the room and up Lily's spine. Then Arlie holds the trap box perpendicular to the opening to the cage and carefully slides up the lid, freeing the snake to glide into the cage. As soon as it's in, its head at the back of the cage, he pulls the box away and quickly shuts the cage door, so hard that several snakes rattle and hiss.

His hands, Lily notes, are trembling.

"Admiring the handiwork of my dear wife?"

Lily turns, looks at the preacher—Brother Stiles. This is how Marvena had introduced him. No first name. And not "Pastor." "Brother," to imply that he stands equally with his congregants—though, of course, this clearly isn't the case. This is Brother Stiles's church.

His wife isn't with him, but he's beaming proudly as he references her. "She's the one that came up with the system of the cages and boxes. I thought you'd like to know we have a role for women. Figured that'd be important to you." He gazes at her badge, flicks his eyes back to her. His grin hardens a mite, just a little clench to the jaw to show he doesn't approve of her taking on a man's job. "Appropriate roles, of course."

Lily looks around. Benjamin, by the door, is scowling at the scene. Marvena, standing by Brother Stiles, is expressionless. Arlie Whitcomb, over by the snake boxes, looks worried, and Lily wonders again about his presence in this church alongside Marvena, given their history. They all stand as if on guard—Lily wonders if snakes can sense human tension.

"I was actually wondering about the snakes," Lily says flatly.

Brother Stiles looks eager. "Well, in Mark, chapter—"

"I know what the Bible says. I'm curious about their well-being. I don't see any bedding. How do they get water? Do you feed them? They're used to certain temperatures outside—"

Arlie laughs. "The woods are filled with snakes. You've seen one snake, you've seen 'em all. I'm one of the snake hunters. They're harder to find in the winter, so we tend to 'em more during the cold months, but they're aplenty, which, a-course, you can't know, being from the big town—"

"Be respectful, Brother Arlie!" the preacher snaps. He looks at Lily with pity. "This soul may yet be saved if she comes to understand our ways. This was the case with you, and even your cousin Marvena, forsaking the sins of liquor, overcoming your past differences to join the body of the Lord."

Out of the corner of her eye, Lily looks at Marvena. Her expression has not changed a whit. Arlie, though, turns a mite red. And there is a pulpy bulbousness to his nose that could be left over from his drinking days—or could be recently worsened.

"The snakes are ours for using to prove through signs of our faith," Stiles is saying. "God has provided them for our use."

Lily stares at him a long moment. She'd been taught that God had entrusted all his creation to mankind's care, and to honor the use of his creatures for sustenance or shelter with humility and gratitude. That's why Mama insisted on saying blessings over each meal.

She turns to the cages, catching a glimpse of the snake that Leroy had been holding earlier now curled up in a corner. She'd never thought she'd feel sorry for a rattler.

She looks pointedly back at the preacher. "I'm not here to mock. I'm here to ask about a man named Colter DeHaven. Zebediah Harkins has testified to me that he saw the man shot, and brought him here. For sanctuary. He wasn't sure where else to take him."

The preacher frowns. "There is no man by that name here. You've seen our church—there are no places to hide anyone. And why would Zebediah have witnessed such a thing—"

"Th'boy was working for me," Marvena blurts. "I—I've taken up shining again. I know that means I need to leave the church, but I did it for extra money for—"

"Sister, if you had need, you should have said something—" Stiles starts.

"I didn't need pin money! I needed real money! And Zebediah, well, I caught him loitering near my still when he should have been in school, and I figured the best way I could keep an eye on him was to have him do a little work for me." She slides her gaze to Arlie, who looks terrified. "He told me he'd learned of my still being back in business through the kids of some of the adults here who're some of my best customers. But I ain't naming names."

The preacher looks genuinely shocked and hurt. "So Zebediah says he saw this man shot . . . but why . . ."

"The man is a revenuer. Another—his partner—came to see me today, said Agent DeHaven isn't expected until Monday. He must have come early, for some reason. If we can find him, return him safely to the bureau, find out who shot him—well, it would be better than agents eventually coming in from the bureau crawling all over this hill, and maybe finding other stills either run by or visited by your congregants, Pastor."

At this, all the piety falls away from the pastor's and Arlie's expressions.

"Not only that, Luther Ross is back in the area. . . ." She hesitates, decides against sharing that he claims to be working with the bureau. She opts for a true, but vague, explanation. "I have reason to think he's now associated with George Vogel—you know who that is?"

Stiles nods.

"Then you know that neither you nor I nor anyone else want any part of this county caught in a cross fire between Vogel's men and the bureau. The sooner I can find out what happened to this Agent De-Haven, the better."

Stiles shakes his head. "But we don't know anything—"

"The boy would have brought Agent DeHaven here on a Wednesday," Lily says. "I noted your sign out front saying you have prayer meetings on Wednesdays." She thinks back to Ruth's comments yesterday. "According to his sister, Zebediah got home sometime between four and six in the evening. So if he got the man here, it would have been early, at three—well before your prayer meeting, but I reckon there might have been people here? Some of the women, to stoke the coal furnace, set up for the supper?" She bites back the temptation to add *serving in their proper roles.*

Brother Stiles shakes his head. "The womenfolk would have told their husbands, or me, if that had been the case."

Lily grits her teeth. "Could you tell me who among them might have been here then, so I can ask?"

"They would have told me," he repeats.

Lily stares him down. "I can get a warrant, right quick, to search this land. Your congregants' homes, to see if any have taken in the agent."

Stiles rubs his hand over his face. "Why would you think we'd hide such a thing, Sheriff?"

"The man was seriously injured. It's my understanding you don't believe in regular medicine. Faith healing a man of the law—well now, that would be quite a sign from God," Lily says. "The failure of such healing—well, that could be another sign altogether, and possibly, under the law, manslaughter."

For a long moment, Brother Stiles stands frozen, staring at Lily. Then he sighs, gives her a look of pity. "How little you think of us, Sheriff Ross. But there is no need for warrants. I will give you the names of the women who would have been here. You can bring back your men and your hounds and search in every cave and crevice and holler. You will not find your missing agent. Zebediah, now he's a good enough boy, but he runs wild and scared, and probably ran away and has no idea what happened after to that revenuer man. Now, his sister? Ruth's the softhearted one. She'd a gotten the man to safety here—if Zebediah had brought the man to their house."

Brother Stiles's words hit Lily like a gut punch.

Ruth had said Zebediah stumbled back to their home around 4:00 p.m., but Zebediah had been at the stand near Marvena's still first thing in the morning. Long enough, maybe, for Zebediah to get the revenuer to the church—but the boy doesn't remember much past finding the man. With alcohol hitting his diabetic system, would he have had the strength to get the man this far and then return to his home?

And why in the middle of all that illness and confusion, would Zebediah have shown Ruth the badge? Why would it have meant anything to a burdened fourteen-year-old girl? Could she understand the import of *Bureau of Prohibition* inscribed on the badge—all on her own, without someone to explain it to her?

Ruth's the softhearted one.

What if the pastor is right? What if the agent and Zebediah had never made it here? Instead had gone, straightaway, to the Harkins home—so much closer to Marvena's still?

CHAPTER 18

FIONA

Friday, November 25, 1927
3:00 p.m.

Fiona and Abe have only taken a few steps from the automobile, which Abe left at the top of the lane, when Lily's mother pops out of the farmhouse's front door, shotgun in her hands.

Abe chuckles, mutters under his breath, "Poor old thing, she'd miss us by a mile."

"Don't be so sure!" Fiona snaps. So ridiculous, this wave of homesickness spurred by seeing Lily's mama, even with her shotgun trained on them. Seeing Aunt Nell, saying good-bye at the train station, hadn't stirred such sentiment. But Mrs. McArthur had always been kind to her, kinder than most Kinship townsfolk, especially after Martin died, bringing comforting pies and stews and canned goods for her and Leon and not just hastily dropping them off to fulfill unwritten social obligations. *Fiona, my bones are weary; mind if I sit a spell?* And then Mrs. McArthur would sit with Fiona, on the front porch or in the parlor, and chat about nothing in particular, which in those moments meant everything in the world.

Well, she can sure understand taking aim at Abe, but Lily's mama must not recognize her, in her fine coat and cloche hat festooned with a feather. Fiona hollers, "Yoo-hoo! Mrs. McArthur? It's—"

"I know who you are."

"Well, we're here to see Sheriff Lily."

"She's in town."

"Checked there."

A slight shift in Lily's mama's stance. *Ah.* Fiona can feel a mother's worry, even from this distance.

"We need to talk to her—about Luther Ross."

"She's not here. Leave a message at her office."

Dammit.

Abe starts to head back to the automobile.

Panic grips Fiona. If she can't get a message to Lily, then the plan will go through for imbibers to drink methanol tonight—and if that happens, men, maybe a few women, will die. Or come so painfully close, they'll have moments of wishing to. And, of course, she won't be able to later take credit for alerting Lily.

Plus, if she delivers this message, she can tell Elias she followed through on his wish. He'll be beholden to her.

She sinks down to the ground. "Oh, Mrs. McArthur! I—I'm not feeling well!"

Inside the house, Mrs. McArthur still regards Fiona and Abe with skepticism. But Fiona sips from a hot cup of tea—mint and chamomile and a dash of dried elderberries, a soothing mixture, Mrs. McArthur says, that she'd learned from a friend of hers, good for calming nerves.

The warmth from the cup itself is soothing, as are the aroma and the mild, sweet taste.

"I added one dollop of honey." Mrs. McArthur's shotgun lies across her lap. "My friend says tea always needs two dollops of honey, but doesn't that seem, well, excessive?"

"I'm sure," Fiona says, eyeing the gun.

Mrs. McArthur hadn't dropped it, even when she'd run up the hill to help Fiona. Nor had she put it aside when she'd finally allowed them in the house, telling them to sit in the parlor while she made the tea to help settle Fiona's light-headedness.

In the parlor, while Mrs. McArthur rumbled about in the kitchen,

Fiona briefly closed her eyes. That way, she could ignore Abe glaring at her, and besides, she became truly dizzy. Well, she'd only picked at her breakfast, had no lunch, and the day had been stressful. As if from a great distance, she heard Mrs. McArthur holler out the back door at the children to just stay outside and work on their snowman a little longer.

When she opened her eyes, Mrs. McArthur was putting the cup of tea on a doily on the side table, before sitting down in her chair with her shotgun and giving Abe skeptical side glances, though all he held was the bag of candy that Fiona had dropped in the snow when she sank to her knees.

"You have to take extra care of yourself," Mrs. McArthur says, and pauses to lean forward and whisper—as if Abe won't be able to hear—"when you're in the family way."

"I know," Fiona says, surprising herself as tears spring to her eyes at Mrs. McArthur's unique blend—rather like her tea—of gentleness and gruffness. Does Lily Ross know—even after all her loss—how lucky she is? "I've just been sorrowful over losing Uncle Henry—"

"Yes, I didn't know your aunt and uncle well, except to see them at church from time to time," Mrs. McArthur says, "but I was sorry to hear of your uncle's sudden stroke."

Fiona nods. "It was a surprise. And now here we are, visiting, and Luther Ross seems to be missing! It's causing quite a strain for Elias, who is of course tending to me for this pregnancy since I'm, well, older."

Mrs. McArthur cocks an eyebrow. "Well, I was forty-one when I had Caleb Junior. You'll be fine, I'm sure."

Three children rush in—a girl and two boys—laughing and whooping. They skid to a stop and fall silent when they see the visitors. Jolene and Micah—Lily's two. And Caleb Jr.—Mrs. McArthur's change-of-life baby. Those apple red cheeks, bright eyes, eager faces. Another set of tears dampen her eyes, and she dashes them away. These children have all grown so much since she last saw them. Two years . . . and truth be told, children can change rapidly in just a few months. It's been nearly three months since she's seen Leon. It's good, with all that's happening, that he's spending the holiday at his school in Philadelphia, but a wave of resentment at George, for breaking his promise to bring her son home, again crashes over her. What are the chances he'll follow through on bringing Leon home at Christmas?

"I told you'uns to stay outside!" Mrs. McArthur snaps. In the thick of rearing them, she brooks no sentimentality.

"We should leave before it gets dark," Fiona says. "Please tell Lily we called, won't you, and that we'd welcome any news of Luther. If she has questions, she can always come out to the farm—she knows where it is. Oh, and if you don't mind, I need to use your facilities—"

"Our facilities is an outhouse," Mrs. McArthur says with a wry tone.

Fiona gives a small laugh. "We've all gotten used to that out at the farm—haven't we, Abe?" She looks at him, still standing in the parlor entryway, a silent shadow-man.

"Well, Jolene, can you show Mrs. Vogel the way?"

Abe leans forward from the entryway, a scowl on his face. Fiona bites back a sigh. He's not going to trust her to be out of his sight, even if she's with Lily's daughter.

Fiona replies to Mrs. McArthur, "I'm sure I can find my way—"

"Wouldn't want you to pass out in the snow," Abe says.

"Of course not." She stands, looks at the children. "I brought along some treats for you—early Christmas, if that's all right?" Maybe the children will beset Abe, long enough for her to be alone in the kitchen, leave the note somewhere. . . .

But Abe just tosses the bag of candy on the coffee table, stares at her evenly as she puts on her coat. He hasn't, she notes, even taken his off. He follows closely behind as Fiona walks through the parlor and dining room. Behind them, she hears Jolene's delighted voice: "Oh, these are the peppermints Uncle Elias always brought us!"

Such a simple comment—but it spoke volumes about the closeness that Elias once had with Lily and her children. What had happened to end that? Fiona wonders.

In the kitchen, Abe comes so closely behind her that Fiona has to step quickly to keep him from touching her. He follows her outside.

At the outhouse, on the slope beyond the garden plot and the frozen, empty clothesline, Fiona turns abruptly. Abe stops short. She cocks an eyebrow at him. "You sure you don't want to come in with me? It'll be tight, but—"

"Just hurry up!"

Fiona steps in and then makes gagging sounds. She wants him to think she's sick again. She pulls out her gloves from her pocket, reaches in her dress's bodice, gets the note she'd written earlier, tucks it in one of the gloves, and leaves the gloves on the neat stack of newspapers.

She steps back out, hands tucked in pockets. "It's all yours—though I have to warn you, it turns out afternoon sickness—"

He wrinkles his nose in disgust but steps toward the outhouse. Fiona's heart pounds. *Oh God.* She can explain away forgetting the gloves—no one would keep on gloves to clean up, after all—but what if he finds the note?

But Abe grabs Fiona's elbow, force-walks her back toward the house. *Thank God.*

Her instinct is to hurry; the sooner they leave the better. She doesn't want him to suddenly turn back to the outhouse, to see if she'd left a message. But she resists just enough that he has to push her along a little—not resisting would raise suspicions—though as she stumbles past the snowman the children had just built, with his goofy coal eyes and dotted smile, she almost smiles back.

CHAPTER 19

LILY

Friday, November 25, 1927
6:00 p.m.

At long last, Lily and Benjamin come around the bend to the turnoff to her farmhouse.

Benjamin's driven in silence since their last stop, and Lily has taken the quiet as a chance to reflect on the events of the day. After they'd hiked from the church back to his automobile, he'd driven them back to Rossville proper. From there, Marvena had pulled Lily aside and asked if it was fine by her if she headed back home to tend to Frankie, and Lily had agreed. Marvena leaned close, said, *If'n Frankie's right well, I'm hoping Jurgis will still be willing to go to the barn dance. You could mention it to Benjamin.* Lily had given a little smile while shaking her head. At Lily's request, Benjamin drove to the turnoff to the Harkins place. She told him to wait in his automobile, but he'd gotten out and followed her, just as he had up to the church. Irritating, but she couldn't order him to stay put.

It didn't take long to assess that the Harkinses weren't back home yet—a curiosity, given Dora's frail state. But if Agent DeHaven was tucked away somewhere on the property, it wasn't anywhere obvious. And without permission or proper paperwork, Lily wouldn't unlawfully search. Or, for that matter, with Benjamin observing, she wouldn't even peek in windows and barn doors, toeing the line of lawful.

Now she ponders how best to leave off with him once they inch to the top of the snowy lane.

Lily ventures a glance his way. So different in looks and nature than Daniel, and yet he has the same resolute air. The same underlying quality of loyalty. The conversation they'd had in the woods overlooking the church, about the Argonne forest, comes back to her.

Might well be that he's aiding out of respect for his friend Daniel, nothing more.

Well, Mama would want her to invite him in for a bite of supper. He'd certainly earned it and had to be famished, as was Lily.

At the sight of light warming the parlor window, Lily relaxes just a little. Sanctuary. Mama. Home. The children. A warm meal. Even the effort of heating water and toting it upstairs for a warm bath in the claw foot tub seems worthwhile. Then sleep. Hopefully, dreamless.

Then again, how likely is she to restfully sleep after a day like this? Her mind will be aswirl. Maybe they should go to the barn dance Marvena keeps going on about.

Lily turns to Benjamin. "You know, Marvena's been telling me—"

Benjamin yawns. "Sorry," he says.

Lily looks back out at the night. "Well, she's been, she's been saying, um, how you get on well with the miners. And you've been such a help today. Thank you. Please know you're welcome to come in for supper—it will more'n likely be Thanksgiving leftovers—"

Benjamin, who has been driving smoothly, jolts to a stop. The sharp movement wracks Lily's body only lightly, but it's sufficient to send a spasm of pain from her stiffening shoulder, still in the makeshift scarf sling.

"Sorry," he says, pointing ahead.

There, in the headlights, is Mama, rushing up the drive.

In the parlor, the note shakes in Lily's hand, partly from what it says, partly because she's holding it on her injured side.

She holds it thusly because Jolene sits tightly against her, head leaned against Lily's good shoulder. When she and Benjamin had entered the house, Jolene and the boys had run to greet her. Jolene had noted the scarf sling over Lily's shoulder, the difficulty with which she'd removed her hat and coat, her winces as the children demanded hugs and she gingerly gave them. Mama had tried to banish Jolene back to her own supper in the kitchen with the boys, but Lily, seeing the fear in Jolene's little face, said she could stay, help Mama serve turkey sandwiches and tea in the parlor, as if they were having a tea party.

I had a mishap with my automobile. It may be a few days before it's repaired, Lily had explained in an overly chipper tone. *Mr. Russo has been my chauffeur today,* she'd added, hoping the fancy word might serve as a distraction.

But that's when Jolene had studied Benjamin, wary eyed. Yesterday, his presence had been unremarkable, mixed in with all the other friends. Tonight, Lily can tell Jolene senses something different about his being with them. Something she doesn't quite trust, isn't ready for.

Benjamin had looked at Jolene evenly, as if talking to an adult and not an eight-year-old girl, and said flatly, *As a Bronwyn County citizen, I'm glad to drive the sheriff wherever she needs to go until her shoulder heals.*

Well, she certainly hadn't asked that much of him. On the other hand, she needs some way to get around that doesn't involve working her poor mule to death.

Now she rereads the note Mama had run up the lane with, thrusting it at Lily after explaining Fiona and Abe had come by earlier to report Luther missing, that Fiona had visited the outhouse, left her gloves with the note on the stack of newspapers. Caleb Jr. had found the gloves of the fancy lady, as he'd called her, and was sticking them on branches to give the snowman arms, when the end of a branch poked the note. Jolene had realized the gloves must belong to the *fancy lady* and grabbed them away—Caleb Jr. all the while howling that he was her uncle and she couldn't order him around.

Lily had smiled at the anecdote. Ever since Caleb Jr.—same age as Micah, two years younger than Jolene—had figured out that he was their uncle, he'd tried to act like he was in charge of them.

But her smile faded when she read Fiona's note, scribbled in pencil—and, from the handwriting, in haste—on a penny candy bag.

Wood alcohol swapped in delivery to Kinship Inn for tonight.

That's all the note says.

But the import is much bigger.

If Fiona's note is telling the truth, tonight many people will be poisoned in the speakeasy. Lily has raided it a few times in the past year, but it always comes back.

People will die.

But why would George Vogel want to do such a thing?

Is he trying to move in on another bootlegger's turf?

That doesn't make sense. The speakeasy is mostly stocked by local moonshiners' brew, or the occasional illicit bottle of homemade gin, or even wine fermented up from grape bricks.

Surely this county is too small for him to care about. From what she's read about his near arrests over the past year, questions arising about his claims that he's simply creating legal Vogel's Tonic, he must have bigger concerns than setting up shop in Bronwyn County.

And yet—he's married Fiona, who has ties here. Abe Miller has now been to her house twice, once with Luther, once with Fiona.

Is George trying to send some sort of message by killing people?

Or is Fiona being used to scare her, to bring Lily into a dangerous situation?

The truth is, Lily doesn't know what she's walking into. But if lives are at risk, she needs to act—though both her head and shoulder are throbbing.

Lily gives Jolene a friendly smile. "Honey, I need a proper sling to rest my shoulder. Could you take your mamaw with you upstairs and go fashion one out of a clean sheet?"

Jolene looks so eager that Lily feels almost guilty knowing she won't wear it once she's at the Kinship Inn—she can't conduct a raid in a sling, after all. Mama sighs, comes over to Lily, and cups her face with a cool, dry hand. She starts to say something but then gives her head a little shake before following her granddaughter, already running up the stairs.

Lily looks at Benjamin. "Since you're driving back to town anyway, would you mind—"

"Yes, I mind." Benjamin folds his arms. "Oh, I don't mind driving you around, but I mind you not even considering asking me to do more."

Lily frowns. "What?"

"You're about to do something big, something dangerous. Probably something you're going to need help with." He waves his hands to shush her as she starts to protest. "Oh, I don't mean 'the little woman needs help' kind of help. Don't think me that much of a pig. I mean the sheriff needs help. A few deputies, maybe. But you're not even considering asking me for help."

Lily stares at him. Starts to speak, then snaps her mouth shut again. Meets his glare with her own, then sees that he is well and truly miffed. That he is being serious.

"Is it because I'm not *from* here?" Benjamin asks. "Because I've been here half a year, working among the miners, writing reports—which, yes, I know how soft that must sound, but to get the information, I've gone down in the mines with them—to do assessments on structure and practices, with the hope that safety can eventually be improved. I've talked to everyone who survived the Widowmaker explosion of '24."

Lily's eyes prickle. Her father, and Marvena's first husband, were among the men who'd died in the aftermath, trying to save other miners, and then were buried alive. If Benjamin's been talking to survivors, then he knows this.

"And I care about people here. Lots of people." He leans forward, cocks an eyebrow. "Some more than others. So, for God's sake, if you need help, then let me help."

CHAPTER 20

FIONA

Friday, November 25, 1927
6:00 p.m.

"What are you doing in here?" Fiona demands.

Klara jumps, turns from the dresser in Fiona's old room, nearly dropping a framed photo she holds in her hand—the photo that had spilled out of her tote bag on one of the sharp curves on the drive over here.

"Mr. Vogel told me that the two of you would take your aunt's bigger room, now that she's gone. And I should move in here," Klara says stiffly.

Across the small room, and without sickness to distract her, Fiona notes that the old photo is of a man and woman, a little boy.

Fiona crosses to Klara, grabs the photo before the older woman can react, steps back. "Is this your family?" She asks the question gently, softly, as if probing a sensitive, never-healed wound, and from Klara's expression, that is the case.

Klara just nods. Fiona hands back the photo. "Must mean a lot to you, bringing that photo on even a brief trip."

"My husband. My son."

"From when you lived in Germany?"

Klara's eyes widen. "Yes."

"Abe mentioned them today. When he was driving me out to Sheriff Ross's."

"Why—why would he bring them up?"

"Oh—I was just trying to get to know him better. Asked how he met George, that he must have been George's first friend here," Fiona says. "He said no, you are a distant cousin to his mother—well, to him, too. And your families came here together."

Klara's expression closes. "That is true."

Fiona bites her lip, looks down. "He said, well, he implied, that something tragic happened after you all came to Chicago." He hadn't, but that much was easy to guess. "That you—you had something to do with the tragedy?"

A complete fabrication—but so easy to say, later, if called on it, that Klara must have misunderstood Fiona's question. She waits a beat, looks up to see Klara's face pale and drawn.

"The boys—George, Abe, Ralf—they were playing in the street."

"Yes, Abe said he'd met George at school?"

Klara nods. "Yes. And Abe was always around. He didn't like being at his own home. His father was hard, cruel. Hard to imagine, but back then, Abe was a scrawny kid, picked on. George watched out for him, at least at school. My boy didn't like him much, though—I think Abe picked on him, sometimes, just to have someone he could think he was bigger than. Anyway, one day Abe and Ralf argued over a ball, and George got mad and threw it—he meant no harm—but Ralf wanted to impress him, ran after the ball. He didn't see the streetcar—" Klara forgets herself, brings her hands to her mouth, drops the photo—but Fiona catches it before it can fall to the floor.

She studies the photo for a minute. After George's nightmare, he'd said something about a boy running. A ball. Had guilt made him protect Klara? And had Klara blamed Abe this whole time for her boy's horrific demise?

Fiona puts the photo on her dresser, guides Klara to the edge of the bed, helps her sit down, sits next to her. "How—how tragic. I'm so sorry. And—and was there then a falling-out between George's mother and father and your husband? Did he leave after? I mean, if he blamed your cousin's son—" Of course, she knows from Abe that Klara's husband died on the boat.

Klara puts her face to her hands. "George's father died back in Germany. My husband and I—we took pity on George and his mother. Thought we'd bring them over with us. But my husband died on the boat over. The four of us, we lived together. George's mom and I worked at a clothing factory, took in washing, whatever we could do to make ends meet. George was just a boy, you see, but he had to watch after Ralf. George got tired of that, especially after he became friends with Abe, who was always over. Picking on Ralf. Putting George up to picking on him, too. I don't blame George for what happened."

"I always get the sense George loved his mother very much," Fiona says, hoping this will nudge more information from Klara.

But now Klara is wiping her eyes, standing up. "I had all your things moved to the bigger bedroom."

"Thank you." Fiona doesn't stand up or make to leave, though. She puts her hand to her neck, by the red marks, gives her hand a little shake so her sleeve falls back and Klara can see the bruises on her arm.

Klara frowns. "What happened to you?"

Fiona drops her hand quickly, as if she hadn't wanted Klara to see. "Abe," Fiona says. "He—he got rough with me. Said George always trusted him before I was around, and I said, well, Abe didn't always seem trustworthy—" Fiona stops, claps her hand to her mouth, as if horrified at sharing that she'd said this—when of course she wasn't. "Oh God. Abe never mentioned Ralf, not by name. But he referenced an accident, said you should have been paying more attention. . . . Do you suppose he's the one who threw that ball? Made George confess—or made George confused, and think he'd caused the accident?"

Klara's eyes narrow, and Fiona worries she's pushed too far. "I paid as much attention as I could—especially since George's mother was sickly much of the time. Abe has always been a bully." There's more to their stories than that, Fiona thinks. "Are you going to tell George?"

"Oh—oh—no. I couldn't." Fiona widens her eyes. "With Abe saying George has always trusted him—well. Would George believe me?" She makes tears well, easily. At last, she stands. "I'm sorry to barge in on you. But I'm glad your photo didn't break. I—I'm not feeling well. I'm skipping supper. Please tell George that I'm going to lie down for awhile and I'll eat something light later."

CHAPTER 21

LILY

Friday, November 25, 1927
8:30 p.m.

Lily and the three men who've accompanied her as deputies—Benjamin and two others—enter the basement speakeasy of the Kinship Inn. For a moment, before they are spotted, the activities continue on as before: a poker game in one corner, other men and a few women talking at the few tables and at the bar. The bar is the only permanently affixed furniture; hastily assembled wooden tables and chairs fill the rest of the windowless room. Each table and the bar are lit by coal-oil lamps, behind which a makeshift counter holds bottles and glasses. In the side wall is the opening to a dumbwaiter for sending illicit drinks up to the hotel's tiny restaurant or food down to the drinkers, but otherwise the walls are bare. A pall of cigar smoke thickens the air, along with side notes of alcohol and ladies' perfume.

As eyes settle on Lily, the room mutes. The hush soon breaks as patrons jump up and run.

Lily had told her men to let them run—all except the barkeep. Her goal was to clear out the place tonight, have armed deputies around the Kinship Inn, put a stop to the delivery that Fiona had forewarned her of. Then she had a few questions for the barkeep.

But something—instinct, maybe—makes Lily look to the other corner.

It seems the room hushes and stills around her as she focuses on him. Luther.

He's with Arlie Whitcomb, Marvena's cousin and the Holiness gospel deacon. But Arlie is just in the periphery of her vision.

Once she spots him, her eyes do not leave Luther.

Their gazes lock.

Well, of course he's here. Playing both sides. Always and only just for himself.

But for a scant moment, his eyes widen. Shame? After all, just that morning, he'd been in her office, claiming to help the bureau. No sorrow floods his gaze. But not at being caught. Something deeper flickers. Regret. Maybe it's just liquor loosening whatever smidge of humanity is left pooling at the bottom of his dark soul, but it strikes Lily that Luther's regret is over a lost chance for connection. For forgiveness.

In the next moment, without so much as a blink, a filament seems to fall over his eyes as they narrow and thin into pitiless, cold dashes. His cigarette falls to the table as he jumps up.

Lily rushes toward him. She needs to catch him, show the bureau they can't trust him.

Luther shoves his ever-present flask in his hip pocket, then pulls out his gun from his front pocket. His hands shake.

She draws her own weapon, and it remains still in her hand, ready to do her bidding.

Lily coldly notes Luther's expression transition to confusion, fear, wonderment: Would she really shoot him?

For just a second, Daniel's handsome face flashes before her. Blood-lust for vengeance at any cost rises scorching and thrumming. The sound of a woman screaming seems to come from a great distance, from far outside this room.

Yes, yes, she would shoot him.

She aims, wanting nothing more than to shoot Luther dead on the spot for his part in all the many threads that had been woven into a net that had snared Daniel from this life, from her. Recklessly, she doesn't care what doing so might cost her later, what ramifications would inevitably thunder out from such a moment. She just wants the moment.

But Arlie picks up a chair, throws it at her, and it crashes against her sore shoulder. The blinding, ricocheting pain is sufficient to make her hesitate for just a moment, and that hesitation is enough for Luther to escape from the room.

From her grasp.

Mr. Kline, who serves as the speakeasy's barkeep, pats his handkerchief across his brow. He's sweating profusely, though the basement storeroom is so cold.

He waves his sweaty handkerchief at a crate. The gesture is enough to nearly tip his considerable girth from the edge of the stool. "The crate doesn't look any different than usual. I don't know what arrangements either Mr. Williams or Mr. Bennett makes—if they both make them, or just one of them." He's referring to the hotel manager, who resides on premise, and the hotel owner, who happens to be a county commissioner. In the past two raids, Lily's interviewed each of them and both denied any knowledge of the speakeasy. It keeps popping back open, though, so the notion that they aren't aware of its existence is poppycock. "Usually, the crates arrive Sunday nights."

Sure, Lily thinks. *Fewer eyes on the streets, in the alleyway.*

"But this time, it came this afternoon?" Lily asks. She sits on another stool near Mr. Kline. Benjamin stands by the door.

Mr. Kline nods.

"I noticed Luther Ross was here—along with an unlikely friend, Arlie Whitcomb. A cousin of Marvena Whitcomb Sacovech's."

Mr. Kline shrugs. "So?"

"Have you seen Luther here often, recently?"

"Just tonight."

"Was he acting unusual? Did you overhear him say anything of note?"

"He did seem agitated—more so than I remember him being in the past, at least," Mr. Kline says. "He asked me and a few others if we'd been bothered by, or seen, a revenuer."

Lily lifts an eyebrow. Did he mean Special Agent Barnaby Sloan? Barnaby had said he was heading back up to Columbus.

"Did he describe or name this revenuer?"

"Didn't give a name. Said he was younger, skinny."

So, not Barnaby. But that could describe Colter DeHaven. Barnaby had said Colter wouldn't arrive in Columbus until today—but Zebediah had been firm in saying the revenuer he'd seen shot, whom he'd tried to get to the Pentecostal church, was Colter.

"Did he mention any injuries to the man?" Lily asks.

"No," Mr. Kline says.

"Well, what did you—or others—tell him?"

"I told him no—hadn't been bothered by any revenuers. Can't speak for anyone else, told him. I was too busy serving drinks—until you showed up."

Lily looks at the crate. "Newly arrived?"

Kline shrugs.

Lily turns to Benjamin. "Do you mind opening the crate? My shoulder—"

Benjamin grabs a crowbar and levers open the top.

She studies the box, full of unlabeled bottles. Lily pulls out a bottle, opens it. A quick sniff—it smells like regular alcohol. She crosses to Mr. Kline, sticks the bottle under his nose.

"Does this smell like the usual stuff?"

He shrugs. "Stronger. But sure."

"You'd have served it."

"Yes." He sighs. "And most folks would have liked that it's stronger. How many nights am I going to be in lockup this time?"

"One, maybe two," Lily says.

But it's widely rumored that the judge enjoys the occasional cocktail, though usually in the privacy of his home. So he will most likely let Mr. Kline off with another warning.

"There's a way to test if this contains methanol that's more telling than smell," Benjamin says. "My chemistry background might come in handy for you."

Outside, in the alley behind the Kinship Inn, Lily trains her flashlight so Benjamin can see to work quickly. Mr. Kline is standing next to her, curious. She knows he's not going to run off, so she hasn't bothered to handcuff him or walk him to the jail just yet.

Benjamin drops a handkerchief into an empty metal bucket. Then he pours a generous portion of the alcohol from the new shipment into the bucket.

"Watch for the color of the flame," he says. "Yellow would mean the alcohol content is ethanol—potable. Pale blue—it would be nearly invisible in the day—means this contains methanol."

"Methanol? Ain't that what's been talked about in news stories about big-city liquor?" Mr. Kline says. "That stuff can kill you!"

Benjamin steps several feet back, lights a cigarette, inhales deeply so that a goodly portion of the cigarette's tip flames orange. Then, quickly, he flicks the cigarette into the bucket, at the same time that he jumps back into the darkness.

The flames jump high, over the bucket's rim. Yellow flames.

This alcohol—though illegal—isn't the lethal methanol.

Why would Fiona have left her a note, sent her on a raid that was—at least in terms of stopping the serving of methanol—pointless? Especially given how risky it would be to do so in the presence of Abe Miller?

She wouldn't have. Fiona must have truly believed that the methanol was supposed to be switched in this evening.

Or, maybe, George had sent Fiona to set up Lily to do this raid.

To what end? To make Lily look foolish? Toy with her?

Lily shakes her head—she's done raids before, so another one wouldn't make her look foolish. Why would George waste his time with her like this?

She thinks back to what Mr. Kline had just said about Luther asking around about a revenuer—and that the description of the revenuer fit Colter DeHaven. To Zebediah's giving her Colter DeHaven's name.

Could Colter have arrived early—perhaps not trusting Barnaby to handle Luther?

Could the "older man" Zebediah had seen shoot Colter be Luther?

For a moment, she considers that she ought to inform Barnaby. But she's not sure, at this point, if she should trust him, either. What had he really told her? That the bureau was looking for a reason to raid the farm where George was visiting.

He hadn't really given a good reason why.

When she'd raided here, looking for the tainted alcohol referenced in the note Fiona had slipped her, there was none to be found.

Though Barnaby was older, he seemed gullible. From the state of his clothing and attitude, she had no doubt that if he saw the bureau as offering a fresh start, then George, via Luther, could easily dazzle him with a better offer. Even after Barnaby and Luther left her office.

You can see she's not gonna be much help, right, Barnaby? Why not just say you did your best, and take a little extra from us—look the other way? Lily can just imagine Luther saying that to Barnaby.

That was the problem with the bureau, even in its infancy. Sure, there were plenty of good agents. But there were also too many on the take.

Well, Lily thinks, as she asks Benjamin if he'll help her get the crate back to the jail, that's all supposition. The only way to find out what happened to Colter is to track him down—and, God help her, to track Luther down.

For the second time that night, they pull around the bend to the turnoff to Lily's house.

Benjamin idles his automobile at the top of the lane. Lily barely discerns her house under scant moonlight sifting through tree limbs. There is no light burning in the parlor.

"Thank you, I—" Lily starts, as Benjamin says at the same time, "I could—"

He laughs as they both stop short. "Ladies first," he says.

"Thank you for driving me home," she says. "And for all of your help tonight."

After securing the crate, tagged as evidence, at the jail in a locked storeroom and getting Mr. Kline in lockup for the night, Lily had thanked Benjamin for his help, especially given her bum shoulder. She then started to walk back in the bitter cold night to her house.

But he convinced her that he could simply drive her home.

He'd even waited while she interrogated the night clerk at the Kinship Inn to see if there was a Colter DeHaven registered at the hotel.

No, the clerk had said.

It was possible, Lily thought, that the agent had arrived on the train and not taken a room yet. On the way to his automobile, Benjamin said, *There are only so many rooms for let in Kinship and I'm guessing my landlady knows about most of them—she's always pointing out to me how hers is the best. Do you want me to ask her, on your behalf, who's renting rooms? Check if a Colter had rented any of them.*

Lily found herself reluctant to further involve him in this case. But she had to admit that his was a clever idea and she could use the help.

She'd nodded in agreement.

Now Benjamin nods in response to her, *Thank you.*

"Gentlemen next," Lily says. In the dark, she can't tell, but she imagines him smiling.

"I could stay the night—in the parlor, I mean, like I did last night. Given all that's going on, I mean. The parlor settee is, it turns out, quite comfortable. Of course, the chickens and the neighbors might take to clucking."

Now Lily laughs, and doing so feels good. The last time she'd laughed had been with Mama and Marvena, toasting one another with Mama's fermented grape juice, not even two full days ago. It seems like much longer ago, or like something she'd daydreamed.

"But last night, you weren't napping when I came home. You were awake."

Awake. Waiting for her. Since then, he's only been helpful. Not in a pandering way. Like he admires her. Respects her.

For a moment, they sit silently, facing each other. Lily's and Benjamin's breaths puff and mingle between them.

Slowly, she leans toward him, desire to bring her lips to his pulling her. He moves forward—but Lily hesitates.

Desire is interrupted by the need to ask a question—an important question, especially if their lips touching might take them into new territory. She speaks softly. "You said you were thinking. What, what were you . . ."

Benjamin leans back. The question trails off into the cold.

"You. I was thinking about—you."

Ah. She waits for him to move forward again. Wills him to.

But he sighs and adds, his voice taut as if the honesty pains him, "About your job. How much you seem to—to like it. To love it, even?"

A different sort of cold ricochets through her. Not shock. His reservations are to be expected. But of flickering hopes, doused by reality. There are to be no barn dances tonight, or in their future.

Her own honesty, in turn, pains her, but at last she answers, "I do. I love my job. And even if I'm not reelected in three years, I'll find some way to—"

"I know." Benjamin's words click evenly, carefully meted out. "That is part of what I was thinking about. It's impressive, watching you at work. But I—I'm not sure what I'd think about you keeping a job like that, long term, if we—"

Before he can say more, Lily opens the automobile door. It creaks loudly in the cold. The sound of her shutting the door echoes loudly across the snow-covered yard.

She walks carefully down the lane, so as not to slip, and even after she steps out of Benjamin's headlamps she hears his automobile still idling and feels him still watching her. *Good,* she thinks. But she's not sure why. She does not want him to follow her, not tonight, when they are both too tired, too cold, too raw from the long day's and night's events. And not if he will, eventually, attempt to talk her out of keeping her job.

And yet, as she opens the front door, and hears his automobile backing up, and then turns and stares into the now dark, cold night, her heart falls, just a little.

CHAPTER 22

※

FIONA

Friday, November 25, 1927
8:30 p.m.

Fiona keeps her eyes closed and her breathing slow and even to simulate sleeping. She lies as still as possible, but her heart pounds as the door squeaks open and George's heavy footfalls come nearer. Well, it had taken George plenty long to come check on her, she thinks. She'd started to wonder if Klara hadn't passed along her message about skipping supper. The bed dips as George sits down at her feet.

He puts his hand gently on her hip.

Now she pretends to stir, then startle awake.

"Oh, Fiona, I didn't mean to wake you," George says.

The room is dim. Fiona sits up. George holds a lit coal-oil lantern. Odd, seeing him with such a rural device. "It's all right, sweetheart," she says, as he puts the lantern on the side table.

"I wanted to check on you," George says. "Klara came to me—said that you weren't feeling well, that you told her Abe had hurt you?"

Though Fiona resists the temptation to smile—*Good, pitting Klara and Abe against each other is working*—she is glad for the shadowy light, lest her expression give away her gratification.

"Is it true? That he hurt you?" He looks at her neck, takes her arm and examines the bruises.

Fiona considers. She could admit now that, yes, Abe had hurt her. All that would result in would be George telling Abe to keep his hands off his wife—unless ordered to punish her.

Or she could deny it, reveal later she'd simply been covering for Abe because of George's friendship with him, use such a dramatic confession to greater advantage. And in the meantime, George might be more harsh toward Klara, and that will rattle Klara's loyalty in George.

Fiona looks down. "I—I just fell. It's so slippery outside."

"Well, be careful, my little spitfire," George says. "That's my baby you're carrying."

With those words, George's voice grates on her nerves. But Fiona forces herself to look back up and smile. "I did tell Klara I wasn't feeling well, but I—I'm sure she just misunderstood about Abe. Tiredness will make people more easily confused. Klara has been working awfully hard for all of us. I feel rested. Maybe I could get a light bite and then help her a bit? In the kitchen?" She'll have a piece of bread and then offer to bring up tea and a snack for Elias—save Klara an extra trip up and down the stairs.

George nods. "Don't overdo it, though."

"Of course not, sweetheart."

A half hour later, her hands full with a tray filled with light sandwiches and mugs of broth, Fiona nudges the bedroom door open with her hip and gives a little call—"Yoo-hoo! Klara told me you also skipped supper, so I brought a little something."

"Come in," Elias replies.

Fiona pushes the door open the rest of the way and enters his bedroom.

Elias is sitting up in bed, reading a book with a well-worn cover—Henry James's *The Turn of the Screw*. Not, Fiona thinks, a book he'd found here. He must have packed it in his and Luther's trunk.

As Elias sets the book aside, he smiles benevolently while watching Fiona carry the tray to the side table. The tray just fits. She pulls a chair up alongside the bed, makes herself smile back at him, hopes the coldness she actually feels doesn't show in her face.

She's had time to think, on the drive back from Lily's and in the time since returning to the farm, about many things—including how to use to her advantage the news of Luther still being missing.

Fiona sips her broth, watches as Elias greedily tucks into his sandwich. His color is improved, his hands steadier, since he's been taking his medicine.

"You seem better," Fiona says. "Have you been up here alone, all day?"

"Klara has checked on me," Elias says. "But I prefer your company." He looks at her like a kindly uncle. Though she keeps her smile in place, Fiona is unmoved.

Then he leans forward, his expression turning darkly serious. He grabs ahold of her arm. "Were you able to convince George—about the wood alcohol?"

"Yes," Fiona says evenly—though of course she had not. There's no *convincing George.* There's only making him think your idea is really his—and that's tricky. She's already nervous about George changing his mind about the property being in her name. It would be so easy for him to change back. And she'd overheard George and Abe reviewing plans while making up this tray in the kitchen. The animals were to be taken away tomorrow afternoon, sold, Fiona was relieved to hear, to a nearby farmer. Trucks hauling in gravel are already set to arrive shortly after that, the gravel to be poured for a makeshift road out the back of the property starting tomorrow and finishing up Monday, just in time for hijacked legal alcohol to be trucked in. Operations start next week, with a small army of armed guards, on round-the-clock duty, posted on both the main lane to the house and along the gravel road.

By a week from today, the plan will be underway—alcohol trucked for manufacture of Vogel's Tonic in Cincinnati but hijacked en route. Not by actual gangsters, but by men George had hired to play that role.

George's tonic company gets the insurance payout on the stolen alcohol—but then it's brought here. Trucked in off the main road and access road at the front of the property. Diluted here and rebottled.

Trucked back out via a gravel road being constructed on the property and connecting up with a local county road.

Then bootlegged at bars, dives, speakeasies, at points south and east of here with the assurance that this alcohol is safe—no methanol.

Ensuring all that will happen will require Abe and George to work closely together, giving Abe plenty of time to convince George to reverse today's paperwork, to not entrust this or any other property to her after all.

But she must be the one, the only one, George trusts. Keep pitting Klara and Abe against each other, so that George sees their squabbling. Make Elias trust only her as well, so she can use him to her own purposes—for information. For doing her bidding.

Still, her moves must be thoughtful. Careful.

Fiona pats Elias's clammy hand. "Well, I didn't exactly convince George." She leans forward, whispers, "But I was able to get word to Sheriff Lily Ross."

For a moment, relief soothes Elias's brow. It's as he relaxes, closes his eyes, that she sees in his face—even with better color—how ill he really is. He looks older by years than he did just a few months ago, when he and Luther first came into George's orbit. But then his eyes pop open, and he stares at her.

"To Lily? Why did you do it that way? And how?"

"Luther and Abe went to get your medicine from Dr. Goshen last night—but the doctor had gone to visit Sheriff Lily. Lily was gone with the doctor on an emergency—something about a child, with alcohol poisoning, near a still run by Marvena Whitcomb Sacovech," Fiona says. "Daniel's old friend."

Elias nods. His eyes grow filmy. He shifts in the bed, as if his back is aching or he needs the pillows fluffed, but Fiona guesses that's not what's really hurting him. She can tell she's stabbing him with the names—*Lily, Marvena, Daniel*—as if they are knives. She doesn't know why, she may never know why, and she may never have to care. But it is worth knowing. Maybe for later use.

For now, Fiona leans forward. She speaks quietly. "Today I learned that Abe and Luther went back to wait at Dr. Goshen's office last night.

When the doctor came back, explained where he'd been, Luther ran off. As if spooked. Why would he be spooked?"

Elias shakes his head. "I don't know. Send him up here—we can ask him—"

"Oh, Elias . . . ," Fiona says. She pauses, knowing her next words will be as a knife to him, and she wants to slip it in carefully. Slowly. She serrates her next pronouncement by looking as worried as she can muster. "That's just it—he hasn't come back."

The old man goes still as death. He stares at her, but she is not sure he sees her.

"We've reported him missing to Sheriff Lily, Abe and I; we went this afternoon. That's when I was able to get word to Lily about the tainted alcohol."

"Why, why would Luther have run off? When I'm—sick?" Elias's voice is a bare, heartbroken croak.

"I don't know," Fiona says—though she does. The Goshens had told her that Luther ran off to the Harkins farm after learning that the Harkins boy had gotten ill after drinking shine near Marvena's still. And that Abe witnessed this.

What she doesn't know is why Luther would care enough about that to run off—or why Abe would withhold this information from George.

She doesn't need to tell either Elias or George this just yet. She has a gift, she's discovering, for saving reveals for when they're most likely to yield outcomes that she wants.

Elias protests, "We have to tell George. We have to find Luther—"

"Not yet, Elias. I'm sure Luther will return. Let's wait to find out why he ran off when he gets back and then combine that with what I've learned about Abe withholding information." She pats Elias's hand again. Offers a small smile. "Then, Elias, we'll help George see that he is better off with you and Luther by his side. Now, you just relax."

Fiona takes the book he'd been reading and puts it on the side table. Puts his plate on the tray. Pats his head. "Just rest for now," she says.

Saturday, November 26, 5:00 a.m.

How easy it is to fall back into old patterns and rhythms.

And how poignantly amusing that now Fiona finds comfort in the early morning chores that she once chafed against.

But she is out here, in an old dress and boots of Aunt Nell's, donned as quickly and quietly as she could while George tosses and turns in his sleep, beset again by nightmares. If he—or Abe or the other men—questions why she is out here, she can tell him, honestly, that she feels sentimental about the farm and the changes coming.

Then she can give a dizzy laugh, play it off as girlish sentimentality.

None of them will question that.

That she *does* feel sentimental does not make it less of a cover for her true purpose.

She, too, had tossed about in her sleep, reviewing more of what she'd thought about on the drive back from Lily's yesterday.

About Aunt Nell's beliefs that Uncle Henry had been perfectly healthy at the time of his death. About Dr. Goshen saying he'd been treating Uncle Henry for stomach ulcers without Aunt Nell knowing. About Elias saying that he'd wandered the land and checked the buildings to see what might need to be modified for George's plans.

Could it be he was looking for Uncle Henry's medicine in order to poison it?

Uncle Henry wouldn't have stashed his medicine inside the house, surely—that was Aunt Nell's domain.

So in one of the outbuildings—Uncle Henry's domain.

That's why she's really out here—looking for that stomach medicine. Whether it was benign or poisoned, wouldn't she be able to tell, somehow?

The springhouse, barn workbench, hen house—none of them had yielded anything.

There is one place left to look. Uncle Henry's woodshop. It's the building farthest down the property, right where the gravel road is going to go in. Uncle Henry's private place to spend time, by himself.

Fiona shivers by the time she reaches the woodshop. No new snow has fallen overnight, but the cold has deepened. It is still dark, before sunrise.

The door to the woodshop is not one that locks—Uncle Henry had not believed in locks on doors other than the main house. He used to say that no one would make it past the house who he didn't know.

Fiona swings the door open, steps in, lets the door slam shut behind her. She takes a moment to let her eyes adjust to the darkness, broken only by the coal-oil lantern that she carries. Then she sets the lantern down on the bench, opens its drawer—nothing in there but a variety of hand tools, a few mousetraps. She holds the lantern up, stares at the shelf over the bench.

There's linseed oil, and a bottle of rat poison, and other cans of oil and then—something different. A blue medicinal bottle.

Fiona stands on tiptoe, reaches up, pulls it down.

Studies it in the lantern light.

It has a label, handwritten, with instructions from Dr. Goshen.

Uncle Henry's ulcer medicine.

She opens up the bottle, sniffs, draws back.

It doesn't smell odd.

Fiona's gaze drifts up, focuses on the box of rat poison. The brand name is Rough on Rats, and it features an almost comical silhouette of a rat, belly up. She's familiar with the brand, a common one; Martin and she had to use it once at the shoe repair shop. It's arsenic—tasteless and odorless.

Fiona's heart pounds. Elias wouldn't have had to go to any great lengths to poison Uncle Henry. Dr. Goshen could simply have told him about the stomach medicine, and Elias would only have had to find it and add in a few spoonfuls of the arsenic.

Woodworking tricks . . . Dr. Goshen had also said he'd come by with the medicine using Uncle Henry teaching him *woodworking tricks* as a pretext so Aunt Nell wouldn't worry about Uncle Henry's ulcer. . . .

Fiona shakes her head. It makes more sense that Elias would have tainted the medicine, at George's behest, to clear the way for eventual possession of the farm.

If the arsenic didn't kill Uncle Henry right away, it would certainly have made him ill enough over a few weeks to eventually kill him— but the fall from the tractor, and the tractor blades running over him, would have finished the job.

Fiona puts the arsenic back up on the shelf and puts the stopper back in the blue glass bottle. She pockets the bottle, not sure when she'll confront Elias but knowing that she will.

She turns and is about to step out when she sees a shape shifting in the far corner of the woodshop. Slowly, she lets her free hand drift back to the workbench. She grasps a hammer, steps forward, holds it high up.

A man comes forward. He's wrapped in a filthy blue-and-white-patterned quilt, over his fine suit. The hair on his head is a bloody mat. He smells of sickness and filth. His eyes are bright with fever and fear.

He manages to take a few steps forward, and Fiona notes his fine, lace-up dress shoes—ridiculous out here in farmland, especially in winter weather. He stumbles forward, lands on his knees on the hard ground.

But even in his pitiable state, he is studying her. Assessing her.

Apparently, he decides that, even though she holds a hammer high over his already-injured head and could bring it smashing down on him, she is not a real threat. *Oh,* she thinks. The way she's dressed—in Aunt Nell's too-large rough and dowdy work dress, worn boots, long hand-knit brown scarf covering her stylish short bob, but that could just as easily be covering long, pinned-up hair. And, too, weariness and morning sickness have no doubt added years to her face. He thinks she's just a simple farmwife.

"Help, please." The man's face is boyish and lean but stretched with the sheen and flush of fever. His voice crackles with thirst and weariness, making him sound like an old man. And his next words make Fiona think he must surely be delirious or insane. "I'm Colter DeHaven. Special agent. Bureau of Prohibition. And I've come for Luther Ross."

CHAPTER 23

LILY

Saturday, November 26, 1927
5:15 a.m.

Though Lily stands by the edge of Coal Creek, it's yet dark enough that she can't really see the water moving, though she hears its sluggish progress between the narrow banks. For now, the snow has stopped falling and the air has warmed sufficiently to turn snow on the ground to tendrils of mist creeping along the earth. She leans against the Kinship Tree, somewhat irritated with herself for having come down here from the house, in the dark and cold, when she has plenty to do.

Yet, she'd been awake for an hour, thinking of the unique tree that is well-known in the county, for it is formed of three saplings—maple, sycamore, and beech—conjoining and twining many years ago. A footpath led from Kinship Road across her property down to the Kinship Tree, and she didn't stop occasional visitors, just as the farm's previous owner had not.

Lovers' initials were carved into the tree. Hers and Daniel's were not, yet this is where their story began. She'd injured her foot here when she was just a teen, coming over from her grandparents' farm next door to jump into the creek on a warm day, and her brother had rushed her to the then doctor's farmhouse across the road—Dr. Elias

Ross. That's where she'd met Daniel the first time. He'd waited a few years to court her.

So much has changed since then—Daniel, her grandparents, her brother, her friendship with Elias all gone. And yet, new paths had been forged by the Kinship Tree. Lily puts a hand on the bark of the maple side of the tree. She and Marvena had made a major decision here, a few years ago, securing the safety of the county—at least for a time. Hildy, after injuries sustained in a dangerous case the year before, had found sanctuary at the farmhouse and under this tree.

Lily's never told anyone that the tree was one reason she'd bought this farmhouse, when it was time to move out of the county-owned sheriff's house. Now she stares up through the limbs making a lattice-work against the slowly lighting, opaque sky.

She'd come down here to think, to contemplate what Daniel would do in her situation about Elias and George and Luther. She'd made herself as still as possible, listening to the wind, the creek, her heart.

But she hears no imagined whisper from Daniel, cannot conjure advice he'd likely give.

And yet, rather than sorrow over this, she realizes, to her surprise, she feels relief.

She is the sheriff. She must untangle the situation. Even if she had a sense of what Daniel would do in her place—it wouldn't matter. She has to do what she thinks is right, within the rule of law.

Lily gives the tree a pat, knowing she'll be back often to seek the counsel of her own thoughts and heart, and then walks up the thin, frozen path.

She needs to get to the Harkins place—though she's told Dora the good news about Zebediah and his improved condition, she still wants to see if she can learn anything more from Ruth about Special Agent DeHaven. Could he be hiding out there? Still alive?

She hopes so. Then she won't have to track down Luther, grill him about whether or not he was the older man Zebediah had seen shoot the agent. DeHaven can just tell her—and Lily would rather track down someone else than Luther.

Even if she finds DeHaven easily and he says someone other than

Luther shot him, Lily will need to find a way to talk with Fiona about why she'd sought to warn her that George had planned to swap alcohol with methanol—when in fact that hadn't happened at all.

That alone means a trip out to the Murphy farm. Could she just pretend she wanted to call on Fiona, as if they were old friends and she was sorry she'd missed her visit?

As she comes into the clearing of her yard, Lily smiles at the snowman the children built the afternoon before. She hadn't paid any attention to it when she came out of the house this morning, but now it provides momentary, whimsical distraction from all of her weightier concerns.

But then she sees a figure coming toward her from the house. It takes her a moment to realize it's Hildy.

Lily smiles as she approaches her friend, happy to see her even though she has so many tasks to attend to. "I didn't expect to see you today. . . ."

Lily's voice trails off.

From the stark, struck look on her friend's face, Hildy is not stopping by on her way to Kinship to check on her mother—as difficult as their relationship is, Hildy remains faithful in watching out for her—or do her Christmas shopping.

Hildy's eyes are wide, worried.

"It's Luther Ross," she says.

Luther's body has been leaned against the front door of the small main office for Wessex Corporation, the same building where Luther used to reign supreme over his family's mining operation before he sold it to Wessex. A thin dusting of overnight snow has settled in the crown and on the brim of his fedora, which covers most of his face, and on his pant legs and shoes. Luther's legs sprawl, his arms fallen to his sides, his palms turned up, as if he'd been pushed or collapsed against the wall, and then slid down.

Lily squats low to study the body of the man who was her brother-in-law, who had betrayed her husband and hurt her friend Marvena.

On the drive over, Hildy told her that Luther had been found early this morning at the start of the day's shift. Some of the miners, recognizing their former tormentor, had whooped upon seeing Luther, thought he was passed out, started throwing rocks at him. But when he didn't respond, when his hat fell away to reveal the shocking condition of his face, the crowd grew silent. Someone thought to cover his face with his hat. Tom and a few others stood guard around the body so no more damage could be done. Then Hildy went to fetch Lily.

By the time they got to Rossville, most of the men had gone on to work, while the current manager of the mines allowed Tom and Jurgis and a few others to stand watch over Luther's body. Now Lily ignores the manager, impatiently looming over her, apparently anxious for the corpse of his predecessor to be moved so he can get in the door and to work. She tunes out the people murmuring behind her, the few remaining onlookers from the town.

Lily calculates. The snow on his hat and pants means that Luther has been out here for at least a few hours.

His hands. It's strange to see them so still. In life, he was always gesturing—pointing, shaking a fist, picking at his nails. Snow has settled into his palms. Why isn't he wearing gloves? His left hand is blue tinged. The right is red and swollen, a grotesque balloon.

The redness extends to his partially exposed wrist.

Lily carefully and slowly pushes up Luther's right coat sleeve. There, two small punctures, purplish blue around the holes.

Fang marks.

Next, Lily reaches slowly for Luther's hat, lifts it carefully with both hands from his face.

Oh. His face is beaten, bruised. His eyelids are puffy, nearly swollen closed. But only just nearly. His eyes seem to still be staring out through those slits.

Though neither sorrow nor relief nor rage rises in Lily at the sight of Luther like this, some emotion wrestles to break free. Dammit, she wants to feel nothing for this man who'd been so cruel to her husband, to so many others in the past.

Lily swallows hard, once. Twice. Forcing the bile running up in her throat back down, forcing herself to observe dispassionately. She'll need to make careful, detailed notes later.

Luther's death, Lily thinks, does not make sense, at least not in the mechanics of it. Oh, there were plenty of people who would have motivation for wanting Luther dead. Marvena, Jurgis, Tom. Any number of past employees. If he had frustrated George one too many times, George would not hesitate to have him killed—though of course he wouldn't have sullied his own hands. And what of the agent Colter DeHaven? Luther had been looking for him just last night; Colter had been shot, left for dead. What if Luther was his attacker and Colter sought revenge? What of, for that matter, Arlie Whitcomb, whom Lily had seen the evening before with Luther?

Knowing Luther, there were undoubtedly plenty of other possible suspects.

So that someone would want to kill Luther Ross, and be pushed to do so, is unsurprising.

The mechanics of his death—*that* rouses curiosity and questions.

Luther appears to have been beaten to death and dumped outside his old mining office, cruel yet fitting given that his greed as mining manager had condemned so many men to die.

But what of those fang marks?

They draw her gaze, and she wonders if he'd been bitten before or after being beaten. If the bite or the beating, or both, had led to his death. Where and when he might have been bitten.

She looks at his bruised, swollen face. How odd—even in this grotesque condition, his face is easier to contemplate than it had ever been in life. He'd always looked so angry, so ready to strike himself—like a snake. Now, at least, beneath the mottling and lacerations, there's a hint of peacefulness. Lily sees his once-superior attitude, so often acted out in cruel and petty ways, as what it really was—a mask for his own emptiness.

At last, the emotion she'd been struggling to push down breaks free.

Pity. She feels pity for Luther.

Luther had had every advantage afforded to a person in this neck of the woods, and he'd still, for whatever reason, wrestled his demons and lost. Or maybe, at some point, like Brother Stiles might say, he chose to stop wrestling and embrace his demons as comrades.

Why had he been like that? She'll probably never know. And death has robbed him of any chance for contemplation, for remorse, for peace. At least in this life. Maybe, even for one like Luther, there's hope for it in the next.

Lily shakes her head at herself. Luther himself would be unmoved by such sentiment, would surely laugh at her for feeling it on his behalf.

But then, Lily wonders, isn't what we think of, and how we treat, our foes really as much for saving our own humanity as judging theirs?

Lily stands slowly, turns toward the people behind her. She sees, in the corner of her eye, the grim, taut expressions of Jurgis and Tom. If she asks them to do what she needs, she has no doubt they'll comply, just to help her. Given how cruelly Luther had treated Tom and Jurgis a few years ago as unionization leaders, she can't bring herself to ask them. So she looks beyond them to the other people.

"I'll need two men to help load the body in Hildy's automobile, and follow after us to Kinship," Lily says. She plans ahead quickly: they'll have to get Luther into the Kinship funeral home, then fetch Dr. Goshen, who serves as the county coroner. "And if anyone knows where I might find Arlie Whitcomb, please speak up. I need to bring him in for questioning."

CHAPTER 24

FIONA

Saturday, November 26, 1927
5:30 a.m.

"C'mon, just a little farther now." Fiona's doing her best to sound encouraging, even sweet, but the man keeps stopping every few steps.

Colter DeHaven, he'd said. *Special agent.*

Sure, he's dressed well enough—slick coat, nice lace-up shoes, suit pants, like a businessman or banker or *special agent* would dress. But he doesn't, as far as she can tell, carry a weapon. Or a badge. No hat, but a mass of hair with dried blood. He's been shot.

Yet he was hiding out, on her aunt's property—*her* property—asking for Luther Ross.

So what could he be, other than a special agent as he claims?

He stops again, panting from the effort of walking up the rise. "How much?"

"It's not a far piece," Fiona says.

She startles at her own turn of phrase, hearing herself as if from a distance. In Cincinnati and Chicago, she'd cleared her voice of her accent she didn't know she had until that encounter with Eugenia at her wedding. But she's lapsing back into it now, easy enough. *Good.* At least she'll be convincing as a farmwife. On their trek so far, she's already worked out the story she'll give him, pulling in as many elements of truth as possible, so it's easier to keep from crossing herself up. In case at some point DeHaven had seen or even met Aunt Nell—the latter notion is doubtful, but after all, her aunt had kept back other information—she'll claim to be Fiona Vogel's cousin, and say she's visiting her relatives at the farm for the holiday. Say she is a widow and lives on another much smaller farm. But she'll only mete out her story as needed.

The man starts up again but skids on the slick leaves and snow. She catches his elbow, and he keeps from falling. His glance her way mixes chagrin and gratitude. She offers a smile. Thinks: *Hurry!*

She's been gone too long. George will be asking questions—where she had been, why she had been outside so long. Especially if she's spied coming back to the farm from this direction. She'll have to go the long way back to the other side of the farm, come down from the cemetery, concoct some excuse about visiting Uncle Henry's graveside.

Fiona and the man walk up the final rise and there it is.

The cabin.

Now it's Fiona who comes to a sudden stop.

Colter stumbles, almost falls to his knees again, but Fiona holds him steady as she stares.

It's so much smaller than she recollects. Just one room, a chimney, no porch, just the one door and a paned window, the cabin's most elegant feature. There's only one other window, in the back by the cast-iron stove.

The front window is shattered. Mama's lace curtains, once pristine and white, hang in tatters, the dingy gray of old snow. Mama had set aside coins, here and there, saving for them.

Won't Daddy be angry? Fiona asked. Her father had been fearsome about controlling money, saying women didn't know anything about it. As far as Fiona could tell, he didn't know much about managing money, either, spending what little he made from odd jobs now and again mostly on booze.

Of course, she hadn't said that. She'd kept mum, wondering what glorious joy Mama must be saving for, dreaming about possibilities like hats in impractical colors—pale blue or yellow—and topped with confections of feathers and silk flowers and lace. Or maybe a fine lamp, its glass shade and oil bowl made fancy with a painted swirl of pink roses and mossy green leaves. She'd seen pictures of such in a Sears, Roebuck catalogue someone had brought to the school she'd attended for a few years, up through the third grade, where she'd been better at her numbers than her letters—unusual for a girl, the schoolmarm had said.

But in the end, the coins had been traded for white lace curtains purchased on a rare trip that Mama and Fiona had made into Kinship. There'd been enough left over for Fiona to buy a pretty item, too—a cut-glass candy dish.

Crystal! little Fiona had exclaimed.

The shopkeeper had laughed at her. *No, just glass. But I guess you can pretend. Maybe get real crystal someday.* Then he'd given Fiona and her mama a look that conveyed he didn't believe for a moment that that would ever happen.

Fiona had bought it anyway. It was pretty, even if she couldn't imagine she'd ever have much candy to put in it. But she could pretend it was crystal.

Later that soft spring day, Mama beamed at the gentle billow of white lace curtains in the open window, so much more pleasant than the dull flap of a burlap bag. Her pleasure dimmed quickly when Daddy came home and glowered at the curtains, then sputtered out altogether when he grabbed up Fiona's candy dish and threw it at Mama. The dish gashed her cheek, before hitting the wall, then falling to the floor. A bit of glass broke off from the rim, but otherwise the dish remained intact.

Flecks of Mama's blood dotted the curtains.

"Lady?" The man sounds even weaker than he had down in the woodshop, and his knees buckle. He falls back into her, clunking against the pocket where she'd tucked Uncle Henry's blue bottle. Fiona twists—she doesn't want the bottle to break; on the slow, plodding trek over here she'd come up with an idea for what to do with it. The hammer, in her other pocket, thwacks against her thigh.

She helps him stay upright. "Go on." She prods him toward the cabin.

At the door, she pushes him across the threshold. When she ran away years ago, she swore she'd never come back here. And she hadn't—until now.

As the man staggers into the cabin, Fiona stills. She can't bring herself to cross the threshold, plunge into the derelict structure's greedy, gobbling darkness.

She opens her mouth to holler for the man to come back.

She'll tell him, *I've made a mistake; Luther's back at the farmhouse after all,* and once there let George deal with him however he wishes. Make an excuse for having come here first with the man. Do as George wishes with the properties. With his business. With Luther, Elias, Abe, Klara—all of them. Give up on trying to draw Lily out to the farm. Why had she ever thought she could get away with playing one person off another, with taking control?

Fiona gasps with panicky breaths. She braces one hand against the doorframe, puts the other hand on her hip as she bends forward, forces her breath to stretch and slow.

As she bends, the bottle in her pocket hits against her thigh. She sees again it flashing blue on the shelf, is shocked anew at what she'd put together upon seeing it, just before also discovering this man. Shudders as she examines the horrid truth: Aunt Nell wasn't just paranoid; George truly had been willing to murder her uncle Henry—well, not by his hand, likely leaving that task to Elias—to make it easier to get his well-situated farm for his own expansion purposes.

This reality smacks her back to the moment, firms her resolve for what she has to do for her future—for her children's futures. She wills herself to focus: *The past no longer exists. It cannot touch me. I will not let it.*

"Lady?" The man's stringy voice tugs at her.

Fiona looks up, realizes she is already in the cabin. The man has stumbled into a chair, by the cast-iron potbelly stove. Milky light diffuses through the cabin's only other window, this one intact, by the stove, on which still sits a cast-iron skillet, slick with old bacon grease, flecked with flies and small spiders who'd sensed they'd found a feast but then got stuck to their doom.

The man's face has pinched and paled. She grabs an old ceramic bowl, left on the table, pulls it free of strands of spiderweb that have tenuously bound it to the log wall, holds it under his chin. His puke is thin and watery. Just stomach acid.

Fiona waits as he leans over the bowl, and considers: He is dehydrated, hungry. Injured, obviously. Filthy. Ill prepared for being in the wild, particularly in the winter. But somehow, he'd come to the farm, asking after Luther, claiming Luther had shot him.

But he's also naive, and being hurt and hungry hasn't helped his judgment. Immediately sharing his name, identifying himself to be a prohibition bureau special agent—foolish. Or maybe it just shows that he doesn't see her as much of a threat simply because she's female. A farm woman—even more harmless.

Fiona sets the bowl aside, pulls out one of Aunt Nell's handkerchiefs, wipes the man's mouth. She leaves the handkerchief on the table.

His eyes start to close, and he droops forward.

"Hey, mister!" Fiona snaps her fingers thrice next to his ear. "Don't pass out on me."

Not just yet.

He looks up at her with bleary, almost glassy eyes, swimming with confusion.

"You said you're Colter DeHaven?"

His head bobs once in affirmation.

"And you're looking for—" She stops. Better to sound, for now, like she doesn't know who he's asking after.

"Luther Ross." Just saying the name seems to perk the man up. He straightens in the chair. "Told you that already; you said you knew where he was, you were taking me to him."

Well, yes. She had said as much, drawing him away from the farm. A special agent looking for Luther, she'd thought, could be useful to her. Letting him be found on the farm would only put him in George's control—or worse.

She just needs to be sure not to get caught helping this man—and to have a good excuse ready in case she does.

Fiona makes her eyes go wide, her voice quivery, like the nervous farm woman she's playacting. "You aiming to bring him in for something?"

"He was working for me—or I thought he was. But he shot me. Left me for dead—" He grabs her arm, grimaces as he stands. "Don't try and play me for a fool. I know he's staying at your farm, and you said you'd take me to him."

Too many memories of her time in this cabin, when she thought she could not fight back, rush up from deep within, propel Fiona to her feet. She shoves him back down, whips out the hammer, holds the claw end under the soft part of his neck.

"Don't think, mister, I won't gash your throat. Or bash in what's left of your head," Fiona says. In her own voice, she hears the mean grittiness of her father, threatening her and her mother. So be it. She is, at last, someone who will fight back. Whatever it costs her. "Yes, Luther Ross has been at the farm. Belongs to my aunt. I'm visiting, because my cousin and her husband are visiting too. I've met this Luther. He works for my cousin and her husband. But he hightailed it outta here the day after Thanksgiving."

"Lady, I've seen the armed men on the farm. I've seen George Vogel there. You gotta know the kind of man he is, your cousin's husband! So why'd you drag me out here?" His hand trails to the inside of his coat. Maybe he does have a weapon.

Fiona presses the claw of the hammer up under Colter's chin. He leans his head back as far as he can, so far that as he stares at her his pupils are half-moons over his bottom lashes.

All right, so Colter has seen George out on the grounds with his men but hasn't spotted her. It was just two days ago—*God, but it seems a lifetime*—that she would have been out walking with Aunt Nell, past the woodshop, on the way to the cemetery. So this man, Colter, hadn't been hiding out in the woodshop then.

"You just up and announce to me that you're a special agent, looking for Luther, with Mr. Vogel and his men wandering all over the place," Fiona says. "You oughta be grateful I didn't just scream for help, then and there."

"Why didn't you?" Doubt and defiance tinge his voice. Weak as he is, he still has some sense and fight left.

"Maybe I don't like or trust them," she says. She pulls back the hammer but doesn't put it away or sit down. "Why'd Luther shoot you?"

His face reddens. "Do you mind if I get out a smoke?"

She hesitates. He could be reaching for his gun. But if he has it—or wants to use it—wouldn't he have already? "Go ahead."

He pulls out a pack of cigarettes and a lighter. Shakily, he lights a cigarette. After his first puff, he says, "Another agent, from the Columbus office, has been working for the past few months with Luther as an insider to Mr. Vogel's, ah, operation. It's very complex, so I won't trouble you with details."

Fiona resists rolling her eyes. *Oh yes. Don't upset the little woman with information she won't understand anyway.*

"I got brought in from a bigger office—Chicago. . . ." He pauses, as if expecting her to ask where that is. She just gives a little nod, and he goes on. "That's because the case got bigger than what Columbus could handle. But I started having my doubts that the Columbus agent was fully on board. That he might be giving Luther the runaround, be on the take." Colter shrugs. "Just some things Luther said."

Fiona could see Luther sowing doubt with one agent, to play off the other. To what end?

"I was supposed to come over next week, take the lead working out of Columbus, but Luther asked if I could come early. He wanted to show me something, he said, that he didn't want the other agent to know just yet."

And you fell for it? But Fiona keeps her face placid. She is, after all, not supposed to be Fiona right now. She's Fiona's naive farmwife cousin. So she infuses sympathy into her tone. "You came before Thanksgiving?"

Colter takes another drag on his cigarette. He doesn't say anything. Not the time for exploring why he's alone for the holiday. Fiona goes down another path. "But Luther shot you?"

Now the revenuer stares at the ember tip of his cigarette. "I thought I could trust him."

Fiona almost feels sorry for him. She sees in him that quality that made Martin so dear—wanting to trust others. Of course, it had led him into foolish mistakes at poker games. And it's a terrible attribute for a man in Colter's position.

She sits back down but keeps hold of the hammer as she rests it on the table—just in case. "Luther Ross has quite the reputation in these parts—from when he ran a coal-mining company over in Rossville. He's duped many a person." The thought of Martin, killed at the hands of one of Luther's hired thugs, makes her heart twinge. It must show in her face, for now Colter looks sympathetic—and a little comforted that he's not the only one Luther's ever tricked. "You must have been shot nearby, but I haven't heard any gunfire around here."

"It was near some still, a place where Luther Ross was supposed to show me evidence that Vogel is . . ." Colter pauses, looking for the right words.

Fiona puts this together with what she'd learned during her visit with Dr. and Mrs. Goshen. So Luther had shot this man at Marvena Whitcomb Sacovech's moonshine stand. Left him for dead. Why would he do that? Surely he'd know that sooner or later someone would find this revenuer, dead at Marvena's site?

It hits Fiona—maybe that was the point? Maybe he wanted to get Marvena into trouble? Marvena had, after all, once rallied miners to try to unionize at the coal company Luther had owned. And Luther hates Sheriff Lily Ross, who is friends with Marvena. Maybe he took some pleasure in knowing how it would hurt Lily to have to arrest her friend.

Would he risk George's ire over the attention this would have surely brought?

In any case, Luther would have later learned at the Goshens', while getting heart medicine for Elias, that a farm boy from the Harkins family had been there—a possible witness. And maybe the boy had helped Colter? After all, this farm is a long way from the Harkins place—at least by foot, and certainly in this weather. No wonder Luther had run off in a panic. Had he gone to the Harkins farm then, to try to find out?

Colter stumbles on. "Vogel is engaged in illicit activity."

Fiona gives him a wide-eyed, perplexed look.

He can't help but explain. "Bootlegging. A big plan, involving your aunt's farm." His look turns concerned. "I'm sorry, ma'am, but I think you and your aunt should know that. Luther revealed that Vogel is planning to buy the farm."

Fiona says softly, "I overheard Fiona say to our aunt that she wanted to talk with her about buying the property." How odd, yet thrilling, to refer to herself as a whole other person. But it's best not to keep focus on her assumed identity. She asks Colter, "Why not just make your way to the sheriff, after he shot you?"

Colter starts to laugh, but the effort turns into a watery cough. "Luther already told me she's on the take with your cousin's husband." Fiona has to bite back a laugh. *Lily Ross? On the take? She's always been so self-assured, self-righteous.* "Just like his half brother was, when he was sheriff. *Now* I know he could be lying. Telling me the reason he wanted to help us with Vogel was to set things straight after his brother was a yes-man for Vogel." Fiona swallows another yelp of incredulousness. She recollects Daniel as a lot of things—curious. Brave to the point of carelessness—he'd gotten shot, himself, in an altercation with a prisoner he was transporting, the prisoner then running away, never to be caught. At least that was the story everyone told—but Fiona isn't so sure. Daniel seemed too clever for that. And he sure wasn't a yes-man. "So I did my own digging, read a lot of news stories about how Daniel Ross used to box for your cousin's husband. Seemed like Luther could be telling the truth."

That was always the problem with snakes like Luther. They always *seem* like they can be telling the truth.

Fiona shifts in her chair, suddenly uncomfortable. She *seems* like she's telling the truth, too—and it's a habit that quickly becomes easy to rely on. So thrillingly easy.

"I don't know Sheriff Ross well," Fiona says softly. "Luther might could be telling the truth about her. And, well, I'd say you ought to go back to your room at the Kinship Inn—I reckon that's where you checked in?"

Colter looks away. "Never got around to it. Met up with Luther first."

"He still has your travel bag?"

Colter turns a hard gaze on her. "By now, I'm sure he's tossed it away. But I still have my gun. Bring him to me."

"Sorry, but he took off Thursday after dinner. I reckon he didn't like our quiet little evening. He's probably back in town, carousing it up—I hear tell there's a speakeasy—"

Colter tries to stand. Quickly sits, moaning.

"Mister, you're weak. Got a fever, I can tell. Not thinking straight, if you're trying to go to town to find him."

Colter frowns.

"Not your fault he double-crossed you," Fiona adds quickly. "Luther has quite a reputation throughout the whole county. Way I hear tell it, he's done that many a time. I—I think it's dangerous to confront him while you're so weakened. But listen—stay here. I can help you get strong, until the other agent comes back, Monday you said. I can bring you food, some ointment. Clean clothes." She smiles at him.

Colter nods. "That—that might be for the best."

"I'll be back soon," Fiona says. "Just stay here—no one comes to this old cabin. It's been abandoned for years."

Colter looks suspicious again. "How do you know about it, then?"

"It was my parents'," she says. "I lived here before I married. I inherited it, but we never did anything with this land. Too hard to farm." Each piece of what she's said is true, though she's rearranged the pieces to suit the meaning she wants him to take. So easy, the more she does it, to do that with bits of truth. Easier, at least, than outright lying. Less to keep track of.

She stands, acts as if she's about to leave, but turns back around. "Who told you how to find my aunt's farm? I know just about everyone here and I could tell you if they're really to be trusted—"

She stops, seeing that suspicion grow in his gaze. Best not to press too hard, too soon. She'd bought herself until Monday, she thinks, with Colter. She has to keep Colter hidden away long enough to figure out how to use him to ensnare George—and Abe. That just leaves the problem of Elias and Luther.

Colter's eyes, though, are narrowing on her. "I'm not sure I should be trusting you. Why would you help me?"

Again, stating the truth, or at least mostly the truth, works to her advantage. Fiona lets her true fear bloom in her face. "Mr. Vogel scares me. I—I think my cousin is in over her head."

Colter nods. "You are wise. He is a bad man."

Fiona gives him what she figures he'll want—and what will work best for getting him to trust her for just a little while: a submissive yet encouraging smile. He'll tell her the name soon. "Just rest. I will be back."

She steps out of the cabin, trudges away. When she gets almost out of sight of the cabin, though, she turns back, stares at it.

This is the first time she'd been back since that last awful night.

Fiona had run to Uncle Henry and Aunt Nell's a few weeks after Mama died—when Daddy had tried . . . things . . . with her. She was fourteen, but she'd sobbed like a little girl when she told her aunt and uncle the truth. Aunt Nell had gone pale, and Fiona saw the truth in her face—Fiona's father, Aunt Nell's much older brother, had done the same with her.

Would she have run back, if Aunt Nell hadn't been so cold with her? Blaming her distance and aloofness on her morning sickness when Uncle Henry whispered to her, *It's not the girl's fault.* She'd heard them, when they talked after they thought she was asleep.

And when she did sleep, she dreamed, of all things, of that crystal—no, cut-glass candy dish, and one night she ran back. Thinking, foolishly, she could get away with sneaking in, rescuing that dish. Her one pretty possession.

Daddy caught her, of course. And thank God her uncle Henry came charging into the cabin before her father could abuse her.

Fiona had taken the dish she'd come for from a box under her cot, stumbled back in the dark with Uncle Henry, crying all the way. He was silent, but she knew he forgave her.

Even after they got back to the farmhouse and found Aunt Nell sobbing, for she'd miscarried while Uncle Henry was gone, he forgave her.

Fiona turns, continues her trek back to the farmhouse.

That candy dish—she still has it. She knows right where it is, in which trunk, in the Cincinnati mansion.

When she's back, she will unpack it. Put it out somewhere. To remind her where she came from. So she never goes back.

CHAPTER 25

LILY

Saturday, November 26, 1927
8:00 a.m.

Hildy is unusually quiet on the drive to Kinship. Not surprising, with Luther's corpse in the back seat.

As Hildy quickly but expertly navigates the rises, dips, and turns of Kinship Road, Lily turns her face to the brisk wind. They have the windows down, even in the frigid cold, because of Luther.

Lily considers: Luther's injuries, though startling, don't seem severe enough to cause death. Maybe Dr. Goshen will say otherwise, but Lily's guess is that Luther must have died from the snakebite.

But when would Luther have encountered a rattlesnake? The creatures usually stayed in the woods in crevices and under rocks, especially in cold weather.

And why would Luther have been out in the woods in the middle of a cold, bitter night, after running from the Kinship Inn? But say he had been, had gotten bitten by a snake. The odds of a chance encounter with a snake are small. Maybe he'd been running, tripped, had the unfortunate luck to fall onto a snake in the woods, and in such a way that the startled, scared snake could strike an exposed bit of wrist. Would Luther have had the strength in such condition to stagger into Rossville? And if he'd been able to, had he sought help? And when did the beating take place—before or after the snakebite?

"Lily?" Hildy's voice is small, thin.

Lily looks over at her friend, whose face is pale, taut. "I'm sorry, I know this is a lot—"

"No, it's just that . . . on Thursday night, and then after the barn dance last night—"

Lily frowns. Odd timing to bring up something so frivolous. But then, Hildy is anything but frivolous. "Yeah?"

"We saw Luther both nights. Me and Tom. Jurgis and Marvena."

Thursday night? She'd spent so much time with Marvena yesterday— why hadn't she brought this up? Especially since Lily had fessed up about her own encounter with Luther?

Lily, I oughta tell you . . .

Ah. Before the wreck, Marvena had started to tell her but then encouraged Lily to go first. Still, she could have told her later, on the walk to Kinship—though Lily had just wrapped up her own confession as they arrived at the town. Or on the way to the Pentecostal church—though Marvena might have been embarrassed to do so in Benjamin's presence, while he drove, and Marvena sat up front, and Lily dozed in the back.

"I know I didn't, and I don't for a minute believe any of them had anything to do with—that," Hildy goes on, twitching her head to the side as a gesture back at Luther. "But you should probably talk with all of us. I think it's better that way. Before someone talks to you."

"What happened, Hildy?"

"I was mainly a witness. I don't want to put words in their mouths." She offers up a thin smile. "I learned that much, helping you out last year with that big-time case."

Lily sighs, turns her face to the cold wind. The *Thrilling Gumshoe* case. She has a feeling that Luther's murder—if she can solve it—will become another one for the detective magazines.

"Mr. Ross appears to have died from a rattlesnake bite." Dr. Goshen points to the bite marks on Luther's wrist. Luther's body, laid out on a table in the shadowy basement of the Kinship funeral home, already seems shrunken, unreal, a husk cast off.

Lily follows the doctor's gesture to the spot. The two piercings are just a quarter inch or so apart. "His injuries from being in a fight appear recent, but not severe enough to indicate a blow to the head sufficient to cause death," the doctor adds, confirming her earlier thoughts.

Lily's aware of the growing impatience of both Dr. Goshen and Mr. Arlington, the funeral home director. The smells of formaldehyde and lamp oil also press in on her, making her head pound, giving her every excuse to leave.

A snakebite. A beating. What did it matter?

But it does.

Because both Luther's humanity and the rule of law matter more than Lily's personal feelings. It matters because it's Lily's job.

Dr. Goshen clears his throat. "Lily, I'm sure this is hard for you—"

She holds her hand up to hush him. Something seems off-kilter.

She stares a moment longer.

Then it hits her. Luther is still wearing his winter coat, but it is un-buttoned, flapping open. His suit jacket is flat against his chest. Doesn't he usually tuck his flask in the inside top pocket? Lily pulls back his jacket. A thin cigarette case, and a Zippo lighter. No flask.

She checks his pant pockets. There's loose change.

Checks the pockets of his overcoat. One glove per pocket.

No flask, and no automobile keys.

Where is his automobile?

And where is his flask?

Maybe it's just a small, pointless detail, but she's never seen Luther without his flask. Why, he'd even had the gall two years before to show up at her first swearing in as sheriff—when she took her husband's po-sition by special appointment—sipping from his flask.

"Lily, for God's sake, can we wrap this up?" Dr. Goshen snaps.

Lily looks up at him with a small frown.

"I'm sorry," Dr. Goshen says. "The last two days have been—long."

"I can sympathize." Lily is too weary to hold back a note of irony. Her gaze hardens on the doctor. "Very long indeed. After I got back home on Thursday night, I learned that Luther Ross, and another man, had come by my house looking for you, for medicine for Elias Ross—he'd been a doctor in the county—"

"I know who he is!" Dr. Goshen snaps. He's glaring at her, but his face has also brightened with red splotches. There's an uneasy defensiveness in his next words. "Luther and the other man—Abe Miller—were waiting for me at my home. My wife, God love her, such a stickler for rules"—he shakes his head—"wouldn't dispense medicine without my say-so. She thought I should go see the patient, but it was so late, and Luther already knew what Elias took—a common enough medicine, which Elias had simply forgotten while packing for his trip—so I gave them the pills."

"You just *gave* Luther the medicine? Without going out to check on Elias?"

Goshen looks away. "It was late, Lily. A common medicine. Elias himself is a doctor."

This still strikes her as, at best, lazy, if not technically malpractice.

"And then what? After you handed over the pills?"

"They left."

"They just—left. Together. No discussion."

"That's right."

Lily reflects. Thursday night, Luther and Abe were out, seeking help for Elias. Friday morning, Luther and Special Agent Barnaby Sloan were in her office and Luther had downplayed Elias's health concerns, which Lily hadn't believed. He'd made it seem like he'd gone back to the Murphy farmhouse, and indeed Elias must have recovered, for Luther to be out in Kinship on Friday night, at the speakeasy.

Yet Fiona and Abe had also come by Lily's house on Friday afternoon, reporting their—well, Fiona's concern that Luther had never returned to the house since Thursday night.

Where had he spent Thursday night, then? And Friday, after leaving her office? And why had he been at the Kinship speakeasy with Arlie Whitcomb, who earlier had been at Marvena's strict Pentecostal church?

Fiona had cleverly left word about the local alcohol being poisoned, sufficient to trigger Lily's raid of the speakeasy. Had she—or George or Abe—had good reason to think Luther would be there, would hope that Lily would capture him?

Why? Wouldn't they be afraid Luther would, in that case, sell George out? Or was that the hope Fiona might have had?

And now Hildy's indicated that she, Tom, Marvena, and Jurgis had seen Luther both Thursday and Friday evening.

It's all a confusing swirl—Luther's comings and goings. And there are just too many people—probably many she couldn't even name—who would be plenty glad to see Luther dead. If she could fill in the gaps of where Luther had been on Thursday night, on Friday between her meeting with him and the raid, and then after the raid, maybe she could figure out how he'd ended up dead, in Rossville, by Saturday morning.

Lily regards Dr. Goshen. "Have you seen Luther Ross since Thursday night?"

"No," he says evenly.

"Even from, say, across the street?"

"No."

"Didn't see him sometime yesterday?"

"No, Lily."

Lily studies the doctor for a long moment. He simply looks weary. She can't think of any reason he'd lie to her, about Luther Ross, of all people.

"Well. I see no reason not to release Luther to his next of kin." She looks at Mr. Arlington. "I expect that Elias Ross will be calling on you later today, or tomorrow."

Lily emerges from the funeral home and stands for a long moment on the front porch, taking in the lengthening light of late morning. Snow has stopped falling, and what has already fallen is packed down on the streets by automobiles and pedestrians, the slightly muted and slower version of Kinship's Saturday morning bustle.

Such a lovely scene. And she would like nothing more than to spend it doing a little shopping herself, but there is much work to be done.

She needs to track down Arlie, the last person she's aware of having seen Luther. Revisit the Harkinses and gently ask Ruth what she might know of the missing agent.

First, though, she has to visit Elias on the Murphy farm.

The very thought staggers her. Lily leans into the porch column. It had been hard enough, that meeting yesterday with Luther, seeing him again for a few seconds last night.

But to confront Elias? Though she'd never liked Luther, she'd loved her husband's uncle Elias. Daniel had seen him as a father, looked up to him, and so Lily had, too. She'd respected and trusted him for years—up until the moment, a few years ago, when she'd discovered the shocking truth: Elias had, more so even than Luther, been a factor in all the threads and conspiracies that eventually led to her husband Daniel's murder.

And worse, to see him in the presence of George? He, too, had betrayed her husband, and though he'd come to regret it, he has clearly moved past caring, given that he's brought Luther and Elias into his fold.

On top of that, Special Agent Barnaby Sloan believes George is planting a bootlegging operation, right here in Bronwyn County, at the Murphy farm.

Should she telegram Barnaby? Let him know of Luther's demise?

But no—according to Zebediah, the other agent, Colter DeHaven, had come to Kinship earlier than planned. Gotten himself shot.

She still doesn't know where Colter might be.

Whether she should trust Barnaby.

This visit to the Murphy farm to deliver bad news is a standard part of her job.

How bitterly ironic—Luther had wanted to draw her out to the farm, into an encounter, she'd suspected, with George.

Now she's going out to the farm to inform Elias and the others of his death.

She'll assess the situation while there, decide whether to bring Barnaby and the agency back in.

Just doing her job . . . but it will test every bit of mettle she has.

"Lily?"

Benjamin's voice lifts her from the darkness of her thoughts. He's standing below her on the funeral home's porch steps.

"I ran into Hildy at the hardware store," he says. "She filled me in on Luther's death."

He fishes in his pocket, holds out his automobile keys. "I'm guessing you have quite a few places to get to. I assured Hildy I'd make sure you can get where you're going. She wanted to get back to Rossville. Tutoring students, she said, who need extra help—even if it is a Saturday."

Well, that sounds like Hildy.

What if she also wanted to forewarn Tom, Marvena, and Jurgis that Lily would want to question them?

Lily shakes her head to clear it. This is what being weary, and caught back up in the world of Luther and Elias and George, would do to her—make her doubt her oldest friend's integrity. If Hildy wanted to cover for herself, or any of them, she could have just not mentioned that they'd seen Luther on Thursday and again on Friday, probably after that damned barn dance.

Benjamin smiles, kindly. Lily's heart pings. So silly, wishing she could have gone to that damned barn dance with him after all. And not to bear witness to Luther's encounter with her friends, more 'n likely after the dance. Lily can't imagine Luther kicking up his heels.

She pinches the bridge of her nose. Her shoulder twinges, just from that small movement. She nearly groans at the notion of driving, at the thought of where she'll be driving, out to the Murphy farm. Barnaby had commented the land was well situated—between an offshoot near the main road, and another local gravel road. She thinks back to her visit with Nell Murphy, after her husband's death. Lily doesn't fully recollect the lay of the land. If Benjamin drives, she can note it carefully, in detail—where are the ridges, the dips. Just in case Barnaby is right and she notes goings-on that justify going back with a warrant and deputies, or the bureau. She'll want to be aware of where George's men might have the high ground, might be hiding to ambush any law officers.

Benjamin had been more helpful than she'd expected yesterday.

That's all this is, Lily tells herself. She just needs a bit of help. Lily puts her hand to her sore shoulder. "I appreciate your offer, but if you can stand me taking more of your time, I could use a *chauffeur*."

Benjamin hesitates. Oh, of course. He doesn't really approve of her job. But then he smiles. "I don't mind."

Lily ducks her head down as she descends, hoping he doesn't see her cheeks flame.

"Oh—and I checked with the three other homes with rooms to let," Benjamin says as she comes up beside him. "No Colter DeHaven."

Lily lifts her eyebrows. Well. That was a lot of effort. Maybe he regrets his comments from the night before. But her only comment is, "That was quick."

"I usually read on my time off," Benjamin says. "This was a change of pace."

She waits for him to wisecrack about playing detective, but he doesn't. Instead, he says, "If he didn't take a room, hasn't left a trace, maybe he thought he was only coming for the day, that his business would be over quickly."

"Interesting point," Lily says. "Did you happen to check at the Kinship Inn?"

Benjamin looks chagrined. "No."

"That's all right," Lily says brusquely, regaining her confidence now that she can switch back to a professional focus. "I need to see if, by any chance, Luther looped back after we left and checked in."

"Slow down," Lily says.

Benjamin isn't going too fast, but the lane to the Murphy farm is roughly rutted, far more so than it had been nearly four weeks ago. The weather isn't enough to explain the deterioration of the dirt lane. Only numerous vehicles would explain that.

Luther hadn't, as it turned out, checked into the Kinship Inn late Friday night, after the raid was over.

So had he and Arlie headed over to Rossville? Gone by the barn dance for some reason? She thinks back to the meeting, just yesterday morning, at her office with Luther and Barnaby. To her doubts that George would come here just to spend time with Fiona and her aunt when he could be relaxing at his well-appointed Cincinnati mansion.

After leaving Kinship, Lily had asked Benjamin to go to her house, where she'd quickly retrieved Fiona's leather gloves, setting the note aside in a drawer in her bureau and writing her own to tuck into the left-hand glove.

Sure, maybe Fiona would come out for the holiday to visit her aunt. But then there was Fiona and Abe's odd visit, to announce Luther missing—and Fiona leaving that note about George tainting the local alcohol supply. A risk Fiona had taken? Or something she'd done, for some reason, at George's direction?

And then the local alcohol supply hadn't been poisoned after all. A change in plans? Or had it never been meant to be poisoned?

It's all such a tangled web. Will she ever be able to sort it all out?

Now Lily says, "Stop—but slowly." She points to a branch that's fallen on the lane.

Benjamin does but protests as Lily starts to exit his automobile. "Lily, I can move that—"

She shakes her head. "The branch hasn't fallen from the weight of snow or ice. Look at the end." There's a clean cut where the branch had been. Someone has sawed it off, left it there deliberately to slow anyone approaching.

She thinks, *If George has men watching, then those who are welcome would have a sign they could give to indicate they're friend, not foe.*

Maybe it's a blessing that her automobile, with its distinctive sheriff's star on the door, is still in the repair shop. For most people, the emblem might generate wariness but also respect. For George's people, it just might cause his hired guns to start shooting.

"Keep your hands on the wheel and if anything bad happens, back up as fast as you can and get out of here and gather up my deputies," Lily says.

Benjamin frowns, puts his hand on her arm. "Lily, I can't just let you—"

"What?" she snaps. "Do my job?"

She jerks her arm away, grimaces at the sharp pain in her shoulder.

She gets out of the passenger side and lifts her hands slowly and as far as her stiff shoulder will allow. "Yoo-hoo!" she calls. "I'm Lily Ross. I have news for Elias Ross and George Vogel."

Two men, one on either side of the lane, emerge just in front of the large limb, rifles aimed at her.

CHAPTER 26

⁂

FIONA

Saturday, November 26, 1927
2:00 p.m.

Fiona enters Elias's room, again toting a tray. With her hip, she pushes the bedroom door nearly shut. She brings the tray to the side table, ignoring Elias's worried gaze as she arranges the food—a bowl of turkey noodle soup, some biscuits, a glass of buttermilk—on the table. She puts the tray on his lap.

"Any word on Luther?" Elias's voice is fearful.

Fiona returns the tray to the side table. "Why, yes, I'll be glad to help you eat your soup, Elias," she says loudly. Then she cuts her eyes to the door.

No one is out in the hallway at the moment—all the men are gathered in the parlor, endlessly reviewing every detail of George's plans with him—but let Elias think differently. Anything to stoke his fear and paranoia, keep him reliant on her.

Elias nods to show he takes in her meaning.

But he whispers, *"Luther,"* his voice breaking on his nephew's name.

Fiona isn't quite ready to tell him what she's learned from the revenuer Colter, who is—she hopes—still in the old cabin. She'd gone back to the main house, gathered food, a spare quilt, and hurried back, mostly certain that she hadn't been seen. She has a story ready in case she has—she'd become sentimental, doing those last chores, and wanted to spend some time in her childhood haunts.

Haunts.

Such a perfect word.

Ever since tending to Colter—bringing him the food, dressing his head wound, bringing him cold water, settling him in, getting a small fire going in the old fireplace—she'd felt nothing but haunted. She'd paused on her trek back to the house, stared back to check to see if smoke from the fireplace was obvious. Thankfully, it is a cloudy, gray day, so any smoke quickly blends into the sky, and a sharp, cutting wind from the northwest whisks away lingering tendrils. The wind also portends worse storms to come in the next few days.

She'd made sure to tell Colter about the coming bad weather, prattling on about signs and portents from nature—some she'd learned from Aunt Nell, others that she just made up to sound authentic enough to this city fellow—to scare him into staying put.

When she got back to the house, she'd stuffed her aunt's dress at the bottom of her trunk, underneath some of her own clothes. So far, Colter hasn't questioned that she's anything other than what she's play-acting. But George will quickly have questions if she's not neat, clean, dressed in the modern fashions that she prefers—so fetching in Cincinnati or Chicago at their fine dinners, but ridiculously impractical here.

Even so, by the time she shook George awake this morning from his fitful sleep she was dressed as he expected.

Her sleek, sleeveless dress made carrying the blue bottle difficult, but she'd found one of Aunt Nell's bulky sweaters and put it on, complaining that the house was cold, implying to George that this was just a symptom of being pregnant. She'd transferred the bottle from the bottom of her trunk and into the sweater pockets a few minutes ago.

Now she shakes her head. "No word on Luther yet." Other than from the injured man in the old cabin, who swears Luther shot him, left him for dead.

She pulls out the blue bottle. "But I found this."

Elias's expression turns solidly passive.

Fiona looks at the bottle, reads the label aloud as if for the first time. "*Two tablespoons each morning and evening. For ulcerative stomach disorder. Dispense for Henry Murphy only.*"

She clicks her gaze to Elias. "You surely have stomach pains, with the stress of working for my husband." She drops her voice to a sly whisper. "I should put some in your soup."

Elias swallows hard, gives his head a little shake. "I—I don't think—"

"Oh, you don't want it?" Fiona pops the cork. "Well, I'm certainly having stomach pains. Probably sore from morning sickness. This would be even more effective on an empty stomach, don't you think?"

She puts it up to her lips as if to take a sip, and Elias grabs her arm so suddenly that some of the medicine sloshes out, dotting the quilt. Elias looks at the wet spot of the medicine in horror, as if it will sizzle right through Aunt Nell's handiwork and onto him.

"I found this in the woodshop," Fiona says. "Next to the rat poison. Arsenic. I'm guessing you mixed it into the medicine, on your and George's visit here."

"It was Dr. Goshen's idea," Elias says.

He's so defensive—as if the doctor's idea was what tainted the medicine, and not his own action—that he doesn't seem to note the quick flash of surprise across Fiona's face. Dr. Goshen? Of course—that fancy ring Mrs. Goshen wore. The doctor's solicitousness toward her and Abe. Goshen's proximity in town to the speakeasy. Of course George would have gotten to him, pulled him in.

She should have put that together earlier.

"He'd been treating your uncle for months anyway, before we came to him to propose he work with us," Elias goes on. "If Henry had just agreed to sell the farm, as your aunt Nell wanted him to—oh yes, she encouraged him to take the very generous offer, said she wanted to leave here, go to Florida, said it right in front of us—then I wouldn't have had to poison him. But, in the end, your aunt loved your uncle more than the thought of Florida, and your uncle loved this land more than her. So I did what I had to do."

"But you didn't *have* to do it."

Fiona puts the stopper in the blue bottle. "Instead, my uncle's stomach pains only got worse as he kept taking more medicine—more poisoned medicine—thinking he was treating the problem. He'd have died in a few weeks if he hadn't gotten so weak he fell off the tractor and the blades hadn't sliced his head open."

Elias winces at the graphic description. *Apparently,* Fiona thinks bitterly, *he prefers murdering from a distance.*

"If it helps, he might have truly died from a cardiac event, triggered by the tachycardia the arsenic could have caused, before he fell from the tractor. That could be why he fell, might have been dead before he hit the ground—"

"Helps?" Fiona's voice grows loud, and now Elias gives a warning glance toward the door. She drops her tone back to a whisper. "I'm surprised you're admitting all this so easily."

Elias's smile is small but sufficient to alarm Fiona. "What are you going to do? Tell George?"

Of course not. Then Elias could reveal that she'd tried to stop the plan to poison drinkers at the Kinship speakeasy. As furious as he'd be with Elias, he'd be even more so with her, and while she didn't think he'd hurt her while she was pregnant with his child, he'd certainly never trust her again. He'd likely reverse the paperwork putting his property in her name. And there would be the time *after* she'd had the child.

"I could tell Sheriff Ross—"

"You could. But even if you could get to her, even if she believed you, how would you keep it from George?" Elias's smile broadens, stretching his dry lips taut and thin. "And how would either of you prove it? Everyone keeps rat poison on hand."

"Why?" Fiona hates that she sounds weak. Pitiable. "Why are you so bent on working for George, just because Luther wants to?"

"Luther is like a son to me. Both my nephews were, but Luther is all I have left. All I have of the family I once had—once wanted to have." Elias's eyes grow watery, and he looks at her as if she is, after all, nothing more than a nursemaid whose role is to be sympathetic. "And Luther wants, more than anything, to reestablish himself in Bronwyn County, in Rossville. I'm sorry, Fiona."

She forces her gaze to soften as she studies him. But he's not sorry he killed her uncle. He's sorry it was necessary, and that she's sussed it out.

The only way to make her uncle's death not a waste is to carry on with her plan to outwit George. She'll deal with Elias in time.

A knock comes on the door, and then the door opens. It's Klara. "Pardon me," she says. "Sheriff Lily Ross is here. She needs to talk with you."

Fiona stills, even as her heart thuds in her chest. *Oh God.* What if the revenuer was right? What if Lily was not to be trusted? She needs to buy time, to grab a few things—just her coat and hat, sturdy boots—and she can go down the back stairs, out the kitchen, run after all.

"Oh well, just give me a minute to finish helping Elias with his meal."

"She's not here for you," Klara says. She looks at Elias. "She needs to speak to *you.*"

As Fiona helps Elias walk into the parlor, holding him by the elbow, she barely notices Elias's sharp intake of breath as he spots Lily, sitting on the edge of a parlor chair.

There's that look in Lily's face again—pity mixed with revulsion, though now it's turned on Elias. And there's an extra measure of revulsion.

Lily does not seem to notice, or doesn't care about, all the others staring at her: George on the couch gazing at her with a mix of amusement and respect; Abe in a side chair, wary; Klara, hovering in the entry to the dining area, affronted. Well, of course. What else would Klara think of a delicate, petite woman who is, of all things, a county sheriff?

And then there's a stranger, a handsome man who'd apparently come with Lily. He doesn't wear a badge, doesn't have an air of law enforcement about him. He looks intelligent, wry, a bit bookish. But he, too, is staring at Lily with—something. Fiona can't quite name it.

As Fiona helps Elias to a chair, she recollects how she and Lily had never gotten along well when they'd both been simple housewives. Lily had worked as the jail matron, and Fiona occasionally helped if it got very busy in Martin's shoe shop, and they both attended the Presbyterian church and Woman's Club. So much alike, on the surface.

Fiona keeps her expression pleasingly placid as she sits down next to George on the sofa. She studies Lily, taking in how delicate she appears, in spite of her heavy work boots and old-fashioned navy blue cotton dress, long sleeved and mid-calf length. Even with those boots, Lily crosses her ankles like a lady, makes herself seem taller by holding her posture even and tall, though one shoulder seems slightly bowed, as if weighted by a great burden. Her hair is swept up in a prim bun, with a few rogue strands flying loose.

But, up close now, Fiona sees that Lily has aged. Oh, she's still blessed with a smooth, porcelain complexion. But there's a wariness, a darkness, about her that Fiona couldn't have noted as she hovered in the bank's doorway yesterday and Lily stood at the top of the courthouse steps.

And Lily's eyes glint with hardness, betraying no emotion, as she locks her gaze on Elias.

Interesting. At one time, Fiona thought, Lily had adored her uncle-by-marriage. But not a glimmer of that adoration remains.

"I'm here because Mrs. Vogel and Mr. Miller came to my house yesterday afternoon," Lily says, measured and unemotional. "They were concerned about Luther having gone missing, while out to collect heart medicine for you."

"Yes," Elias says, though his wobbly tone belies his affirmation.

And in Elias's expression, Fiona sees several emotions besides worry over Luther or his own health. Sorrow. Longing. And, oh—even more interesting than Lily's flat affect. *Fear.*

Fiona presses her lips together to mimic concern and to disguise a smile at a realization: How Elias and Lily feel toward each other can be another tool for her to use somehow. She doesn't need to understand the *why* of their feelings.

"I'm better, thank you," Elias says, though Lily hasn't asked. "What have you learned about Luther? Is he in lockup? He struggles sometimes with his habits, so if he needs bail—"

"I know from Dr. Goshen and his wife that after Abe and Luther got the medicine on Thursday night they left quickly," Lily says. She looks at Abe. "And I know, from your and Mrs. Vogel's visit to my house on

Friday afternoon, that you all were concerned that he hadn't shown back up here. Has he been back here at all?"

Abe studies her, carefully assessing. Even Abe, Fiona notes with fascination, looks a little rattled under Lily's gaze. "He has not," Abe says finally.

"Any idea where he might have been all this time, since Thursday night?"

Abe shakes his head.

"Odd, him running off, entrusting Elias's medicine with you," Lily says. "Not that you can't be trusted, of course. It's just that I know how close Elias and Luther are." She looks at Elias, and he flinches. "Like father and son."

"Sheriff Ross," George says, "this is all quite—fascinating, I'm sure. But I have work to do, and I'm hoping you'll get to your point sooner rather than later?"

"Lily, please, if you know anything—" Elias stops, his voice knotting up in a pitiful strangling sound as Lily holds up a hand to hush him. God, Fiona had no idea Lily could be so cold. "Do you know why Luther might be away so long, after being so worried about his uncle?" Lily presses George.

George chuckles. "No, I don't. Luther is a bit—unpredictable at times. You know that."

Lily gives a cold smile. "No, I'd say he is predictable. I spotted Luther at a speakeasy at the Kinship Inn. I got a tip that led to a raid."

Fiona's heart pounds. What if Lily betrays that Fiona tucked a note inside one of her gloves?

But Lily shrugs. "Nothing unusual. It seems that no matter how often we raid the Kinship Inn, the speakeasy is back a few weeks later. I spotted Luther at the inn—along with Arlie Whitcomb. A cousin of Marvena Whitcomb Sacovech's. Does anyone know how Luther might have come to be connected with Arlie—especially given that Luther and Marvena haven't been on friendly terms, to put it mildly?"

George and Abe just stare back flatly. It seems clear that they don't know what's going on with Luther, at least since Thursday night.

"When did Luther arrive here?" Lily asks.

"Thursday, with us," Abe says.

"'Us' meaning?"

"Myself, George, Elias, security guard who drove us."

"But not Fiona, or—" Lily looks at Klara, who flinches. Fiona bites back a smile. "Who are you?"

"Mrs. Klara Schneider," Klara says primly. "I work for Mr. Vogel, have for a long time. Mrs. Vogel, myself, and another driver came on Tuesday. To help Mrs. Murphy prepare for Thanksgiving."

"Another driver—but not Luther."

"He came as they say. Thursday," Klara says smoothly.

How easily she lies, Fiona thinks with some admiration—but also makes a mental note.

"I see." Lily turns to Fiona so rapidly that Fiona almost startles. "I'd like to speak with your aunt Nell. Where might she be?"

The question catches Fiona off-guard. She's nearly forgotten about Aunt Nell, with all that's happened. George squeezes her hand, too hard. The message is clear: *Answer carefully.*

Fiona's face reddens. A flash of worry crosses Lily's expression. But Fiona can use the flush of fear flooding her cheeks to her advantage. "Well, you see, I—I am in the family way. And I've been corresponding with Aunt Nell about that, and since this farm is overwhelming to her without dear Uncle Henry, she wondered about selling it to me. As a place to get away. A country retreat, if you will. And I agreed! Isn't that good news, Lily?"

"Delightful," Lily says flatly. "I'd still like to speak with her."

"I'm afraid she left Friday on the train, Lily," Fiona says. "She's moving to Florida."

At that, Lily finally looks shaken. "Just like that? She didn't want to say good-bye to anyone in town?"

"She didn't have many friends. Most have passed, or moved away. She just wanted a fresh start after losing her husband." Fiona tightens her tone, drives home the point. "I'm sure you can understand, Lily."

But Lily is not so easily rattled. She keeps her gaze tightly clasped on Fiona, who dares not look away. "I do," Lily says. "Well then, if I could speak to Leon. Surely he is here?"

Oh. Fiona's heart clenches. It was one thing to not give a passing thought to Aunt Nell over the past hectic hours. But Leon—*oh.* She hadn't thought of him all day, either. "He is back at his private school." Her voice sounds wispy, and she clears her throat. "Philadelphia. Short holiday, and all—"

George interrupts, "What is the point, Lily?"

To Fiona's relief, Lily's gaze clicks back over to George. Fiona forces herself to inhale slowly. Suddenly the room, with its overstuffed furniture and so many people, feels suffocating.

"Just making sure Luther truly came on Thursday," Lily says. "To eliminate the possibility he had time to go into town, stir things up as he tends to do, and get in trouble."

Lily turns back to Elias and fixes her stark gaze on him for a few seconds, long enough for the room to still again. "Luther is dead. He was found this morning in Rossville," Lily says, each word hard as a slap. "He'd been beaten, but also, it appears, bitten by a snake."

Elias falls back in his chair, hands clasping at his heart. For a moment, he's so silent, so shocked, that Fiona fears he's expired instantly from the shock of losing his beloved nephew. But then a long, thin wail rises from him.

Fiona checks George and Abe. They look surprised but not shocked—it's not shocking that death would come to a man like Luther, who made enemies more easily than friends and blustered with bravado at every turn. It's more shocking that he's lived this long. But the surprise tells Fiona that her husband and his right-hand man had nothing to do with it.

She glances at Lily, who has looked away from Elias, not because of his pained bereavement, but to also study George and Abe. She, too, sees the surprise on their faces.

"So was it an accident or did someone kill him?" George asks.

"I don't know," Lily says. "That's why I'm trying to establish exactly when Luther arrived, who he might have interacted with. But from your testimony, he came here on Thursday and the only time he would have had to see others was between late Thursday night and whenever he died, probably in the early hours of this morning. I'm hoping to find Arlie Whitcomb, who may be the last person who saw Luther alive. You're all sure you don't know Arlie, or where he is?" Silence. "If anyone has a sudden recollection about Arlie, let me know." She stands up, stares down at Elias, who is now bent forward, head in his hands, crying softly. "But you're free to arrange for his burial. His body is at the funeral home."

Lily pauses. Fiona watches her carefully, sees that Lily is trying to decide whether or not to say what's on her mind. Does she know about the revenuer? She's a law woman—would the bureau have already been in touch with Lily, if they think their man is missing?

In spite of her best intentions to remain calm, her face flushes. She's afraid of Lily Ross.

Lily pulls Fiona's gloves out of her pocket, walks over to Fiona, holds the pair out to her. "Oh, I almost forgot. You left these at my house the other day. You might want them. Feels like another winter storm is coming."

Fiona takes the gloves. Abe is looking at her, so she just coolly tucks them into the pocket of Aunt Nell's bulky sweater, while patting Elias with absent-mindedly offered comfort as Lily says to George, "If I learn anything new about Luther, I'm assuming I can return with the information without fear of one of your men shooting me?"

George chuckles. "I suppose. Depending on why you're returning."

Lily's only response is to arch an eyebrow.

As she leaves, the man accompanying her follows, and Fiona finally interprets how he looks at Lily: With admiration, yes. But also respect.

No one, certainly not a man, has ever looked at her like that.

CHAPTER 27

LILY

Dusk drapes the hills and nestles into the hollers by the time Lily and Benjamin are on the topmost rise of Kinship Road, just before plunging into the coal town still called Rossville, though Wessex Corporation now rules. Lily can barely see to add to the notes she's been writing out on the drive over, but she quickly looks them over.

So, on late Thursday afternoon Luther had left with Abe Miller from the Murphy farm to get medicine for Elias. They'd arrived at Dr. Goshen's, then, sometime after 4:00 p.m. They'd come to Lily's later that evening, looking for Dr. Goshen, then gone back to the doctor's house, gotten the medicine in the evening. But for some reason, after getting the medicine Luther had entrusted Abe with it and not returned to the Murphy farm that night or at any point since—assuming George and Fiona and Elias were telling the truth.

On Friday morning, Luther had turned up at her office with Barnaby and both men claimed Luther was working undercover for the Bureau of Prohibition. Luther said he'd arrived in Bronwyn County on Thursday, along with George and Elias and Abe—but they could have easily been lying. On the other hand, they seemed genuinely surprised at the news of his death.

Yet she's verified he did not check in at the Kinship Inn before Thursday, and Benjamin had confirmed for her that Luther also hadn't checked in Friday night. He hadn't been back to the Murphy place. So where had he been staying? With Arlie?

After all, Lily and Benjamin spotted him at the Kinship speakeasy on Friday night. He ran off with Arlie and, according to Hildy, turned up in Rossville and had a run-in with her, Marvena, Tom, and Jurgis—an event that Lily needs to check into.

Then Luther turned up dead in Rossville on Saturday, the next morning, from a poisonous snakebite, according to Dr. Goshen's assessment.

Lily finally closes her notebook and stares out at the stark iced tree limbs flickering by as Benjamin drives slowly on the slick road. His carefulness, for one thing, had ensured she could write out her notes. Even more than his caution, Lily appreciates that he's been silent since they left the Murphy farm. She senses that he's unsettled by how cold she'd been about Luther's death and in delivering that news to Elias, but he hasn't asked her to explain.

She wouldn't know exactly what to say if he did ask. She can't imagine revealing, not yet, the complete truth about how Luther and Elias betrayed Daniel in ways that led to his death.

Seeing Luther had been unpleasant, but she'd never cared for him in the first place. He'd always been crude and unkind, always mocked Daniel as a "half-breed" because Daniel's mother—the second wife of his and Luther's father—was Indian.

But Elias—brother to the father of Daniel and Luther—had been more like a father to Daniel than an uncle. Elias's steady, constant presence had been a source of comfort and reassurance while Daniel was away in the Great War.

Elias's betrayal had rent her to her depths, left behind a rankling cold thorn. Seeing him had only ripped her open again, made her see that all this time since Daniel's death she'd just been pushing that thorn deeper, as if she could bury it.

Benjamin pulls to a stop in front of one of the squat, simple miners' houses that line up along either side of the road like sentries.

"Is this the right one?" Benjamin's question is the first time he's spoken on the drive.

Lily looks at the house, the neat lace curtains in the window, the handmade wreath on the door. Hildy's touches, though Hildy doesn't live here—not officially at least. Lily suspects her friend spends more nights here, in Tom's house, than she does in her own.

"Yes," Lily says. "It's Tom's place."

She should get out, go inside, get a move on with interrogating Tom, and later Jurgis and Marvena, about their encounters with Luther. Lily swallows hard, her stomach turning at the awfulness of having to interrogate her friends about the murder of a man she reviles.

"I can go in, or I can stay here, either way," Benjamin says.

Lily looks at him, his dark eyes wide and encompassing, while he waits for her to tell him what she wants.

All at once, what she wants is to not have to ask anything of anyone. Lily wants to pull him to her, feel his warmth, his touch, his kindness. For that to be enough to at last expel the venomous cold that's rankled deep inside her all along since Daniel's death, numbing her from the inside out, as if her soul has been frostbitten.

But Benjamin cannot heal her. Only time, and her own choice to let go of the cold deep inside her, can do that. Maybe then she'll be ready for Benjamin. Or someone like him. She has no way to know when that might be, though.

"It's up to you," she says.

Lily opens the automobile door, steps out into the cold, shuts the door behind her. She forces herself to stare straight ahead as she ascends the porch steps.

But when she hears Benjamin get out of his automobile and follow her, she smiles, just a little, to herself.

Tom's company-owned house is crowded: Jurgis, Marvena, Nana, and Frankie have come down from Marvena's cabin on this Saturday night to share supper and, Lily guesses, to face her together. From their somber expressions, Hildy has forewarned them.

As Lily and Benjamin take off their coats and get settled, Nana shoos Frankie and Alistair into the kitchen to help her make rolls for Sunday morning breakfast. Warm, sweet scents soon waft out, as does Nana's tender fussing at the children not to eat *all* of the sugar-cinnamon filling—a rare treat—before it can be used in the rolls.

Here, in the tiny room—Jurgis and Marvena on a small couch, the rest of them on kitchen table chairs pulled from around the table—the atmosphere is cold, even with the coal-fired stove in the kitchen warming up the house.

"I'm here to talk with each of you about the death of Luther Ross," Lily says. "Now, I haven't seen any of you since Thanksgiving at my house"—dear Lord, has it only been two days since they'd all gathered at her house, cheerfully enjoying one another's company, no idea of the storm that was to descend on all of them?—"except Hildy when she fetched me this morning, and Tom and Jurgis briefly after I arrived to the scene of Luther's being found. I won't say 'murder' site, because I don't believe he was killed outside the coal-mining company. I spent a good deal of time with Marvena on Friday. Yet it was Hildy who told me this morning that you all had run-ins with Luther both Thursday night and last night after the barn dance."

"Started to tell you on Friday about the night before," Marvena mumbles, still looking down at her nervously clasped hands, "but in the end, I didn't. Had a fool hope that his presence would amount to nothing. But that vermin ain't nothing but trouble."

"Just speak plain, Marvena," Lily says.

"You don't have to speak at all!" Jurgis snaps. He puts his hand on Marvena's back, a tender gesture that, in spite of the stifling tension, Lily is relieved to observe. He might be disappointed in what he sees as Marvena's lack of faith, but he still believes in her.

Marvena takes Jurgis's hand into her own, and finally, she's no longer twitching. "After we left your place, Jurgis and me, we got into a fight over what I done. He said I ain't given our church's way the time it needs. Then Tom got into it, defending me, and Nana and the children got upset, and Hildy used her toughest schoolmarm voice to shut us all up."

Despite the grimness of Marvena's description, Lily allows herself a small grin.

"We went on in silence, until we got here. Hildy was helping them unload things, before heading to her place, of course—" Well, more likely, from Hildy's blush, she was going to stay the night, and though Lily knows that's frowned upon, she can't help but think, *Good for you, Hildy.* A twinge of envy, that Hildy can embrace love again, spikes Lily's heart. She twists on the chair, tries to find a more comfortable angle. "And we were fixing to load up the mule cart, and figure how to get Nana and Frankie to it without waking them up—they'd fallen asleep the last little bit of the drive—when, well, Luther staggered by. He was by himself—no hired men with him. So drunk, he was staggering around like a rabid racoon. Meaner, too. Spotted us, started yelling that he'd show me. That's all he said—*I'll show you.* Like he was fixing to do something."

"You sure he put it like that, like he'd do something in the future?"

Marvena nods. "That's what he said. Then again, his speech was slushy."

Lily considers what she'd already wondered—could Luther have shot Colter, left him for dead at Marvena's still, make it seem like Marvena had killed him? "Go on."

But Jurgis speaks next. "Lily, I shouted at Luther to get lost. I know I shouldna 'cause of course that just egged on the sot. He laughed, said he was back, had *been* back for a while and staying at the boardinghouse in Rossville, right under our noses."

Ah. So everyone at the Murphy farm today—Elias and George, Abe and Fiona, even the housekeeper, Klara—had lied. Luther has been back in the area for a while, but not staying at the Kinship Inn. Staying, instead, at the boardinghouse.

That would put him in the area at the same time as Colter. And could explain how he might have run into Arlie, who lives in this part of the county.

"He said we were all too dumb to catch on," Jurgis is saying, "and that soon he'd have Wessex Corporation sell the mine back to him and it'd be Ross Mining again and he didn't have to listen to miners and their—well, he used an unsavory term."

Hildy glances at the entry to the kitchen, where the children and Nana are still caught up in their own chatter. She leans forward, whispers, "He said '*whores,*' Lily. He called us whores."

"Oh God." Lily swallows hard. Though no one cares about Luther's opinion, words like that still sting. Her gaze is drawn to Benjamin, to wonder what he thinks of all this, but she can't read his face. He is calm. Inscrutable.

"But we ignored him," Tom adds, "until he ran over and grabbed Alistair by the arm. Alistair was about to shake him off, but Luther just spit in my boy's face. Said he'd be back in the mines soon. And this time, he'd see to it that a dynamite blast would lay open his guts and what little brains he has."

Lily's teeth clench until she feels the pressure in her temples. How had they kept from killing Luther on the spot?

"Well, I started beating on Luther, first to get him off Alistair," Tom confesses. "But then I couldn't stop—"

"And I joined in," Jurgis says. "I wanted to kill him, Lily."

"We all did," Marvena says.

Even Hildy nods.

Well, Lily doesn't blame them for such feelings. Maybe even for acting on the impulse, as awful as Luther has been to all of them in the past. But the rule of law applies, even to one as loathsome as Luther. Maybe especially. If exceptions are made, where are those lines drawn?

"Hildy put a stop to it," Marvena says. "By then, Nana and Frankie were awake, and terrified. Hildy pulled Alistair out of the melee, ordered Jurgis and Tom to stop acting like damned fools. They released Luther—and Hildy looked him dead in the eye, told him to *get his sorry ass*—them's *her* words—*outta her sight.*"

Lily can't help but look at her once quiet friend. How she's changed and grown. She gives Hildy a small smile.

But Hildy says, "I'm not proud of what happened—of any of us."

Lily nods. "You did the right thing, telling me that you all saw Luther

Thursday night. But you said you saw him here yesterday as well—that had to be after Benjamin and I saw Luther at the Kinship Inn. I'd gotten a tip that wood alcohol would be swapped into the speakeasy supply. We didn't find it. But I did see Luther at the speakeasy, along with your cousin, Marvena—Arlie. Any idea where he might be? Or why he was with Luther?"

"Heard tell Arlie moved from his old cabin," Marvena says. "Not sure exactly where to. Brother Stiles might know. But Arlie, well, he always did have a predilection for trouble—"

"He was saved just a few months ago, baptized in the river—" Jurgis protests.

"Well, I reckon he's backslid!" Marvena snaps. "Seems to be in our blood."

"Now, Marvena—" Tom starts to admonish his sister, but Hildy gives his hand a squeeze, and he hushes.

"So you don't know why Luther and Arlie would have taken up?" Lily asks.

"No," Marvena says. "I even approached Arlie when I went back to—well, you know. Brewing. But he said he wouldn't do it, warned me not to. Told me to just have faith." Her gaze softens with worry as she looks toward the kitchen. From the sounds of it, the children have settled down, fallen under Nana's spell, but Frankie is singing a hymn. Her sweet voice is so clear, so steady, that it's hard to imagine the same child can be wracked with asthmatic attacks.

"All right." Dark is already falling. Lily will have to wait until the next day to track down Arlie. "I need to ask where each of you were last night, after eight p.m."

Hildy starts to speak, but Tom cuts her off. "Hildy, you don't have to—"

"It's all right," Hildy reassures him. She looks evenly at Lily as if daring her to pass judgment. "I was here, with Tom. Alistair can vouch for Tom. I'm sure neighbors can, too."

Lily nods. She has no inclination to pass judgment on Hildy. Her passing thought is, *Good for you. For both of you.* Then she refocuses on the question at hand.

"And I'm guessing Marvena and Jurgis, you can vouch for each other, and Frankie and Nana can also—"

But Marvena abruptly stands. "Friday night, we had another special prayer meeting, for Dora Harkins. And for Frankie. Arlie showed up, with Luther."

"Why was Luther there?" Lily is taken aback. Luther was not the spiritual type.

"I don't know how or why they connected Friday night—or before—but Arlie had some cockeyed idea that Luther could find God. Be redeemed. They were both drunk, though." Marvena snorts with disgust.

Jurgis tries to pull her back into her chair. "Marvena, no, you don't gotta—"

But Marvena holds her ground, slaps his hand away. "It's better this way, Jurgis. You just take care of Frankie for me." Tears are running down her face when she looks back at Lily, but Lily knows they're not for what Marvena is about to confess. They're tears of worry for her child. She'd do anything—sacrifice anything—for Frankie. "Well, Luther disrupted our service. Some of the men pulled him out. And I ran after him. I—I was handling a rattler. He'd gotten away, but had fallen down. I set the snake upon him, Lily. I killed him with that snake. I tossed the snake into the woods, and Luther staggered away."

Jurgis stands, too, puts his arm around his wife. "She's just saying that to protect me. After he got bitten, I ran after Luther, caught up to him, and beat him up. Left him unconscious in the woods. I didn't come back home until late in the night. I knew I'd killed him."

Lily looks at Marvena, then at Jurgis. Maybe both of them are lying. Maybe only one, to protect the other. But neither is going to say they believe the other murdered Luther.

"You realize what you have done? You've both confessed to murder. I'm going to have to bring you both in—at least for a few days, until I can get this truly sorted out."

Lily looks at Benjamin. His demeanor remains still, calculated, and Lily can't help but take comfort in his steadiness. "I need you to do me a favor. Could you go to the boardinghouse, see if they'll tell you when Luther arrived?"

She returns her attention to Marvena and Jurgis. "I'll wait here, while you let Frankie and Nana know that you need to come to town with me for a bit." She fights back tears as she sees them streaming down Marvena's face and turns to Hildy and Tom. Hildy's chin quivers, but she, too, holds back her tears. "Maybe Nana and Frankie can stay here?"

"Of course," says Tom.

CHAPTER 28

※

FIONA

Saturday, November 26, 1927
10:30 p.m.

As she nears the farmhouse, Fiona shuts off the flashlight she'd found earlier on the kitchen shelf. She stands still in the near-total darkness, savoring the sensation of being, for just a moment, totally alone. She tilts her chin so that snow and ice crystals fall on her face. Not new snow; a harsh, stirring wind has unsettled earlier snowfall.

She's just come from Colter, bringing him food, making sure he's not well enough to consider leaving for the night. He still has a fever, probably from the head wound being infected. The skin around where the bullet had grazed him is red and puffy. But just to be sure, she'd put a dollop—not enough to kill him, of course—of Uncle Henry's rat-poisoned stomach medicine in a cup of tea. When he was looking away, she'd put the bottle on top of the pie safe. She doesn't want to run the risk of being caught with it. How would she explain to Abe or to George that she's discovered Uncle Henry's poisoned medicine—for they would know it was poisoned—and is carrying it around?

Then there is the news about Luther. His death has devastated Elias. He is in shock. And being in shock means he is vulnerable, and Fiona can work with vulnerability.

And what about Lily bringing back her gloves—with her own note?: *I'll be at Luther's funeral if you need help.*

The raid on the inn must have gone well or, at the very least, the forewarning had convinced Lily that Fiona was on the side of right and thus might need help.

On her slow trek back through the dark and cold, Fiona puts together the next step in her plan to unseat George and take control of all of his wealth.

She takes a deep breath of the delicious cold, steps inside the kitchen door. Now to just get back upstairs without stirring anyone.

Someone grabs her from behind, pinning her arms behind her back. She yelps, struggles to pull away, but her arms are pinned more tightly.

"Stop," Abe says. Just the one word, but it's suffused with anger. If he could get away with it, he'd snap her neck, right there in the kitchen.

"I'll tell George—"

Abe chuckles. "Yes. Yes, you will."

He shoves her, and Fiona stumbles through the kitchen to the parlor, where she sees George sitting in the wing chair in the far corner, his face partially shadowed, as there are only two coal-oil lamps lit in the dark room. The pale white skin of his fleshy ankles shows between his slippered feet and silk pajamas. He wears his robe over his pajamas, and yet he looks as confident and in charge in his nightclothes as he does in his usual suit.

Klara, too, is up, putting a cup on the side table next to George. She turns to go, but George says to Klara, "You, stay. You've been tending to my wife since you both got here last week. I might want your input."

Klara sinks down onto a settee. She doesn't meet Fiona's eyes. They haven't talked since Fiona told her of Abe's unkind remarks. Had Klara believed her? Hardened her heart toward Abe? Or had Fiona turned Klara even more against her?

As Abe finally lets Fiona go, he gives her a little shove toward George. Abe—still dressed in a suit as usual—*Does the man ever rest?* Fiona wonders—moves to stand beside George's chair. Every self-protective instinct tells Fiona to turn and run, but she knows she won't get far and trying to escape will only make whatever this is worse.

She meets her husband's unflinching, dark stare with the prettiest gaze she can muster and adds a soft smile for good measure.

"George, darling, you're awake! You were sleeping so deeply when I left our bed. And coffee, so late?"

"Chamomile tea," George says flatly. "Klara says it will settle my nerves." Even in the shadows, even as he picks up the cup and sips noisily, Fiona can tell his stare is hardening. Abe has succeeded in making George suspicious of her.

A shadow shifts in the entry behind George and Abe—tall, thin, leaning on the bannister for support. It's Elias, who has crept down the stairs, like a little child listening in on the adults. *Just stay put,* Fiona thinks. Her heart is beating so rapidly, so hard, she can hear it thudding.

"And I was quite unnerved, because yes, yes, I was asleep," George says. He takes another sip, smacks his lips in satisfaction, and sets the cup down so hard that Fiona jumps. Miraculously, the cup doesn't crack. "Abe awakened me. Alerted me to your actions."

"You left the house earlier this afternoon, and then this evening after you thought everyone was to bed." A satisfied smile pinches Abe's lips. "One of the guards noticed you disappearing this afternoon. I told Klara to stay up, keep watch, and from her window upstairs she saw you leave this evening."

This afternoon, this evening . . . she hadn't been observed this morning. Nothing's been said about anyone following her. She nearly smirks. Are they that afraid of the cold, hard weather? So, they've just noticed her leaving.

Fiona relaxes a little. "Just what do you think I'm up to?" She directs the question to Abe, hardening her voice. He looks taken aback. *Ah—he doesn't have any ideas.* He's just desperate to make George doubt her. "Well, if you must know, I promised Aunt Nell I'd visit Uncle Henry's grave in the afternoons for her, as she used to do, and reassure him she's fine. Oh, smirk if you must, Abe. What do you know of love?" She is surprised but pleased at the flash of pain that crosses Abe's face. Something else to dig into, use later, perhaps.

Quickly, though, Abe's expression closes and he snarls, "Oh please.

She's up to something! And what about this evening? Surely you're not hiking up to a grave after dark!"

Abe is suspicious of her—nothing new. He doesn't know, though, what she's doing.

"I don't like to talk about womanly things, but I find I need fresh air often. Even at night. Women can have odd cravings, especially when they're in the family way." She looks at Klara. Cruelly, she reminds her with a soft yet piercing question, "Isn't that true? I'm sure that was your experience?"

Klara looks down at her hands. "It is true. Usually, it's food—but I suppose fresh air, even at night, makes sense, too."

Fiona gives George a hurt look. "Are you satisfied? Why are you doubting me?"

She lifts her hand, lets it float to his knee, speaks the truth: "Haven't I been faithful to you every step of the way? Haven't I done your bidding since the moment we met?"

And she had, at least until now. The plotting she'd done before they came here—well, that was all in her mind. She could have written it off to imagination run wild, the effects of a late-in-life pregnancy. Doesn't everyone say women get hysterical during such times?

It wasn't until Aunt Nell shocked her with her suspicions of foul play in Uncle Henry's death that she began putting such plans in action. And it wasn't until acting that she realized how pinned down, like a flower to his lapel, she's felt since marrying George. But soon she'll be free. At least as free as a woman can be. Maybe as free as any person can be.

"I don't know," George says. "On the one hand, Abe is quite concerned about your comings and goings. Seems to think you're hiding something." He looks at Klara. "You've been here the whole time with her. Do you think she's hiding something?"

"Klara—" Abe says, a warning tone to his voice.

Klara looks at him, hurt flashing across her face. *Good,* Fiona thinks. "I don't think she's hiding anything," Klara says flatly. "I think she needs fresh air. Whenever she needs it."

George takes another sip of his tea as he stares at Fiona. "So you see, darling, I don't quite know who to believe. My longest-employed servant, or my right-hand man?"

Fiona wants to say to Klara and Abe, *Do you hear that? Not kin-who-was-like-a-mother, not friend.* But Fiona doesn't even look at them. She doesn't need to point this out, even with a sharp look. From the growing cold stiffness of the room, they're hearing quite clearly.

She keeps her gaze pinned on George. "Why don't you believe *me*? I've been honest and true, well, except for one thing." *Now is the time to use the marks and bruises to her advantage.* She sets her voice aquiver. Let George think she's nervous because she's afraid of Abe. "You see, I have kept something back. I visited Dr. Goshen after our trip to the bank. I felt faint, and Abe was kind enough to take me." She looks up at George through her eyelashes. "You have so much on your mind, darling, and I didn't want to worry you over nothing. Or maybe Abe mentioned the visit to you?"

Silence. A harsh look at Abe, who shifts his weight, crosses his arms.

Well then, no. Abe hadn't mentioned it—and George is unhappy about this. *Good.*

George abruptly moves forward on the edge of his seat. He takes Fiona's hands. "Are you all right? Is the baby—"

"Yes, I—I think so. But Dr. Goshen asked me if I was under any stress. Course I mentioned poor Uncle Henry. But also that Luther was missing. I hope that was all right. I mean, I knew Luther and Abe had gone to him to ask about getting medicine for Elias."

Fiona swipes a loose strand of hair from her forehead, uses the gesture as cover to glance at Elias. He's standing so deeply in the shadows that he's barely distinguishable.

"And I asked if Luther had made mention of where he might have run off to—I mean, it had to be pretty important, for him to not come back to check on Elias." As Fiona shifts her gaze, she studies Abe for just a moment. His jaw is tense, his fists clenched. But she knows he dare not hurt her in front of George. Fiona focuses on George, eyes wide. "Dr. Goshen said that he had told Abe and Luther that he'd gone with Lily to the Harkins family farm. Seems the girl, Ruth, accused Marvena of letting her little brother keep watch at her shine stand, and he must have gotten into the drink, because he'd stumbled home but fallen into a coma. Luther got agitated, and ran off." Fiona offers a soft smile. She notes from the corner of her eye that Elias is no longer in the shadows; he's gone at least partway back up the stairs. She hopes he's still listening, though. "And I told Abe this, on our drive out to Sheriff Ross's house, and that we should tell you, but he didn't want you to know."

Abe leaps to his feet, lunges forward. "That's not true; she didn't tell me the doctor told her that on the drive out—" He stops, just from George holding up a hand. His tone deflates as he adds, "And I didn't tell her I didn't want you to know—"

"But you also didn't tell me about that visit with Goshen. Or about this girl or boy," George says. "Is it true? That Luther ran off, to find a boy who kept watch at Marvena's still?"

Interesting, that George should care so much about Luther running off to find the Harkins boy. Of course, she knows from Colter that Luther shot him, but she's assumed that Luther was acting on his own. Had Luther, playing both sides, told George and Abe about Colter? Had they, then, ordered Luther to get rid of the revenuer?

From Abe's silence and taut, pinched lips, he's struggling to find the right words to appease George.

"Is Fiona telling the truth?" George's voice thunders around the parlor.

Fiona makes her voice sound sad. "George, if you don't believe me, you could just check with Dr. Goshen."

"Yes," Abe bursts out.

"And you didn't think to tell me?"

Each tick of the parlor clock ratchets the tension.

Finally, Abe says, "Because we're better off without Luther. God knows why he ran off because of some farm boy in a coma, but if the boy witnessed Luther paying off the revenuer and now he's in a coma, he can't exactly talk about it, can he? And if he's just a poor farm boy with diabetes, he's probably already dead. So the revenuer's gone, the farm boy dies of his illness, and Luther's running around like a fool—as usual—getting the shit beat out of him or bit by a snake. Great. All our problems are taken care of with no effort from us. It will be easier to make progress on our plans without Luther."

Fiona inhales slowly. Abe's deep, calculated coldness washes over her, and her hand rises instinctively to her neck, where he'd pinned her against the automobile seat on the way to Lily's farmhouse. His cold, menacing words echo: *George never questioned my loyalty or competence until you came along, Fiona.*

George's shoulders relax. "Good point. But I want you to check to see how the kid is. Find out from Goshen. If he's come around, find out what he knows, if it was a good reason for Luther to be panicking, or if he was being a fool."

"And if the kid knows something that gave Luther reason to panic?"

"If the kid's that sick, a little coin thrown the family's way should suffice. Otherwise—"

Abe nods.

In the dim silent stillness of the parlor, Fiona understands that protecting George's enterprise knows no bounds.

"Is there anything else you ought to tell me?" George's question is brusque, proffered as he waves Abe to sit back down. Abe complies, flashes a taunting smile at Fiona. *See? The men are back to business.*

Fiona puts all of her focus back on George. "Yes. I—I was covering for Abe yesterday. I didn't want to have to say this—but those red marks? And bruises? They weren't from a fall. They were from Abe being, well, rough with me, over not wanting to tell you about Luther's actions on Thanksgiving night."

George's eyes, even in the dim parlor, go so cold and dark, so fast, that Fiona involuntarily shivers. "Abe? Is this true?" His voice is equally cold, flat.

"No! Well, we hit a patch of ice, and I held her back as we skidded, until I could straighten the automobile—"

"I told you! She showed me the marks and bruises when she first came back yesterday." Klara's voice is a soft but shocking surprise, floating out across the room. "Poor thing. She was distraught. I can see why she covered for Abe, though. Neither of us want to get in the way of your business. And we know how much you rely on Abe."

Fiona wills her gaze to remain wide yet unflinching. She cannot show surprise at Klara's pointed comment, a not-so-subtle criticism of George for trusting Abe too much. The hurt Fiona had planted with Klara, about Abe's supposed comments, is already paying off.

"What the hell, Klara? How dare you? When did you decide to take up with this—this—"

"Careful," George says. His eyes click over to Abe. "This is my wife. And Klara is like a mother to me."

Ah, now she's like a mother, and not just a longtime maid. How easily his allegiances shift, depending on what he wants. Fiona ventures a darting glance at Klara. Even in the low light of the coal-oil lamp, she sees that Klara is beaming.

George looks at Fiona. "Darling, Abe and I have a lot to discuss, given these revelations." He stands, takes her by the elbow as if she is so fragile she needs his help to rise. Good Lord, she'd just been out hiking these hills at night. She smiles gratefully, though, lets him help her up. "But no more forays away from the house without Klara to accompany you. All right?"

"Of course," she says.

"Or one of the guards." His gaze sharpens a bit. He trusts her more, but not yet entirely. He never will. That's all right. She just needs him to trust her *enough,* for a time. "I wouldn't want you to be simply following doctor's orders but be mistaken in the shadows for someone who shouldn't be poking around here."

Here being *her* farm—technically.

But she lets him walk her to the stairs, thinks for a moment that he is going to go up to the bedroom with her.

He releases her arm, says, "Don't wait up. Now that I'm awake, I want to review a few plans with Abe. Having Luther out of the way sooner than expected means modifying a few things." He hands her the lantern. "Klara, brew up some coffee. Abe and I have a lot to discuss."

Klara nods, rushes out of the parlor and back to the kitchen.

Fiona moves slowly up the dark stairway. She sees Elias sitting in the shadows on the top step. He is slumped with his forearms on his knees, his head dangling between his arms.

Fiona puts her hand on his shoulder, and when Elias looks up she sees that the hard planes of his face have broken with hurt and the realization of betrayal, crumbled into one another, slicked with tears. He's heard everything.

Good.

CHAPTER 29

LILY

Sunday, November 27, 1927
11:00 a.m.

For a moment, the cold air snatches Lily's breath as she exits the telegraph office. She'd just sent a telegram to Special Agent Barnaby Sloan about the death of Luther Ross: *Foul play suspected.* She had not gone into details or mentioned that Zebediah Harkins had helped a man he said identified himself as Colter DeHaven, or her suspicion that Luther may have been the man who shot Colter, or that she had two suspects under arrest in Luther's death. Not only was all of that too overwhelming for a telegram—heaven help her, it was overwhelming just to think about—but she still is not sure whether to trust Barnaby. If only she could find Colter—preferably alive, of course, and able to answer questions—then she might better know what her next step should be.

Letting Barnaby know about Luther in the vaguest way seemed safe enough for now.

So wearying, not being sure who to trust.

But the cold air is refreshing, and so Lily takes her time to appreciate that overnight a brisk wind whisked away clouds, rendering the sky a deep cold silver blue. Though of course the Kinship General Store is closed on Sunday, she pauses to admire the store's Christmas display of evergreen swags and ornaments. It's the first store to decorate for Christmas.

The window is also filled with the latest temptations for everyone: pipes and cloche hats and, for the children, toys—the popgun that Micah wants, and so of course Caleb Jr. covets one as well, and a collection of dollhouse furniture. Jolene still plays with the ornate dollhouse that Daniel had made for her several Christmases ago. Lily's heart pangs as she stares at the tiny stove and sink, both miniatures more modern than her own farmhouse appliances, and for a moment she longs for the innocence of childhood, of blithely trusting in the good intentions and honest motivations of others.

Well, childhood is long past, and both life and her work have taught her wariness.

She shakes her head to clear it, makes a note to go in soon, put several of these items on layaway, though Jolene's been asking for a real pony or horse of her own. Oh, and buy one of the fancy hats that Lily knows Mama covets but won't own up to desiring. Well, Lily's going to get Mama one anyway.

Snow swirls in behind Lily as she opens the women's door of the Kinship Presbyterian Church. At least it's the women's door for now, though there is much debate in the church about allowing men and women to sit together at church.

She knows she is hesitating in part because going to church has become an obligation, a respectful bowing to Mama's wishes. Doubt and unanswerable questions beset Lily, it seems, at every church service.

Now in the church's vestibule, Lily shrugs off her coat, hangs it in the coat closet, tucks her hat on the shelf over the coatrack. The sanctuary door squeaks as she opens it. Several people turn to look at her, then quickly resume attention to the opening hymn. Benjamin, who had shown up at the house early this morning to see if Mama and Lily and the children would like a ride to church, sits near the back on the men's side. His arrival at the house had been welcome; Lily had not looked forward to the ride into town in the mule cart, but neither could they miss this particular Sunday.

Benjamin is not so forward as to give her a smile, but their glances touch for a moment, and his eyebrows and the corners of his lips lift briefly, pleasure at the sight of her. But then he turns back to the hymn.

She hurries down the side aisle, wanting to get to the pew where Mama and the children sit, before everyone sits, and her boot heels click on the hardwood floor and echo in the hymn's aftermath. She slides in, ignoring Mama's sidelong glance, and focuses on the children. Jolene's relieved look melts Lily's heart. Had her child really thought she'd miss her big moment? Lily puts her arm around her daughter's shoulders, prim in her carefully ironed dress and neatly plaited thick black hair, her red ribbons tied perfectly at the end of each braid. Mama and Jolene had fussed this morning over getting those ribbons tied into perfect bows—Jolene not much caring, but Mama insisting that God smiles on neatness, even in hair ribbons.

The pastor says, "Today we celebrate the first Sunday of Advent," and Jolene slides out from the pew past Lily and walks evenly—no lollygagging—her slender shoulders squared, her chin tilted up enough that the tips of her beribboned braids brush the waistline of her new gingham dress that Mama had finished sewing just yesterday.

As Jolene proceeds to the front of the church, the pastor continues. "Hope is belief that an expectation will come to pass. But hope must be grounded in faith—confidence in a person or idea or belief even without proof. . . ."

"Don't see why she gets to light a candle, I'm big enough, and she's a girl—" Lily shushes Micah with a stern glare. He draws back, cuddling up to Mama. Lily sighs. She will reassure him of her love later, but for now, her attention is only on Jolene. Jolene's eyes are steadfastly set on the altar as she ascends the wooden steps. The pastor strikes a long match and carefully hands it to Jolene, who lights a blue candle on the Advent wreath, the first candle, signifying *hope*.

The light blooms, casting warmth on Jolene's face. For a blessed moment, all the tension and sorrows of the past three days—the missing revenuer, the illnesses in the Harkins family, Luther's death, George's worrying presence, the possibility of wood alcohol poisoning the community, taking in both Marvena and Jurgis on suspicion of Luther's murder, even her confused feelings for Benjamin—fall away.

Lily sees only the flickering light of hope as Jolene returns to the pew, her gaze seeking reassurance that she's done well. This, Lily can give without doubt or hesitation. She nods at Jolene, and Jolene smiles.

At the carry-in lunch after the service, Benjamin had again offered to lend Lily his automobile until hers was repaired. She'd accepted, ignoring Mama's glare as Benjamin nodded, gave her his automobile key, and walked out of the fellowship hall.

On the way back home, Mama had been uncharacteristically quiet, harrumphing as she got out of the automobile, *You shoulda let that boy drive you!*

Because I'm such a bad driver?

Well, you did run your automobile into a ditch, Mama groused. *And you shouldn't be working on a Sunday, anyhow!*

Lily'd driven on to Rossville, left Benjamin's automobile parked at the bottom of the hill, and hiked up.

By the time Lily makes it to the River Rock Holiness Church, their service is nearly over. Quietly and respectfully, Lily stands at the back of the sanctuary near the coal stove, thankful for the warmth wrapping around her legs and feet. She gazes over the gathering—a thinner collection of people than when she'd come here with Marvena and Benjamin—and notes that here men and their wives and children sit together, not separated by gender. Of this, at least, Lily quite approves.

She's taken aback to spot, a few rows up, Nana and Frankie, Hildy and Tom and Alistair.

"Brother Billy Sunday has preached long and hard against the many sins that liquor lubricates," Brother Stiles is saying, referencing the popular evangelic preacher who tours throughout the South and Midwest. "And there will surely be a special place in heaven for him, for his role in getting Prohibition passed."

"Amen!" a man shouts, an affirmation echoed by others.

"So what are we to do when one of our own backslides, brothers and sisters?" Brother Stiles goes on. "Do we turn our back, judge them, harden our hearts unto them?"

"Amen!" shouts the same man.

"No, dear brother," Brother Stiles says sadly, "no. For hasn't temptation come a-knocking at all our doors? We must pray for our brothers and sisters who let it in—even if their doors are like the swinging doors of a saloon!"

There's a tittering of laughter, hesitant, but Brother Stiles blesses his tiny flock with a forgiving smile. "We must pray for them continually, and for ourselves, too. We must never lose faith or hope that they'll find their way back to righteousness, by the grace of God."

Lily smiles to herself. Both pastors she'd heard today would find each other's approaches odd, even irreverent. And yet both focused on faith, on hope.

Her smile fades. The return of Luther Ross—and his last days and his death—had shown her how fearsomely thin her own faith had become. Not just in religion—she'd long lived with doubts and questions. But in others. In her community. Even in the power of the rule of law.

"I'll close with these words from Billy Sunday," Pastor Stiles is saying. "I was so blessed to hear him speak at a revival meeting in Kentucky this past summer. *The law tells me how crooked I am. Grace comes along and straightens me out.* Let us pray for forgiveness and grace."

Lily bows her head respectfully, though she tunes out Brother Stiles as her mind drifts back to the hike up here. Truth be told, she'd been grateful for the solitude. The effort of climbing the hill while observing snow glistening on tree limbs had given her a chance to sort and settle her emotions and thoughts, particularly about Marvena and Jurgis. It hurts to the core to see her friends at odds with each other, even as they're each trying to protect the other. But the solitude of moving through nature had eased her troubled mind more than any church service—hers or this one—could. If she could make a request of God, it would be that she could clear Marvena and Jurgis, let them find their way back to peace with each other and a way to help Frankie. But God, Lily knows, isn't a mere granter of wishes, and so all she can pray for is faith that she will find the truth, and if the truth is that one of them did kill Luther, she'll have to find a way to be at peace with that. Not just because the law would demand it, but because her life—as the sheriff, as a mother and daughter, sister and friend—would demand that she carry on.

After Brother Stiles at last reaches "Amen" and service wraps up, most people avert their gaze from Lily as they linger to chat with friends. Lily makes her way to Nana and Frankie, Hildy and Tom and Alistair.

Hildy leans close and half-whispers, "After last night, we insisted Nana and Frankie stay with us. This morning, Nana wanted to come up here. Tom didn't want to bring them, but he didn't want me coming by myself with them, so . . ." She pauses, gives a little shrug.

"You did the right thing, Hildy," Lily says. After all, what is any community for, if not solace?

Hildy nods. "I know." Then she stands aside, to let Nana approach.

Lily's heart crimps as she takes in Nana's splotched face, her red-rimmed eyes, her usually neat bun askew.

"Oh, Nana," Lily says, "I'm so sorry—"

Nana lifts her hand to Lily's face, to cup it gently. Nana shakes her head. "Don't ever apologize for doing your job, young lady. Have faith in yourself!"

Tears spring to Lily's eyes.

Nana gives a tremulous smile. "You are cold, child. And life is hard. Have tea."

"I will, Nana," Lily says. She turns to little Frankie, who also looks like she's been up crying half the night. Lily kneels before Frankie. "I know you miss your mama and stepdad right now. . . ." She pauses, wishing she could offer hope that Frankie'd have her parents back soon. Instead, she offers what she knows is true: "They love you. And so do Nana and Hildy and Tom and Alistair. So do I and Jolene and my mama—and even those two stinky boys back at my house." At that, Frankie gives a small smile. "We'll all do everything we can for your parents—and for you, OK?"

Frankie flings herself at Lily, who returns the child's tight hug with one of her own.

She turns back to Hildy, says softly, "I'd offer them to stay with us since it's closer to . . ." She trails off, not wanting to say *jail*. "But . . ." And she trails off yet again, not wanting to add *it'd be a conflict of interest.*

"I understand," Hildy says. Lily squeezes her friend's hand, seeing that she does, and then she heads down the aisle, for the real reason she came here before heading to the Harkins household—to talk to Brother Stiles.

She fights back tears at her friends' faith in her.

She's dry-eyed by the time she approaches Brother Stiles, who regards her with reluctant civility. "Sheriff Ross. It's nice to see you coming forward to the altar." He offers a half smile.

"I just have a few questions," Lily says. Several people are looking at them with curiosity. "In your back room would be best."

Brother Stiles looks at another man and gestures with a head tilt for him to follow them. Lily would rather talk to the preacher by herself, but she realizes that in this sect, though men and women might be sanctioned to worship together, they're not to be alone together unless married. So she doesn't argue. Besides, it appears that word spreads quickly in this congregation.

In the back room, Brother Stiles offers her a chair, but Lily declines—she just has a few questions—and so they stand on either side of the table, while the other man stands near the door, arms crossed.

Lily says, "Marvena told me that Arlie came here with Luther for a special prayer meeting Friday night."

"That's right."

"How did others react?"

"Most of us were startled. A lot of the men work in the mines. Luther Ross—well, let's just say he'd test anyone's capacity for forgiveness."

On this they can certainly agree.

"And of course, there was some disappointment at Brother Arlie's— condition. But he struggles mightily, we all know." The preacher smiles. "I used to wrestle with the devil's drink, myself." He offers this insight with more humility and less sanctimoniousness than Lily would have expected.

"And how did Luther and Arlie act?"

"Well, truth be told, Luther didn't look well, and Arlie was worried about him. Said he'd been sick on the way over," Stiles says.

That's odd, Lily thinks. As much as he drinks, he should be able to hold his liquor. But maybe for once he couldn't, and he'd tossed aside the flask. "Any idea where Arlie might be now? As you might understand, I need to question him."

Brother Stiles frowns. "I thought Marvena and Jurgis confessed? That's what Nana told us this morning."

"I need to question him."

"All right. He lives with his daughter, Sally Mayfield."

"Any idea where?"

Brother Stiles nods. "I can direct you there. I'd go with you, but from what he told us, his daughter doesn't think much of our views—or believe her father truly found redemption here."

Well. Arlie's actions seem to bear that out.

The pastor smiles as if reading Lily's thought. "As I said, judge not. Anyway, you'd have better luck questioning her, if he's not there, without me present."

"I'm not a judge," Lily says. "But I am the law. And I need answers to a few questions."

Brother Stiles gives Lily directions and she jots them down. She can drive part of the way, but she'll have to walk a good stretch of it.

When she finishes taking her notes, Lily says, "Marvena says both she and Jurgis ran out after Arlie and Luther. And that Marvena was holding a snake at the time."

"Yes."

Lily gazes at the cages. All but one hold a rattler. She looks back at Brother Stiles.

"She was holding the one that's now missing," he says.

Lily takes a moment to push aside her disappointment. She'd so hoped she'd learn something that would contradict Marvena's and Jurgis's claims.

"Have you ever been bitten by a snake, Brother Stiles? While handling?"

Surprise at the question lifts his brow, but he nods.

"Do you bear a scar?"

"Yes."

"May I see it?"

A few moments pass as Brother Stiles studies her. Lily thinks he's going to say no. But then he takes off his jacket, unbuttons his shirt cuff, rolls up his left sleeve. He holds out his arm so she can see the top of it. There are two raised spots, just above his left wrist, and a raised welt, reddish brown. The spots are about a half inch apart.

"Thank you. Can you tell me about how it happened?"

The pastor frowns.

"I'm just trying to understand how a bite might happen to a person handling a snake, or from one person handing a snake to another."

"Well, in my case, it was last summer. It was a smaller snake, so smaller fangs. Had to have the top of my arm lanced, and some of the flesh cut out, to release the venom and remove the infected flesh. But, praise God, I was only sick for a while after that."

Lily lifts her eyebrows, questioning.

"I don't consider the bite a failure of our practice, Sheriff Ross," Brother Stiles says patiently. "It was a sign of my own lapses of living as God would have me do, and that I should correct them and improve my faith. I've handled snakes many a time, been bit just the once."

"The missing snake, the one Marvena had, how big was it compared to the one that bit you?"

"Much bigger, I'd say just over four feet."

"So would its fangs be the same distance?"

"No—more like three-quarters inch, an inch apart."

Lily considers. The punctures on Luther's wrist were closer.

"How fast did you swell up?"

"Nearly right away."

"Would that be the case for everyone?"

"I've only seen a few snakebites. It depends on the snake—its size, how long its fangs are, how deep the bite, and even if it releases venom. Not every bite means a venom release. And it depends on the person." He smiles. "It's just like being exposed to the word of the Lord. Not everyone reacts the same way."

Lily's not sure a comparison of God's word to a snakebite is the best analogy the preacher could make, but she sees his point. Dr. Goshen had said the puncture wounds were deep in Luther's bite. Yet there was no swelling on his arm, just the red discs around the punctures. And if Brother Stiles had to have his arm lanced to remove poison and infected flesh, wouldn't Luther's arm have swollen, too—even if he wasn't as reactive to venom as the pastor?

"And how did it happen—I mean aside from it being a sign." Lily says this as respectfully and sincerely as she can. "How were you holding the snake?"

"I held it just below its head, and up high, over my own head. I was taken by the Holy Spirit, in prayer, and speaking in tongues, but I was told later that my left arm was pretty close to the middle of the serpent's body. It was able to reach down, strike me."

So there is some technique in handling the snake to avoid bites—not pure faith. But that's neither here nor there right now.

For Marvena to harm Luther as she said, she'd have had to chase him down in the dark, while carrying a writhing four-foot rattler, pin Luther down, and get the snake to strike on the inside of his wrist, through a coat jacket and shirt.

So unlikely. Most likely, she'd dropped the snake soon after running after him.

And the puncture wounds are too close for the fangs of such a snake. The swelling doesn't equal what Brother Stiles just described. So someone had put those puncture wounds on Luther, to make it look like Marvena had attacked him with the snake.

Not Jurgis. It's possible he'd beaten Luther, hit him so hard or caused him to hit his head so that he'd died.

Or more than likely, Luther had passed out somewhere—maybe even where he'd been found—and frozen to death.

But why make it look like he'd been bitten?

The only person who can tell her that, she guesses, is Arlie.

Soon Lily finds her way to Arlie Whitcomb's daughter's house. The daughter, Sally, is a haggard-looking woman of only thirty-two, with four children, one a baby bouncing on her hip as she answers the door of her meager hillside cabin.

"My husband's out hunting," Sally says as she leads the way inside. "Just fixing myself sassafras tea. Care for a cup?"

Lily smiles. *Life is hard. Have tea.* Then she nods.

"And as for Daddy, well, he can go to hell, for all I care." Sally's pleasant tone doesn't match her harsh comment. She's at peace with how she feels.

Lily sips the hot tea, between jotting notes in her notebook.

"Pa did well enough, getting off the liquor—after years of being on it. I grew up with him drunker-'n'-a-skunk half the time. Said it was the Lord and prayer'd saved him. Don't know about that. 'Bout drove me crazy with his constant Scripture quoting and preaching at us, trying to nag us to church. Where was all that fervor when Ma wanted us to go, when I was a kid? Seven of us—Ma died with the last one. . . ." Here, Sally pauses to point at a boy, about age ten. "None of my brothers or sisters would take Pa and Junior in, so we did, and figured we was doin' enough work for the Lord with that. Well, soon as that snake Luther Ross came around a few weeks ago, flashed some coin, told him he needed Pa to take him to round up men who might want to work for his boss—some big-city fella, George something—Pa went back to his carousing ways. Never thought I'd miss the Scripture spouting and Bible thumping. Anyway, Pa disappeared nights at a time. Cried myself to sleep worrying, then I recollected Pa said he'd left his drinking troubles on the altar. Well, I mayn't go to church much, but in my mind, I just decided I'd leave my troubles on the altar, too."

"Did your father ever say anything about a revenuer coming around?" Lily asks.

"No."

"All right. When did you last see him?"

"Lessee, that'd have been late Friday night—well, really Saturday morning. Pa came back by hisself, looked shaken up, grabbed some clothes, said he was going to head down to Portsmouth, get a job at some manufacturing company there. We don't know nobody 'cept folks here; whole family is here!—but he said that he had it in his head to start over for a while, Luther had told him there were good jobs there, and you know what? I just laughed. Said what skills you have for some fancy manufacturing company—you're old and you don't know nothing except grubbing out a life farming, and you ain't done that for years.

Anyways, Pa said he'd write and send money when he got settled. And send for that one."

Sally waves toward her little brother, the languid gesture showing she doesn't believe that will ever happen. But when the boy looks over and grins, Sally's return smile shows she doesn't much mind.

Lily heads back to her borrowed automobile. So, if Arlie had headed down to Portsmouth, had he gone on foot back to Kinship? Taken the train? Taken Luther's automobile? The best she can do is see if Arlie had bought a train ticket in Kinship, alert the police department in Portsmouth.

An hour later, Lily trudges on to the Harkins house. When it comes in view, she stops short, partly from her calves cramping up at the last bit of uphill walking and partly because the house feels, even across the snowy stretch of yard, lifeless and empty.

She goes to the kitchen door on the side porch anyway. Knocks. Waits. Starts turning back when the door creaks open.

Ruth stands in the doorway. Her face is ashen. "Sheriff Lily. How did you know to come? Did you bring help?"

"Mind if I come in? It's mighty cold out here."

Ruth steps back, and Lily enters. Dishes are piled up in the pump sink, and there's a gag-inducing smell of food scraps piled up too long in the compost bucket by the door. Ruth, who has on two sweaters over her dress, shuts the door, but it's not that much warmer inside.

"I came to talk to you about Zebediah."

"Oh—is he still all right?"

Lily nods. Well, at least she hadn't heard different. As sheriff, she'd expect a telegram from the hospital if there was a change, so she could take news—good or bad—out to the family. "Ruth—you told me that Zebediah came home, groggy, around four, but he was at Marvena's still in the morning, and you told me you found the revenuer badge on Zebediah." Lily puts her hand gently on the girl's shoulder. "But I think though the man was hurt, he was the one who helped Zebediah home."

Ruth breaks down sobbing. Lily gives her a little shake. "Child, look at me! I need to find the man. Tell me what you know."

Ruth gulps back sobs as she explains. "He did come here. And I tended to him in the barn. When I—when I could get away. He was in and out, sleeping a lot, but when he came around on the morning of Thanksgiving, he was able to talk, and wanted to know where the Murphy farm is. Wanted to go there. I reckoned I'd get in trouble for hiding him away, but I felt so sorry for him. I told him I'd tell Daddy about him—ask him to take him over."

Lily's breath catches. She forces her voice to remain steady, soft. "Did you?"

Ruth shakes her head. "The man was right adamant—told me no. It was too dangerous. He'd light out by himself to the Murphy place. When I took a bit of food to him at noon, he was gone. By then, Zeb still hadn't come around, and so I lit out to find Dr. Goshen. Daddy—none of the others—knew he'd ever been here. Just me and Zeb."

Lily considers the implications of this. The Murphy farm—where George and his men are ensconced. Including Luther and Elias. And this Bureau of Prohibition agent—who wasn't even supposed to arrive until tomorrow but who showed up early, who was shot at Marvena's shine stand near her still—wanted to go by himself to that farm. It might make sense—if he was on the take with Vogel. He could want to get back to Vogel but still have the heart not to involve this girl and her family.

But him being on the take doesn't explain who shot him.

Unless, as Lily has theorized, it was Luther.

In that case, would Colter have tried to go after Luther, even at the Murphy farm? He would have to be delusional, naive, or stupid to wish to do so.

Lily lets go of Ruth's arm but tightens her hard stare, willing the girl to tell the full truth. "Did he say why he had to get to the Murphy farm?"

Ruth nods. She rubs the back of her sleeve across her face. "Said the man who shot him was there. Said it was Luther Ross."

The revelation, though not entirely unexpected, hits Lily like a sucker punch to the gut. *Oh God.* The image of Luther, grinning and taunting, emerges—in her office on Friday morning, with Barnaby, knowing he'd shot Colter, thinking he'd left him dead at Marvena's still, setting Lily up to look incompetent just before Mabel Walker Willebrandt's visit—a revenuer getting shot on Lily's turf—and Marvena to look guilty of Colter's murder. Forcing Lily to arrest her friend.

And she had—along with her husband—but for Luther's death.

Could Barnaby have been in on Luther's plan? She considers how solicitous the agent had been toward Luther.

"Ma'am?"

"Sorry, Ruth. Please repeat what you were saying."

"Just that I remember the name Mr. DeHaven gave 'cause that's your last name. Kin?"

"Distant," Lily says. "Very distant."

"Well, I said we should fetch you, but he got really mad, said he didn't need to talk to you, he just needed to get to the Murphys. I don't know why your kin'd be staying with the Murphys?" Lily's heart hurts for the poor girl. She's glad Ruth's not aware of the likes of Luther, but to be so cut off from her family's earlier community that she doesn't know Mr. Murphy's died—well, that's sad.

"It's a long story, Ruth. I promise I'll fill you in sometime." Well, sometime in the far future. "Please go on."

"Well, Mr. DeHaven was scary mad, and I reckoned anyone who could be that mad had to be getting better, and it was getting too hard to help him and Mama, too, and to tend to Zeb, so I told him the whereabouts of the Murphy place. Back when we were at our old church, sometimes all of us would go after for Sunday supper, all of us, me and Zeb and Daddy and Mama, but it was to help them a bit, too, even though it was a Sunday and Daddy and Mama used to say you can't work on a Sunday, but Mama told me it was all right, 'cause we were doing the Lord's work and the Good Book says we need faith, hope, and charity, but the greatest of these is charity, and it was a charitable thing, helping them out a little. They were getting older, Mama said." Tears course down Ruth's face again. She whispers, "I don't think Mama would say I did the right thing, the charitable thing, tellin' that man what I remembered about finding the farm. I shoulda told Daddy about the man, had him fetch you, but—"

Lily pats the girl's back. "It's all right, honey. You did the best you could, in really awful circumstances."

"Well, late Thursday night after you left with Zeb and the doctor, the other man, the one he said shot him, Luther Ross, he came here, demanding to know where he was, with this fellow from the church—Arlie—and Daddy, he ran them both off, threatened to shoot them dead."

"I need to know, did you say anything to anyone about the revenuer?"

Ruth shakes her head. "I didn't. I was just glad Daddy ran them off, and, and I'm sorry, Sheriff Lily, I gotta go; Mama is in a bad way."

Lily hears a moan from upstairs. Dora. "Isn't your daddy with her?" She'd assumed as much, and that the twins were napping.

But Ruth shakes her head again. "Mama took a turn. Pa went to fetch Brother Stiles, thought maybe hands-on prayer would help."

Fear sparks up Lily's spine. "Where are the twins?"

"He took them with him. Told me to tend to Mama, keep her well until he gets back."

Another moan. Lily recognizes the sound from her days tending flu patients. This isn't just a moan of pain—it's a death rattle.

Ruth looks terrified. She starts crying again. "I—I can't—I—"

Given the new information Ruth's shared, there is so much to consider, to do. She should go to the Murphy farm—she has a reason, bringing Elias news of Marvena's and Jurgis's arrest, though it rankles. She's honor bound to do so, as she would for the family of any other victim. Still, she can hold back what Ruth told her. How bound is she to share that with Barnaby, though? Can she—should she—trust him?

Yes, so much to do, to consider, but Lily takes Ruth's hand. "Come on. You can do what you must—but you don't have to do it alone."

As they start up the stairs, Lily already smells the suffocating odors of dying. She follows Ruth into the room where her mother lies.

Dora is even more shrunken than on the day before yesterday, a bare scrawl of life, like she has no more substance than a bit of unraveled yarn, head curled forward, knees pulled up nearly to her belly. Her face already has the waxen look of the dead.

Lily gazes across the bed at Ruth, whose eyes are wide. Anger rises in Lily, like the white-hot sparks of flint on stone. How could Leroy have left his wife like this, left Ruth behind?

Lily hurries to Ruth's side. She puts her arm around the girl's shoulders. "Honey, this is just the natural order of things. It's hard, but that's the truth."

Ruth looks up at her. "You'll stay?"

Lily nods. "I'll stay."

Dora shifts, opens her eyes, stares at Lily. Lily looks into her eyes—shiny and glazed and unfocused, the eyes of the blind, she thinks, but then Dora says, "Sheriff?" Her voice is raspy. "You come with news of Zebediah? He's still fine?"

Ruth inhales sharply—joy at her mama reviving. Lily's seen it before—a last rally, before the end. She takes Dora's thin, dry hands between her own, as she sits in a chair, pulled close to the bed. Truth has always been a cornerstone value of Lily's. She doubts Zebediah will be fine for long, not unless his father accepts the boy needs insulin and finds a way to make sure he gets it for him, and even then, Zebediah's life will be more fragile, and likely curtailed, with the sugar diabetes.

Sometimes, though, offering solace and peace matters more than the hard-striking flint of truth. *Hope.* Earlier today, she'd watched Jolene light a candle for hope. Let Dora die with hope in her heart. Hope for her boy is the release that Dora needs.

"Zebediah's going to be just fine, Dora," Lily says.

Dora coughs. Ruth gets a glass of water, cradles her mother's head, so she can take a few sips. "That's enough, honey." She looks up at Lily. "Don't let Leroy put the children in an orphanage."

Lily nods, although there is no law she can apply to enforce Dora's dying wish.

"Tell him I want him to remarry."

Lily swallows hard, nods again. Dora stares at Lily a long moment. Then she looks at Ruth. "Tell the young 'uns—" The words catch and crackle.

"Mama!" Ruth cries.

Dora finds the strength to give Ruth's hand a small squeeze. "Tell them about me, when they're older. Oh, how I love you." She touches her daughter's cheek, lets her fingertips course along the river of tears. "You are my brave girl. The best of me."

Then her eyelids drift close.

They sit like this, for a long time: Lily next to Ruth, Ruth holding her mama's hand, murmuring to her, occasionally looking up at Lily, who nods at her—*You're doing the right thing,* this incredibly hard thing, as Dora's breathing slows, a ragged, rasping meter halving itself with every exhale.

Two hours later, Lily knocks at the door of the house where Benjamin rents a room.

His landlady invites Lily inside to wait in the parlor, but Lily says she will wait outside, by Benjamin's automobile.

Lily stares up at the cold, dark, still sky. Still. But it seems to be swirling around her, and she imagines herself one of a million motes, swirling in it, and as impossible as the notion is, Lily feels she will, any moment now, fall up into the sky.

"Now, Lily, I said you could keep my automobile for as long as—" Benjamin stops, his voice halting, his grin fading as Lily looks from the sky to him. He pauses on the porch.

"Dora Harkins died," Lily says. "Her daughter Ruth was going to be there alone with her, but thank the Lord—oh, if there is a Lord in heaven"—Lily's voice hitches, and tears finally overflow down her face—"I was there with Ruth and Dora. I stayed until Leroy got back—"

Benjamin does not say anything, but he rushes to Lily, and he pulls her to him, an enveloping embrace, and slowly the world starts to slow and steady again.

CHAPTER 30

FIONA

Sunday, November 27, 1927
9:30 p.m.

There is something new between Lily and the handsome man, something—intimate.

Not sex—well, there could be sex, Fiona supposes, although Lily has always struck her as traditional, if not prim, except in her tomboyish hobbies—letting it slip once at a Woman's Club meeting, to more than a few gasps, that she enjoys hunting and fishing—and of course in her embracement of working as a sheriff.

No, there's something different, and possibly even more intimate than that, developing between them. Though the man again stands in the parlor entryway and Lily sits across the room on the edge of a wing chair, somehow he holds her in his gaze; somehow, she leans with complete trust back into it.

Fiona wonders if they're aware of how they are with each other.

She wonders at jealousy rising, thick and choking, within her at what courses between and around them, slowly binding them.

She wonders at the sorrow washing over her, as if she's been plunged in a river but will never rise again, at the realization that she's never had *this*—whatever this is, which they'll probably take for granted like fools—even with sweet, gentle Martin.

"Fiona!"

She jumps at the sound of George barking her name.

She turns to him on the settee. "I'm sorry, darling." She puts a hand on her stomach. "It's just that Lily and her—" She gives a quick appraising look at the man. Fiona transfers her hand to George's knee—a show of intimacy for everyone in the parlor—as she goes on, "—her *friend* have called on us so late, and I'm rather tired these days."

"I wouldn't have bothered you if I didn't have urgent business," Lily says. "I was asking if Luther had mentioned any encounters that he may have had with several parties of interest."

Fiona's heart pounds, and she pulls her hand back from George. Had Lily been talking to the Harkins boy—assuming he'd come around? If so, had he mentioned Luther shooting the revenuer? Would there be some way the boy would know Luther or that Colter is a revenuer?

"She wants to know if Luther has brought up working with Arlie," Abe says impatiently. He's pacing in front of the window. He'd been preparing to leave for Kinship, to talk with Dr. Goshen about the boy, when Lily had arrived. "We've already told her no, but I guess she needs to hear it from everyone in the room, well, everyone who matters."

He cuts a cruel glance at Klara, standing off to the side, at the ready with a teapot in case anyone needs a refresher, though neither Lily nor the man accompanying her had touched the cups George had insisted must be served to *their guests*. As if the sheriff and her deputy—that must be his role, even with no badge—showing up so late is a social call.

Fiona glances away to cover her flash of a smile at the harsh look Klara returns to Abe. Their mutual animosity is now hard-set. Through the window, Fiona notes another man, one of George's guards, also pacing. Other guards are posted at the main entrance. Surely Lily's noted them. What would happen if Lily knew of the other men, working on clearing land for the gravel road at the back edge of the property?

Fiona focuses on Lily. "Luther and I rarely talked. I'm sure you can understand that we—didn't have much in common. No, he never mentioned Arlie to me or in my presence."

Lily nods somberly. For a moment, her expression reminds Fiona of the night Lily had come to tell her, *Martin's been shot. . . .* Of course Lily understands. Better than anyone else in her life, Fiona thinks. She clears her throat, looks away for a moment.

"Well, I think you all should know that both Marvena and her husband, Jurgis, have confessed to murdering Luther," Lily says.

Fiona catches her gasp before it blooms large enough for anyone to notice. Marvena and Jurgis confessed? A glimmer of an idea arises in the back of Fiona's mind.

Lily says, "Arlie brought Luther to a church they all attend, hoping he'd reform—"

George laughs, and Abe stops pacing long enough to give Lily an incredulous look.

"I'm only sharing what I was told. I have Marvena and Jurgis in custody, but I'm hoping to track down Arlie," Lily says. "They're protecting one another, but Arlie is a bigger suspect as far as I'm concerned. If I can clear Marvena and Jurgis, they can get home to Marvena's daughter Frankie. Marvena is rightly worried about her little girl, who has asthma." Lily gives Fiona a pointed look, as if sharing this motherly concern might stir enough empathy in Fiona to say where Arlie is. But she has no idea.

"We told you before, we don't know anything about Arlie. He's not here," George says. His laughter has ceased abruptly and he sounds impatient.

Lily gives him a small smile. "I didn't think he was. I'm wondering if Luther's automobile is here?"

George and Abe exchange looks. George's glance gives Abe the go-ahead. "It is not."

"Do any of you happen to know his license plate number?" Lily asks. After a brief silence, she adds, "I think Arlie took Luther's automobile. I have an idea where he is going, so with the number, if he's spotted in that area . . ." She stands. "Where is Elias? I can ask him."

This makes sense—Elias knew Luther better than anyone. But, Fiona realizes, Lily had hoped to avoid talking to Elias.

George frowns, reluctant to let Lily talk to him because in his state

God only knows what Elias might say. But he says, "Of course. Klara, would you show them—"

Ah—here's an opportunity. "Klara has her hands full." It's true—and not just holding a teapot. She's been run ragged, constantly cooking for and cleaning up after George and his men. "So I've been tending to poor Elias. He's been so distraught since the news of Luther's death. Taken to his bed." She quickly tired of how pitiful he's acting, all but refusing to eat. Still, for right now she manages to look sympathetic about him. She stands, looks at George. "Let me help out and take Lily to him. I can make sure Elias answers Lily's questions *suitably*—but that he doesn't get too tired."

George's grimace unfurls just a little as she emphasizes *suitably* and Fiona sees he's pleased with her—and how he interprets her careful choice of words. That Fiona will cut off Elias's comments if he starts to say too much. Also true—though not for the reason George thinks. She hopes Lily doesn't know about the revenuer—not just yet. The news about Marvena has given her an idea.

"That would be fine," George says.

Fiona leads Lily upstairs. She waits at the top, notes how wearily and slowly Lily moves.

In his bedroom, Elias lies curled up on his side. The room is fusty. Fiona turns up the wick on the coal-oil lamp.

"Elias, you have a visitor," Fiona says, almost chirpily. When he doesn't move, she can't keep the snappishness out of her voice. "Elias! Sit up. Lily is here to see you."

At that, he rolls to his back. As she helps him sit up in bed, Fiona observes how piteously he looks at Lily. But Lily's face remains impassive as she repeats the news and questions she'd shared downstairs.

Elias looks to Fiona for guidance. She doesn't encourage him to confide in Lily, and that is enough for him to simply say he doesn't know anything about Luther and Arlie's connection, that they'd all just come here for the Thanksgiving weekend, had planned to leave this evening, until Luther passed.

"Do you happen to know the license plate number for Luther's automobile?"

Elias stares at Lily. If he's looking for pity or softness, Fiona thinks, he's going to be bitterly disappointed.

Lily presses her lips together for a moment, then adds, "Come on, Elias. You've always had a perfect memory for such."

"Six-one-eight-six-two-six," Elias says.

Lily makes a note of it, turns to leave without so much as a thank-you. At last, Fiona is moved to feel some sympathy for Elias. She pats his shoulder.

"Lily—oh, Lily, will you be at Luther's funeral?" Elias cries out.

Lily pauses in the doorway, turns, and fixes Elias with such a hard stare that Elias shrinks back in the bed.

"Oh, I meant to thank you for returning my gloves yesterday," Fiona says. Lily lifts her eyebrows at the reminder. "I—I will have the funeral home leave word with you. We are hoping to make plans tomorrow for a service and funeral on Thursday."

"No need to go to the effort to leave word," Lily says flatly. "I'm sure I'll read the funeral notice and obituary in the *Kinship Daily Courier*, along with everyone else."

Elias drops his head to his hands.

"We'll see you there, then?" Fiona keeps her tone polite—not too eager, just in case Klara has come upstairs after all. While she's succeeded in turning Klara and Abe against each other, she hasn't—and knows she won't—turn them against George. Klara will surely report any odd flicker in Fiona's voice to George.

But Fiona widens her eyes, as if begging Lily to understand. *I need to see you there.*

Lily gives a curt little nod that only Fiona sees.

Then the sheriff leaves.

Fiona gives herself a moment, just a moment, to close her eyes. Breathe slowly. Is it possible that Luther's murder, Marvena's arrest, is a gift to her? Yes, yes, the shimmering outline of her plan floats before her, beckoning. Rash—yet offering hope for full escape from George, and control of her own fate, far sooner that she could have dreamed. She reviews the steps in her plan. Tonight, she'll lay awake after George is again lost in his restless nightmares and hone every detail until her plan is solid and gleaming in its polished perfection.

Monday, November 28, 8:30 a.m.

"Pull over there." Fiona points to a spot a little farther up on this stretch of Kinship Road.

Elias keeps driving at the same creeping rate, his hands clenching the steering wheel so tightly that the hairs pop up on his knuckles. He stares intently out the windshield, as the wipers clear a light freezing rain.

"Did you hear me?" Fiona's voice is shrill. "I said pull over!"

It's nearly impossible to keep her patience with him, though she knows she must. This morning, she'd finally gotten him to dress, to go downstairs to breakfast, to say what she'd instructed him to say: that he was feeling better and needed to go into town to the funeral home.

George had looked annoyed, as Fiona knew he would. He was intent this morning on getting the men started on putting in the gravel road before the weather got worse; he'd even talked to her about it this morning before breakfast. He wouldn't want to spare any of his men.

If Elias feels up to driving, I can keep an eye on him, Fiona had offered.

Abe had not returned yet, and George is fuming over his right-hand man's absence—and no news about what, if anything, the Harkins boy had observed happen at Marvena's still.

Abe's absence and George's resulting fretful mood worked to Fiona's advantage. George, preoccupied with plans he'd written out in a notebook, waved his hand, as if shooing them out the door. *Go on.*

Now Fiona snaps again, "Pull over!"

This time, Elias listens, gliding to a stop alongside the road.

"Look at me."

Elias stares straight ahead.

Fiona takes his chin, nudges him to look at her. When he does, she nearly gasps. Elias is a broken man.

She can use that.

"Elias, you yourself said a few days ago that you were worried that Luther and you would become expendable to George. You didn't want the liquor supply poisoned, and we thought we stopped it because I was able to warn Lily Ross. But she didn't mention anything about finding tainted liquor and George has complained to me that the plan was not pulled off. Last night, George laughed at the notion of Luther finding solace in the Lord. But what if Luther changed his mind, didn't want to poison others?" Fiona in no way believes this, but Elias's face is slowly brightening at the notion. "What if Abe killed Luther? Doesn't that make more sense than Arlie? Sure, Lily saw Luther and Arlie together at the Kinship Inn, but Abe was gone that night, too, looking for Luther."

Elias frowns but then shakes his head. "What does it matter? Luther is gone. Daniel is gone. I have nothing—"

"Listen to me! I have a plan, but you have to trust me. What if we can take George and Abe out—but in a way that shows Lily that you're a good man?"

Elias's eyes widen and he shakes his head again. "That will never happen—"

"Whatever you did to make her hate you"—at this, Elias recoils as if Fiona has spit in his face—"I don't know. I don't need to know. And maybe you can't get her to care for you again, but if that's the case, don't you want people to talk about how you did this good thing—stopping George from bringing this business into the county? Her children—Daniel's children—will hear that talk one day. And don't you want to avenge Luther's death? If he was all you had to live for, and now he's gone—well, especially since he had changed his mind about hurting people, don't you want to fulfill what he started?"

Elias looks confused, and Fiona knows he's turning over the question—had Luther changed his mind, found a need for goodness at the end with Arlie?

Fiona is quite certain he hadn't.

But she sees that in his grief, Elias wants to believe in her. Have faith in her and, more important, in the improbable fiction she's weaving.

Fiona gives him another nudge. "Elias, I believe Luther found redemption. The truth is, I know you're weak, even with your heart medicine, and none of us know how long we have. I have a way for you to find redemption—if not in Lily's eyes, then in God's. In the community's. You don't want Luther to have died at the hands of George and Abe in vain, do you?"

Elias sighs. "What do you want me to do, Fiona?"

Fiona smiles, her relief sincere. "Your brother established the mine in Rossville, and Luther ran it. I'm guessing they talked about blasting new entrances and tunnels. If we could get our hands on dynamite, would you know how to safely set it?"

Elias stares at her, and for long moments the only sound in the cold automobile is of the ice pelting on the roof and windshield.

At long last, he nods.

"Good," she says. "First, there's a man you need to meet."

Colter is still in the old cabin, but Fiona suspects that that's mainly due to how weak he is.

Elias pulls a rickety wooden chair up to the bed and stares at the man, taking in his long, raspy breaths. He presses his hand to the man's chest, and then to his forehead. Colter doesn't bother to open his eyes.

When Elias turns to Fiona, she nearly jumps—he's transformed, his expression animated with concern.

"This man has a fever and slightly elevated heart rate," Elias says briskly. "He has an infection and is dehydrated."

"What can we do?" Fiona asks. Colter will be no good to her dead. She needs him to be alive for at least another week.

"Plenty of fluids. An antiseptic, such as Listerine, for the head wound, which needs to be cleaned," Elias says. "Rest and warmth . . ." Elias pauses, considering, and for a moment Fiona admires how smart and efficient Elias must have been as a doctor, how much he'd loved his work. "He's young, otherwise healthy," Elias says. "If we can stabilize him, he has a good chance of recovering—otherwise the infection will take over his body."

"Do you think you could get what you need in Kinship?" Fiona asks.

Elias nods but narrows his eyes, questioning. "Who is he? Why is he here?"

"He's an agent from the Bureau of Prohibition. He came looking for Luther. . . ." Fiona hesitates, unsure how her next bit of news will impact Elias. Push him back in his well of despair—or motivate him further to fulfill her plan. "He told me Luther shot him at Marvena's still. Left him for dead. He found his way here, and I found him in the woodshop."

Elias has gone still, his eyes wide. Though he seems to be staring at her, she's not sure he sees her. Fiona kneels beside him, puts her hand on his arm. "Elias, listen to me. That was, that was before Luther went to the church. Remember? And this man has a family. I found his wallet." She stands, goes to the table, grabs the wallet. "Look. There's a letter tucked inside, addressed to his mother back in Chicago." She holds the wallet open, so Elias can see the folded letter—no envelope—alongside a few bills. "I've read it to him, several times over, to remind him to fight to get better."

Well, she'd read it, a long apology for some undetailed slight, which explains why he wasn't home at Thanksgiving. But she had not read it to the man. A lovely thought, though.

"So we need him to get better. For his sake. Because if he does, the Good Lord will judge Luther less harshly. For Luther's redemption."

Elias hasn't moved or blinked.

Anger rises in Fiona's chest. She grabs Elias's arm again, this time to give him a shake. "And for yours. Remember, you helped kill my uncle? If you can help save this man, help me take down George, won't that repay the debt—"

Elias jerks his arm free, shakes his head. "That's not how it works, and I can never make up for what I've done." Fiona is pretty sure he's not referring to Uncle Henry. "But yes, I can get those items. If we can get back quickly enough, we can still save this man."

"Why in the world would I tell you that?" Marvena eyes Fiona with skepticism. "And why do you want it?"

Fiona glances around the jail, a new addition to the county courthouse, with twice as many cells as the old one that once stood behind the sheriff's old house. But no one—save Jurgis, who is in a cell across from Marvena—is paying any attention to them. Marvena is in a cell by herself, while the other cells each hold several men.

Fiona refocuses on Marvena. "I can't answer that just yet." She's just asked Marvena where she might find some dynamite near or in Rossville. Martin had talked with concern about rumors of miners sometimes sneaking back sticks of dynamite to use as a threat—or defense—against Luther and the thugs he'd hired to thwart talk of unionization.

Fiona leans closer. "But what I can tell you . . . you tell me where I might find some, and I will find a way to help you with whatever you want."

"Are you trying to bribe me? I killed Luther; I've already admitted it." Marvena scowls. "Glad to see the sum'bitch dead. There's no getting me off the hook."

"I'm not trying to get you off the hook," Fiona says. "I'm saying I've heard tell of your little girl's trouble with asthma. Lily came by yesterday asking about Arlie's connection to Luther, and mentioned it. I think she thought my hearing of it would stir sympathy in me for you, and make me say where Arlie is. I don't know that, but I read the Cincinnati newspapers diligently, and I do know that there's a children's hospital in Cincinnati that has new treatments. I'll pay for it, as long as it takes; all you have to do is tell me how to get my hands on a few sticks of dynamite."

Marvena stares at her, askance. "How are you going to convince your new husband of footing that bill?"

Fiona smiles. "Don't worry about him."

Still, Marvena looks worried. "Is this for something he's up to?"

"No one you care about will get hurt, Marvena. But your young 'un just might *live* with the right treatments. You have to believe me."

Pain treads over Marvena's face, as if every gasping wheeze and coughing fit of Frankie's is replaying in her mind's eye. And, Fiona can see, Marvena wants to believe her.

A vulnerable moment. Fiona leans closer, practically pressing her face to the cell's bars. She puts her hand on her abdomen, whispers, "I'd do anything for my children. Wouldn't you?"

Marvena's expression shifts to distaste and sorrow, as if she's about to make a deal with the devil.

And, Fiona thinks, perhaps Marvena is.

But Fiona is not going to back down from her plan now. It's genius.

Ten minutes later, Fiona joins Elias at the Kinship funeral home. When Mr. Arlington excuses himself for a moment, she whispers to Elias, "Did you get what you needed from Dr. Goshen?"

Elias, stony faced, nods.

* * *

Fiona's foot slips, and she catches hold of a tree branch. She waits for a moment for her heart to settle, then pulls her scarf back up around her face.

Tears spring to her eyes, from the cold and from frustration. She doesn't see anything like the rock formation Marvena had described, an overhang of shale a hundred paces or so directly north from the Rossville boardinghouse.

She dashes her eyes, scans the icy white landscape again, and this time relief floods over her. Snow has blurred trees and hills and rocks, but there, behind the trunk of a large oak, looks like the hiding spot that Marvena had finally told her about.

Dusk comes as Fiona enters the old cabin. She's just hidden the dynamite—a bundle of four sticks, tightly wrapped in a rag rug—in a woodbin, where the sticks should stay dry, at least until Thursday. Elias is already tending to Colter.

"He's gotten worse," Elias says as he removes the bloody, soiled cloth from Colter's head and gently begins washing the wound with water—snow that Fiona had melted and then boiled, over a small fire in the old stove, then cooled.

Fiona's exhausted, and she catches a whiff of herself from her labors in the woods. She's already worrying about how to explain that she and Elias ended up spending almost the entire day in Kinship—simply to plan Luther's funeral and burial. It is set for Thursday.

Well, she'll just have to worry about George when they get back to the farmhouse.

For now, she stands ready, with fresh bandaging and Listerine that Elias had gotten from Dr. Goshen, telling him one of the guardsmen had injured himself working on the gravel road.

Fiona had bitten back a smile when Elias told her that. It turns out that Elias can be surprisingly devious when he wishes.

When Fiona and Elias finally return to the farmhouse, George is too preoccupied to ask why it had taken them almost all day to arrange for a funeral.

But Fiona's breath is taken away when she sees why.

There, in the parlor, is a young boy she guesses is about ten years old—or maybe he's older than that but just looks younger because of how pale and gaunt he is. He's wearing filthy brown pants that have been cut off at the bottoms.

When Fiona found Colter in the woodshop, his head was bandaged with filthy brown strips of cloth.

George sits to the side on the settee, while Abe towers over the boy, sitting on the same wing chair Lily had occupied the past two nights.

Abe regards the child with narrowed eyes and a thin slice of a smile.

Oh God. This must be the Harkins boy. Zebediah Harkins. He's pale and shaky, but he meets Abe's stare with his own resolute gaze.

"Luther seemed upset when he learned you had been at Marvena's still. Why would that be, boy?"

The room spins around Fiona and she cannot breathe. She grabs Elias's arm, and he offers her support. Manipulating adults to her end—that's one thing. Not one of them deserved any pity, and she has no remorse, not after what happened to Martin, to Uncle Henry, what would happen to her if she doesn't take control. But—but this is a child.

George is intent on the boy and doesn't notice Fiona's distress.

"I-I don't know," Zebediah says.

"The nurse told me Sheriff Ross and Marvena came to visit you." Abe puts his hand on the armrest of Zebediah's chair, leans forward, so close that his face nearly touches Zebediah's. But the boy doesn't lean back, even when Abe barks at him, "What did they ask? What did you tell them?"

"Nothing! Just—I had a drink, several drinks, of Mrs. Sacovech's shine, and next thing I knew, I was coming around in the hospital."

Abe doesn't believe him—neither does Fiona. She's quivering. How long will the boy hold out?

She pulls away from Elias. "Please, the boy's tired. Maybe some food—"

Zebediah starts crying. "I don't know nothin'! Can I go home? I want to see my mama; she's sick—"

"Go upstairs, Fiona." George's voice hits each word as sharp and hard as a hammer on a nail. "Abe and I are working."

CHAPTER 31

LILY

Wednesday, November 30, 1927
1:00 p.m.

Lily stares in disbelief across her desk, first at Assistant Attorney General Mabel Walker Willebrandt and then at Special Agent Barnaby Sloan—shifting from shock at Mrs. Willebrandt arriving with Barnaby to disappointment.

Barnaby has just announced, *I've investigated to my full satisfaction. I'll be taking my leave tonight, after Mrs. Willebrandt's speech. . . .*

"I don't understand," Lily says.

"Sheriff Ross, I went to the hospital in Chillicothe first thing this morning. The boy that you told me alleged Luther shot at Colter? Well, he's no longer at the hospital," Barnaby says.

"He's been released?" Zebediah was supposed to be at the hospital through the end of the week. His father, Leroy, must have found someone in the church who could get over to Chillicothe, bring the boy home. She can understand wanting the children all gathered for their mother's funeral, but for Zebediah's sake, he should still be in the hospital.

"Yes, late afternoon, Monday. I talked to the nurse who works on the children's floor. She told me that you asked very leading questions. That the boy was delusional, having come out of his coma."

Lily clasps her hands and leans forward. "He was not delusional. And I didn't ask him leading questions. I have a witness who was with me who can attest to that."

"Marvena Whitcomb Sacovech? The union organizer and moonshiner who you've arrested for killing Luther Ross?" Barnaby's smile stretches into a smirk. "Now there's a reliable witness. I've done my research, Sheriff Ross."

"I've brought her in only because she and her husband each have confessed—but I don't believe their confessions. I think they're covering for one another."

Barnaby looks askance. "So, each thinks the other killed Luther and you don't think either one did so?"

"There are plenty of people who'd want to kill Luther," Lily says flatly. "Regardless of who actually killed him, last we knew, your agent—your injured agent, shot by Luther—was headed to the Murphy farm!"

"Right. What we really know," Barnaby says, "is that Luther is dead and Agent DeHaven has been missing all this time."

"No—he showed up at the Harkins farm, was headed to the Murphy place—"

"So said a distraught young girl who, by your own account, lost her mother right after telling you that."

"So now both children are confused, and you're accusing one of your own?" Lily can't keep the incredulousness from her voice.

"Ma'am," Barnaby says, "with all due respect, you're getting too emotional—"

Lily inhales sharply as Mabel clears her throat. Barnaby stops, chagrined by Mabel's subtle sign of annoyance.

"Agent Sloan filled me in after I arrived this morning," Mabel says. Lily looks at the petite woman. She's demurely, modestly dressed and coiffed, hair pinned back in a low bun, only a bit of powder on her nose. Only the finer quality of dress material, the luminescent strand of pearls, her soft floral perfume, suggest that Mabel might be from a station higher than the richest folks of Kinship. Her eyes belie a deep intelligence, the set of her mouth a determination, the fine lines by both that she, too, has endured despair and trials—and overcome them. Mabel Walker Willebrandt, no matter her lofty position, would fit in well with the women of Kinship—though of course, her ambition would not let her rest easy here. "Agent DeHaven's job was to befriend Ross, which he did in Chicago. Then DeHaven offered him quite a sum—three thousand dollars, I believe you said?"

Lily's eyebrows rise at that princely amount as Barnaby nods in confirmation.

"Yes, quite a lot, as payment for any leads that would help us nab Vogel."

"But Agent DeHaven was supposed to arrive with me this week to complete the sting."

"In time for your speech," Lily says.

Mabel gives a small smile. "In this war on alcohol, I've found that it's dramatic stories—not statistics or studies—that draw people's attention. We've had some magnificent wins in New York, Chicago, San Francisco—even along the East Coast and down in the warmer waters around Florida. But we've also had a lot of bad press about rogue agents—"

"You can't blame the newspapers and radio news for reporting both types of stories—"

"No." Mabel gives a small huff. "But they surely seem to revel in the negative."

"Such as the government allowing methanol into legal industrial alcohol? Knowing people will defy the law, try to cook it into something potable, and get sick, go blind, or die?"

Mabel lifts her eyebrows, draws back, but looks at Lily with new respect in her willingness to speak to her without kowtowing. "That fact isn't hidden."

"Thanks to those reporters," Lily says. "But that doesn't mean it's widely known. The rules and attitudes around Prohibition are confusing and even self-contradictory. Rich senators and businessmen were able to stockpile huge amounts of liquor before the Volstead Act went into effect—and can drink it legally. Why, a farmer can even have a barrel of cider by the door. . . ." She hesitates, not because Mabel is now pinch lipped with displeasure at Lily's outburst, but because she'd been about to blurt about Mama's grape bricks—just add water, stick in a dark place, and allow natural fermentation to take its course. "But some poor sap, whether in the city or in my county, who doesn't know better, maybe doesn't know how to read, can get legal wood alcohol, try to brew it up, not know better, die a gruesome death—"

"You seem very concerned about this," Mabel says.

"That's because I had it from a good source that George Vogel was planning to release a supply tainted with methanol into my county. I haven't entirely worked out why yet, and thank God it didn't happen, but—"

Mabel smiles thinly. "Perhaps you should give a speech."

Lily sighs. She has, when necessary for campaigning, done so. It's her least favorite part of her job. "I'm sorry. I'm—tired. I just don't understand why I can't get bureau help to look for DeHaven at the Murphy place."

"You're the one who told me you believe in the rule of law. That you just can't raid the farm because Vogel's there, without evidence he's breaking the law and a warrant," Barnaby says. "Well, that's what Luther was working to provide us. Now he's dead. You ask me, DeHaven killed Ross, took off with the cold, hard cash he was trusted with."

"How does that square with the shield, the hat, the bullet, we found? The testimony of the Harkins children?"

"You've told us their mother was ill for a long time, and just passed away. They're under stress. And for all we know, if Luther shot at Colter, it was in self-defense," Barnaby says.

"And then didn't tell you about it. Came here with you Friday morning, didn't say a word. Even though he was still on the bureau's side, right?" Lily delivers each word like a sharp jab. "Because there's no way Luther would have tried to play both Vogel and the bureau and gotten himself killed, somehow, in the middle—"

"You have a husband and wife who've confessed, and by killing him, they've ruined our operation! And again, you're letting your personal, emotional issues with your brother-in-law—"

"Enough!" Mabel's retort is hard as a slap. Barnaby turns red. Mabel goes on. "Sheriff Ross makes an excellent point—if Mr. Luther Ross were really, fully committed to aiding the bureau, he'd have told you immediately about Agent DeHaven's presence."

Hah! But Mabel turns her probing gaze onto Lily. Her *take that!* smile immediately fades. She wouldn't want to be on a witness stand, trying to hide so much as a hangnail, under this woman's interrogation. *No wonder she's gone so far in her career.* Even squirming, Lily thinks, *Good for you.*

"On the other hand," Mabel says, "none of this theorizing gets us closer to cause or evidence for a warrant to raid the Murphy place, does it."

Lily nods.

"Do you think you can get it?"

That initial note from Fiona—her begging look for Lily to come to Lily's funeral. Surely that look was in response to Lily's own note, indicating an offer of help. Meeting at Luther's funeral.

Lily clears her throat. "Possibly." She's still not sure if she should trust Barnaby, but she's probably not going to have much choice. She can't take on Vogel by herself, with only local deputies. That would be a slaughter. "But I won't know until Luther Ross's funeral."

"When is that?" Mabel asks.

"Thursday."

Mabel looks disappointed.

Well, of course. Her speech is scheduled for tonight.

"Any way you can speed that up?"

"I'm sorry," Lily says. "Not and follow the rule of law."

At that, Mabel smiles. "Well, I see we are kindred spirits, Sheriff Ross. At least in some ways." She turns to Barnaby. "Well then, you had best get back to Columbus, assemble as much help as Sheriff Ross says you will need. I have a speech in Louisville on Friday evening. I will rearrange my schedule, have my speech here next Tuesday, say?"

Mabel gives Lily a sharp look. "I'm assuming that will be fine."

"Of course," Lily says. "But I can't guarantee you'll have anything exciting to add. A, ah, compelling story. I can only work within—"

"I know, Sheriff Ross. I understand." She opens her purse, pulls out a card, pushes it toward Lily. Lily picks it up, stares at the fancy embossing, Mabel's full name and title and a number. "My telephone number."

Barnaby snorts. "The closest telephone is—where?"

"Chillicothe," Lily says. "I could send a telegram."

"Sheriff Ross, do you have someone you can trust who can get to a telephone quickly? To reach me if you find you need, ah, additional help?" Mabel shoots a hard look at Barnaby.

The face of someone Lily can trust comes to mind. Gently smiling. Always willing to help. *Benjamin.*

"Yes," Lily says. "Yes, I do."

Mabel nods, starts to rise. Barnaby also begins to stand. "No need," Mabel says. "I can see myself out."

After she leaves, Lily and Barnaby sit for a long minute in Lily's office. Barnaby stares at the poster of Lady Liberty hanging on the wall behind Lily, while Lily gazes through the gaping door at the hallway's black-and-white-checkered tile. The only palpable hint of Mabel having been here is her floral scent.

Finally, Barnaby says, "All right. Now what, Sheriff Ross?"

In the parlor of the Harkins home, Leroy sits in his armchair, gazing past her and Barnaby out the window behind the settee.

"How are you doing, Leroy?" Lily asks.

"Fair to middlin'," Leroy says. There's no irony in his voice, just flatness.

"I'm so sorry about Dora," Lily says.

Leroy twitches at his wife's name, then shifts his dull gaze to Lily. "Thank ye for staying with her and Ruth—" He stops, choking up.

Lily ignores Barnaby's questioning look. They had driven out in an automobile she'd gotten on loan from the only dealership in town. Barnaby had sheepishly said his tank was low and he had just enough gasoline to get back to Columbus.

While driving, Lily had explained about Dora's passing, but not about how Leroy was gone with the twins in search of a miracle and that she'd found Ruth here alone with her mother.

One of the twins climbs up into Leroy's lap, but he ignores the child as if she's a pesky gnat he can't be bothered to swat away. She begins to cry, and Ruth, who is sitting in a rocking chair and already looking terrified and overburdened, opens her arms to invite her little sister into her lap. This sets off the other twin, who jumps up from his blocks and runs toward Ruth.

Poor girl. "Hey, sweetie," Lily says to the little boy. He stops in mid-run, clambers up in her lap. She pulls a handkerchief from her dress pocket and wipes his nose. "How about a snack for you and your sister?"

"We just had break—" Ruth stops as Lily gives her a gently reprimanding look.

They carry the twins to the kitchen, settle them at a small table with biscuits and jam.

"We need to discuss a few things they don't need to hear." Lily aches to pull Ruth to her in a comforting hug, but the girl just nods.

Satisfied the twins will be fine for the time being, Lily and Ruth return to the parlor. As she sits back down on the settee, Lily notes that Leroy hasn't moved a twitch or reacted to any of this commotion. He's in shock. Gently, she says, "I was glad to help the other night. If I can help in any other way—"

"We'll be fine."

His dismissive tone stings, but Lily nods. "I understand. Well, we will try to be right quick. This is Agent Barnaby Sloan. From the Bureau of Prohibition. When I was here the other night, Ruth told me that Luther Ross had been by very late on Thanksgiving night, wanting to talk to Zebediah."

"Yep," Leroy says.

"With Arlie Whitcomb."

"Yep."

"Did he say anything about looking for another Prohibition agent—a Colter DeHaven?" Barnaby asks.

"Didn't get a chance. Ran him off right quick. Didn't have time for his—or Arlie's—foolishness. They were both drunk, and we don't approve of such."

"Luther has been found, dead," Lily says. "Possibly bitten by a snake." Leroy frowns; even in his shocked, grieving state, this strikes him as

unbelievable. "Possibly beaten. Both Marvena and Jurgis have confessed that they killed him—not together, but individually."

"Huh," Leroy says. "Seems unlikely. And why're you botherin' us
with this?"

"Well, we have a witness who tells us that the agent, Colter DeHaven,
has claimed Luther shot him when they were at Marvena's still. And this
witness claims that Zebediah brought Colter here and Colter stayed out
in the barn. . . ." Lily pauses, looks at Ruth apologetically. The poor girl,
who'd been so still and quiet in the rocking chair, now trembles.

"I'm sorry, Daddy!" Ruth bursts out. "You and Mama taught us not
to lie or keep secrets and this has been weighing on me something
awful. I'm the witness Sheriff Lily's talkin' about. That agent and Zeb
came here Wednesday. You were gone and Mama, Mama—" She starts
crying. "And I didn't know what to do, and Zeb was sick, and the man
was hurt, and—"

Leroy stands, moves swiftly to his daughter. Lily jumps to her feet,
ready to defend Ruth.

But Leroy sinks to the floor, pulls his daughter from the rocking
chair and into his arms. He holds her, rocking back and forth. "Oh,
baby girl, it's all right, it's all right. You done the best you could."

Lily sinks back to her seat, stares down at her hands. For a long moment, the only sounds in the parlor are the ticking of the mantel clock
and the soft crying of father and daughter.

"Perhaps if—if we could talk to Zebediah?" Barnaby finally asks gently.

Leroy looks up from his daughter, confusion interrupting the sorrow
in his tear-slicked face. "He's at the hospital in Chillicothe, so if'n you're
asking my permission, sure."

Lily and Barnaby exchange looks, Barnaby bewildered and Lily
concerned. If Zebediah is not at the hospital—but also not here—then
where the hell is he?

A sickening possibility grips her.

"Actually—" Lily starts.

But Barnaby gives her a small frown and a discreet shake of his head.

"Thank you so much, sir," Barnaby says. He stands up. His eyes
soften, and his face widens with genuine sympathy. "I'm so sorry for

your loss. And that we've intruded on you at this time. I—I'll be praying for you."

Leroy looks up, surprised, and then grateful. Barnaby is sincere. Something in his eyes conveys that he's suffered so much loss, too.

Lily glances at his tattered, frayed coat, recollects how just before they came out here he said he was low on gasoline. Because he'd neglected to refill his tank—or because he's economizing?

Agents don't make much—a reason some are on the take with the criminals they're supposed to pursue. But if he'd been on the take with Luther or George, wouldn't he have spent a little on himself? Sure, he might be smart enough to not display newfound wealth.

But usually people on the take can't resist flashing around wealth—just a little.

Something about that thought snags at Lily, bothering her. . . .

"Come on, Sheriff Ross," Barnaby is saying. "Let's let ourselves out."

As they head to the door, Leroy calls after them, "Dora's buried just up the road."

Lily turns and looks at him. Nods. "I will pay my respects." Not today, but soon. "Listen—I'll be back to check on you all. All right?" She doesn't mean as sheriff, and Leroy must know that. He nods in turn.

Outside, snow has started falling.

When the door has closed behind them, she turns quickly to Barnaby. Starts to snap at him but is taken aback when she sees him wiping his eyes.

She gives him a moment, then says, "The boy is gone from the hospital, and not here!" *Oh God. One of George's men—Abe or another—must have taken Zebediah. But how did they find out that the boy was a witness to Luther shooting Colter?*

"We have to get to the Murphy farm. We can assume Colter is there, and now, I hope, Zebediah, too—"

Barnaby sighs. "Funny as it might sound by now, I hate to argue with you, but suspecting Colter and Zebediah are at the Murphy farm, against their will, isn't enough. Like I said on Friday, under the new search and seizure laws we don't need a warrant to raid an establishment if we suspect Prohibition violations. But a private residence isn't an establishment." He shakes his head. "And even if Colter is there, we don't know that he hasn't turned. As for the boy, why, boys run off all the time. Maybe he found his family too restrictive, took this as a chance to run off."

Zebediah working alongside his father on her farm, eager to learn, flashes across Lily's mind. Helping her. Carefully and proudly handing her the pie-filling apples that Ruth had canned. Lily's eyes sting as she shakes her head. "The boy's not like that."

"Colter and I were supposed to get Luther to turn over any documentation he could get his hands on, not just of violations of Prohibition, but of tax law. You said you'd have proof Thursday morning to support backup. No matter what Mrs.—what Assistant Attorney General Willebrandt said this morning, I'm going to need proof to convince the men in between me and her to sign off on sending in agents on a raid."

Lily thinks furiously as they walk in careful, halting steps down the narrow path through the snowy forest. Does she trust Special Agent Barnaby Sloan or not?

Trust yourself. Nana's words come back to her.

Well, sure. Barnaby had been solicitous of Luther. But he'd also been trying to get Luther to turn over copies of tax documents and such. And her judgment of Barnaby had been clouded by Luther, his very presence making her doubt not just Luther, but her own thoughts and instincts.

Yet away from Luther, Barnaby, though still wary of her, had been respectful. And his reaction to the Harkins family, whom he'd only just met—well, he was sympathetic.

Trust yourself.

"All right," Lily says. "Here's the proof I'm hoping to get. I'm—well, not friends, but sympathetic with Vogel's wife. I'll be at Luther's funeral on Thursday morning. Fiona will be there. I think I can get a sign from her about whether or not the boy or the agent—or both—are at the farm. Would that be enough to go on?"

"I think so. I can go back up to Columbus, assemble a team on standby. Can you get a telegram to me, fast? Let's see, by the time it gets through—"

"Better than that. I can send a—a friend to let you know to come. His name is Benjamin Russo. He works for the Bureau of Mines, and they, too, have a branch office in Columbus. So he knows the way, and the city, well. He could be there in an hour, hour-and-a-half."

Barnaby nods. "Better to deputize him, make it official." He looks warily at the gray sky speckled with sifting snow. "I'll jot down my home address, too, in case he needs to find me after hours. And if you're the praying type, pray for good weather by tomorrow."

Back in her office in the courthouse, Lily holds her hands over the radiator heater just under the window. Even with gloves, she'd gotten cold on the drive back from the Harkinses. She wishes for a cup of tea, but there's no time for that, so she indulges in closing her eyes for just a moment to focus on the goodness of the warmth emanating from the heater.

Lily sits down, opens her notebook, writes up what's happened so far today.

Then she loops back, rereads everything.

Something is off, though, about the timeline.

Luther had been in Rossville for several days at the boardinghouse before Thanksgiving. Then, on Thanksgiving, at the Murphy farm. That night, at Dr. Goshen's. Later, at the Harkinses' place and in Rossville. Friday morning in her office, Friday night at the Kinship speakeasy, later still that night at the gospel church. Then dead on Saturday.

But where had he spent Friday night? Not with Arlie—his daughter, Sally, would have told her that. Not at the Kinship Inn after the raid. Not at the boardinghouse—Benjamin had confirmed that.

At the Murphy farm? That seems unlikely. If he'd gone back there and George—well, Abe or one of George's other men at George's behest— had killed Luther, they'd have just dumped his body somewhere. Not set his corpse up so dramatically all the way over in Rossville.

What's more, Lily's notes remind her that not only is Luther's automobile still missing, so is his flask. It's next to impossible to believe that he'd found the Lord and tossed it aside. And another question mark— Pastor Stiles's comments make it seem unlikely that Luther had actually been bitten by a snake—

Lily startles at a knock on the door. She looks up to see the clerk of courts. He looks alarmed. "Couple'a deer hunters here, Sheriff. Seems they came across an automobile, in a ravine, off Kinship Road. You know—the sharp turn afore you turn on the state route to Portsmouth? And there's a man inside. Dead, they say."

Arlie is in the driver's seat of Luther's automobile—the automobile license matches the number Elias had given Lily—and from the look of him, he's been dead several days. The cold has at least mitigated the smell of death.

She shuts the driver's side door carefully—it's not that slamming it could startle poor Arlie, but doing so seems disrespectful. Lily and Dr. Goshen climb up the incline to the men waiting on the road. The snow is falling faster now, along with dusk.

"Can you pull the automobile out?" Lily asks the tow truck driver. She'd gotten him, Mr. Arlington, and Dr. Goshen to all follow her out to the site.

"Yes, ma'am," says the tow truck driver. He works at the only dealership in Kinship—the only one in the county.

The others walk down the side of the road to where they've carefully parked their own automobiles.

"How long you reckon—" Lily starts.

"From the rigidity, and other signs, I'd say three, maybe four days," Dr. Goshen says. "Could be longer. The wreck wasn't enough to kill him, though. Could have been a heart attack, he goes off the road, his body heat would have kept the interior of the automobile warm for a little bit. Then the freezing temperature seeps into the vehicle."

So it's possible Arlie wrecked just a few hours after seeing his daughter.

They wait in silence while the tow truck driver finishes his work.

Next comes the gruesome task of extracting Arlie from the automobile and loading him into Mr. Arlington's hearse.

"Ma'am, you don't need to—" the tow truck driver starts as it's clear Lily is going to help.

Both the doctor and the undertaker suppress small smiles, even in this grim situation. They know better than to tell Lily she can't do something because she's a woman. Yet her half eye roll is for herself as much as for the men who think it's still 1890—why does she remain surprised by these lingering attitudes?

"He's a big man," Lily says, and indeed it takes the four of them to move Arlie to the back of the hearse. The task is difficult, strains her still-aching shoulder, but she's not the only one affected by it both physically and emotionally. Even Mr. Arlington, who is used to dealing with the dead, looks ashen.

Yet as she's starting back to her automobile she notes Dr. Goshen leaning into the back of the hearse, lingering over Arlie. Lily pauses, cranes her neck to see the doctor patting Arlie's pant pocket, then quickly checking his coat pockets. She turns her head, continues her trek, but out of the corner of her eye she sees that the doctor looks relieved.

Lily swallows hard, as a theory quickly rises in her mind.

Dr. Goshen gives her a long look. Lily smiles and hollers, "I'll meet you later. I need something checked on my automobile!"

She gestures the tow truck driver over to her automobile and kneels by one of the tires.

"What seems to be the trouble, Sheriff?" he asks politely. "The axle was bent when we got it back to the shop, but I know the boys took extra care—"

"Just keep looking over my tire like you're concerned," she says.

Finally, the hearse pulls away. She waits a beat, then says, "I want to take a look in Luther's automobile."

He frowns. "Here? It's getting dark—"

Lily pulls a flashlight out of her tote bag, switches it on.

"All right then."

He cranks the wench to lower Luther's automobile, and Lily climbs in the passenger side. She gags a little at the smells that have collected inside the automobile—besides the smell of body fluids, there's stale cigar smoke and alcohol scents.

But a ten-minute search is worth it.

In the glove box, there's a packet of money. A quick examination reveals that there's at least five thousand dollars, probably the money Luther was supposed to receive from the undercover agent, plus—*oh.*

Lily guesses that the rest is money Luther had from George to try to bribe the agent. He'd played both sides—thought he'd get away with it—but then Elias had a heart event.

She checks the back seat, under the front seat—and there it is. The flash of Luther's flask. She pulls it out, studies the fancy etching with his initials.

Lily steps out of the automobile. "You got a lighter?" she asks the tow truck driver.

He nods.

She opens the flask, sniffs. It's alcohol, more rank smelling, though, and the flask is a little over half-full. She pours a bit on her handkerchief, carefully seals the flask, puts it in her pocket. Then she holds out her handkerchief, dampened end dangling. She looks at the driver. "Light it," she says.

He does, and it flames quickly.

She drops it almost immediately, and it extinguishes in the snow.

But she's had time to see: those flames burned a deadly pale blue.

CHAPTER 32

LILY & FIONA

Wednesday, November 30–Thursday, December 1, 1927

LILY, NOVEMBER 30, 6:00 P.M.

Mrs. Goshen peeks out through her barely open front door and frowns out at Lily. "The doctor isn't back yet." She starts to shut the door, but Lily sticks her foot in and jerks the door from Mrs. Goshen's hands.

Lily had sped back from the crash site, hoping to get to the doctor's while he was at the funeral home helping to move and prepare Arlie's body.

"I need to come in, Mrs. Goshen."

"It's after hours, so unless you have a medical emergency—"

"I'm here as sheriff. Let me in. I'd rather not force my way in."

"You can't do that! You don't have a—a—warrant or anything—"

"I'm here on suspicion that you are harboring illegal alcohol. Under the law, I don't need a warrant. I just need a suspicion." Lily shoves the door with her shoulder, grimaces as sharp pain reminds her that she'd dislocated it just a few days ago.

Mrs. Goshen stumbles back as Lily enters. Her eyes dart to the door, but Lily has brought along a deputy.

"Please," Lily says. "I think you should have a seat."

Mrs. Goshen sits down in her own waiting area, while Lily's deputy sits down across from her. His other job is to keep watch for Dr. Goshen and not let him run away. He pulls his pistol, holds it on his knee, and Mrs. Goshen stares at it like she's about to burst out crying.

Lily sighs. "I don't think it's necessary to hold a gun on Mrs. Goshen," she says.

Lily finds the case of liquor quickly, tucked in a storage cabinet in the examination room, other bottles of Listerine and hydrogen peroxide and such pushed aside. She's relieved at finding it quickly for her own sake but also because she's glad to save Mrs. Goshen the indignity of a search of their private abode upstairs.

The case has already been opened, and a bottle is missing. Lily opens an overhead cabinet and pulls out a rolled bandage from a neat stack and then drops the bandage in a metal pan. She pours on some of the liquor, then opens the drawer, pulls out a lighter—useful for sterilizing needles for splinters and such. She sets the cloth aflame, and again, the flames are a barely visible pale blue.

By then, Dr. Goshen has returned and is sitting next to Mrs. Goshen. He has his arm around her, and she leans into him, crying.

Lily sits down across from them, ignoring Mrs. Goshen and giving the doctor a cold, pitiless stare. "I just found a case of industrial alcohol with methanol, repackaged in liquor bottles, in your examination room cabinet," Lily says.

"How do you know that's what's in there?" Dr. Goshen sneers.

"I tested it. Flames burned pale blue—methanol."

The doctor looks away.

"I was warned that the supply might be delivered to the Kinship Inn's speakeasy. That's why I held the raid the other night."

Dr. Goshen looks back at Lily. "Well, it wasn't delivered. I—I have that alcohol for . . . medical reasons."

"Medical reasons? For industrial alcohol?"

"Sterilizing examination and surgical instruments. And such."

"Or you're working with George Vogel and he wanted the alcohol to sicken the locals and send along a message—work with him, or else."

Dr. Goshen narrows his eyes. "Why would you think I would do something like that?"

"I wondered about that, too. Then I realized. Money," Lily says. "You haven't exactly hidden it—your new automobile." She nods toward Mrs. Goshen, the flashy ring on her finger. "Jewels for your wife."

"Our spending habits aren't your concern," he says coldly. "Or proof."

"A few days ago, at the funeral home, I noticed you checking Luther's pockets—and I noticed something else. He didn't have his flask on him," Lily says. "And today, you checked Arlie in the same way—no doubt also looking for that flask. Luther was never without it."

"So?"

"I found it, in Luther's automobile, after you left the scene of Arlie's wreck. It had fallen under the passenger seat," Lily says. "I tested the alcohol. It also burned blue. And though Luther had such a drinking problem he wouldn't have noticed—or maybe not even cared—about the taste, witnesses say he was acting ill at the Holiness gospel church. It would take a great deal of alcohol to make Luther ill—unless it was industrial alcohol that had been substituted in his flask. A splash of that alcohol in a mixed drink would make someone sick. Consumed straight up, and in the quantities and at the rate Luther drinks, well. Even with his tolerance level, you knew he'd quickly get very ill—and soon it would kill him. What I'd like to know is when you substituted his alcohol. It had to be sometime on Friday—"

Mrs. Goshen sits up, pulling away from her husband, who looks perplexed. Through her tears, she says, "It was on Friday night. Luther came back for the case of alcohol, while Arlie waited outside, but—"

"But I wouldn't give it to him," Dr. Goshen says. "I'd had a change of heart, was planning to tell you, Sheriff, and—"

Mrs. Goshen shakes her head. "You said that Luther had changed the circumstances, made it too dangerous to do, that all Luther was supposed to do was pay off that revenuer, then stay put at the Murphy farm, but instead Luther had been running around, and you demanded to know where. Luther screamed it was none of your business. While you all fought, I realized this nightmare would never end, unless Luther was out of the way. It all started with Luther not following orders. It was easy enough—I slipped out, got his flask from his coat pocket, and quickly switched the alcohol."

"You—you don't have to say any of this," Dr. Goshen says. He looks at Lily. "Please, she doesn't know what she's saying—"

"You were looking for something on Arlie," Lily says. "Was it Luther's flask?"

Dr. Goshen nods, looks away, defeated, as Mrs. Goshen wipes her eyes and focuses on Lily. "Arlie brought Luther back late on Friday night, realizing how sick he was. And then Arlie took off in Luther's automobile. Luther was too sick to protest."

Lily calculates: *Arlie might—or might not—have known about the money in the glove box of the automobile. Either way, he thought he was escaping to start life anew—again—in Portsmouth in the southeastern tip of Ohio. And had Arlie simply wrecked, or been drunk while driving, or drank from Luther's flask, dropping it when he became ill? She would never know for sure.*

Dr. Goshen drops his head to his hands for a long moment. Mrs. Goshen puts her hand gently on his back. "We have to tell her the rest."

Finally, he looks up at Lily. "Luther passed while I was trying to save him. I got him in my automobile, left him in Rossville."

"And the snakebite marks?"

"I punctured his wrist. Arlie said they'd been to service, so I thought—" He drops his head back to his hands.

"We got in over our heads with Luther and George Vogel," Mrs. Goshen says. "We know George's plans for the Murphy farm. If—if we spelled it out in detail for you, would that make things . . . easier . . . for us?"

"I can't make promises, but it wouldn't hurt," Lily says. "I'm listening."

FIONA, NOVEMBER 30, 6:00 P.M.

Fiona gazes up at George. "Darling, I'm feeling so much better."

They are alone together in their bedroom, getting ready to head down to dinner.

George takes her chin in his hands, too tightly. His smile is tense, too. "That's good to hear—but we don't want to take any risks, now do we? With our baby?"

He asks the last question as if there is doubt that she's pregnant. It's Abe who must be putting doubts into George's mind. They've been working long hours together.

"It's just that . . ." She pauses, considering, but also because it's hard to talk clearly with his hand vise-clenching her chin. "I've gotten close to Elias, tending to him—"

George lets go, pushes her away, so she lands on the edge of the bed. "Have you? He seems quite fine now," George says. Elias had been caught the day before, coming back from the cabin where Colter is still hidden, and had passed it off as taking a long walk for fresh air, for his health. Elias had been able, though, to hide the dynamite in the woods along the newly made gravel road. He'd been able to whisper that much to Fiona. Thank God.

"Well, physically," Fiona says. "Emotionally—" She shakes her head to indicate how pitiful Elias has been since Luther's passing.

"Fine in that regard as well," George says as he straightens his tie in the mirror. Even here, he insists that they dress well for dinners. Tonight, he's requested Klara cook sauerbraten, red cabbage, schnitzel. George chuckles. "I think he likes having a patient to tend to."

He means the boy—Zebediah Harkins, who had finally said that he'd witnessed a man they know to be Luther paying off another man and that the man and Luther had shaken hands and parted ways. The only other thing the boy will say is that he'd been diagnosed with sugar diabetes at the hospital and wants to go home to see his mama, who is sick. When Elias protested that the boy would die without insulin, George had ordered the medicine be brought in—it seems there is nothing that he can't conjure with his money and his will.

And he's right; Elias has seemed to find purpose in treating the boy. George refuses to let the boy go back to his family. Fiona is not sure why. Because George wants Elias sharp and alert again, for overseeing the creation of diluted liquor? George can use Dr. Goshen for that.

More likely it's because George doesn't believe the boy—neither does

Fiona, for that matter. He's holding on to him—for now, while he might be useful in some way. She'd overheard George and Abe talking about using the boy to trade to Lily, if she gets too suspicious and comes snooping around, for her silence on their plans. Something about knowing that she can compromise. Working on their plans, George seems to have forgiven Abe for his recent flubs and indiscretions.

"Well, I just think Elias might need someone with him at the funeral tomorrow—"

"Abe and I will be with him!" George snaps. "You can stay here, and get packed up. You'll be going back to Cincinnati in a few days."

Dammit! Abe really has gotten to him. Already, Fiona's hold on George is waning. The sooner she can put herself in control, get him and Abe locked away, the better. For now, Fiona says mildly, "All right, darling. You won't be coming with me?"

"It's nice to know you'll miss me," George says. He comes over, takes her chin again, more gently, but his eyes are still steely. "Abe will accompany you back—just to make sure you're safe, of course. Shortly after the funeral."

Of course—George doesn't trust her to be alone. But why right after the funeral? She considers for a second—*oh*. Because George and Abe want to be seen at the funeral, supporting Elias in his time of loss.

"Will—will Elias also come with us back to Cincinnati?" she asks as lightly as possible. "I'd like to have a doctor on hand since I'm, well, a bit older."

"I'll make sure you have a doctor in Cincinnati," George says. "Elias will leave directly after Luther's funeral on other assignments."

In other words, Fiona thinks, after Luther's funeral, after everyone gets a chance to see Elias there—because it would be too odd if he disappeared before the funeral—Elias will be conveniently disappeared.

Dr. Goshen will take his place, working on the operations here.

Fiona's heart quickens. This completely scrambles the plan she and Elias had put together: Fiona would pass along the letter from Colter's wallet, which Fiona had retrieved on her walk to the cabin this morning, to Lily at the funeral. Alerted that a federal agent is being held here, Lily would come in after the funeral, undoubtedly with others, and George would seek to escape down the completed gravel road. But by then, Elias and Colter will have snuck down to the road, and strung the dynamite across it.

They will just need to set the fuse and blow up the road right before George's automobile gets there and block his escape.

Or, even, kill him. But if Elias doesn't come back from Luther's funeral, what then?

"I'll be sure to tell Sheriff Ross you send your regards," George says with a small smile that reveals only the tips of his teeth.

"Of—of course," Fiona says, and offers up the brightest return smile she can conjure. She stands. "Shall we head down to dinner?"

LILY, NOVEMBER 30, 8:00 P.M.

"With the deputies I have, I think we'll need about a dozen more men," Lily says, glancing up from sketching a map of the Murphy farm, the road leading up to it, the layout of the buildings, the hills around it. "I counted less than that at the Murphy farm, but Vogel could have brought in more—"

Lily comes to a halt as Marvena looks as ill as if she'd held a plug of tobacco too long and swallowed a mouthful of tobacco juice.

"Marvena? Are you all right?" Jurgis asks.

The three are gathered in Lily's office. Ten minutes or so before, she'd finally released both Jurgis and Marvena—after she booked Mrs. Goshen for murder and Dr. Goshen as an accessory. She'd updated Marvena and Jurgis and now was telling them that she planned to raid the Murphy farm, not just because of Vogel's plans as divulged by the Goshens, but also because she suspects that both the federal agent DeHaven and the Harkins boy are being held there. Lily has spelled out the whole situation and that as soon as they finish speaking she'll send Benjamin to Columbus to alert Barnaby to come back the next morning with agents. With what the Goshens have told her, she has enough to justify the raid.

At Luther's funeral tomorrow, she'll see if Fiona offers any indication that Zebediah or DeHaven are on the farm, useful information to have before the raid, though Lily is still not fully convinced she can trust Fiona. After all, she, like Luther, could be trying to trick Lily on George's behalf.

Either way, she needs to attend that funeral—especially since she'd let Elias and Fiona know she'd be there. Keep appearances going. Not alarm George. That will buy time for Barnaby to assemble his agents and get them down here.

Even so, she also needs willing, trustworthy locals who are good with firearms—without being hotheads.

Marvena looks stricken. "It's—it's just Fiona came to see me Monday morning," Marvena says. "She recollected as to how I'd threatened a few years ago to blow up the mines if'n the men weren't allowed to discuss unionization. She remembered that I'd told you, Lily, that I'd hidden away dynamite sticks. Seems Martin had told her about this. And—and she wanted to know where that dynamite is—"

Lily drops her pencil to her desk. She takes a long, slow breath. The room feels too close, too stuffy.

Jurgis's jaw clenches. She understands his anger, but wrath isn't going to help either Marvena or this situation.

"Did you tell her?" Lily asks.

Marvena wipes tears from her eyes. "Yes."

"Why?" Jurgis's voice cracks on the simple question.

Marvena turns to him. "Pure 'n' simple—she offered money for Frankie to get asthma treatments in Cincinnati. And I was desperate, and she pointed out she'd do anything to help her child if he truly needed it, and—"

"I've been desperate to help Frankie, too!" Jurgis cries. "But this—this—"

"She said no one I cared about would get hurt!" Marvena exclaims. "I didn't know about the boy Zebediah being there, and—"

"She came to you on Monday morning?" The question rolls slowly from Lily.

"Yes," Marvena says.

"Zebediah wasn't at the farm at that point," Lily says. "Barnaby told me earlier today that he learned that the boy's father—really though, it was Abe who went posing as him, I'm guessing—came and got him Monday afternoon." Lily stares past Marvena and Jurgis, thinking. They quiet, giving her the stillness and silence she needs for contemplation. "So I think Fiona was sincere—at the time she came to ask you about the dynamite, no one was at the farm you'd care about. And why would she ask you for dynamite? It can't be to help George in some way. He has access to everything he needs, whenever he needs it. So she must have another plan for it. Something to hurt George."

"I thought she was more'n happy to be his fancy wife?" Marvena says.

"I thought so, too," Lily says. "But she talked about caring about her son—and yet he is not at the farm with her for Thanksgiving. I'm guessing that was George's doing. Her aunt Nell, who was supposedly hosting them all for Thanksgiving, has left for Florida." Marvena and Jurgis look surprised at the notion of such a big change. "And something else—in Dr. Goshen's confession, when I pressed for every detail, every interaction they'd had with the Vogels, he said Fiona seemed upset when he'd mentioned giving ulcer medicine to her uncle. When I talked to Nell Murphy after her husband's sudden death, she was adamant that he was perfectly healthy, that she believed foul play was involved. I didn't believe her at the time, but now I'm wondering if I should have. Mr. Murphy would not have sold the farm to the Vogels, but what if Mrs. Murphy's hand was forced in some way—and Fiona knows or suspects foul play, too, regarding her uncle?"

Lily looks back at her friends. "I think she wanted that dynamite to hurt or stop her husband somehow. Marvena, did she ever come back, say if she found it?"

Marvena shakes her head. "No. And I have my doubts she could find it—it's well hid, and she's not exactly the type suited for backwoods trekking."

Lily lifts an eyebrow. "I don't think we should make the mistake of underestimating Fiona. She managed to cleverly get a message to me, right under Abe's nose."

"So now what do we do?" Jurgis asks.

"You all gather reliable men here," Lily says. "And I go to Benjamin—and ask him to take a message for us to Barnaby."

FIONA, NOVEMBER 30, 8:30 P.M.

"Is it all right if I go check on the boy?" Fiona asks George. She smiles at him as though his word is her command—and God help her, for now it still is. She tries to keep her smile loose, casual, hoping he doesn't see how much she seethes, how she regards his stolid face—once so comforting—as loathsome.

Fiona inhales slowly. Her head pounds, a sick throbbing just behind her left eye in particular, not just from nerves but because the parlor roils with cigarette smoke.

"It's just, I've overheard the boy crying for his mama. And, well, I hate to complain since it doesn't usually bother me, but the smoke—"

"Just go," George says.

"But—" Abe starts.

George cuts him off with a glare. "What in the world do you think she's going to do?" He dismissively waves his hand, then returns to reviewing his notes.

Fiona quickly leaves the room before George can change his mind and hurries up to the semifinished attic, where a cot has been set up for Zebediah.

He's sitting up on the cot, a confused and scared expression overwhelming his thin face. He only seems at ease when he talks about his family, especially his mother and his sister Ruth. Fiona's heart pangs at the sight of his slender shoulders even as he tries to hold a tough posture; he reminds her of her son, Leon.

Elias sits on the edge of the cot next to him, watching as the boy injects himself with insulin. Slowly, Zebediah's getting the hang of the dosing and process. Elias's concern is obvious. How can the willingness to kill exist so easily alongside the obvious need to care for others? Fiona will never understand Elias.

She shakes off that concern. She doesn't need to understand him. She just needs for him to do as she asks.

Fiona approaches the cot. The light from the coal-oil lantern dances with the sharp shadows of the steeply pitched ceiling, casting eerie lines on the walls and on Elias's and Zebediah's faces.

The wind outside howls, making Zebediah jump. Fiona smiles gently at him. "Don't be afraid," she says. "We have a plan and soon you'll be home."

The boy's face lights up, but Elias looks dejected, as he has ever since he learned Fiona will not be going with him to Luther's funeral.

Fiona quickly reaches down, into her boot, and pulls out Colter's letter from home. "Here," Fiona says to Elias, offering him the letter. "Get this to Lily."

"She won't—"

"Yes she will!" Fiona hisses. "And if she won't talk to you, her mama will."

"How do you know she'll be at the funeral?"

Fiona considers. "I don't—but I'm guessing she will. Her mother values family above all else, and Luther is Lily's children's uncle, whether Lily likes it or not, and you're their great-uncle."

She looks at the boy, smiles as she asks him, "Do you trust Sheriff Ross?"

He nods.

"You should," Elias says, a shadow of sorrow crossing his expression.

Zebediah says, "Well, my dad says she's good people, though it's weird she's a lady sheriff. And she's always nice to us when we work on her farm. And Ruth sent along home-canned apples—and she's stingy with those. Sheriff Lily said how much she liked them."

"Good," Fiona says. She points to the letter Elias is holding. "I've put your initials up in the corner, just below the stamp. I think she'll understand when she sees. Just in case, when Elias passes the letter, he's going to whisper, 'Canned apples,' and quickly point to the stamp."

She gives Elias a somber look. "You must do this," she says. She looks back at Zebediah. "We have to get word to Sheriff Ross."

Elias pats the boy's shoulder. "I'll get word. You remind me of my other nephew. Daniel, when he was a boy. Always showed a tougher exterior than he really had on the inside."

Zebediah frowns. "I'm tough." He crosses his arms.

Fiona smiles. "Course you are." She pulls off her watch, almost reluctant to let go of it, it's such a pretty thing—rose gold chain wristband and a diamond inset for the *12*. "Can you tell time?"

"Yeah." Zebediah sounds insulted. "I'm no fool."

"I know, I know," Fiona says. "All right, tomorrow, when it's ten thirty, I want you to start hollering, something fierce, that you have stomach pains and you're going to throw up."

Ten thirty is the set time for Luther's funeral. Elias, George, Abe, and probably another man or two will be there. That would leave two men here in the house, a few more out front, and Klara, who had been bringing the boy his meals. But when Fiona retrieved the letter, she'd also nabbed the poisoned stomach medicine, hidden it in the back of a kitchen cabinet. She has been helping Klara in the kitchen, and Klara has started to warm to her at last.

So tomorrow morning, she will make Klara's customary cup of tea for her, bring it up, whisper how grateful she's been for how well Klara's been tending to the boy and everyone else, and wouldn't just a wee break from taking care of the boy, while the men are away at the funeral, be nice? She'll have dosed Klara's tea, just enough so she feels ill, and Fiona will again play the ever-concerned mother figure.

"All right," the boy says slowly. "I can do that. Then what?"

"Don't worry about that just yet," Fiona says gently. It's better to tell him tomorrow, at the last possible minute. She turns a harder look on Elias, pushes back regret that she can't warn him that George's plan is that Elias won't be coming back from Luther's funeral. "Just play your part. We're counting on you."

LILY, DECEMBER 1, 9:00 A.M.

Lily's heart trembles—a mix of relief and joy at seeing Benjamin standing just outside her office door. Relief that he is fine, for snow started coming down heavily yesterday evening right after he left for Columbus to track down Barnaby.

And joy that he immediately brightens upon seeing her.

Once in her office, Lily takes her seat, and Benjamin—after closing the door as Lily asked—sits across from her.

"I found Barnaby," Benjamin says. "He'll have his agents here later this morning. I gave him the map of the Murphy farm."

"Good," Lily says. She'd drawn several copies. "Marvena and Jurgis are gathering men, too, and they have a map. We have enough to go on with the Goshens, but I hope Fiona comes through today at the funeral. She seemed to be hinting she wanted to tell me something more—" Lily shudders. She is not looking forward to the funeral.

"I want to go with you," Benjamin says.

"To the funeral?" Lily's confused. Why would he want to do that? Though she's glad to see him—with an intensity that surprises her—she doesn't need him by her side.

"Yes," he says. "Because I sense it will be hard for you. And I think you need a friend by your side."

Lily stares at him, struck mute by the kindness of his offer.

He smiles. "I'm guessing Marvena or Hildy won't be there?"

Lily shakes her head softly.

"Well then, let me come with you."

"All-all right."

"And also on the raid."

At that, Lily gives her head a hard shake. "No. No, I can't let you do that, it's too dangerous, and—"

"Lily, for pity's sake, I fought in the trenches!"

"I know that, but this is a different scenario. We may take them by surprise, but they may be ready for us, shooting upon sight—"

Benjamin smacks his cap against the edge of her desk, and Lily jumps, more in surprise at his outburst than at the sound. She has come to see Benjamin as a gentle man. "Dammit, Lily! The other day, you told me you would not give up your work as a sheriff. That you love it. And I told you I'd been thinking about that—"

"About how it's not suitable for a woman?" Lily regrets her snappish tone as soon as the words fly from her lips.

Benjamin sinks back in his chair. "Yes," he says.

Though the simple answer is not surprising, it still stings. Lily looks down at her hands, rigidly clasped together on her desk.

"And how I need time to turn that over in my mind. See if I can reconsider my opinion." Now Benjamin's voice is soft as butter. "Clearly I'm going to have to, if we, well, if we can grow from friends to—to . . . Well, to more. But you need to let me into your life, your thoughts. Let me see what it's like for you, being sheriff. Not just driving you to a church, or asking a few questions at a boardinghouse, or running an errand for you up to Columbus—"

Lily looks up, sharply.

"Oh, not that I minded that!" Benjamin amends quickly. "But I want to understand all of your life. Even the hardest parts. The bad and scary parts. . . ." He pauses, swallows hard, his Adam's apple bobbing up and down an enchanting sight, and Lily flushes a little. "Like you, I imagine, had to do with Daniel, when he was sheriff?"

"He tried to protect me from that. Shield me," Lily says.

"Sounds like him. But how did that feel? To you? *Between* you—and him?"

It's a question meant for her to consider—not answer in the moment. For now, Lily pushes it back and considers instead: Does she want Benjamin to come closer? To trust him with seeing her in the toughest situations, in her hardest moments?

Lily stands.

"Well, c'mon then. We need to get to the funeral. And prepare for the raid."

In the Kinship Cemetery, the pastor speaks quickly to the small gathering, as if trying to outpace the weather with the few words he has to say over Luther's coffin.

Lily is paying only the scantest of attention to the pastor. All part of her mind can think is, *Thank God.* Thank God that Luther's internment is on the opposite edge of the cemetery from Daniel's grave. Thank God it's in a corner she will not have to walk past when she wishes to visit Daniel, or her brother, Roger, or her father.

The other part of her mind is thinking, *Where the hell is Fiona?*

Had she not seen the note Lily had passed on in Fiona's glove?

Or had she shared the note with George—or been found out in her attempt to warn Lily of the industrial alcohol?

Lily sits in the back row of folding wood chairs—three rows, enough for twenty or so people, and the only ones at Luther's funeral are the pastor, Elias, George, Abe, and one of George's guards, who leans against the tent pole, languidly smoking a cigarette and staring at her as if she might jump up, knocking aside chairs, and shove Elias, George, and Abe into the grave after Luther.

Benjamin sits next to Lily, taking in the unfolding scene with the same distanced objectivity he'd had at Tom's place, when Lily had interrogated her friends about the night of Luther's murder.

Now Lily finds herself studying Elias, as she had at the Murphy farm, this man whom she had loved for acting as a father to Daniel and then betrayed them all so terribly. As Lily looks from Elias to Luther's casket, she realizes that at one time she'd have felt spiteful relief at either Luther or Elias being gone.

If she feels anything beyond coldness, if she mourns anything, it's her own lost sense of trusting others, of mostly assuming the best of others, her surprise when people acted in shocking ways. Now she's no longer shocked, and she holds in reserve her assessments of other people until she has enough facts to make an educated judgment—and even then, each judgment is rendered with a reserve of doubt.

It makes her a better sheriff.

And it has cost her in other ways.

Maybe trusting Benjamin, letting him get a little closer to her—the real, raw her—is a way of healing?

As the pastor asks them all to bow their heads, Benjamin reaches for Lily's hand. She lets him take it. She does not pull away.

Lily stands before the "Amen" finishes echoing under the tent. She starts to walk away—she'd come for Fiona, but Fiona is not here—but then she catches Elias's gaze. He looks a broken man, but there's something else. A pleading in his gaze, for her to come over to him.

She notes something else, too—both Abe and George intently watching him. He cannot, she realizes, come to her without raising suspicion.

And yet it feels as though her feet are frozen to the ground. Her legs quiver as she tries to take a step and can't. It had been hard enough, seeing him at the Murphy farm, but walking over to him, of her own volition—no. She cannot.

Benjamin stands so close behind her that his coat brushes her back. He leans forward. "Lily," he says softly, "do you need to talk to him?"

She nods ever so slightly.

"Then you can."

He doesn't push her. Doesn't take her arm. He steps back, away from her, to give her space. And somehow, this is enough for her to go forward to Elias.

For a long moment, she stares up into the broken face of this man.

"I'm so sorry for your loss," she says. She cannot bring herself to hug him, even as his eyes overflow. She holds out her hand for a handshake, and quickly he pulls his hand from his pocket and takes hers.

Lily feels a folded square of paper in his hand. She quickly moves her hand from his, puts her hands in her pockets as if for warmth as she sees Abe approaching out of the corner of her eye, but she does not look away from Elias.

He clears his throat, says, "Please give your best to your mother and the children, Lily." Elias forces a wavery smile as Abe comes within hearing distance. "Tell your mama I miss her home-cooked meals, especially her canned apples."

Canned apples?

He's trying to tell her—Zebediah really is at the Murphy farm.

Lily keeps her expression carefully still. "Of course," she says. "I will tell her."

"Are you done visiting?" Abe gives Lily a tight smile. "Elias was not feeling well on the way over. I think we need to take him to see Dr. Goshen."

Lily's heart quickens at the realization that they will all soon learn that Dr. and Mrs. Goshen are in jail for Luther's murder—and surmise that they have revealed all they know about George's plans to Lily. Her face remains frozen with expressionlessness as she turns her cold gaze onto Abe, who flinches a little.

She does allow herself the satisfaction of a slight quirk of a smile at that.

Then as she turns and walks away, Lily knows they will need to move quickly. The thick snow has treacherously turned to icy sleet.

FIONA, DECEMBER 1, 10:30 A.M.

Fiona sits in the parlor, trying to focus on reading *The Turn of the Screw,* which she'd borrowed from Elias. Words swim before her eyes. Not that it matters. She's just trying to look normal for the guard, though he's half asleep in the other chair, an occasional snore sneaking out before he jerks back awake.

Right on time, Zebediah comes running down the stairs.

"I gotta—I gotta go—I'm gonna be sick again—" He stumbles into the parlor, making extreme retching sounds. Under any other circumstance, Fiona might have been amused by wondering how often the boy play-acted illness to get out of school.

The guard jumps up as Zebediah lurches toward him.

Fiona's practically quivering with the desire to rush, but she, too, must playact. She takes her time to set aside her book, stands up slowly, smooths her skirt, and rolls her eyes. "Oh for pity's sake. Come on, boy, I'll help you out."

At that, the guard looks at her warily. Fiona returns his gaze evenly. "Do you want to take him?" Zebediah clutches his stomach and gags. "Hope he makes it."

The guard looks up the stairs. "Where's the maid?"

Fiona shrugs. Klara is still in bed—the tainted tea had worked quickly on her. She starts to sit back down.

"This is woman's work," the guard says. "Get him outta here before he pukes on me."

Fiona sighs. She grabs Zebediah's arm. "Come on then, hurry up!"

They leave the parlor, hurry through the kitchen, pause on the back porch to grab her coat and one of the men's coats, all the while Fiona cajoling him and Zebediah retching. They continue the act until they get to the outhouse. She quickly explains what she needs him to do next—if he wants to see his Mama and his sister again.

Dammit, there's one guard coming around the corner. Now that he's spotted them, he'll watch until Zebediah goes inside the outhouse, comes back out, and they both return to the farmhouse. There will be no time to repeat the act. George and Abe will be on their way back, and if Elias has done his part, then Lily and whatever backup she has should be close behind.

Fiona tightens her grasp on Zebediah's arm so much that he grimaces. Through gritted teeth, she says, *"Run."*

They're all the way past the springhouse when the guard's first shot rings out.

LILY, DECEMBER 1, 1:00 P.M.

The mix of snow and sleet brings misery down upon Lily and the others, gathered in the cemetery at the top of the hill overlooking the Murphy farm. Winter has cleared leaves from brush and trees so that if she looks the other way, through her binoculars, standing here next to the as-yet-unmarked grave of Henry Murphy, she has a sharp enough view of Kinship Road as it winds past the turnoff to the farm. If she zooms in, she can see three men outside the house, two by each other in the back, and one out front.

And across the holler in which the farm nests, on the next hill, about a half mile away, she notes a cabin. It looks abandoned, but a spiral of smoke rises from the chimney.

She sees, too, the gravel road that's been laid across the back of the farm, dissecting it and connecting to a smaller county road that, two miles on, connects to a state route. Zooming in, she sees two automobiles pull off and several people—Jurgis, several of Barnaby's men, one of Lily's deputies—get out. Scanning, she doesn't see any guards that George has posted at the rear of the road he's created.

He's not prepared for an ambush—leastways, not at the back of the property, the direction he'll likely flee. He's assumed that only he and his people know about his new road. Eventually, she guesses, he'll have guards at either end, but for now, he has them just at the main entrance by Kinship Road.

Her visit with Nell Murphy, and coming to Henry's funeral weeks ago, plus the two visits out here over the past few days have prepared her, though, along with Dr. Goshen revealing George's plans.

Lily lowers the binoculars, turns to face Barnaby, Marvena, Benjamin, and two other men. She hands the binoculars to Benjamin, and he immediately scans the Murphy farm.

"All right, our primary goal is to get George to realize he's outnumbered, and to retrieve Zebediah and Colter DeHaven—"

"Our goal is to arrest George and bring him in," Barnaby interrupts. "Remember, Lily, our conversation with Mabel—"

"Shut up!" Marvena snaps, glaring at him.

"Now, ma'am—"

"What?" Marvena says. "I don't have to follow you all's rules, or whatever. And this is Lily's plan, so you might oughta *shut up*."

Even as tiny as she is, and with her hat slouched ridiculously over her eyes, Marvena cuts an intimidating figure, standing with her booted feet apart, and holding a shotgun in a way that shows she's quite comfortable with it.

Lily is weary—physically and emotionally. The past week has been relentless. And yet here is her friend, just released after Lily had to arrest her, coming to her defense. The wind stings her eyes, makes watery eyes inevitable, and Lily is glad for this cover for her emotion.

Marvena's support builds her up, and Lily says firmly, "Special Agent Sloan makes a good point—we want to shut down Vogel, preferably with no one getting hurt, and also retrieve the boy and agent." An image of Ruth's sweet, sorrowful face flashes before Lily. She cannot bear to bring that family more bad news. "We need to sweep over the farm before George returns. Take the three guards by surprise, hopefully with no gunfire. Search the house, grab the boy and agent. We'll need to be careful of Abe—he's ruthless when protecting George—"

"Lily!" Benjamin looks away from the binoculars, alarm marking his expression. "There's a man and woman coming down hill to the farm." He points to the hill with the cabin and passes the binoculars to Lily.

She grabs them, peers down: there's a man in a suit, with a gun pressed to Fiona's head, coming into the yard behind the house. Lily shoves the binoculars at Barnaby. "That your man? DeHaven?"

Barnaby quickly looks, then stares up at Lily, shock registering in his expression. "Yes."

"Then why the hell is he holding Fiona hostage?"

"I have no idea."

Lily grabs the binoculars back, staring, trying to make sense of this. Has DeHaven been working for George all along? But why hold a gun to Fiona's head? Then movement catches her eye to the north, along the gravel road. Maybe a deer—but no. It's a figure, male. She zooms as much as she can. *Oh God. It's Zebediah Harkins. He's running—*

Another movement—an automobile, coming in through the front entrance. It must be George and Abe.

Lily looks up. "We have a hostage situation and a runaway—the boy." She looks at Marvena. "You're with me. We must stop Zebediah running out the back—he doesn't know what he's running into, and several of the men at the back don't know him. Barnaby, you get down there, talk to your agent, figure out what the hell is going on, and see if you can get Fiona. Everyone else, cover Barnaby, but don't fire unless you must. Barnaby! For God's sake, take your bullhorn!" He'd started off without it.

Benjamin gives Lily an appreciative smile, then follows the other men.

"You're the faster runner," Lily says to Marvena. "You get to the men at the back, and I'll find Zebediah."

FIONA, DECEMBER 1, 1:30 P.M.

Fiona shivers, wishing she had her coat, but they'd left their coats in the cabin, to make their ruse look more believable. Colter shoves his revolver into the back of her head, and Fiona stumbles forward. He's holding her wrists with one hand, and she tries to twist her hands, irritated. He's recovered well and is stronger than he looks, but must he hold her hands so hard to make this look believable? They stop by the woodshop, Fiona tripping into the pile of scrap wood, a jagged end of a piece ripping through her dress and into her shin, and then she stumbles forward again, toward the one confused guard staring at them. Sure, his gun is drawn, but—*ah*.

There's George's automobile, coming down the lane, screeching to a halt. Perfect timing. Except—the doors open, and out comes George and Abe . . . and Elias.

Elias is not dead. She'd thought George and Abe would dispose of him—

Abe pulls out his own gun, aims it at Colter and Fiona.

"I—I—want your automobile. Give it to me and she won't get hurt," Colter says.

And . . . Come on, remember your lines, Fiona thinks.

"And she has to come with me," Colter adds. "Collateral."

"No," George says. "She stays here."

Fiona looks at him, arranges a mix of fear and gratitude on her face. Except . . . he looks perfectly calm. And he is staring at her coldly. He lights a cigarette.

Fiona's gaze clicks over to Elias. Oh God—what had he told them? From the mix of sorrow and exhaustion and anger on his face—everything.

"Seems we need Elias after all," George is saying. "Found out that Dr. Goshen is in jail as accessory to his wife in the murder of Luther." He flicks his ash into the snow. "Good thing we found out. You see, my dear, Elias here—when he realized our plans for him, and that you'd heard them last night but didn't warn him—confessed all."

Fiona's heart pounds. She looks at Elias. *All?* Even Zebediah, ready to set the fuse to the dynamite as George's automobile approached?

"Darling, I—I'm so sorry; the boy just ran away earlier when I took him outside because he was sick, and I followed and then this man grabbed me, and I don't know who—"

"He's a revenuer," George says. "The one Luther was supposed to simply pay off. But you know that. You know because you've been tending to him for the past week, haven't you."

Fiona ventures a glance at Elias. *Is that all he has told them?* He gives a small nod. Even knowing she hadn't warned him about his death, that's all he'd revealed. Relief rushes through her—then puzzlement. *Why not tell George everything?*

The sorrow on Elias's face says it all. He believes he deserves this— any—betrayal. And he wants to die.

"Get out of the way and give me the keys to your automobile!" Colter barks.

"Oh, that's not going to happen," George says.

Fiona feels Colter shaking in the cold, and she shivers, too. She's afraid he'll lose control of the gun, shoot her accidentally. No. No, she wants to live, wants to see her son, Leon, again, wants this child, even though it's George's—and wants control of all George has.

It's not hard to make herself cry, sound pitiable, in this cold. "I'm sorry, I just found him and felt sorry for him and—"

"Is this how you're going to be, with other men?" George barks.

What? He's jealous? Fine. Let him discount any other motives or intelligence on her part. She can work with that. "No, I'm sorry, but let me go with him; he'll let me go later, I'm sure—"

Another automobile races to the yard. Two men jump out—the handsome one who'd been with Lily, and another man. Both have guns drawn. As a second automobile comes racing up, the man intones through the bullhorn, "George Vogel, you are under arrest for—"

Out of the corner of her eye, Fiona sees Abe coming around to the side, pulling his gun—

"No!" Fiona screams, too late, as Abe shoots Colter in the side. Colter falls backward.

George grabs Fiona, shoves her toward the automobile.

"No!"

Another scream, but it's from a distance, down the gravel road, traveling over the bare ground, carried on the icy air.

Lily. Screaming, "No, no, no!"

George shoves Fiona again, as the men behind them holler for them to stop. Another shot rings out. Colter writhes on the ground. Abe stands over him, about to take the kill shot.

But Elias—who has been as still as a frozen statue in the middle of this pandemonium—suddenly conjures strength and energy, and lunges forward, grabs a piece of wood, knocks Abe to the ground. Abe's gun goes off into the air, as Elias runs in the direction of Lily's screams.

More shouting, another shot, George shoves Fiona into the automobile, Abe makes it around to the driver's side, but he's been hit in the right arm, at close range, is bleeding badly, dropping the keys, fumbling, gasping for air, as George curses at him to drive.

LILY, DECEMBER 1, 1:40 P.M.

"No!" Lily screams.

Zebediah has run up the new gravel road and grabbed the end of something and is trying to light it.

Oh God. It's the dynamite.

Fiona has gotten Marvena's dynamite after all and strung it across the road—and sent Zebediah to light it. But when he drops the fuse end, in the ice and snow it goes out.

Still, though shaking, he's trying again.

"No!"

Lily runs across the road, grabs the boy.

He tries to fight her, to get back to the dynamite.

"It's the only way I can get home! See Mama! And Ruth! That's what the lady told me!"

Lily tightens her arms around him, pulls him back into the woods, pulls him down to the ground, holds him still as best she can though he sobs and thrashes. "Sheriff Lily, please, I gotta get home. Mama—"

Oh God, forgive me. She must let Zebediah believe he will see his mama again. "You gotta trust me, boy! Do you trust me? Ruth trusts me!"

He settles a little, though he's still crying.

She hears Elias, gasping for breath. He's right over her.

For a moment, their eyes lock.

For a moment, just a moment, she sees past all that he's done, all the terrible things, all the wonderful things, all the mundane, boring things, into his soul, and sees his sorrow and desperation.

"Forgive me."

Elias whispers the words so softly that for a moment, just a moment,

Lily thinks she's hearing simply the echo of her own prayer in the icy cold.

Then, as she realizes Elias has spoken out loud, he grabs the fuse of the dynamite and runs to the middle of the gravel road.

She hears an automobile speeding toward him.

While still clenching Zebediah, Lily jumps up, sees that the automobile is driven by Abe, carrying George and Fiona.

Lily looks back at Elias.

The fuse is already lit.

But instead of dropping it and running, Elias holds the stick of dynamite in his hand, staring straight ahead at the automobile, now careening, sliding on the road, too much snow and ice for the gravel to offer traction so it can stop in time.

"No!" Lily screams.

Elias does not look her way.

"Elias, you don't have to do this!"

He is frozen. Resolute.

Holding the dynamite with the sparking, burning fuse up, like a candle. He is perfectly . . .

Still.

Somewhere, deep in his soul, he's found the strength and will for this last act.

Lily staggers backward with Zebediah, holds him tightly with one arm, covers his eyes as the dynamite explodes.

EPILOGUE

LILY, SATURDAY, DECEMBER 24, 1927, 8:40 P.M.

At the pastor's cue, the elders rise and lower the wicks of the coal-oil lamps near the altar. Shadows dance around the Kinship Presbyterian Church sanctuary, making the church seem colder than it really is.

Micah snuggles in close to Lily, as Caleb Jr. does to Mama. Lily puts her arm around Micah to still his wriggling.

"Look," she whispers. "Jolene's going to bring the light from the Christ candle, and then Frankie's going to sing!"

"Do we get presents tonight?" Micah asks. There will be another service tomorrow morning, but the church is celebrating the lighting of the full Advent wreath tonight.

Lily can't help but smile. She nuzzles the top of his head with her nose and whispers, "One each—but only if you're good. And hold your candle upright, lest I need to take it away!"

He immediately stops wriggling, sits up straight with his candle, and Lily's smile widens. Benjamin, who is seated next to her, chuckles softly. Just in time for Christmas, the church council, three-to-two, had voted that men and women could sit together, after all.

And so Benjamin sits next to her, and in the pew in front of them Jurgis and Marvena sit together, as do Hildy and Tom. They'd all come over to share in Christmas at Lily's house and even agreed to attend service—at Nana's insistence—with Lily's family. Jurgis and Marvena have fallen away from the Holiness gospel church. Mama had arranged for Frankie to sing for this service; the pastor had been reluctant at first, but Mama is such a stalwart of the church that he'd finally given in.

Now Lily focuses on Jolene and four other children standing around the Advent wreath in front of the pulpit.

A child takes a lit taper from the pastor and lights the first candle of the Advent wreath, *Hope*, as Jolene had the first Sunday after Thanksgiving.

Benjamin glances at her and gives Lily's hand a quick squeeze.

Lily ventures a glance at him and finds herself noting, in the dim light, the silhouette of his sharp features. Heat flushes up her neck and face, and she is grateful for the darkness to hide her romantic inclinations—in church, for pity's sake!

Is it too much—having work she loves and perhaps another person to love as well? A calling that fulfills her during the day, and comfort and love on cold, hard nights—is that too much to hope for?

Only time will tell.

The child passes the lit taper on to the next child.

Faith.

Lily glances over at Marvena and Jurgis, happy to see them at ease with each other.

Last week, Mama asked Lily to take her to visit them, and when Lily picked her up all Mama would say on the way home was that she and Nana *gave Marvena and Jurgis a talking-to.* At that, Lily had bitten back a smile—she wouldn't want to be on the receiving end of that.

Before they left, Marvena had drawn Lily aside, asked if she could, after all, borrow money for Frankie's asthma treatments, and Lily had not been able to resist teasing, *So long as you wait to pay it back with honestly earned dollars—no moonshining!* Jurgis is still in the mines, and Marvena's lost her job with the United Mine Workers.

I'll find a way, Marvena grumbled.

Lily grinned. *How about you become a part-time paid deputy in this part of the county? I'd need the county commissioners' approval, but—*

I can't take a charity job.

Not offering you one. I'm also asking for another part-time deputy in the western part of the county.

Oh, well then. Yes. So long as it helps you out. Marvena hadn't been able to suppress a pleased grin—but then she'd looked worried again. *Oh, Lily, thank you, but how will I get Frankie to her appointments each month?*

Lily had smiled. *Have faith in your friends. Between me, and Hildy, and Benjamin, and others, we'll make it happen. After all, I needed each of you to help me take down George Vogel.*

Thank God for friends. It would be so hard, in this life, this world, to be friendless.

The image of Fiona crosses Lily's mind, in those last jumbled moments back at the Murphy farm.

After the explosion, George's automobile crashed. With the help of everyone else at the site, Lily had gotten George, Abe, and Fiona out of the automobile. All had sustained injuries, but all had survived. Fiona is now back at her Cincinnati home, as far as Lily knows—they'd talked only enough for Lily to gain the information that Fiona had happened upon Colter DeHaven, hiding in the woodshop, and she'd helped him because she was furious that Elias had poisoned her uncle Henry at George's behest. Colter had corroborated the story and asserted that Luther had shot him—apparently trying to play both George and the bureau for money so he and Elias could run from George's grasp and start over.

Lily suspects that there's a lot that Fiona is leaving out about her part in how everything had panned out over those chaotic, challenging days between Thanksgiving and December 1—and that she'll never know.

George and Abe are now in the state penitentiary, awaiting trial on violations of the Volstead Act and, in George's case, tax evasion. It's been reported in various newspapers that all of George's properties are in Fiona's name. And Lily has to wonder, *Did Fiona get what she wanted all along? Is she happy now?*

FIONA, DECEMBER 24, 1927, 8:45 P.M.

"Ma'am?"

Fiona slaps her hand against the top of George's desk—now *her* desk in the study of the Cincinnati mansion—which makes the stack of mail, still untouched from earlier today, slide over top of her ledger. God, how she hates being interrupted.

She looks up at the source of the interruption. It's Klara, hovering, as she so often does, in the shadows.

Maybe Fiona should have fired her when she replaced all the other employees.

"What?" Fiona snaps.

Klara hesitates.

"For pity's sake, come in, I can't hear you, mumbling from the doorway."

As Klara enters the expansive study, Fiona rubs her eyes, looks up and around. Even with plentiful gas-powered wall sconce lights and a massive chandelier hanging above the desk, the room is always dim. And somehow dusty. Fiona blames the shelves of George's lawbooks that Fiona will never read, even though the bookcases are outfitted with glass-fronted doors that remain shut. The bookcases look nice, though. Official. Professional. Just like the leather-upholstered chairs in front of the desk—those are new. They don't quite work with the tapestry-covered sofas or the dark rug.

Fiona makes a mental note to replace the sofas with leather ones that match the chairs. And the rug with something exotic. Perhaps red. From Persia.

Klara stands in front of the desk between the two leather chairs. The scents of ginger and cinnamon waft off her dress. Fiona supposes she's been baking all day. The old woman certainly looks like it. A dusting of flour smudges her forehead.

How cozy—but Klara's dark eyes glint cold and hard in the light of the gas lamps.

Ah yes—that is why Fiona hasn't fired Klara.

Wasn't there an old saying? *Keep your friends close—and your enemies closer.*

Well, these days, Fiona doesn't have to worry about friends. But she needs to keep an eye on the likes of Klara.

"Leon is, ah, eager to see you," Klara says.

Fiona glances at the grandfather clock in the corner. *Oh.* Time had flown as she'd pored over the accounts. Next week, she'd be going to court to get most of George's remaining assets in her name. It was stunning, how quickly the attorneys and businessmen flocked to her side to help her, now that George and Abe were disposed of, likely for a good decade or more.

She isn't pressing for divorce—not yet. She'll have better luck as his wife getting the rest of the assets legally switched over to her in order to, her attorneys will argue, tend to her baby. Oh, and her other son. Leon.

She's stopped all of George's illegal work, cooperating with the Bureau of Prohibition. She's not, after all, greedy like him, she tells herself. She'll do just fine—making money through running the very legal Vogel's Tonic.

Oh, she'll have to make a show for him—telling him it's the only way to salvage what she can. Put it in her name. For their child. Visiting him every so often.

The thought repulses her.

But she'll have control, not just of property, but of bank and cash assets.

Then she can file for divorce.

And maybe, just maybe, eventually, when legal eyes are no longer staring at her, she can execute the plan George had put together for her aunt's old farm, after all. She'd meant it when she told him it was brilliant.

Meanwhile, she wants to keep an eye on Klara. Not have her running free to go visit George in prison.

"Tell Leon I need another half hour or so."

"Ma'am, if I may, he got in on the train more than four hours ago." Yes, Klara had interrupted her then, telling her of Leon's arrival. The new chauffeur had gone to the station, picked him up, brought him here. Fiona had dismissed Klara, ordering her to tell the boy to get settled in for his holiday break from that expensive school in Philadelphia.

"He's unpacked," Klara says, allowing just a bit too much judgment in her tone.

"Why didn't you tell me?" Fiona says.

"You dislike being interrupted when you're working," Klara says. She gives a small, hard smile. "Even more so than Mr. Vogel did."

For a long moment, the two women glare at each other. *I'm nothing like George!* Fiona wants to snap. But then—she'd just asked to put off seeing Leon, though it's been months since she last saw him. "Send Leon up right away."

Klara leaves. Fiona looks down, spots the mail on the ledger. Picks up the stack of Christmas cards and postcards from well-wishers, starts thumbing through. They all are from people whose names she barely recognizes or doesn't at all. George's associates—but all addressed to her. One is from Mrs. Eugenia Chantelle. Sycophants.

She tosses it aside, unopened. Sees that next in the stack is a postcard that isn't Christmas themed. Picturing a beach, in Florida.

Fiona turns it over. It's from Aunt Nell, and there's just a quick dashed note: *Fiona—I am well. I hope, at last, you have found happiness. And peace. Love, Aunt Nell. P.S. Don't forget the last thing I told you at your uncle Henry's grave, before we walked back down.*

Fiona shakes her head impatiently. How in the world was she supposed to remember whatever that was, after all that happened? Something about not becoming—something. What you fear? What you hate?

She chuckles as she tosses the mail back on the desk. She's won. She no longer has to fear anything. Wonder what Aunt Nell would think if she knew Fiona already has sold the piece of land that held the old cabin—after she'd had the cabin burned to the ground?

Fiona stands, stretches. She's past morning sickness but not the weariness of being pregnant. So much more to do—but first she needs a break.

The bar across the room—topped with a decanter of whiskey, quite legal as it is from barrels purchased before Prohibition and stored in the basement—catches Fiona's eye.

She shouldn't—the baby—but it's Christmas Eve. She crosses to the bar, pours herself a neat, stiff drink from the decanter. Next to it is her old chipped glass candy dish. A reminder, of where she'd come from—not Kinship. That cabin. And that she will never go back. Now, though, the dish overflows with peppermints.

But she doesn't want candy. That's for children. Fiona takes a sip of the whiskey. It burns, going down, a fire that feels good.

As Fiona stares at the desk, she notes how big, dark, heavy it is. Such a George desk.

Her eyes prickle as it hits her—no one will have purchased a present for her this year. Well, maybe Leon had brought something he'd made at school, but that hardly counts.

That handsome man who accompanied Lily crosses her mind. Were they an item? Had he bought Lily a gift?

Fiona shakes her head to clear it, takes another deliciously burning sip. Never mind Lily.

Oh sure. She's thankful Lily pulled her from the automobile. But after that, she'd done no more than ask her a few curt, necessary questions.

She studies the desk, takes another sip.

Why stop at ordering a new sofa and rug? Fiona doesn't need anyone to get her gifts. She'll get one for herself—a new desk.

The door opens again, and this time, Leon walks in, Klara just behind him.

Fiona lights up, about to eagerly rush to him. Her heart softens toward her son—oh, this is why she's done all she's done, worked so hard, not just for herself, or new desks. For Leon. For the new baby.

But Fiona stops mid-stride, catching Klara's cruelly amused expression. She must know, even without seeing his face, that Leon stares at his mother with a mix of fright and confusion, as if she's become a stranger to him.

LILY, DECEMBER 24, 1927, 8:55 P.M.

Lily smiles as the next child lights the third Advent candle, *Joy,* for that makes her think, despite all their sorrow, of the Harkins family.

Zebediah had returned home. Lily has checked on the Harkinses a few times, and she's pleased that Leroy has agreed that Zebediah can have insulin. Zebediah is cold to her, though, when she visits. Lily understands—he needs someone to blame for not being home before his mother passed, and even if it doesn't make sense, he's blaming Lily. He's a child, and he will grow out of it, eventually.

But Ruth is always glad to see her. Two days ago, when Lily visited, she pulled Ruth aside, asked her to come out to the front porch.

Brought you a little something, for Christmas, Lily had said. She pulled from her tote bag a glass jar of seeds, a red ribbon tied around its neck. *Store it somewhere dark and dry—in a cabinet.*

Then she pointed to Dora's container on the front porch, still filled with withered zinnias. *Took some seeds, that first time I visited. Can you hang on to them till spring? Start them in little peat pots, with good rich soil and water, and when they sprout, plant them wherever you like.*

Ruth had stared at the jar like it held everything she needed in the world. With damp eyes, she'd finally looked up at Lily.

Sheriff Lily, maybe you could, could come help me?

Of course.

Maybe we can plant some by Mama's grave? Get Zeb and Daddy and the others to help?

Lily had nodded. *If they want to.*

Ruth had smiled. *They won't always be sad, or mad, you know. Zeb already gave me a gift, too! A book—*The Blue Castle. Then Ruth had leaned forward, whispered, *Talked Daddy into getting him a better hunting rifle. A Winchester!*

The fourth candle: *Peace.*

Peace.

Perhaps *peace* is the hardest of the four tenets of Advent.

Neither Luther nor Elias could hurt Lily or anyone she knows for now. George and Abe will be in prison for a good long time.

Sometimes, at night, Lily wakes up in a cold sweat, the horror of Elias stopping George's automobile by detonating the dynamite— and blowing himself apart by doing so—repeating in her nightmares. Sometimes, she sees it again during the day. Elias had wanted peace, his last words the request for her: *Forgive me.*

That horrific ending, even if it led to the capture of George Vogel and the shutdown of his operation, an event that made the newspapers across the land, was not anything she would have wanted or imagined for Elias, though it made for scintillating copy. Lily had turned down requests for interviews, including with *Thrilling Gumshoe,* though they'd written up the story anyway, drawing from news reports. Lily just shook her head and said nothing whenever anyone brought it up to her—whether teasing or with admiration.

She didn't have anything to add to the story, as Mabel Walker Willebrandt—who gave quite the Prohibition speech in a packed Kinship Opera House a few days after the takedown of George—offered up plenty of interviews fully crediting the Bureau of Prohibition, with Special Agents Sloan and DeHaven filling in all the colorful details.

Those details revealed that Elias had murdered Henry Murphy and, along with Luther, worked with George Vogel on plans to bring a bootlegging operation directly to the heart of Bronwyn County. So Mama and Lily had been the only attendees at Elias's funeral. Mama, who'd wept upon reading the stories of Elias's betrayals, insisted they go. *It will bring peace,* Mama claimed.

And, at least to some degree, Mama had been right.

Their pastor, who led Elias's funeral service, had scant words to say beyond the formalities, but in the gray, swirling snow this had struck Lily: *Sometimes the best we can do for loved ones who hurt us deeply is leave them on the altar.* Lily understood: leave their souls to God's judgment, and go back to tending to life. And to the loved ones who remain.

Now Jolene takes up the light from the last child and tips the flame to the candle in the middle of the wreath, the Christ candle, symbolizing light spreading to one and all.

Then as she carries the light to the person on the far end of the first pew, Frankie begins singing a cappella in her clear, pure voice, "O holy night, the stars are brightly shining. . . ."

The first woman lights her candle from Jolene's. The next person lights her candle. By the time Frankie sings, "A thrill of hope, the weary world rejoices," the church is filled with light.

AUTHOR'S NOTE

For the first two novels in my Kinship Historical Mystery Series, Prohibition plays a significant role, but mainly in the background.

For this novel, I decided it was time to bring Prohibition to the foreground, and really explore how the national law might impact one specific, rural area.

It turns out that 1927 is a fascinating year in which to make Prohibition almost a character in its own right in a novel.

For one thing, it is absolutely true that as Prohibition wore on, sixty million gallons (give or take a gallon here or there) of industrial alcohol were stolen each year to supply the "wets" of the land. By 1926, the government required industrial alcohol be denatured with bitter chemicals, but syndicates hired chemists to "renature" it. So, in turn, the government required industrial alcohol to be made more deadly—with methyl alcohol the most deadly. Reports began to emerge in 1927 of imbibers becoming very ill or dying from consumption of drinks made with industrial alcohol. "Blind drunk" wasn't just a cute turn of phrase.

While New Jersey Senator Edward I. Edwards called the federal government's actions "legalized murder," the Anti-Saloon League's Wayne B. Wheeler said anyone who drank industrial alcohol was engaging in "suicide," and that "to root out a bad habit [drinking alcohol of any kind] costs many lives and long years of effort."

Indeed, Prohibition was a complex issue. Many scholars and documenters, including Ken Burns in his documentary *The Roots of Prohibition* (a fascinating series that I highly recommend), refers to Prohibition as the United States' first "wedge" issue, with politicians and lobbyists on either side ("dry" and "wet") working to use it to divide Americans on other issues—from women's suffrage to equal rights for Black Americans.

A fourteen-foot-tall bronze sculpture called *The American Issue* in Westerville, Ohio—headquarters of the Anti-Saloon League, one of the organizations that pushed mightily for Prohibition, and now home of the Anti-Saloon League Museum—recognizes Prohibition as the United States' original wedge issue. It depicts a wedge, pushed down by a barrel, splitting a large rock in half, just as the country was divided by the debate over alcohol, by the Constitution's Eighteenth Amendment, which made Prohibition national law (previously, the wet versus dry decision was made by local municipalities and states); the Volstead Act, which enforced it—sort of, with plenty of loopholes for the wealthy and powerful; and the Twenty-first Amendment, which finally ended the failed experiment.

I've tried to accurately capture the nuances and loopholes and arguments both pro and con regarding Prohibition as part of the fabric of this novel.

Mabel Walker Willebrandt truly was Assistant Attorney General from 1921–1929. I could only include her for a few pages, and of course her dialogue with Lily is entirely from my imagination, but how could I not have these two meet? I'm hoping someone out there is writing a nonfiction book about Willebrandt, or working on a documentary about her!

The iron production industry in Ohio helped the state to grow and develop, but it was relatively short-lived, from the 1840s or so to the late 1890s or so. Smelting furnaces, which processed iron ore extracted from sandstone, flourished in southeastern Ohio, with much of the resulting iron used to support the Union Army during the Civil War. Many of the industry's furnace owners were abolitionists. By 1900, almost all of the furnaces were shut down in the southern part of Ohio, and iron production moved on to other parts of the country. Now, only a few of the old furnaces exist as relics of an industry in southern Ohio that's nearly forgotten. (I wasn't aware of it until I started writing this series.)

Finally, I wanted to explore health issues from the perspective of nearly one hundred years ago. In an era when many aspects of medicine that we now take more or less for granted had yet to be developed, how would people deal with health issues that were relatively common then, as they are now, such as diabetes or asthma? Or, tragically, cancer— for which scientists are still researching treatments? What's more, how would people of limited means or knowledge handle such health issues?

One way is through faith—and I offer that statement with no intention of disrespect. I do believe faith helps people in myriad ways. Of course, exploring extremes—such as snake handling—as a way of showing faith always makes for dramatic scenes. But, in this novel, it also gave me a chance to show how Lily is struggling with her own faith, not just religious, but in those around her and in her community.

However, just for the record, I did all of my research on snake handling by reading and by watching YouTube recordings of modern-day snake handling at several churches. (It is a very rare practice.) That was more than enough for me!

One last note: Asthma cigarettes. Yes, these were real, and were a common treatment for asthma in the 1920s, and Page's Inhalers were considered a fine, top-notch brand. Some things just can't be made up.

ACKNOWLEDGMENTS

While writing the first dreadful draft of any novel takes place alone (thankfully), the other stages require a community that rallies around the writer (also thankfully).

In the research stage, I'm indebted to Teri Kistler, who spent a good part of a day off from her work at the Westerville Public Library going *into* work on my behalf. The Anti-Saloon League Museum is housed at the Westerville Public Library in Westerville, Ohio, and Teri graciously arranged for me to talk with the museum staff and spend much longer than I'd scheduled studying the museum's displays and materials, which preserve the history of Prohibition, particularly that of the Anti-Saloon League and of the "dry" movement in Ohio. (I'm also grateful that no one looked too alarmed when I yelped in glee at the display of a Vino Sano Grape Brick, the existence of which I'd learned about in earlier research.)

Thank you to Karla Hollencamp who, when we met at a book club visit, told me about the "Bootleggers, Bandits and Badges" exhibit at Carillon Historical Park (daytonhistory.org) in Dayton, Ohio; visiting the fascinating exhibit provided surprises and insights for my research for this novel.

Nonfiction authors also provided valuable and necessary context for my fictional imaginings. Though George Vogel is only inspired by real-life George Remus, I'm also grateful to two authors who have written fascinating books about Remus: *The Bourbon King* by Bob Batchelor and *The Ghosts of Eden Park,* by Karen Abbott. *Last Call: The Rise and Fall of Prohibition* by Daniel Okrent, proved to be (and will continue to be) both a valuable resource and fascinating deep dive into the Prohibition era.

Finally, I'm always grateful for my family's patience when I drag them along on my research adventures. This time around, it was to Hope Iron Furnace, near New Plymouth, Ohio, in Vinton County. Thank you, David and Gwen. I'd be lost—metaphorically and literally—without you, still wandering the hills of southeast Ohio.

On to that dreadful first draft . . . ah, perhaps it wasn't written entirely without community support. Because we had our wooden floors resanded as well as a bathroom gutted and renovated as I wrote, I had to find writing spaces outside my home office. I'm indebted to Reza's Roast (www.rezasroast.com), for delicious caffeinated beverages for brain fuel as well as for a gorgeous writing space, as well as to Washington-Centerville Public Library, for public work spaces.

For the later stages of revising, editing, and proofing, I'm ever grateful to my agent, Elisabeth, and my editor, Catherine. Every book has production milestones to meet, and I'd be lost (yet again!) without Nettie keeping me on track. And of course, Sarah and Joe always make sure my books reach a wide audience—thank you!

In every stage, I'm grateful to my writing buddies. Even in the pandemic era, we manage to find socially distanced, safe ways to get together and cheer each other on.

I'm especially thankful for our daughters, Katherine and Gwen, and for my husband, David, who never show any doubts about my wild creative journey—made sweeter by sharing it with you.